A Universe
Less Traveled

A Universe Less Traveled

Eric von Schrader

Weeping Willow Books

ISBN 978-1-7329706-2-5

Library of Congress Control Number 2020909072

Weeping Willow Books
Santa Barbara, CA

Dedicated to the memories of Sarah Linquist and Bob Reuter, whose brilliance and tenacity inspired me to take a creative risk.

"listen: there's a hell of a good universe next door;
let's go"

— e.e. cummings

CONTENTS

STRANGE DOINGS ON ARSENAL

1908

From the Most Secret Archives of the Knights of The Carnelian. For Founders Circle Members Only.

January 2, 1908

Following is a summary of police reports from December 27, 1907, compiled for the Knights' archives by Chief of Police William Creecy:

On the evening of December 27th, the police responded to a disturbance at 2025 Arsenal Street. Patrolman James Cooney reported that two men, who appeared to be identical twins, were engaged in a vigorous altercation. Fists and insults were flying. With the assistance of Patrolman William Stinger, he separated the combatants. They both claimed to be Edward Runkelmann, married to Emily Runkelmann, who was present and extremely distraught.

One of the men asserted that the other was an intruder who had burst into his home during his supper with his wife. The other man insisted that he was the rightful husband of the aforesaid Mrs. Runkelmann, and that the first man was a usurper and impostor. He also demanded to see a baby, a son that he claimed was his, who would be sleeping in the rear bedroom on the second floor. The first Mr. Runkelmann said there was no such baby. Mrs. Runkelmann supported this statement.

As a precaution, the officers handcuffed both men and then led them up the stairs. The rear bedroom contained a sewing table. There was no crib or other indication of a child's presence.

This revelation did not comfort the second Mr. Runkelmann, who strained against his bonds and loudly accused the others of foul play. The officers decided that the wisest course of action would be to take both men into custody.

At the Soulard district station, Detective Paul Throckmorton interrogated both men, to little avail. Each stood by his story that he was the rightful Edward Runkelmann. One of the men demanded that the police arrest the other for the abduction or murder of an infant, Thomas Runkelmann. The detective was unable to calm the man, even with an offer of brandy. Throckmorton noted the uncanny resemblance of the two men to each other, not only in appearance, as would be common with twins, but also in voice and mannerisms. Interviewed in separate rooms, both men were able to give identical accounts of the wedding of Mr. and Mrs. Runkelmann, including minor details likely known only to the bride and groom. The wedding took place on June 16, 1904, at the Fair.

Given the unusual nature of the case, Chief of Police Creecy decided to withhold information from the pack of reporters who frequent the station. Furthermore, he requested that a delegation from the Knights interview the two suspects. He hopes that the capable minds of leading business men might be able to resolve the mystery.

Respectfully submitted,
Christopher Sherman, Esq.
Recording Secretary

From the Most Secret Archives of the Knights of the Carnelian. For Founders Circle Members Only.

January 4, 1908

Knights Endeavor to Solve a Mystery

Following are notes from the meeting of representatives of the Knights with the members of the family involved in the curious December 27 incident on Arsenal Street. The meeting was held at Police Headquarters on January 3, the earliest convenient date following New Year's festivities.

Present: Knights LaBeaume, Heiskell, Wiegand, and Hubbard. Also present was your humble servant, who has summarized the meeting below.

The first interview was with Edward Runkelmann, the homeowner.

I reside at 2025 Arsenal Street and am married, since 1904, to Emily Runkelmann. I am employed as a foreman at the Crunden Manufacturing Company. On the evening in question, I was having a quiet supper with my wife when there was a pounding on our front door. I went to open the door and saw a man there who looked upset and, as became clear, was drunk.

He was about my height, my coloring, and my age. Later, my wife said he looked exactly like me, but that did not occur to me at the time. He challenged me and claimed that I was in his house. I held my ground. "You must have the wrong house, sir. I live here." He flew into a rage and demanded to know where some child was. Emily, who had joined us at the front door, was frightened. He spoke with her in an overly familiar way.

He attempted to force his way into our home and I wrestled him to the floor. Emily ran outside to hail a policeman. Fortunately, two foot patrolmen were nearby.

Wiegand: What is your assessment of this man?

He was obviously drunk, a lunatic, or both.

The second interview was with Mrs. Runkelmann:

I have been happily married since June 1904 to my husband, Edward, who is devoted and a good provider. Our home is modest, but comfortable.

This man who came to our door was very rude. He addressed me as if he himself were my husband, not Edward.

He ranted about 'our baby.' I assured him there was no such baby. Edward and I have not yet been blessed in that way. But nothing we said would calm him. I could smell the drink on his breath.

Hubbard: Who do you think this man is?

He bears an astonishing resemblance to Edward. At first, I thought a friend or relative had found this man and, as a prank, sent him to annoy us. But he persisted in speaking to me in a most unseemly way. It was very disturbing.

Heiskell: Why do you think he insisted that he is your husband?

Are you asking me who my real husband is? I'll tell you. My Edward has a long scar on his left calf from a childhood skating accident. Just look at this drunk's leg and you'll know he's a liar.

The final interview was with the other Mr. Runkelmann, the intruder. He rambled and seemed to be confused by the proceedings. Here is the gist of his answers:

I left my home that morning to look for work. I've been unemployed since November, when the Reed Rubber Company shut down because of the recent panic. (Note: There was no panic and this company is still very much in business.)

I kissed my wife and our little baby, Thomas, goodbye. He was wheezing and ill, as he has been for most of his short life. I bought a newspaper and perused the employment listings. I called on several companies, but no positions were available. The streets were filled with other job seekers who had the same intention. In despair, I visited a tavern in the afternoon. I freely admit that alcohol and friendly companionship are my weaknesses. After a few hours, I saw that night had fallen. Realizing that I would be late for supper, and remorseful that I had left Emily with Thomas all day and had nothing to show for it, I raced out the door. I slipped in the snow and hit my head on the sidewalk. But no harm was done.

I rushed towards home. The sidewalk was now dry. My remorse grew. What would Emily think of me? At the front door, I turned my key in the lock, but the door did not open. Emily must have shut the deadbolt, which we only did when we were both safe inside. She must be angry at me, I thought, for visiting the tavern again. I pounded on the door and tearfully shouted "Forgive me, Emily."

After a few moments, the door opened. Instead of Emily, it was a man. "Where's

Emily? Where's my little Thomas?" I asked. He told me I was at the wrong house. But I know my own home! Then Emily came to the door, looked at me, and screamed as she cowered behind the other man.

LaBeaume: Why did she do that?

It was as if she were afraid of me. My dearest Emily! (Note: The gentleman struggled to compose himself.) The man denied there was any child in the house. Emily asked me in bewilderment, "Who is Thomas?" Then this man, the 'mirror man' I call him, demanded that I leave the house.

Wiegand: Why do you call him the 'mirror man?'

Have you not seen him? He resembles me. That is part of his scheme. He has somehow bewitched Emily into rejecting and denying Thomas and me. Why did she let this awful man into our home?

I decided to push past them both to go to Thomas' bedroom. The mirror man grabbed me and we fought. Soon, the police arrived.

Hubbard: Did the police show you the bedroom?

Yes. Emily and the mirror man changed the furniture in Thomas' room.

What have they done with my poor baby? (Note: The gentleman could speak no more. He became agitated and lost his composure completely. Two policemen had to restrain him.)

Knight LaBeaume asked the police to lift the man's left trouser leg. The scar described by Mrs. Runkelmann was clearly visible. The Knights asked to see the other Mr. Runkelmann once more. When he entered the room, Knight LaBeaume asked him to lift his left trouser leg. Though puzzled, he did so. The same scar was on his leg also.

The Knights summoned a photographer who took pictures of the two men side by side, and of their two scarred legs.

Afterwards, the Knights and Chief Creecy repaired to the Knights' club to discuss the situation over brandy.

Wiegand: The man's story about the missing baby is preposterous. He is obviously looking for a payoff from Mr. and Mrs. Runkelmann to go away.

Hubbard: Or, he is a poor, deluded fellow who imagines himself to be a member of this happy family. Perhaps he was once rebuffed by Mrs. Runkelmann and has developed an unhealthy obsession with her.

LaBeaume: He certainly appears unhinged.

Heiskell: The two men were like twins. But for their clothes, I doubt I could tell them apart.

Chief Creecy assured the Knights that there was no birth record for a Thomas Runkelmann. Also, the birth record for Edward Runkelmann, on July 11, 1878, makes no mention of a twin.

The Knights asked the Chief the fate of the intruder. He said that, as the Runkelmann couple had declined to press charges, the police could no longer hold him. Because he persists in the delusion of the missing child and is in a state of extreme agitation, he will be sent to the State Asylum. They will prevent him from harming himself and endeavor to help him recover his wits.

The Knights approved of this wise course of action.

The Chief said he had one final item for them to consider. He produced a copy of the Globe-Democrat from December 27. It had been found in the intruder Mr. Runkelmann's pocket. He laid it on the table and asked the Knights to examine it carefully.

All did. The Chief then asked, "Do you recognize any of these events on the front page? I don't." The Knights agreed to give it further study.

Everyone adjourned for the evening. Knight LaBeaume summed up the sentiments of all present, "It's a rollicking good mystery. A toast to Chief Creecy for bringing us this intriguing diversion. Mr. Conan Doyle himself could not conceive of one better!"

Respectfully submitted,
Christopher Sherman, Esq.
Recording Secretary

From the Most Secret Archives of the Knights of the Carnelian. For Founders Circle Members Only.

January 15, 1908

Postscript to Entry of January 4

The Knights shared the newspaper in question with fellow Knight Robinson, editor of the Globe-Democrat, for his perusal. A few days later, he declared that it was a clever forgery, probably created by idle typesetters. He pointed out that it contained both a purely fictitious story about a bribery scandal in the city government and an obituary for himself (Knight Robinson). Most likely, some of the typesetters, who are known to have anarchist leanings, were making mischief.

Also, Chief Creecy reported that, sadly, the disturbed Mr. Runkelmann has disappeared from the State Asylum. The asylum staff were baffled by his escape. They insisted he had been in a completely secure area with no possible means of egress.

Respectfully submitted,
Christopher Sherman, Esq.
Recording Secretary

A Man Without Hobbies

2010

Once again, the numbers sucked. May was no better than April, which had been a notch below March. This year's sales were starting to look like a world's record piece of crap.

Billy Boustany pushed back from the computer screen. To clear his head, he wandered from his office into the showroom of the Crestwood location of Duke's Digital. This store was the oldest of his four stores in the St. Louis suburbs—and the most troubled. He passed the wall of thirty-six large-screen TVs, all showing a cartoon of a princess dancing with tubby little animals. He glanced into the high-end stereo section, separated from the rest of the showroom by glass walls. This had always been his favorite part of the store. Years ago, when he still had time for indulgences, he had been quite an audiophile. But now customers were shifting to tinny earbuds and low-fidelity MP3 files. Like a lot of things about the business today, this was an unwelcome surprise for Billy.

One of his salespeople in the computer area who was helping a customer beckoned Billy over. The customer, Dave, was interested in Billy's advice about which of several laptops to buy. Billy asked him about how he planned to use the laptop, his favorite applications, his budget, and other devices he owned. Billy prided himself on his ability, honed during twenty-three years in the electronics business, to zero in on a customer's needs and preferences. He had a knack for getting the customer to think about issues and tradeoffs not considered before. Often, customers were grateful for Billy's ideas and bought the product. This was the most satisfying kind of sale for Billy. After the customer left with their purchase in hand, Billy would have an avuncular talk with the salesperson involved to pass along his wisdom. Whether the salesperson actually acted on Billy's advice was anybody's guess. These days, nothing seemed to make any difference. The business kept spiraling toward the drain.

Today, the customer hesitated, even after Billy had pointed out a great value in a model that he had not considered. Billy demo'ed the product for him, let him feel the comfortable, tactile action of its keyboard, and offered the store's help in migrating data from the customer's old laptop.

"You have given me some fantastic ideas," Dave said. "I really appreciate your time, but I need to think it over a little more."

Billy knew what was going on. Dave had been picking his brain. He had no intention of buying anything from Duke's Digital. That very night, he would go home and order online the exact laptop Billy had recommended. Even if the online price was the same as Billy's, Dave would avoid the 8 percent sales tax. Billy exploded.

"You and I both know you're ripping me off. I spend a ton of money to keep this store open, so I can give you a 'fantastic' idea."

Dave mumbled something inaudible and took a step backward to open up some distance between him and Billy.

"And, in case you weren't paying attention, the idea I gave you *is* fantastic," Billy continued. "It'll save you a lot of headaches—and some real money. But you're not going to give me the courtesy of a penny in sales, are you?"

Shocked, Dave just stood there. His lips moved, but no sound came out.

"You're a 'customer'," sneered Billy, making air quotes with his fingers, "and I'm supposed to treat you like you're always right. But you came in here to rob me of the massive fucking investment I've put into this business. And of twenty years of my sweat."

Dave turned and scurried toward the front door.

"Get out of my store!" Billy shouted after him.

He was shaking with rage. He glanced at the startled salesperson, who was frozen in shock. Billy stormed back to his office.

He flopped into his desk chair. His whole body shuddered. Why the hell did he do that? What an idiot! The instant he figured out Dave's game, a self-righteous tidal wave erupted inside him. He thought about running to the parking lot to intercept Dave and apologize, to give him the laptop for free if that is what it would take. But he knew it was too late. Dave was gone—and would soon tell everyone he knew about the flaming asshole at Duke's Digital.

Billy sat in his office, stewing over his outburst with the customer. He shut the door and then turned out the lights and the computer monitor with the disturbing numbers.

Darkness soothed him whenever he felt overwhelmed by guilt and humiliation—feelings that came to him all too easily. He had learned them at an early age.

A compulsion to atone for his father's huckster legacy had driven Billy's adult life. Throughout his childhood, the old man had peppered the dinner table conversations with scorn for his idiot customers. Big Bill Boustany, the original Duke of Discounts, delighted in pulling fast ones on the unsuspecting fools. His strategy was to screw them softly, so they didn't even realize what was happening—then, when they complained, to turn on his goofball charm from the TV commercials. That was his secret weapon. The Duke of Discounts could get a laugh out of anyone.

The old man was a local celebrity in St. Louis because of the zany stunts he pulled in the crude TV commercials for his store, also called the Duke of Discounts. He roller-skated around the showroom. He drove a real fire truck into the television studio, then jumped out, shouting, "We're having a fire sale this weekend at the Duke of Discounts. Women AND children first!" as he clumsily brandished a fire hose and struggled with an oversized fire helmet that tilted over to cover his eyes. He was awkward and skinny, with a prominent Adam's apple and a loud voice that had the raw, strident quality of a bullhorn. He called himself Big Hearted Bill Boustany. His trademark was the visible thumping of his big heart underneath his shirt. It was actually a whoopee cushion attached to a plastic tube which ran out the back of his shirt into the tip of a turkey baster. An assistant off camera would squeeze the little ball on the turkey baster rhythmically to make the "heart" beat in the close-up at the end of each commercial. The on-screen title would come up: "Big Hearted Bill Boustany" as Bill, under his ill-fitting toupee, smiled his goofy smile and said his catch phrase, "I'm just an old softie!" That phrase reinforced the theme of all the commercials, that Big Hearted Bill was such a nice guy that he just couldn't resist giving customers amazingly good deals on their refrigerators, washers, stereos and TVs.

Once, at age nine, Billy got to squeeze the turkey baster off camera. He was so flustered by this great responsibility that he missed the cue on the first take, then squeezed too fast on the second take, which made it look like his father had a gerbil under his shirt. Bill hollered at him, "This TV crew costs real money, you little shit!" The production assistant for the TV station assumed the turkey baster responsibility once more. Billy was humiliated. He never attended his father's commercial shoots again.

Big Hearted Bill died suddenly, in 1987, just after Billy graduated from the University of Missouri. When Billy, his mother, and his sisters met with the accountants and lawyers, they discovered that there was a mountain of debt behind the façade of success. The Duke of Discounts business was close to going under. Billy's older sisters, Anita and Vera, along with their doctor and lawyer husbands, wanted to sell the business as quickly as possible. That rubbed Billy the wrong way. With all the debt, they would hardly get anything for it, and, despite his troubled relationship with his father, Billy didn't like the idea of the old man's life's work being tossed in the trash.

On the spur of the moment in the lawyer's office, without a second of prior reflection, he said he would step in and try to salvage the business. His sisters and their husbands objected loudly. "What do you know? A few weeks ago, you were a college kid smoking pot in your dorm room!" His mother, Rose, hated conflict, but she had never been comfortable with her husband's rough treatment of Billy.

She ended the argument by supporting her son's idea.

The die was cast. Billy planned to go for a Master's in Electrical Engineering—his dream was to design high-end stereo systems—but that was no longer an option. Instead, he got a very fast hard-knocks education.

At first, Billy tried to follow his father's formula—even doing a wacky commercial. But it flopped, and he pulled it off the air after only two days. Despite that embarrassment, Billy managed to stabilize the business over the next few years. He changed the name to Duke's Digital and bet heavily on computers, stereos, and high-end TVs. As the business began to grow, he was able to set his mother up with a comfortable lifestyle in the old house. His sisters were already married to successful guys, so he didn't have to worry about them. In 1989, Billy married Carol Sprague, a customer who walked into the Crestwood store to buy a PC with graduation money. She needed it for her first teaching job. Their daughter, Meredith, was born just over a year later.

There was a knock on Billy's office door, followed by a voice, "Hey, boss, are you okay?" It was Dennis, the store manager, who always called Billy "boss." Dennis was the last remaining employee from the days of Billy's dad. He got his first job for the Duke of Discounts right out of high school and patiently worked his way up. Billy appreciated Dennis's ability to solve problems and calm ruffled feathers. Dennis proudly described himself as a "people person." Billy was definitely not a people person. He had learned to fake it, especially with customers. Today was an exception. Billy was most comfortable when he didn't have to deal with anybody.

Dennis opened the door. Billy blinked as the shaft of light surrounded him. "Don't beat yourself up over that guy. You were right. He was playing us."

"I'd do the same thing if I didn't own this place."

"It's the crazy world we live in."

"Yeah." Billy sighed. "I guess we don't get to pick a different one."

"Whatcha gonna do?" said Dennis with a shrug. This phrase was his all-purpose comment on the foolishness of life. Dennis let silence linger for a few moments. Billy sensed the first glimmer of his funk lifting.

"Boss, why don't you take the rest of the day off? I've got a feeling that tomorrow's going to be a big Saturday. We'll need you fresh."

It was barely one o'clock. Billy wasn't used to having free time on a weekday and had no idea where to go. Just sitting in the car in the parking lot without an obligation hanging over his head felt like a tiny victory. An idea popped into his head—he would take a drive to look at his old house in the city. Why the hell not? He hadn't seen the place since he sold it sixteen years earlier, after his mother's death. He pulled out of the parking lot and headed east on Highway 40, or I-64 as it was now known, toward the city of St. Louis.

Twenty-five minutes later, Billy turned his car onto Flora Place. Little had changed. All the same houses were there and the same leafy trees towered over the street. A mother pushed a stroller on the sidewalk. Sprinklers waved lazy fingers of water back and forth on a few lawns.

He pulled up across from his old house, a turn-of-the-century, three-story brick home with a large covered front porch. A Volvo was in the spot where his dad had always parked the Cadillac. Memories raced into Billy's head. Every snowman he had built in the front yard, every shouting match with his father. The taste of water from the old kitchen sink, different from the taste of the water in the bathroom.

Billy also remembered the last time he had been inside the house. On the day before the sale closed, he had done a final walk through. He had brought along his daughter Meredith, who was four. He surprised himself by crying as they looked around the empty rooms. He missed his mother, whose quiet presence was everywhere. He even felt a soft spot for his father, dead seven years by that time, despite all the insults he had heaped on Billy—like mocking him as "Billy the Kid, the Royal Pipsqueak" to every guest who stepped through the front door.

The insurance agents, dentists, and business owners who were the backbone of Flora Place didn't know what to make of Big Bill Boustany. He was undeniably well-known, which was a plus, but known for something kind of uncouth, which was a minus. They kept him at a polite distance. He proudly parked his gold Cadillac convertible in front of his house and bellowed loud greetings to the neighbors. Whenever he had the chance, he promised them AMAZING deals on televisions and washers. "Just come on down, and Big Hearted Bill will take care of YOUSE." None of the neighbors ever took him up on his offer.

By the time Billy was a teenager, he was embarrassed by stuffy, old-fashioned Flora Place. Most of his friends at the elite Catholic high school he attended lived in sprawling suburban homes, with big yards and swimming pools. But Big Hearted Bill considered Flora Place the symbol of his rise to success, so moving to the suburbs was not in the cards.

After the debacle of his TV commercials, Billy made Duke's Digital a regular advertiser in the Sunday supplements to the Post-Dispatch. The advertising flyers folded right in with the color funnies. Being in the Sunday paper pleased Billy no end, because he had grown up reading those funnies. As a child, he had always been the first one up on Sunday mornings and had raced out to the sidewalk to bring in the paper. Billy laid the paper out neatly on the dining room table—his father got upset if he found it jumbled—then removed the funnies, which were of no interest to anyone else in the family. He took them over to the corner of the dining room, next to the radiator –the warmest place in the house on a winter morning.

On sunny days, shafts of light painted an enchanted circle on the rug. Bits of dust sparkled and danced in the air around Billy as he immersed himself in the worlds of L'il Abner, Beetle Bailey, Hi & Lois, Pogo, Prince Valiant, and Mark Trail. He always saved his favorite, the local cartoon, Our Own Oddities, for last. It contained humorous and weird items drawn from snapshots readers had sent in. Things like two sisters who married husbands with the same birthday, then had babies born on that same day. Or deformed vegetables, like a radish that looked like Liberace or a tomato that resembled Santa Claus.

When Big Bill came down, his first destination was always the stack of advertising flyers that Billy had separated from the comics. He didn't advertise in these flyers himself ("I'm a TV guy!"), but he liked to see how his competitors—and others—were presenting themselves, including the hardware stores, supermarkets and even the basement waterproofing companies. He was especially interested in flyers from the Twyman Brothers, who he viewed as his greatest rivals. The Twymans had another local appliance store, with three locations, that went after the same blue-collar customers as the Duke of Discounts.

Big Bill would intently study the flyers each Sunday morning, then offer his commentary to Billy. "Too much focus on the price. Not friendly. Doesn't make me want to come in." Or, "Great photo. I want those pork chops TONIGHT!"

He reserved his greatest scorn for the Twyman Brothers' ads. "Look at that face with the 5 o'clock shadow! Reminds me of Nixon. Too damn many little pictures! Customers will want to see every one of these deals in the flesh. You'll spend two hours making a piddly-ass sale!"

When Billy was a teenager, his slope-ceilinged bedroom on the third floor became his sanctuary. Big Bill had bad knees, so he never came up there and Billy's mother was too polite to interfere with her son. Billy had a big TV and a VCR, perks of being the son of the Duke of Discounts. So his room was a natural hangout for Billy and his high school buddies after walking back from the dollar movies at the Ritz Theater.

Looking at the house, Billy remembered the pizza joint that he and his friends swore by. It was called Pizza-a-Go-Go, at the corner of Grand and Gravois. It had harsh fluorescent lighting and battered Formica tables, but served the finest thin crust pizza imaginable. Boxes from the place overflowed the trash can in Billy's room.

Pizza-a-Go-Go was right across the street from the Southside National Bank building, a ten-story, gray limestone tower, the tallest in the neighborhood.

Billy and his buddies adored the Southside National Bank building, not for the muscle-bound Art Deco eagles and cornstalks embedded in its gray bulk, but for a gaudy 1960s addition. To remind customers shooting by in their tail-finned DeSotos and Pontiacs that the bank was still there, a 30-foot mast was erected on the roof. It supported a series of horizontal neon rings. At night, they became a pulsing red beacon, visible up and down both Grand and Gravois. One night, stoking up on the bong before a run to Pizza-a-Go-Go, Billy called it the "Martian Landing Pad." His buddies erupted into laughter that went on for several minutes before tapering off into teary-eyed snorts. A legend was born.

Billy smiled at that memory as he looked up to the third-floor window of his old home. He decided that this would be an excellent time for a slice of Pizza-a-Go-Go.

He drove the mile and a half south to Grand and Gravois. The Southside National Bank building looked stubbier than he remembered and, sadly, the Martian Landing Pad was no longer there. Neither was Pizza-a-Go-Go. The space was now a nail salon. Anyway, he parked on Grand next to the bank building and got out to look around. He walked over to the main entrance, where a sign advertised rehabbed condos that were coming to the building "soon—Spring 2008!", two years in the past. Apparently, nothing had been built.

Billy studied one of the carved eagles above him. He heard a voice shouting off to his left, "Listen, you motherfucker, I'm sick and tired of your bullshit!" He turned his head to see what was going on and felt a sudden chill and a brief twist of dizziness. He stumbled forward and almost lost his balance. It was over as quickly as it began. The shouter's tirade had stopped in mid-sentence.

Billy turned back to the stone eagle and the carved plant patterns. Like the design on an old quarter, he thought. He heard music up ahead and walked around toward the west side of the building. There was a three-story annex with a large arched doorway under a yellow-and red-striped awning. A sign said "Asian Market Open Today."

Two young musicians, a man and a woman, stood in the doorway. The man was playing an instrument that looked like a cross between a hurdy-gurdy and a guitar. The woman was playing a flute. They were colorfully dressed and the music was strange, but interesting. They looked at Billy as he passed by without tossing any money into their open instrument case on the sidewalk. He stepped through the open doorway.

Inside, there was an atrium with two levels of balconies. An aisle ran down the middle of the space, which was moderately crowded with shoppers. Billy saw stalls on both sides of the aisle and more on the balconies above. Banners with Chinese characters hung from the dim, distant ceiling. They swayed in the breeze from large, slow-moving ceiling fans. He wandered down the aisle, dodging shoppers. The stalls sold everything—fresh fruits and vegetables, piled high in colorful pyramids, barrels of dried fish and mushrooms, buckets of tightly packed flowers, garish plastic toys, and costume jewelry. A seafood case emphasized eels, squid, and octopus. One stall offered cheap ties and men's hats. Another had silk kimonos and scarves draped on hangers and fluttering slightly in the gentle air currents.

The shoppers were as varied as the stalls. Squat older women in bright patterned dresses haggled with the merchants. Tall men with tattooed faces stared intently at the seafood display. Children darted through the atrium to cluster at a toy stall where a clerk demonstrated puppets that danced and sang. Billy spotted a stall with a rainbow of snacks laid out in a glass case. Geometric shapes of lime green, pale orange, and intense purple.

"What are these?" he asked the young Asian woman behind the counter.

"Very sweet. A little spicy. The best! Only one dollar." She pointed to a tray with little lavender domes, like igloos, dusted with powdered sugar.

"This is our most popular. People come from all over to get these for parties."

"I'll take one."

Billy gave her a dollar and she handed him the sweet in a little paper wrapper.

Billy took a bite. It was spongy and soft with a deep purple interior and a fruity, peppery taste. Really amazing. He nodded. She smiled.

"Call us for your next party. We'll take care of everything."

The wrapper had Chinese writing and a phone number on it. He put it in his pocket and continued down the aisle, eating the sweet as he examined a stall with paperweights and snow globes.

Billy circled the space, checking out more stalls and watching the people. Serious young men wearing dark jackets, ties, and shorts. Black women in billowing, African-style robes. He thought to himself how much the neighborhood had changed since he was a kid. He had never even heard of this market. *I should bring Carol here*, he thought, *She'll love this place.*

For a moment, Billy stood still in the center of the market, taking in its sights, sounds, and smells, and enjoying the spectacle. He took his time wandering back to the entrance. The two musicians were still on the sidewalk, playing a loopy, vaguely gypsy tune. He pulled out a dollar bill and dropped it in the guitar case. The man with the hurdy-gurdy guitar nodded.

"How long has this place been here?" Billy asked.

"You know, like...forever."

Billy noticed the smooth skin under the musician's scraggly whiskers and thought that their ideas of "forever" were probably pretty different.

Billy turned up the sidewalk toward where his car was parked. As he passed the main entrance to the bank, a voice behind him shouted: "Watch out! Coming through!" Billy reflexively jumped to the wall. Three young men whizzed past, riding shiny, sleek contraptions that looked like a cross between a one-wheeled scooter and a skateboard.

"Pay attention!" one hollered to Billy. He thought they might be the same ones he had seen inside the market, wearing jackets, ties, and shorts. Just as Billy was about to yell at them to fuck off, he felt another swirl of dizziness and a shot of cold air from above. He looked up, but saw nothing. When he looked down again, the skateboarders had disappeared.

Billy found his car and pulled into a parking lot to turn around and head back north on Grand. At the Gravois intersection he glanced in his rearview mirror and saw the Southside National Bank building. There was a vacant lot on the west side. Isn't that where the Asian Market was?

Billy drove home with his head spinning.

Carol Boustany chopped vegetables into precise pieces and tossed them into a large salad bowl. She had recently taken a knife skills course, titled "The Way of the Knife," at a nearby cooking school and now she could mince an onion into perfectly uniform bits in no time. When Carol set her mind to do something, it was done right.

The orderliness of preparing food soothed Carol after long days teaching middle school adolescents, with their rowdiness, mood swings, and theatrical outbursts. All she had to do was learn some basic techniques, follow the steps in a recipe, add a dash of creativity, and she could make dishes that everyone appreciated and enjoyed.

She finished the salad and sealed the bowl with plastic wrap. She checked the clock above the stove. Where the hell was Billy? They were due at their nephew's high school graduation party in half an hour. She called him one more time. It went straight to voice mail. This was just like him—flaking out again. Carol knew that things weren't going well at the store, though it was like pulling teeth to get him to talk about it. He had always been a "suffer in silence" kind of guy, but she was beginning to really worry. She sensed that his reticence really meant "I'm scared and have no fucking idea what to do!"

Carol had tried various strategies to get him involved in things outside of the damn store, but it wasn't easy. For years, she had gone out of her way to stay close to Billy's sisters. More than anything, she believed in family. Without her efforts, Billy wouldn't have any relationship with them at all.

Billy breezed into the kitchen.

"I've been trying to call you for the last hour," Carol said.

Billy took his phone out of his pocket. It was dead. "The battery must have drained. Sorry."

"We're supposed to be at Vera's in thirty minutes. It's Elliot's graduation party."

"Didn't we just do that a few weeks ago?"

"That was the family party. This is the big family and friends party."

Billy tried to regain his bearings after this very difficult and strange day. When he left for work this morning, he was looking forward to a normal evening watching a World War II documentary on the History Channel. There was an endless parade of these programs, with black-and-white battle scenes, diving fighter planes, and marching Nazis. Billy never got tired of them.

But he knew not to question Carol's judgment that their presence at the party was mandatory. She was acutely attuned to delicate webs of duty and etiquette that extended from them out to half the city. She frequently reminded him of obligations that had never crossed his mind, but were important and obvious to her.

"You should call your friend, Sam. His uncle is in the hospital" or "Have you gotten a holiday gift for the trash men yet?" Or "We have to make a donation to the Humane Society this year'" Why? "Because Alice Twombly, who is on their board, invited Meredith to her daughter's debutante party." She usually had a good point, Billy admitted, but he wondered how she kept track of all this stuff.

"We need to leave in ten minutes," Carol said.

Billy did not enjoy these parties. Most of the time, he knew hardly any of his sister's guests. How did she get connected to all these people? Who did all the Mercedes and Audis in the driveway belong to?

Meredith wandered into the kitchen. She was wearing shorts and a T-shirt and typing into her phone.

"Are you coming with us to Elliott's graduation party?" Billy asked.

Carol put the salad bowl and a jar of dressing into a large picnic basket. "It would be really nice if you came. Your cousins will be there."

"I've got plans. I'm going to a show at the Art Museum. It's work by my video production professor, Mr. McElwee."

"You never told me you were taking video production."

"It's a summer class. I like it."

"TV. Following in your grandfather's footsteps."

Meredith looked up from her phone and gave Billy a dead-eye stare.

"Mr. McElwee makes video *art*. Nothing like Grandpa's stupid commercials."

"Hey! Those 'stupid commercials' built this house."

"Whatever. Give Elliott my congratulations."

Billy went down to the basement to get a clean shirt. He slipped into his home office, got on Google Maps and entered "Grand and Gravois, St. Louis." He looked at Street View and saw the fisheye version of the Southside National Bank. West of the bank was a vacant lot. He Googled "Asian market. Grand and Gravois." All the stores that came up were several blocks away.

Carol was in an animated conversation with Vera and a few other women as various dishes were being unwrapped and arranged on the kitchen counter and dining room table. Billy left her and wandered out into Vera's expansive back yard. The sights and sounds of the Asian market were still rattling around in his head.

The patio was half filled with guests. Rambunctious teenagers, Elliott and his recently graduated friends splashed in the pool. Cannonballs off the diving board were followed by loud guffaws. Billy grabbed a beer. A group of men gestured for him to join them.

"Hi, Billy. Good to see you again."

Like Vera's husband, Jeff, these were lawyers. Crisp and presentable in bright polo shirts, loose pants and deck shoes or tasseled loafers. Billy's encounters with them were limited to once or twice a year, at Vera and Jeff's parties.

Except for one guy who once bought a home theater system from him, he had never run into them anywhere else.

They were talking baseball, a topic that Billy understood and enjoyed. He drank his beer and happily joined in. His opinions about the Cardinals' pitching problems were as good as anyone's. But after a little while, the conversation migrated to boats, wine vintages, and European vacations. Billy was lost and sank into silence. The discomfort he usually felt in large groups began to well up.

Billy didn't know what to talk about in most social situations. The Duke's Digital stores were his overwhelming focus. He had been going nonstop on it since he was twenty-three—half his life. In college, he was a big music fan who spent his weekends in the clubs around the University of Missouri listening to the progressive rock and country bands. He had an impressive collection of CDs and a sonic boom-worthy sound system in his apartment.

But after he took over the business, music withered to an afterthought in his long days. A few cuts in the car on his way to and from work. Today, he didn't recognize the bands that the kids who worked for him talked about. And the ear-splitting thumps and sing-song rhymes of hip-hop baffled him.

In all those years, Billy had never developed a hobby or serious recreational interest. He didn't collect anything and wasn't a connoisseur of anything. He enjoyed his classes in college and was a big reader of history and philosophy. But that habit was also snuffed out by the demands of the business. His literary outlet became the bedtime readings with Meredith, from *Goodnight Moon* and *Each Peach Pear Plum* and eventually to *Anne of Green Gables* and *Harry Potter*. When Meredith turned twelve, Billy's children's literature phase ended abruptly. She didn't want to read with dad anymore.

Billy sometimes felt guilty about not having a hobby. Real grownups had hobbies, but he couldn't figure out what his hobby would be—if he had time for one, which he didn't. It was too depressing to think that the stores were both his job and his hobby. A hobby gave you something to talk about and made you interesting—a person who cared about life's charming, intricate whirlpools and backwaters. Not just someone preoccupied with customer traffic, cash flow, and lines of credit.

His doctor and lawyer brothers-in-law had hobbies, even though, he assumed, they were just as busy professionally as he was. One was into fly fishing and craft beer, the other into golf and first edition books and maps. Somehow, they had figured out how to arrange jobs, families, and hobbies into their apparently stress-free lives. Like the way some people had perfectly organized closets and garages, while others, like Billy, crammed clothes and tools randomly into shelves and boxes, and prayed that no one opened the door to look.

Billy wandered away from the lawyers as the topic of conversation turned to tennis, another subject he knew nothing about. As he browsed the appetizer table, fragments from the day kept fluttering through his mind—tattooed faces, pyramids of sweet buns, the scraggly musicians. A voice startled him.

"You must be Billy Boustany. Vera said you would be here. I grew up watching your father. His commercials were better than most of the shows."

A guy about Billy's age introduced himself and reached out to shake Billy's hand. Billy forgot his name immediately as he launched into a recitation of his favorite Big Bill Boustany commercials. Billy was still embarrassed by conversations with his father's many fans. But he was instinctively reluctant to alienate a potential customer.

"Come by the Crestwood store sometime. We have a wall of photos of my dad, and a little kiosk with clips from the commercials."

"Really? That sounds fantastic. We could have lunch."

"Uhh, maybe. But I'm on the move a lot. The business never lets me go."

Billy squirmed around for a graceful way to extricate himself. "I'm sorry, but I need to see how my wife is doing."

The guy looked at Billy with sad, pale blue eyes. "It's been an honor to meet you. I can't wait to see those photos."

These encounters always creeped him out. Didn't these people have anything better to think about than thirty-year-old TV commercials? Billy made small talk all the time at the store, but there he had a purpose. Make a friend to make a sale, his father had always said.

But big parties like this one were chaos to him. People showing off, talking too much, and laughing too loud. Everyone knew how to play a game that he didn't understand. No one had ever explained to him the rules for getting along with people. Had he missed that day at school?

Carol immediately recognized his "get me out of here" look. They were in the car five minutes later.

"Rough day at the store?" she asked.

"Yeah." Followed by the usual silence. Carol had been through this drill way too many times. What was it going to take for Billy to let her help him?

"I blew up at a customer today. He was picking my brain, then he was going to buy the damn laptop online. I'm sick and tired of being a showroom for Amazon."

She put her hand on Billy's shoulder. "I'm sorry. We'll find a way out of this."

Billy was silent again, then he gingerly asked, "Have you heard about an Asian market down around Grand and Gravois? I saw a picture of it somewhere."

"Do you want to go?"

"It sounded like fun. But I couldn't find it on Google."

"Sometimes they photoshop pictures of places that aren't built yet to make it look like they're already there."

"Maybe that's what I saw."

Carol was puzzled by Billy's abrupt change of subject. But at least he had opened up for a moment. That was a small victory.

Lying in bed that night while Carol slept, Billy scoured his memories of the Asian market. He replayed every moment, step-by-step. Getting out of the car. Looking up at the carved script above the bank door. The asshole yelling from behind. The musicians on the sidewalk. The awning over the wide door. The crowd of shoppers jostling around him, the banners fluttering in the breeze from the giant ceiling fans. The booths with food, flowers, and toys. The guys with tattooed faces. The glass case of sweets. The lavender bun with the paper wrapper … Yes! He had put the wrapper in his pocket.

Billy jumped out of bed and fumbled in the dark for the pants he had been wearing. He found them draped over the back of a chair, then went into the bathroom, closed the door and turned on the light. The wrapper was in a pocket, crumpled into a tight lozenge. He unfolded it and saw Chinese characters and a phone number. *This is fucking weird*, he thought.

He tossed and turned all night. After a while he noticed a faint, gray glow around the closed bedroom drapes. Dawn on the way. He nudged Carol.

"I'm going to hit the gym before the store opens. Feels like it will be nonstop there today."

"Sure," she mumbled as she cocooned herself in the covers and went back to sleep.

Billy drove into the sunrise on I-64 and hurried south on Grand, impatient at red lights when there was hardly a vehicle in sight. He pulled up to the same parking space as yesterday at Grand and Gravois, then sprinted around the front of the Southside National Bank building. He saw a vacant lot, just like in Street View.

He drove to a diner on South Grand and ordered breakfast. He laid his memories out in a line, then walked along it, inspecting each one, hoping that, somehow, the pieces would fall into place and reveal an answer. He couldn't construct a logical bridge between yesterday's detailed sights, sounds, and smells of the market and this morning's vacant lot with cracked concrete, weeds and cigarette butts.

A waitress brought Billy a mug of coffee. He asked her if she knew when the market at the corner of Gravois opened.

She scrunched her face, "The Tower Grove Park farmer's market opens at eight."

"No, an Asian market. Other direction. At Gravois. Right next to the tall building on the corner."

"I don't know it. But I'm new here. Want me to ask the manager?"

"No, that's okay."

Billy finished his coffee, paid for breakfast, and stepped out onto the sidewalk. He looked up and down the street. A few more cars, but still pretty quiet. He fished the wrapper out of his pocket, got his phone, and dialed the number.

It rang several times, then "H'lo."

"Is this the bakery?"

"Huh?"

"I got your number at a shop selling sweets. They said you provided desserts for parties."

"You got the wrong number, man. Don't be calling people so early in the morning." The call ended.

Billy compared the number on his phone's screen to the one on the wrapper. Exactly the same.

I'm not crazy, he thought. I'm not goddamn crazy.

Saturday was busy at the store. Lots of traffic, and even a few big purchases. Not bad for early summer. By late afternoon, the salespeople were walking around with a bit of a swagger, greeting each new customer with especially wide smiles. Billy didn't notice. He went through the motions of being a friendly, responsible owner, answering every question that came his way, even posing for a selfie with an older customer who gushed about how much she had loved his father's ads. She brought her daughter to the store to buy her first laptop. It reminded him of how he had met Carol long ago.

Billy's mind kept dissecting the events of the previous day like a film editing machine. Play a few seconds, pause, examine the still frame. Whirr back a few seconds, play the scene again. What is different? Is there a clue in there somewhere? If he closed his eyes, he could play it in slow motion. Getting out of his car, walking around the front of the bank, the shouted "motherfucker!", the annex with its awning, the musicians cross-legged on the sidewalk … hoping that, somehow, the pieces would fall into place and reveal an answer. But nothing emerged. These replays haunted Billy for the next few days, whenever he had a few moments of down time.

On Wednesday afternoon he went back. By then, he had a theory that hinged on one moment—when he heard the shout from behind and spun around. Everything was different after that. He parked his car in the same spot. A little more traffic buzzing by on a weekday, but no pedestrians on the sun-scorched pavement. Billy got out and slowly, carefully retraced his steps from Friday. He stood in the shade at the front door of the bank building.

Gusts of wind ruffled his shirt as they swirled around the limestone mass of the ten-story building. At the spot where he had heard the shout, he turned around to look south on Grand, then toward the front of the bank. He proceeded to the west side of the bank and saw...the trash-strewn lot. Hmm. He walked back to the spot and tried again, looking left, looking up, jerking his head around. Still the vacant lot. He kept trying. Four or five more times, he did a little pirouette, looked up at the eagles, looked down at the sidewalk, then dashed around to the west side. The vacant lot. He changed his position, moving a few feet farther along the sidewalk, then spinning again. Every time, the vacant lot.

Then he walked over to the spot where the entrance to the market had been. Billy closed his eyes and stood still, replaying the mental film clips from Friday. He remembered the strange sound of the hurdy-gurdy guitar, the burbling voices from when he had stepped into the market. As he breathed slowly, the music and voices got a little clearer. He could almost hear them. Was it more than a memory? He felt a touch of cool air. There was a slight throbbing in his ears. He opened his eyes a tiny bit. The afternoon glare was diminished. Above, he saw both the blue sky and an indistinct, slow turning. The ceiling fans? The fluttering banners?

A voice startled Billy. "Sir? Sir? Can I help you, sir?"

Billy opened his eyes to see a bearded young man in a Cardinals tank top looking at him. He blinked. The afternoon sun was full strength again. The turning faded away like a wisp of smoke. Traffic noise overwhelmed the music and voices.

"You looked like you were having a problem."

Billy was flummoxed and embarrassed. "No problem."

"Do you need some water? The sun is a killer today."

"No. Thanks, but I'm fine."

"White Castle is right across the street. I can walk over there with you. Get you a drink or a burger, if you're hungry."

"Thank you very much. Really, I'm fine. My car is right around the corner."

The young man looked at Billy with concern. "Okay, then. But get out of the sun. Get hydrated."

"Yes, of course, hydration. I will."

The young man walked away. Billy stood there. Sweat trickled down his face. He was exhausted. A cold soda sounded good.

Down Then Up

1929

James Whittemore Hines was ruined, and he knew it.

Everything had looked so very different when the morning began. He had been leaning back in his leather swivel chair, imagining a genteel conversation with the red-coated English gentlemen in the fox hunting print across from his desk, when the full body goosebumps pulsed through him. They had always been the unerring sign of his genius intuition.

"Of course!" he realized. Yesterday's drop in share prices, frightening as it had been, had found the bottom. The morning papers were calling it Black Monday. Today, Jim was certain that everything was primed to rise again. The cowards and sheep might not see it, but Jim Hines did. As clear as day.

His genius instincts about the stock market had made boatloads of money for his clients, who would happily follow him into a burning building. He and they would be in the big money again today. They would be toasting him at the club this evening. The goosebumps had spoken.

He bought every stock in sight that morning, He borrowed every dime he could, he used every client's margin account to the hilt. Then he sat back and thanked the red-coated English gentlemen for their wise counsel.

Ticker tape drizzled into lazy loops around his ankles as the machine clacked away. Prices sank immediately at the opening bell—General Electric, Union Pacific, U.S. Steel, all of them. He was sure that it was just a blip before the inevitable rebound. Before long, the ticker was running ten minutes behind, then twenty, then thirty. The numbers below each company's symbol continued to shrink. But, with the delay, he didn't trust them. They just showed ancient history.

What if the rebound had begun, but he just couldn't see it yet? He tried to call New York to get the real story, but the operator said no lines were available. A few minutes later, he called again and even the operator didn't answer. The market had disappeared without a trace, leaving him blind and helpless in his sixteenth-floor office in downtown St. Louis.

Only after the market closed that afternoon was Jim Hines able to see the actual damage. Stock prices had dropped as much today as they had yesterday. The papers would name it Black Tuesday. Two disasters in a row. He was wiped out. More than wiped out, he was in a giant hole. A client called to ask about his money. Jim mumbled some nonsense about being positioned for the long term. Don't worry about these little ups and downs. The client was panicky.

"I need to get my money to a safe place."

"Sir, you don't have any money."

After that, Jim ignored the ringing telephone and stared at the wall. The red-coated English gentlemen seemed to be avoiding eye contact with him.

Jim had arrived in St. Louis from Mississippi in 1926. Though he didn't know a soul at first, he parlayed his Southern manners and financial insights into a new life as the charmed wizard boy of the moneyed set. It happened so easily that he never gave it a second thought. He could look at a stock or an entire market and instantly know what was driving it and where it was headed. It was like prying the back off of a pocket watch to see the fine-toothed gears delicately marching in lockstep to propel the hands forward.

Jim made money reliably and fast. His clients came to believe that he was infallible. He believed it himself—until today. The pocket watch had exploded in his face. Tiny gears and springs were scattered everywhere and he couldn't see any way to put them back together. He was finished.

He walked out into the corridor. Fortunately, it was empty. He couldn't face seeing anyone. A thick miasma of shame saturated his body, drowning the remnants of the morning's goosebumps. He wandered into the stairwell and, before he knew it, he was outside on top of the building. Pigeons scattered as he meandered across the flat tar roof. There was no coming back from this disaster. Everyone would see that he was really a sham, had always been a sham, and they would hate him for deceiving them. He stood at the edge of the roof. Beyond the low parapet, it was a straight shot, twenty-one floors to the sidewalk.

Did he have the courage to do this? What would be worse, smashing into the sidewalk or being hated forever by everyone he knew? A loud commotion erupted behind him. He spun around to see pigeons madly flapping into the sky. He lost his balance...

Jim's eyes opened to see a pale rectangle. His head throbbed. His eyes slowly focused and he saw that the rectangle was a large window covered by a thin white curtain. He glanced left and right and saw more windows. He was in some kind of enormous room.

A face came into his line of vision. "How are you, sir?" said a woman's voice.

"I don't know."

"Would you like a drink of water?"

"Where am I?"

"Barnes Hospital. You've been in a coma. We're so glad you have woken up. The doctors were very worried about the swelling in your brain."

His mind began to cloud over again. She asked him his name. He instinctively responded, "James Whittemore Hines" as he drifted off to sleep.

"Did I fall?" he asked, as the nurse cranked the bed to raise him into a sitting position.

"Yes, but only about ten feet from the roof to the balcony just below. If you hadn't hit your head on a pipe, it would have been just a few bruises."

"When did this happen?"

She looked at his chart.

"October 29, three weeks ago. They found you about four p.m. Do you remember how you got up there? The people at the Chouteau Club said that they had not had any lunch guests who fit your description."

"No idea. I'm still pretty groggy."

Actually, he was feeling much better, but he thought it best to play dumb until he could figure out what was going on. Jim had never been one to reveal more than he absolutely had to. Saying too much could give up an advantage, and he didn't want to do that, no matter how small or insignificant it might be.

He remembered the chain of events—the big bet, the market's disastrous crash, walking across the roof, looking down to the sidewalk. Pigeons. But the despair that had driven him to the roof was gone. It was as if that had happened to someone else.

They brought him lunch and a newspaper. The Globe Democrat from November 20, 1929. He read it feverishly, from front to back. There wasn't a word about the crash. The stock market seemed to be doing just fine. He saw a full-page ad for the line of new model cars from Dorris Motor Company. He remembered Preston Dorris, a pathetic drunk who hung around the Racquet Club, boring everybody about the injustices done to him. His company had gone bust in '26, soon after Jim had gotten to town. Why were they advertising now? Something is odd here.

A nurse helped him get out of bed and walk to the bathroom for the first time.

"It looks so far away. I feel like Lindbergh crossing the Atlantic."

She didn't get the joke and responded with a thin, forced smile, as if he were babbling nonsense. She probably chalked it up to his head injury.

They asked him his address, so they could bring him some of his own clothes. He said he lived at 324 North Newstead. Later, the nurse came back and asked if that was the right address. The hospital sent a messenger and the person who answered the door did not know a Mr. Hines.

"Maybe I was wrong. I don't know. Anything with numbers is all jumbled up in my head. It will come to me in a few days."

It dawned on Jim that nobody here knew who he was. Compared to the shattered fortunes he had left behind, this was fantastic. Between the newspaper and the jokes that fell flat, people seemed to have no awareness of recent events. Were they the real amnesiacs?

"We've asked a neurology specialist to examine you tomorrow. He's brilliant. Dr. Vernon Cantwell."

Jim cringed inside. Vern Cantwell was one of his clients. The crash had wiped out his account along with all the others. Jim was certain that Dr. Cantwell would recognize him right away.

Like many doctors, Cantwell thought he was smarter than everyone else. That had irked Jim, whose whole life had been based on the premise that *he* was the smartest guy around. During long conversations, Cantwell had resisted Jim's pitches for his investment services. Then, Jim found out that Cantwell was a fanatic for playing cards, bridge, in particular. Jim read up on the game. It was child's play, compared to the stock market. He joined in the nightly tournaments at the Racquet Club. He learned the basics of strategy and played well enough to earn a reputation as a solid competitor, but not so well as to scare anyone off. One evening, Jim and a partner teamed up against Dr. Cantwell and his partner, who were the reigning club champions. Jim destroyed them. It was the bridge equivalent of a no-hitter. After that, Cantwell accepted him as an intellectual equal and invested his whole portfolio with him.

Cantwell was sure to tear Jim into little pieces as soon as he saw him. His safe haven of anonymity was about to end. He thought about running, but he still didn't have any clothes, just the hospital pajamas. He was going to have to take his lumps.

At ten the next morning, Dr. Cantwell, in a white coat, entered the room. He was looking down at his clipboard. "You are James Whittemore Hines?"

"Yes, sir," said Jim. "But everyone calls me Whit." He thought that using his middle name might throw Cantwell off the scent.

The doctor looked up from the clipboard and squarely into Jim's eyes. There was not a flicker of recognition.

"Interesting. You're suffering from acute memory loss, Whit, but you know what 'everyone' calls you. How is that?"

"I don't know, I just do."

"The brain is a wonderful organ, but it does play tricks."

Dr. Cantwell proceeded to examine Jim. He tested his reflexes and shined a flashlight into his eyes. He asked a series of questions: "What do you remember about the day of your fall?" "Where are you employed?" "What family do you have?" "Who is the president of the United States?" Jim, who was a skilled liar, feigned confusion about most of these questions. From the paper he had read, he knew that the president was Albert Fall, so that was safe ground. He did let on that he had been in the investment business. "I have this idea that I worked in finance, but it's very hazy."

Dr. Cantwell nodded. Jim let his guard down as he realized that Cantwell, by some miracle, didn't recognize him. The medical questions transformed into pleasant banter between them. The doctor viewed this patient as a charming fellow who might be good company after he recovered from his temporary memory loss.

"Whit, by any chance do you play bridge?"

A few days later, Jim stepped out onto the sidewalk, wearing a donated suit and with twenty dollars in his pocket, courtesy of the Barnes Hospital Indigents Fund. Dr. Cantwell had approved his discharge based on Jim's made-up plan to take the train to Mississippi for further recuperation at the home of a fictitious aunt. And the promise of an evening of bridge when he returned to St. Louis.

He looked around. The city glittered on a sunny November morning. Something about the street and the people and the streetcars looked a little off, but he couldn't put his finger on it. The important thing was that the slate had been wiped clean. His past and his debts had vanished. *Don't look a gift horse in the mouth*, he thought.

He had made a fortune in this city once. He could do it again.

IF AT FIRST YOU DON'T SUCCEED

2010

AFFAIRS AT THE STORE FILLED BILLY'S DAYS for the rest of the week. Vendor reps pressured him to make bigger commitments and put in new displays of their companies' stuff. He had meetings with the retail consultant almost every day about plans for a makeover of the Crestwood store. This location had suffered the worst sales decline in the past few years, due to the closing of Crestwood Mall, just a few blocks away. The area, once thriving with traffic all day on weekends, now had the first whiffs of retail death. Billy learned to be acutely sensitive to this smell.

When he first took over the business after the Duke's death, the original store, on Gravois in South St. Louis, was still the flagship. The old man had featured it in all his advertising. It had the most loyal customers and most senior employees. But when Billy first saw the sales numbers, he realized that it was a money pit—the Crestwood store, then only a couple of years old, was the only one making a profit. That's when Billy first smelled the retail death stink. He closed the Gravois store within a year. His sisters howled that he was desecrating his father's memory, conveniently forgetting their own plan to sell off the whole business. The old-guard employees grumbled and shunned him—until he laid them off. He sold the building at a loss to a developer who bulldozed it to build a Jiffy Lube. But the business stopped leaking cash.

He put his money into Crestwood and, eventually, three more locations in fast-growing suburbs. He stopped carrying kitchen appliances and cheap stereos. It was the dawn of the home theater craze and Billy was out in front. A few years later, he would become the first in St. Louis to sell DVD players. He also purged the business of his father's style. Though he did create that wall of photos to commemorate his father and the TV ads.

These moves were a gamble, but he couldn't see any other way forward. They paid off. Billy, at age twenty-eight, had a better business going than the Duke of Discounts ever could have imagined.

Employees and business colleagues treated Billy like he had the golden touch. Everyone wanted to be his friend. He kept working his twelve to fourteen-hour days without let up, but fear of failure no longer haunted him. He relaxed a bit

In 2006, the good times began to peter out. Billy had survived the onslaught of the big box stores, like Circuit City and Best Buy, in the 1990s. But this was different. People he knew were starting to buy computers and electronics online, from Dell and Amazon. He never thought online sales would amount to much with complex products. Customers wanted tech support and reassurance from someone they viewed as an expert. But now, he was hearing about "the web" more and more. Retail death was swirling everywhere.

In early 2010, Billy's banker, Dan, pressured him to hire a retail consultant, Justin, to develop a new strategy for the stores. Dan said Justin had done great work for a local shoe store chain. "He worked miracles. Think what he could do for a high-tech business like yours." Billy, who had big outstanding loans from the bank, was in no position to blow Dan off.

With his nonstop consultant doublespeak, Justin was rapidly ascending to the top of Billy's Most Hated list. He spewed buzzwords and big talk at the drop of a hat— "analytics" and "customer intimacy" and "destination experiences." What the hell are those?

Even if Billy matched Amazon's prices, they didn't have to charge sales tax. How much customer intimacy will he need to analyze to compete with that? Should he install ice cream machines and bounce castles?

Billy wondered what the Duke of Discounts would do. More television ads? Do people even watch TV any more without first recording it to zip past the commercials? Billy was surprised that he wished for his father's advice.

The week got away from Billy. One meeting or crisis after another. Each evening, he fell asleep before finishing his evening glass of wine on the patio with Carol. The weekend brought no respite. He spent Saturday with the pool repair guy fixing the crapped-out filter pump. Another seven hundred bucks out the door. Then on Sunday he had a long-planned ride with his neighbor, one of his few friends. Billy liked the rides because they involved very little conversation. They rode the Riverfront trail to Alton, then to Pere Marquette State Park, a 46-mile distance. Their wives met them for a late lunch at the park's lodge. That night, he was wiped out.

Still, whenever the tiniest sliver of time opened up, whether he was getting a cup of coffee between meetings or riding along the Mississippi under the magnificent Illinois bluffs, replays of the Asian market ran back and forth through his head. He had no choice. He would have to check it out one more time.

Billy slipped away from work the next Tuesday afternoon, swearing to himself that this would be his last visit to Grand and Gravois.

He slowly paced back and forth in front of the Southside National Bank building. He watched the cars in the White Castle drive-through across the street. Standing in the alcove, he spun around in quick half-circles like he had done the week before. Nothing. He tried rewinding his mental movie back to the moment when he felt the little shudder of cold air that, perhaps, signaled the change. Nothing.

He leaned against the building and tilted his head up to see the beaks of the carved eagles on the wall above protruding from the surface of the limestone. They looked weird from this angle. He thought back to the Carlos Castaneda books he read in high school, up on the third floor of Flora Place. What would Don Juan tell him to do?

Billy closed his eyes and tried to empty his mind. He sensed a slight movement in the darkness behind his eyelids, something hovering off in a corner, just out of range. It seemed like he should know what it was, but he couldn't quite pin it down. Then he felt an unpleasant twinge of vertigo and a throbbing in his ears. He opened his eyes and moved his head, but it got worse. He hunched over and squatted down. Good thing that nobody was around. He didn't move his head, fearing that the vertigo would overwhelm him. He stared at the sidewalk and noticed the bits of gravel embedded in the concrete, like the peaks of a mountain range emerging from clouds.

He took a long, deep breath and tried to relax. Everything slowed down. His ears continued to throb, muffling the sounds of the street. He took another breath. The whoosh of the inhale was all that he could hear. The vertigo began to recede. Just as he thought he could try to stand up straight again, he was bumped from the side and pushed into the side of the building. He shot up and shouted indignantly, "Hey, watch it!"

"Sorry, pal. I didn't see you down there."

Billy turned to see a fat man in a blue jumpsuit pushing a large cart piled high with boxes of fruits and vegetables.

"This thing is tricky to maneuver when it's loaded. My mistake."

"No problem," Billy said. The man pushed a button on the handle of the cart and, with the whirr of a motor, it rose up and pivoted on its wheels. He guided it down the sidewalk toward the Asian market, just a few feet to the west.

Billy grinned. He had done it!

He turned around and looked out at the street corner. The time before, he hadn't paid attention to anything but the market. Instead of the White Castle across the street, a building of green glass filled the corner. A billboard on the roof had a huge image of a beautiful woman in a flowing gown. It was animated, almost 3-D. She appeared to be floating; the folds of the gown fluttered in slow motion. Billy thought she was smiling at him. Lettering faded in, 'Reifenschneider's…just for her."

On the far corner, he saw an ornate brick structure, six stories tall, with wide windows punctuating the façade. A subtle, vine-like pattern of light and shadow in the brickwork swirled up the building, framing the windows. The roofline was sheathed by a shaggy fringe of actual shrubs and vines. Broad shade trees lined both Grand and Gravois. A blue double decker streetcar whooshed by silently. A knot of people waited to cross the street— purposeful men and women carrying briefcases, children holding hands with their mothers. When the light turned green, they flowed around Billy, paying no attention to him.

Billy drank it all in. He couldn't make any sense out of what he was seeing. Where the hell am I? he wondered. He blinked his eyes a few times to make sure that he was not imagining or hallucinating this scene. Everything looked real. As he recalled it later, odd little details stuck with him. Many people were wearing bright red shoes. A sign in a window said "Ski Kirghizstan. 7-Day Excursions." A man in a business suit sped by on a motorized scooter that weaved deftly around cars and pedestrians. It had a slender, scimitar-shaped frame, a larger wheel in front and a smaller one in back.

Billy decided this was his chance to explore. But, first, he wanted to check out the market again. He headed toward the entrance. The street musicians weren't there this time. Inside, he saw the same booths and the lazily turning ceiling fans up high in the dim light. He smelled the same jumble of food and spice aromas. There were fewer customers than before. After all, it was Tuesday, not Friday. The vendors were still setting up. He saw the fat man straining to maneuver the cart through a narrow aisle between stalls. Billy found the stall with the sweet buns again. The same smiling lady was there. He bought a green bun at her suggestion. It tasted of lime and kiwi. Then he got a coffee from the stall next door.

Fortified, Billy went back outside. The building across the street, where Pizza-a-Go-Go had been, was the same one that he knew. It had storefronts on the first floor and offices or apartments above. Tan awnings hung above each window on the upper floors and a broad, continuous awning wrapped the building at the first floor, shading the store windows.

He decided to cross Grand to get a closer look. He stood at the corner with other people waiting for the light to change. He studied them closely. All the men wore shorts and most had wide brim hats. Women wore loose, gauzy dresses. Children fidgeted in brightly colored, short-sleeved jump suits. More one- and two-wheeled scooters shot by, ridden both by men in shorts and women whose dresses fluttered behind them.

There were fewer cars than he would have expected. They were rounded, almost egg-shaped, with front wheels splayed out from the body, like spider legs. Some had three wheels, rather than four. He noticed one with a raised compartment in the rear with the driver up high while other people sat in the front seats. Maybe it was a taxi.

The light changed and Billy crossed the street. Between the trees and the wide awning, the sidewalk in front of the Pizza-a-Go-Go building was completely shaded. As soon as he stepped under the awning, he felt a cool breeze. Very pleasant, though he couldn't tell where it came from. Sipping his coffee and taking a last bite of the bun, he checked out the storefronts.

"DE Repair—Same Day Service" had electronic equipment in the window—polished wood boxes opened to reveal knobs and screens inside.

"Manfred's Fine Meats" was a butcher shop with skinned rabbits and chickens hanging on hooks.

"Schmidt's Canary Cove – Your Bird's Home Away from Home" appeared to be a pet shop. Billy saw shelves of cages with colorful inhabitants.

Photos were definitely in order. Billy reached into his pocket for his phone. It was dead. He tried to restart it, but nothing happened. Damn! He had no way of capturing any of this. He glanced at his watch, a digital Timex, but the screen was blank. Also dead.

He looked east on Gravois. In his world, it was a six-lane street with auto parts stores, fast food joints, and nail salons scattered between parking lots. But now he saw an elegant boulevard flanked by wide tree-shaded sidewalks. A streetcar line, with more smooth blue cars, ran down the middle. Three- and four-story buildings lined both sides of the street. Some were older brick structures; others were newer, with glass walls and ribbons of balconies. Many had small trees and shrubs on their roofs and greenery hung from the balconies.

Billy strolled east. As he walked under one of the wide awnings that extended from every building, he heard a whirring sound, looked up, and saw the awning extend itself a foot or two. No one was attending to it, so it was apparently automated, adjusting to the changing angle of the sun.

There were more people on the sidewalk than he would have expected on a Tuesday afternoon. Women and men going in and out of shops, walking dogs, or sitting at sidewalk tables, chatting and reading newspapers. A boy of about seven was eating ice cream at a sidewalk table as his mother was talking with her friend. As Billy walked by their table, the boy stared at him. Billy smiled and nodded.

The boy kept staring with his mouth open and ice cream dribbling down his chin. The mother and friend glanced up and both gave Billy a hard look. He continued on, a little shaken. What was that all about?

He looked around and it hit him. The men all wore shorts, some with matching socks and ties, and others with billowy loose shirts. Most wore hats, none wore sunglasses. Billy, in his normal summer outfit of a polo shirt, khaki pants, and running shoes, was very out of place. He took off his sunglasses and put them in his pocket. He was not used to being thought of as weird-looking.

A little further east, Billy spotted a sign "Whittemore's." He peered in the window. It was a bar. He stepped inside. The place was dim and almost empty. Two ceiling fans spun slowly. One man was seated at the bar and another at a table. Billy sat on a barstool. A bartender appeared out of the back room. She was a black woman with braids of hair piled high on her head and a big, friendly smile.

"What can I get you?" She pointed to a contraption of steel tubes that was attached to the bar. It looked like some kind of dental equipment. "Innies are half-price until six." Billy looked puzzled. "Inhalants. We have stims, relaxers, and sidies. Pretty much every flavor."

"What's a sidie?"

She laughed. "You know, the kind that twists your way of looking at the world for a little while. Not really my thing, but a lot of people like them."

"Just a beer."

"On draft, we have Lemp Light, Anheuser Gold, and Kahok Lager."

"Kahok. Haven't had that before."

The bartender drew a tall glass of beer and set it on a coaster in front of Billy.

"Fucking Kahoks," muttered the man sitting a few bar stools away. He looked to be in his mid-fifties with a lot of barstool time behind him.

"I'm so tired of seeing them everywhere, with their filthy hair and messed up faces. They're taking over. Mark my words," said the man emphatically. The bartender came over and gently put her hand on his.

"Walt, this gentleman just came in. He doesn't want to hear you go off on the Kahoks. Let him have his beer in peace."

"Mary Jo, you know I'm right. Ten, fifteen years ago, you hardly ever saw one of them on this side of the river. Now, they're everywhere, even on the Southside! I hear they're buying up property to build more of their damn mounds over here."

"Where are they going to put a mound?" Mary Jo said. "It's not like there's empty space in the city. The Kahoks aren't that rich."

"Just you watch," Walt said.

Billy took another drink of beer. It was pretty good. He looked down at the cardboard coaster. It read Kahok Fine Lager, and had an image of a flattened pyramid, which looked vaguely familiar to him.

"Are you from around here, buddy?" Walt asked.

"I grew up nearby, but I live in West County now. I run a couple of electronics stores. Duke's Digital."

"Don't know them."

"What about the Duke of Discounts? Back when you were a kid?"

Walt looked confused and shook his head.

"The TV ads? 'I'm just an old softie?'"

"Sorry, pal. I must have missed those."

"Those ads were my dad's. He was pretty famous back in the day."

"He wasn't a Kahok, was he?" Walt broke into a wide grin. "Just giving you crap, pal."

Billy had never met anyone who had grown up in St. Louis who hadn't heard of his dad. They always responded to the catch phrase. He looked down at his beer coaster again. What was a Kahok anyway? He put the coaster in his pocket as a souvenir. He decided one more time to make conversation with Walt.

"You a baseball fan?"

"Sort of."

"Cardinals?"

"Do I look that old? They left town before I was born. I follow the Brownies."

"Yeah, me too," Billy said, not wanting to get into another standoff.

"I just wish they could beat the White Sox now and then. Those Chicago people piss me off. They got a chip on their shoulder about us. The Sox are the only thing going in that pathetic little town. When they beat big, bad St. Louis, you never hear the end of it."

"Yeah, damn right," Billy said. He had no clue what Walt was talking about.

Walt finished his beer and stood up. "Thank you again, Mary Jo, my dear. I'll see you tomorrow. Don't let any of those damn Kahoks in here. And keep an eye on our friend here. He seems a little lost."

Walt walked to the door. Bright light flooded into the bar as he opened the door, which closed behind him with a swoosh.

Mary Jo filled Billy's glass with another draft of Kahok Lager.

"Don't pay attention to Walt. He's just got too much time on his hands. He was a big-time designer at the brickworks. His claim to fame is that he was on the team that developed the custom lightweight Ampies. Anyway, something happened a couple of years ago and he lost his job. Very mysterious. Long story short, a Cahokian replaced him."

"A Cahokian?"

"An Indian from the East Side. Now all he does is bitch about them. Walt's a good guy underneath the bluster. What was that you were asking him about, Duke of something?"

"Duke of Discounts. A store my dad owned. Everyone in St. Louis knew it. It was weird that Walt didn't. Have you heard of it?"

"I just moved here about ten years ago."

Billy had an idea. He would try a list of famous St. Louisans on her. "Have you ever heard of … Stan Musial?"

Mary Jo thought for a second. "No. Who's he?"

"Greatest baseball player ever for the Cardinals."

"Way before my time."

"How about…Chuck Berry?"

Mary Jo thought again, then shook her head. "Another baseball player?"

"Musician. Started rock 'n' roll. Famous all over the world."

"I thought Scott Joplin was the musician everyone talks about here"

"Tina Turner?"

"I think there was a kid in my third-grade class named Tina Turner."

"Another world famous singer. "Ted Drewes?"

"Now, he sounds like a baseball player."

"No! He sells ice cream."

They both started laughing. Then Mary Jo had an idea.

"If you're into music, you should come to the street supper on Saturday. The Sons of Rest supper, the best one in the whole city. And it's on D-Day this year. So everyone will be in a mood to celebrate. It's kind of a secret, but I'm told that Milo's going to play."

"Who's Milo?"

"You're messin' with me!"

"No, I'm not. Who's Milo?"

"Milo Riley, the biggest singer ever from St. Louis. He's a lot more famous than Chuck...Cherry ever was. Saturday night at Grand and Arsenal. Great food and the surprise concert. They start serving about 8:30. We'll be by the stage."

Billy was pleasantly surprised to be invited to something. "Sounds like fun."

Just then, the guy who had been sitting quietly at a back table came up to the bar to pay his tab. "Mary Jo, I'll take one of those half price innies. Dinner with the in-laws tonight, so I could use a sidie. Make it mint."

Mary Jo took a plastic breathing mask from under the counter and attached its tube to the contraption on the bar. She twiddled some knobs, then handed the mask to Mike. He put it over his nose and mouth and took a deep breath. He put it down, said "thanks" with a dazed grin, and headed out the door.

Out of habit, Billy looked down at his watch. The face was still blank. He saw a clock on the wall that read 4:30. He thought for a moment.

"What's the date today?"

"Tuesday, June 22."

"Year?"

"2010. Are you lost, like Walt said?"

"Just wanted to be sure."

It was the same time, date and year that he expected it to be. Billy finished his beer and stood up.

"One last question," said Billy. He pointed to a large black-and-white photo on the wall behind the bar. A man in an old-fashioned suit with a carnation in his lapel was holding a shovel at a construction site. "Who's that?"

"Whittemore. I think he was a big shot from a long time ago. The first owner named this bar after him."

Billy could feel the two beers as he stepped outside onto the sidewalk. The throbbing in his ears started again. He stopped to steady himself. A shot of vertigo erupted in his head. He closed his eyes and took a step forward. The sounds of the street receded and changed pitch. The vertigo subsided. He opened his eyes. There was a parking lot and a Chinese carry out place across the street.

He turned around to look back at the bar. Instead, he saw an auto parts store with a big banner in the window, "Batteries—40% Off." He looked up and down the street. No tree-lined sidewalks, no streetcar tracks, no elegant buildings. He was bewildered for a moment, then glum. He walked toward his car.

He looked at the familiar corner of Grand and Gravois—the White Castle, the nail salon, the Southside National Bank building with the vacant lot on the west side. A smile came over him. I did it! I wanted to make it happen and I did. I fucking did it!

He got into his car and checked his phone. Still dead. He plugged it into the charger. As he drove home, all he could think about was the street supper on Saturday.

Collapse

1931

It was a glorious May morning—sunny, gentle breeze, a flock of gauzy clouds meandering across the sky—but Jim Hines was in a foul mood. The whole city was decked out with banners and bunting. Festive crowds lined Market Street from Union Station to the Old Courthouse. It upset him to see that almost everyone was enthusiastically waving little flags.

At the entrance to the VIP grandstand, Jim showed his pass to a policeman, then made his way toward his seat, shaking hands with other businessmen as he walked up the steps. Jim found his assigned seat with his name written on a white ribbon. He pulled a fat Cuban cigar out of his jacket pocket, lit it, and took a puff. The smell of the sweet, sharp filigrees of smoke drifting around his face was usually a sure-fire bet to soothe him. But not today. Jim just couldn't get comfortable with what he was about to witness.

He had adjusted to a lot since waking up from his fall eighteen months earlier. Though everyone here spoke

English and the streets of the city were familiar, he had come to realize he had, in some inexplicable way, arrived in a foreign land. No Babe Ruth. No Lindbergh. No Prohibition. No Louis Armstrong. But Jim was a practical man. He didn't go for dwelling on questions that most likely had no answer. He quickly learned how to navigate this place and figured out how to earn a buck—a lot of bucks—and make a name for himself. He succeeded without breaking a sweat.

Once again, powerful men sought out his financial advice and doted on his every word. He had known some of them, like Vernon Cantwell, in his previous life before the fall, but they never showed even the slightest glimmer of recognition when he met them again here.

Jim looked around the VIP section, which was rapidly filling up. Most of the men he had business dealings with were there, wearing their best suits with small flags in their lapels. Their wives looked like rare tropical birds in their long, flower-printed gowns. What disturbed Jim were the military officers in their medal-bedecked uniforms. They chatted amiably with the other guests. Everyone was all smiles, even when the language barrier made for amusing misunderstandings. Jim saw F.L. Wright, wearing his distinctive floppy hat and cape, in an animated discussion with an officer whose tunic was encrusted with a truly impressive number of medals and who was wearing a gleaming, silver spiked helmet. The damn helmet made Jim's blood boil. Leave it to Wright, thought Jim, to buttonhole the most important of the visitors. He had an unerring nose for power. Wright was talking a mile a minute, pointing out details of his latest triumph, the recently completed Hydraulic Building, to his companion.

Jim's seat was just a row behind the ribbon-draped chairs reserved for Mayor Chouteau, a few other dignitaries, and the guest of honor, Kaiser Wilhelm II of Germany. The Kaiser was on a triumphant farewell tour of the United States. The rumors were that his health was poor and he wanted to bask in glory one more time before passing from the scene. The newspapers lauded the visit with gushing hyperbole that made Jim want to vomit.

"Three Cheers for the Man of Peace!"

"St. Louis Welcomes the Savior of Europe."

"Long May He Reign!"

These headlines brought back memories of 1918 that Jim had long fought to erase. Jim had arrived at the front with thousands of other fresh-faced doughboys only to be slammed by the vast, senseless carnage. Jim, of course, got himself out of the putrid trenches as quickly as possible. Though only a private, he maneuvered his way into a job as a colonel's aide de camp. His primary qualification was his ability to procure good French wines when no one else could. The war had been his first taste of the rarefied world of powerful men. He liked it.

Still, Jim saw plenty of death and destruction. He lost many friends and, like every American soldier, developed a deep, visceral hatred of "Kaiser Willy" and all he stood for.

When he read the papers this morning, the stench of rotting corpses and the sting of mustard gas came back to him, almost as real as in 1918. He didn't want anything to do with this bizarre event, but he knew he had to make an appearance. It was going to be the grandest show St. Louis had put on in years. All the important people—the people responsible for his good fortune—would be there.

A shadow passed over the grandstand. Jim looked up. The Kaiser's immense silver zeppelin, the *Barbarossa*, moored to the mast at the top of the Hydraulic Building, was shifting direction in the breeze. The eagles of the imperial crest painted on its tailfins glinted in the sun.

A roar of applause and cheers swept through the crowds on the sidewalk. Everyone in the grandstand stood up. A long, open limousine had just pulled up. The mayor of St. Louis, Philippe Chouteau, stepped out and waved. He turned to offer his arm to a frail little man so bedecked with medals that Jim wondered how he could even stand up.

The Kaiser, smiling beneath his famous upturned mustache, raised his good arm to greet the crowd. The withered arm clutched a small baton. A brass band struck up the German national anthem. The mayor put his hand on the Kaiser's shoulder to steady him and, together, they walked, slowly and laboriously, across the red carpet and up the steps to their reserved seats. The Kaiser sat right in front of Jim. The gold eagle mounted atop the Kaiser's helmet was practically in his face.

Mayor Chouteau stood and approached a microphone. The papers had proudly announced that he would be speaking through the largest "electric sound projector ever used west of the Mississippi." *It's just a goddamn loudspeaker,* Jim thought. He had seen many technical marvels in this new city, from steam-powered buses that glided silently through the streets to little electric shavers that fit in your pocket. But some of their stuff was laughably primitive.

As the mayor began his introductory speech, Jim stared at the back of the Kaiser's helmet. A strong urge to strangle the old man rose up inside him. He closed his eyes and let it pass. Jim tuned out the mayor's voice and daydreamed through the rest of his speech. He sat stone-faced as the Kaiser rose to give brief remarks, first in German, then in English.

A band began to play and a contingent of the Missouri National Guard paraded past the grandstand. Everyone stood to salute the flag. Jim saw this as a good opportunity to get away without attracting attention.

He slipped through the police barricade at Sixth Street and walked north, away from the crowd. He was glad that ordeal was over and he needed a little breathing room. People were still walking toward Market Street to get a glimpse of the Kaiser and the big parade. Jim took a few deep breaths and began to feel a little better. He became annoyed with himself for getting upset. "Never show weakness" was one of his rules.

Ahead, there was a clump of people gathered in a semicircle, facing someone or something he couldn't see. Jim moved closer. A man stood in front of the brick wall of this side of the Hydraulic Building. His clothes were unkempt. He was speaking to the small crowd with fervor and intensity.

"Don't be duped by that thing" he pointed to the zeppelin above, "or the fancy parade. This man is a butcher! His Huns mowed down good American boys, like Bill McKenzie from Chicago, Herb Walton from Chattanooga, Tommy Sykes from Madison. Good Marines, every one of them, killed by Willy's murderers."

The man pointed to a woman in the crowd who was holding her son in her arms. The little boy had a German flag in his pudgy hand.

"Shame on you for letting your son wave the flag of a Hun! Shame on all of you for cheering this monster!"

Jim saw people whispering to each other as the man continued. They weren't sure what to make of this spectacle.

"He gassed us, too. Do you know about the gas, the mustard? No? You're living in a dream! What's the matter with all of you?"

Jim didn't like the way this was going. People were looking at each other nervously, confused by the man's harangue. He saw flickers of doubt and fear in their faces. Jim walked past the clump of onlookers and up to the man. Softly, so no one else could hear, he asked, "Where did you do your fighting, pal?"

The man turned to him with a surprised look. "Belleau Wood. First battalion, Sixth Marines."

"That was a pretty rough go, a meat grinder."

The man looked at Jim incredulously. "Were you there, too, brother?"

"No. I was Army, Third Division. We got chewed up at Chateau Thierry, but we heard about what happened to you Marines."

The man threw his arms around Jim.

"Oh my God! You know! You know!"

"Yes," said Jim as he returned the man's hug.

"You know about the war! You're the first in months." He waved his arm around at the crowd. "These idiots have no idea. They're too busy cheering for that rat bastard Kaiser."

Jim pulled away from the embrace and put his hand on the man's shoulder. He looked straight into his eyes.

"They're never going to understand, my friend. It didn't happen to them, not to anyone in this whole city, except maybe you and me."

The man began to sob quietly. The righteous anger drained out of him. Jim led him over to the wall.

"Sit here and rest a while. Don't waste your breath on these people. This damn parade will be over soon. We'll get a drink and talk some more about the old days. Would you like that?"

The man nodded, not quite believing that he had actually met a fellow veteran. He crumpled limply to the sidewalk.

"Stay here and take it easy. I'll be back," Jim said.

Jim turned and started to walk away. A woman came up to him. She was carrying her son, who was still clutching his German flag.

"What was that man talking about?" she asked Jim. She looked anxious.

"Don't worry about him, ma'am."

"Something about a war? Against Germany?"

"It's nothing, ma'am. I think he had too much to drink."

A man approached.

"Have you heard of this war? He made some interesting points."

All of a sudden, several people were gathered around Jim. They were talking with each other and peppering him with questions. Jim, a little rattled, quieted them down, then spoke slowly and firmly.

"There's no war. There never has been a war. The man is disturbed, obviously."

Jim extricated himself from the group and walked away. This was the first time he had run into another person from his world. Jim was discreet, but this guy was shooting off his mouth, making people upset. What would happen if rumors started to spread?

At the corner, Jim approached a policeman at a barricade. A brass band was parading by, so Jim had to lean in close and speak loudly.

"I'm Jim Hines, an associate of Mayor Chouteau." The policeman looked Jim up and down.

"There's a man up the block who has been frightening people. Very aggressive. He's clearly a lunatic. Probably drunk, too. You need to take him to the asylum right away. Like I said, he's a dangerous lunatic."

The policeman was skeptical, but nodded.

"What's your name, officer?" Jim asked.

"Jenkins, sir."

"Good man, Jenkins. I'll let the mayor know how helpful you've been." Jim took out a business card, wrote something on the back, and handed it to the policeman. "Give this to Dr. Cantwell at the asylum when you deliver the man there."

Jenkins pulled his billy club from his belt and started up the street.

The meeting with the mayor and his business council was due to start in half an hour. Jim Hines left his office to walk to the New Southern Hotel. Even though the elevators no longer worked, his third-floor office was still accessible.

The building commissioner had not gotten around to condemning this building. That could happen any day now. The damage was borderline, compared to neighboring structures. Cracks in the walls traced the path of forces that had wrenched the street below and turned most of the surrounding blocks into a heap of rubble. Hines had noticed that the cracks grew a little each day, but, when the aftershocks stopped, he stopped worrying about a collapse. He had an automatic faith that his good fortune would revive and refused to let anything cloud that sunny prospect.

The earthquake had happened early on a Sunday morning, just four weeks after the triumph of the Kaiser's visit. The ground began to shake, people screamed, and homes and buildings swayed drunkenly. Then, as the tremors grew more violent, the proud structures of downtown St. Louis, one after another, sank in clouds of smoke and dust. The whole thing lasted less than three minutes—157 seconds, according to the geologists at Saint Louis University.

Mayor Chouteau studied the conference table intently. Getting the seating arrangement right would go a long way toward making the meeting a success. Chouteau had known most of these businessmen for years and was acutely sensitive to the nuances of their power dynamics.

Keeping the bankers separated was one of his maxims. Thompson of Boatmen's despised Scudder of Planter's, and neither had any use for Hargadine of First National. Yes, Chouteau thought, keep them as far apart as possible. He walked around the table, setting name placards in front of each chair.

But, what about the industrialists? Dorris was pleasant company who got along with everyone. He could go anywhere. Wright was another matter. His arrogant manner rubbed most of the others the wrong way. And, these days, he was all worked up because of the collapse of his brand-new Hydraulic Building. For him, it was a major source of embarrassment. Never mind the thousands of ruined homes or the destruction of the Eads Bridge, which had cut the city off from the east.

Chouteau put Wright's name card at the far end of the table, next to the beer barons. Griesedieck and Busch could easily ignore him. They spoke German with each other most of the time.

But, what about Hines? He didn't own a company or employ anyone, but he was an idea man. And new ideas were in short supply with this group. Chouteau didn't trust Hines—he had popped up out of nowhere, with no family connections—but most of the others doted on his every word. He set Hines' name card at the head of the table, right next to his own. If the "financial Svengali," as the papers called him, went too far off on a tangent, Chouteau could give him a kick under the table.

Satisfied with his preparations, Chouteau walked over to the window and lit a cigarette. From this twelfth-floor conference room at the New Southern Hotel, he had an unobstructed view of the river. Most of the intervening buildings had collapsed into jumbled piles of brick and steel. He saw the barges gathered around the twisted girders of the Eads Bridge that had sunk into the water. Workmen with cranes were trying to remove the wreckage, which had blocked river traffic from the north. They were making progress, but there was a long way to go.

The levels of destruction were mixed in other neighborhoods around the city, but, all in all, it was a catastrophe. This hotel, the most modern in town, had miraculously survived. Chouteau took some pride in that. He had been pressured relentlessly—and offered a sum of money not to be sniffed at—to relax the new seismic building code. But he stood his ground. His political career hung by a thread. Now, after the earthquake, his "fussy obstinance" and "hatred of progress" had been vindicated.

Still, tears welled up as he looked out the window. What was the point of being right if the city was ruined?

Jim had to take several detours to avoid impassable rubble as he made his way toward the New Southern Hotel. He saw groups of men, women, and children picking through the debris in search of bits of copper or other potential valuables. Years earlier, he had seen people like this in the war-ravaged wastelands of France. They worked silently, with hollow faces of exhaustion and desperation.

Off to his left, he heard an eerie, keening sound. Voices echoed off the brick and masonry stumps of the ruined buildings. A small cluster of people stood at the base of a wall singing a hymn. Jim had heard about the impromptu gatherings of singers that had sprung up around town after the earthquake, but this was the first one he had witnessed. It was both touching and pathetic, he thought. A futile response by humans powerless in the face of the sudden, senseless immensity of destruction. Singing, no matter how beautiful, wasn't going to bring the broken city back.

He arrived at the corner of Broadway and Chestnut. To his right, the fluted tower of the Hydraulic Building had been snapped in two. The upper stories lay in a heap that blocked Broadway. Pieces of the fallen spire were scattered for several blocks. He followed the handmade signs that pointed the way around the piles of debris. Each brick was stamped with the word "Hydraulic."

He entered the hotel lobby and glanced at his watch. The meeting would start in five minutes. Rather than head to the elevator, he stopped at the bar for a coffee. He always liked to be the last to arrive—the unspoken hint of nonchalance would give him an advantage over these earnest businessmen, who, these days, were in barely controlled panic. He needed every angle he could find, no matter how small, if he were going to convince them to agree to his audacious plan.

Hines had been mulling over his idea for months. But he hadn't seen any plausible way to convince the timid leaders of St. Louis to sign onto it. Too many toes would be stepped on, especially those of the bankers. That would be fine with Jim, who despised every pompous, dull-witted banker who had gotten in his way over the years.

The earthquake changed everything. The city, and the men in the room he was about to enter, had no other options. Jim complimented himself for again being in the right place, at the right time, with the right idea. His intuition, despite the regrettable lapse in '29, was infallible once more. In a sleepless marathon the night before, he had run the numbers a final time—all in his head, without benefit of paper or calculator, as was his custom. They looked good. He was ready.

The conference room was full when Jim walked in. Despite the death and destruction that had engulfed the city, the twenty or so businessmen and politicians present were still well-fed and well-dressed. *These guys are so used to being in charge, they can't imagine anything else,* Jim thought.

He had been coming to these meetings of the Mayor's Business Council for months. Time after time, he had warned them of the slow decline that threatened St. Louis. About the imminent irrelevance of Mississippi river commerce, about the reluctance of the New York and Chicago banks to invest in the city. They hadn't wanted to hear it, much less do anything about it. "We don't need New York or Chicago money," they had insisted.

Now, after the earthquake, the crisis had instantly grown from a trickle to a waterfall. He was determined to finally convince them to try something new, if it was the last thing he ever did. These guys always loved his stock tips, but when he tried to tell them something really important, they hadn't been interested.

Mayor Chouteau gestured for Jim to take the seat next to him, then called the meeting to order.

From around the table, men began to give their reports. Jim sat quietly as the tale of woe unfolded:

"Damage assessment continues. Seventy percent of downtown buildings will need to be replaced or significantly repaired. Damage in other parts of the city varies from fifteen percent to forty percent by neighborhood. The Southside National Bank, the tallest building in that area, suffered only minor damage."

Once again, a result of my "fussy obstinance, thought Mayor Chouteau. He refrained from commenting.

"Another month of bridge debris clearing will be needed before river traffic can resume."

"Scores of businesses have ceased operations due to lack of supplies and transport. Many will declare bankruptcy. Employment is collapsing."

"Hundreds of families have left by train in the past week. Union Pacific says that all available seats for the next several weeks have been purchased. The exodus appears to be increasing."

"Initial meetings with leading banks in New York, Chicago and Cleveland have not produced any commitments to finance rebuilding. The possible terms of financing that the banks proposed were onerous. They would have us completely under their thumbs."

The mayor thanked those who reported, then opened the floor for discussion.

"Well, gentlemen, what proposals do you have to solve these sobering problems?"

The room was silent. Jim scanned the faces around the table. Some of the men glanced nervously at each other. Others stared down into their laps. Wright sat with his eyes closed in contemplation. None of them wanted to be the first to speak. No doubt, more than a few of these upstanding civic leaders were already plotting their own departures from the city. Jim sensed their fear. Good, it might make them more receptive to his plan.

After a long, awkward pause, Mayor Chouteau turned to him.

"Mr. Hines, you've always had strong views on financial matters. How do you see our current predicament?"

Jim said nothing for a few seconds. Always better for his listeners to think they were getting the benefit of his immediate, spontaneous thoughts. He had a reputation for unerring instinct.

"For one thing, we don't need money from bankers in New York, Chicago, Cleveland, or anywhere."

That got everyone's attention.

"Present company excepted, of course. Support from the esteemed financial institutions of St. Louis is always vital."

Nervous smiles and chuckles rippled around the room.

"Seriously, I'm confident that all the money needed to revive commerce and rebuild the city can be raised right here. But we have to be willing to do things differently."

R.G. Cabell of Mercantile Bank spoke up. "The significant wealth in this city is represented by the men in this room. And it isn't nearly enough for this crisis. Jim, you know that as well as I do."

"I'm not proposing that the funds needed will come from you."

"From where then? Will you raise the money from paupers?"

A few chuckles bounced around the room.

"Actually, yes. By himself, a pauper has next to nothing. I grant you that. But the beautiful thing is that the good Lord made thousands and thousands of them."

"Why would thousands of these paupers—common men—part with their meager dollars to rebuild the city?"

"Because we will make them owners."

Guffaws and harrumphs.

"Owners? Did the earthquake rattle your brain, Jim?"

"We need their money, not to mention their labor. Of all the discouraging news I heard this morning, the exodus of common people scares me the most. So, we must make it worth their while. Paupers may be poor, but only a few of them are fools."

"Sounds like socialist-anarchism," said Ward Wallace of the Wallace Law Firm, "that's what got that fellow Ulyanov in Russia hanged."

"Call it whatever you want, but the fact remains that you have only two choices today. Remain in complete control of a failing city in danger of abandonment, or own part—still a very significant part—of a thriving enterprise. I know which I would prefer.

"Let me explain. I propose that the city government and all its assets be converted to a joint stock enterprise. Additionally, companies wishing a St. Louis business license would transfer ten percent of their stock to this new enterprise."

"Outrageous! That's thievery."

"No, it's the price of a business opportunity. The plan I propose will make this city the envy of the nation. Any firm that participates will profit handsomely."

"Where do the paupers come in?"

"The joint stock enterprise—call it St. Louis, Inc.—will grant shares to every adult man and woman who resides in the city. Those free shares give them a stake, to prime the pump. They also will have the opportunity to purchase additional shares. That's how we generate cash to invest in reconstruction and, later, new ventures. Shares can only be owned by city residents. If they move away, they must sell their stake back to the enterprise."

"Why would anyone purchase these dubious shares?"

"Dubious? Today, our citizens are theoretical owners of public assets, but they get nothing in return, other than collected trash and filled potholes. That's what I call dubious. The enterprise I propose will pay dividends, which over time could become substantial."

"Since when have you been so concerned about the common man?" said Harry Wickham of Consolidated Grocers.

"Harry, I don't give a tinker's damn about the common man, any more than you do. But I give a great big damn about what the common man can do for this city, and for the fortunes of all of us in this room. It'll be more than money. When people feel like they're part of the action, they'll work harder. They'll go the extra mile. That's how we get out of this mess we're in."

Mayor Chouteau thanked Jim for his "provocative" idea, then asked if anyone else had other proposals. There were some embarrassed squirms as he looked around the table, but no one offered a different idea. "Then, I move that we discuss Mr. Hines' proposal."

"What about the coloreds?" said Ward Wallace.

"What about 'em?"

"Surely, you don't propose giving them shares in this enterprise."

"Don't they have money to spend? Labor to contribute?"

"Most of them are lazy good-for-nothings."

"Hell, most of everyone are lazy good-for-nothings. Look out the window, Ward. We're in no position to turn down help from anybody."

"If you give stuff to the coloreds, you just attract more of them."

"Right now, people, both white and colored, are leaving town in droves. I'm not worried about attracting too many. Everyone has to be in this plan or it won't work. If you don't like it, don't support it."

The discussion moved on. Jim answered every question and countered every objection. He outlined the operating principles, cash flow, investment priorities, and marketing strategy. He insisted on the need for immediate action by city government to establish the new enterprise. He sugar-coated, cajoled, exaggerated, and waxed poetic. Even Jim didn't know what was going to come out of his mouth next. It was the greatest sales pitch of his life.

F.L. Wright of the Hydraulic Brick Company, who had been silent throughout the debate, raised his hand and was recognized. Jim thought, *Oh no, here we go. What nonsense will Wright spew out this time?*

"Gentlemen, I fear we must take great risks to achieve great outcomes. Such has always been the way of the world. Mr. Hines has laid out a daring plan. Very daring. Perhaps too daring. But also brilliant. And I haven't heard any plausible alternatives. I am but a humble architect, not a financier, so I don't have a better strategy to offer myself. I'm happy to commit the support of the Hydraulic Brick Company for St. Louis, Inc. As soon as the legal work is done, we will proudly be the first to transfer our required shares."

Good lord, thought Jim, *he must be desperate for financing for his new skyscraper.* It was the first time that Jim, or any of the men, had heard Wright praise an idea that wasn't his own.

"And I further propose," Wright continued, "that Jim Hines be the chief executive of St. Louis, Inc. In my view, Hines is the only man who can pull it off. Though I truly hope we can come up with a more resonant name for this entity."

And so, St. Louis, Inc. was born. J. Whittemore Hines was put in charge. The coloreds were included. A different name was found—the Citizen Shareholder Plan. It quickly became known as the CSP.

SONS OF REST

2010

ALL WEEK, BILLY WORRIED ABOUT ONE THING—what if he can't get back to the other place for the street supper? He had managed to slip over one time on purpose, but he still didn't understand what he had done to get there or even what or where "there" was.

It became harder and harder for him to pay attention at work. He went through the motions, but barely heard what people were saying to him. Again, the editing machine in his head whirred back and forth through the sights he had seen and his visit to the bar. He couldn't stop doing this. He felt like one of those conspiracy nuts who dissected grainy splotches in each frame of the Zapruder film of the JFK assassination. They were convinced that the truth was in there, but it was always just out of reach.

In the evenings, he was also only half present. Carol, who had long ago gotten used to Billy's withdrawal, didn't notice anything different. Meredith, busy with college and friends, was home only occasionally.

Billy was dying to tell Carol what was going on. He came close a couple of times, but he couldn't think of a way to explain it that would make sense. He had visited this place twice, but he had no idea what or where or why it was.

Carol was intensely rational and had no use for what she called "wish-based thinking." Billy imagined her skeptical "what is the matter with you" face. The more he thought about how she would react, the more he questioned what he had experienced. What if it really was just a hallucination? He dropped the idea of telling her.

Most evenings that week, Billy retreated to his home office in the basement. He opened his desk drawer, pulled out the bun wrapper and Kahok beer coaster, and stared at them. He tried to place them, like jigsaw puzzle pieces, into the logical framework of real life. But they didn't fit.

As the week wore on, he made his plans to go back for the street supper Saturday night. He told Carol that a vendor had invited him to a boy's night out at the baseball game. He picked out clothes that wouldn't make him look so weird—shorts and a loose shirt.

He was ready to go.

Saturday came. Billy was still unsure of his ability to slip across successfully. He wanted to give himself plenty of time, so he left the store about 6 p.m. and drove to Grand and Gravois.

He parked his car, then walked over to the front of the Southside National Bank building. He looked out and scanned the intersection—White Castle, gas station, nail salon, sleazy adult lingerie store. He tried to reconcile it with the other version he had seen last week. There's no way that could be real, he thought. If it was a dream, it was the best damn dream he'd ever had. He slowly paced up and down the sidewalk in front of the bank building. He looked up at the now familiar carved eagles.

He wasn't sure what to do. The first time had been a total surprise and the second was triggered with a sudden attack of vertigo. He stared up at the eagles, hoping for the vertigo again. Nothing. He stepped into the alcove of the main entrance where it was a little quieter and sheltered. He closed his eyes and tried to empty his mind, as Carlos Castaneda's Don Juan would have advised. He wondered if anyone would see him disappear at the moment he slipped across. Would he just pop into view in the other place?

He shoved that thought away and took a few long, slow breaths. He felt the air flowing through his nostrils, then, with greater precision, he felt the hairs in his nostrils tingling with each inhalation and exhalation, like stalks of wheat in a breeze. He sensed something hovering just outside his field of awareness—a vast expanse behind him, though his actual back was up against the wall of the alcove. He was momentarily afraid that he could fall backward. Then he decided to turn toward the openness.

He took one small step. His foot couldn't find the floor. He started to panic, then it landed on a solid surface. He opened his eyes. He was still in the alcove. He turned toward the street and there was the animated Reifenschneider's billboard. The smiling model floated with her billowing dress. She seemed to be looking right at Billy.

He had done it again—and it was getting easier! In front of him was the entire vista he had seen last week—the building covered in vine patterns, the tree-lined boulevard, men in shorts, a streetcar gliding by. He decided to walk north on Grand toward where the street supper was supposed to be held. He glanced at his watch to see how long before it would begin—but, of course, the screen was blank again. He reminded himself not to wear it next time. He didn't want to have to keep replacing dead watch batteries.

As he strolled north, he noticed a mix of familiar and unfamiliar buildings. The branch library he had used as a kid was there, as was the church across the street. But, in many places, taller buildings with greenery-draped balconies had replaced the two-story brick flats and homes he had remembered. In Billy's St. Louis, this stretch of South Grand was a mix of funky stores and ethnic restaurants. But, here, retail was more varied and shoppers filled the sidewalks. Wide awnings shaded the sidewalk on the east side of Grand, but on the west side, where he was walking, they had retracted. The buildings themselves provided shade at this time of day.

At one corner, there was a slender triangular tower, much taller than all the buildings. It was covered in latticework. As Billy approached it, he felt a cool breeze. He figured the tower was a device for dealing with St. Louis summer heat, though he couldn't quite see how it worked.

Billy saw a hat shop advertising everything 30 percent off. On a whim, he went inside. A hat would help him fit in a little better. He asked the clerk what was in style for men this summer. After trying on several samples, he selected one. As he paid for it (he had brought lots of cash, so he would be ready for the street supper), the clerk asked, "Where are you from?"

"California. This is my first visit to St. Louis."

"You picked a great time to come. Tonight's street supper is one of the unique St. Louis experiences. There's nothing like D-Day to put people in a good mood."

"So I've heard."

Billy walked out sporting his new hat. Saying he was from out of town made the conversation go much easier. A good tip for future encounters.

Up ahead, he saw the back of a big stage erected across the street. Beyond, men were setting up rows of long tables in the street, all the way to the corner of Arsenal, about two blocks. He still had time to kill, so he decided to walk into Tower Grove Park, which began at the corner. of Grand and Arsenal.

Tower Grove Park had long been seared into Billy's mental landscape. Designed in the nineteenth century as a Victorian walking park, it contained long paths, stately trees, a bandstand, a pavilion, and faux ruins and fountains. It was also dotted with fanciful gazebos, which served as picnic shelters. Mostly built in the 1870s, their styles ranged from Chinese to Turkish to Victorian fantasies with bright colors, carvings, and ironwork curlicues.

The park had been his retreat and oasis from the Flora Place house, which was just a few blocks to the north. He knew every path, every viburnum shrub with a secret hiding place beneath its branches. He had played in the wading pool with his sisters as his mother watched, reading her book. He had tried, unsuccessfully, to catch frogs in the lily pad pond. As a teenager, he had lounged with friends on picnic tables under the gazebos, spinning tales and learning to tell dirty jokes. His best memories of the park were from ages nine to twelve, when he roamed at will on his bike, racing from one end of the park to the other.

That period came to a crashing end the day three older kids surrounded him and stole his bike. Billy made a meek attempt to resist, but it was hopeless. The biggest one grabbed Billy's shirt and said: "Don't you be calling the police. We'll find you and we'll slice you good!"

Billy walked home, shivering with shame. His mother comforted him, but Big Bill busted a gut when he got home that evening.

"Why didn't you fight 'em for it, you little chicken?"

"There were three of them. They were bigger than me."

"Still, you put up a fight, goddammit. A black eye might be good for you."

Billy stared at the floor, withering under his father's tirade.

"Look at me. Stay out of that park. And I'm not throwing my money away on another bike. You can walk from now on."

Billy turned and dashed up the stairs to his room.

Big Bill hollered after him, "Like I said, fight the bastards!"

All of these memories, good and bad, flittered through Billy's mind as he crossed the street into the park. He strolled up one of the long central pathways lined by tall trees which filtered the early evening light. He had not set foot in the park in years. He saw young couples walking their dogs. A family was packing up its picnic supplies at one of the gazebos. The children ran around screaming and laughing as the adults loaded their car, a sleek, silver, lozenge-shaped three-wheeler. He watched a softball game on one of the fields along the Arsenal side. A handful of fans sat in lawn chairs drinking beer and eating snacks as the teams stumbled through an inning with shouted jokes and clumsy plays.

The park was exactly as the one etched in his mind. Even in this strange version of the city, almost nothing had changed. Looking across the street, he could see high rise buildings poking up above the trees, in contrast to the unbroken line of red brick homes and two-families that lined his Tower Grove Park. But that didn't make much difference. The feel of the park was the same.

Billy wandered farther to the main crossroads of the park. He saw the gazebos he was familiar with, then noticed two additional ones. The first was in the style of a Greek temple, with white columns and a triangular frieze above that depicted children riding bikes and playing ball. The other had an undersea theme. Its columns were carved as intertwined octopus tentacles. A smiling octopus face hovered over the front entrance. A metal comb of mermaids and leaping dolphins adorned the roof line. These gazebos were nice additions.

Ahead were the large pavilion, wading pool, and playground. To his left was the most magnificent of the gazebos, the Turkish one, with its red and white turbaned confection of a roof. He wandered over to the lily pond and spotted a few tadpoles darting about in the dark water. No little boys were trying to catch them today. As evening softly descended, Billy heard the gradual rise and fall chirping of cicadas. He breathed in the long, slow waves of sound, which brought back the comforting reassurance that all was well in the world. A reassurance that went back to long before his bike was stolen, long before the customers started drifting away from his business.

In the deepening darkness, Billy retraced his steps down the stately path underneath the trees. It was probably time for the street supper to start and he didn't want to miss anything. After a few minutes, he noticed a slight green glow on the path ahead of him. It was barely visible. He saw it brighten then fade. A moment later, a more bluish glow replaced it. What was this?

Billy stopped and stared at the path to watch this odd phenomenon. Then he looked up. About thirty feet up in the trees, he saw swirling ribbons of green and blue. They silently pulsed like the Northern Lights. He looked down the path. The curling ribbons of light wove through the trees, crisscrossing over the path, all the way to the end. They formed an enchanted canopy that was leading him back to Grand Avenue and the street supper. Billy turned around and saw that the canopy of light also extended back to the center of the park. For a moment, he wondered if aliens had come for him or if one of Don Juan's visions was coming true.

Then it hit him. He was seeing the street lighting system for Tower Grove Park in this new, very odd and wonderful St. Louis.

Billy left the park and walked toward the gathering crowd on Grand Avenue. People were streaming into the street supper from all directions. Families with children and grandparents picked out tables. Pods of teenagers roamed through the crowd. Young men and women hopped off electric scooters, folded them up into briefcase-sized packages, and looked for their friends. Waiters circulated between the tables with pitchers of beer and wine.

Billy scanned the faces. He tried to imagine the stories behind each person. Where did they come from? How did they end up here? An old lady with a walker moved laboriously toward a table. Her large family protected her from the jostling crowd. What had she seen over the years? Teenage boys laughed and smirked as they scanned the crowd for girls. He had once been like them, standing on this street corner thirty years ago.

But this version of the corner wasn't the same. Green cascades of plants draped over balconies rising up eight and ten stories. Behind the balconies, walls retracted as night fell, opening up the interiors to the evening breezes. And there was a surprising swirl of cool air, coming from no direction in particular.

He looked around and saw slender towers on the sidewalk every fifty feet or so. He hadn't seen them when he walked down Grand earlier, and they were much smaller than the cooling tower he had seen then. Probably portable units brought in for the event.

Workers were unloading carts with flowers and decorating long tables with gorgeous arrangements of lush blooms of all types—zinnias, orchids, roses and more.

They don't hold back, Billy thought.

Slowly threading his way through the crowd, Billy headed toward the stage at the end of the next block. A ragtag marching band of ten-year-olds was pounding drums and tooting trumpets. They stopped in front of a table to serenade the people sitting there. A man tried to shoo them away with a dismissive wave, but the woman next to him took some coins out of her purse and gave them to the bandleader, a girl with a top hat two sizes too large. The band ended their tune with a flourish and headed off in search of their next victims.

Billy spotted the bartender, Mary Jo, at a table near the stage. She saw him as he approached and lit up with a big smile.

"You made it!" She slid over to open up a space on the bench for him. Walt, Billy's barstool companion, poured a glass of beer and handed it to Billy.

"This ain't no goddamn Kahok. Enjoy." Walt introduced his wife, Mildred. She gave Billy a soft handshake and returned to a conversation with another woman at the table. Mary Jo introduced three of her other friends, but Billy didn't catch their names. Recorded music from the speakers on the stage was pretty loud.

Mary Jo waved her arm across the crowd. "What do you think?"

"It's amazing. Where do all these people come from?"

"The neighborhood. The South Side. A lot of the street suppers around town are full of tourists. If you go to some of the big suppers on the North Side, half the people are speaking Russian or Chinese and sticking their movie cameras in everyone's face."

"That's too bad."

Mary Jo shrugged her shoulders. "Street suppers are part of the city's mystique. People travel here and they want to see them. But this one is still the real deal. And with the size of this year's CSP checks, it will be quite a party."

Billy nodded and drank his beer. He looked out over the sea of flower-festooned tables which stretched for almost two blocks. There were people of all ages, shapes, and colors. At one table, everyone was laughing. At another, a fierce argument was under way. At yet another, three generations were on display. An ancient couple sat stiffly as their children talked and gestured with each other and grandchildren gamboled about.

Billy saw something bouncing above the tables in the distance. It was a large, softly inflated ball, six feet in diameter. People were pushing it above their heads from table to table. There were cheers as a table gave the ball a huge push, then laughter as it landed on a group at another table who hadn't been paying attention, knocking over their drinks. They looked up in mock anger, then playfully knocked the ball to the next table.

"They do this ball thing every year," said Mary Jo. "Never seem to get tired of it."

Waiters started to set platters of food on the table—pasta, roasted vegetables, chicken and sausages. More waiters scurried around with trays of wine and beer.

"Don't I need to pay for this?" Billy asked.

Mary Jo handed him some metal tokens.

"I already paid for you. Just use these."

"What do I owe you?"

"Twenty bucks. Give it to me next time you come into the bar."

The meal was amazing. Billy could taste basil and other Italian spices, but there were also unfamiliar flavors and aromas. He almost felt a little high, like from one of his high school bong nights. Could there be something laced into this food? That seemed crazy, but who knows what they do around here?

As he ate, Billy listened to the small talk at the table and watched the people at neighboring tables. He wanted to pinch himself—or stand up and scream. Could this possibly be real? How in hell did he get here? On one hand, the questions racing around in his head were exhausting. On the other hand, he knew that this was a perfect moment that he would never forget.

There was a loud thumping behind him, and he turned around to see a middle-aged man on the stage tapping a microphone. He seemed to be unsure of how to use it. A technician whispered in his ear, then the man spoke.

"Welcome, friends, to the fifty-second annual Sons of Rest street supper. My name is Wayne Mizukowski, the president of the Sons of Rest."

A smattering of polite applause rippled through the crowd.

"Let me give the benediction." He waved a glass in his hand. That gesture got the crowd's attention. Everyone was quiet.

"Here are the words we Sons of Rest live by: Life is short, and often hard, so let us do all we can to make it sweet."

He raised his glass and the crowd repeated the saying. Then everyone took a drink.

"The men who founded the Sons of Rest almost 150 years ago knew hard lives. They worked long, grueling hours to pull this city up after the Civil War and to provide for their families. They wanted to make the most of the little time that they could call their own. That's how our beautiful organization began. Those men knew that sweet times came from the company of those they lived and worked with. The city has grown beyond what any of them could have imagined. We have welcomed people from all over the world. But we have also stayed true to the sweet life."

He raised his glass once more, and the crowd roared, "To the sweet life," and everyone drank again. He raised his glass yet again, "To the CSP." The crowd repeated "To the CSP" and cheered loudly. Billy was getting the distinct impression that much more drinking was on the way. Though he had never cared much for alcohol, that sounded just fine to him tonight.

"How many of you are here at our street supper for the first time?"

Mary Jo gestured to Billy to stand up. He did, sheepishly, and saw that a few others were standing here and there.

"To our new friends! To the sweet life!" Another toast.

"How many of you have been coming to the Sons of Rest street supper for at least ten years?" Most of the crowd stood up.

"We congratulate you. To the sweet life!"

He went on to ask who had been coming for twenty years, thirty years, and forty years. Fewer stood up for each decade, but the toasts and the cheers grew ever louder. Walt refilled Billy's glass a couple of times.

Then Wayne asked, "Is there anyone here who was at the very first Sons of Rest street supper, fifty-two years ago?"

The crowd was completely silent. Then, from the far end of rows of tables, applause began. As it spread through the crowd, Billy, in his excitement, stood up on the bench so he could see. One person was standing. It was the old lady with the walker whom Billy had seen coming into the supper. She held one arm high. Her children were helping to keep her steady.

"Yes," Wayne said. "Mrs. McGivern! I remember you from when I was one of the children running around here, getting into trouble. You are a true Daughter of Rest. You are a soldier of the South Side, forever true to the sweet life."

Glasses were raised, then emptied. The cheering went on for a full minute.

"This city has given much to the world, including our ways of celebrating the sweet life." On cue, the crowd raised its glasses once more and said, "To the sweet life." Wayne had not meant to say "the sweet life" and he tried to stop them, to no avail. Everyone laughed.

"But one of the greatest gifts that St. Louis has given to the world comes from right here on the South Side. It is a man who has made life sweeter for millions of people everywhere. He is without a doubt a Son of Rest!"

From behind the curtain that hid the rest of the stage came a long, wailing song, Ahhh–eeee–oooo–eeee. Billy couldn't make out any words. The crowd erupted into applause, gasps, and screams. Mary Jo turned to Billy and mouthed "I told you."

The singer stepped out through the curtain. The screams became deafening. He was in his thirties, with straight, dark hair. He had a stocky build and a friendly face with a wide smile. He wore a loose, silky, black outfit, with pant legs gathered around his ankles. A rounded guitar-like instrument hung from his shoulders, which Billy later discovered was an oud. It was Milo Riley.

Everyone was standing. Some climbed up onto tables. Looks of disbelief and joy rippled across hundreds of faces. People lifted up children so they could see better. Milo continued the keening billows of his song. The deep thumps of a bass boomed out as the curtain opened to reveal a large band that began to play. There were oboes and clarinets, large, unfamiliar-looking stringed instruments, male and female backup singers, and a percussionist surrounded by massive drums. They all wore similar loose clothes with colorful, wild patterns. The sound was rhythmic, swirling, and complex. It sounded vaguely Middle Eastern to Billy, but it was like nothing he had ever heard.

It took a little while for Billy to connect with the layered rhythms, but soon he was just as hypnotized as the rest of the writhing multitude. Milo ranged back and forth across the stage as he sang. Here and there, he stopped to unleash swarms of notes from his oud. The horn section sent smoky tendrils of melodies into the night sky. Dancing with castanets and tambourines, the backup singers delivered precise, purring choruses as counterpoints to Milo's wails.

After a few minutes, the music settled back to a deep, pulsating rhythm. Milo stood still at the center of the stage.

"Life…is…sweet!" he slowly proclaimed. The crowd roared. He said it twice more, getting a bigger response each time. He waved for the crowd to settle down, then delivered a monologue, dramatically punctuated by lightning riffs from his oud:

"I love the Sons of Rest supper. It's one of my first memories. You can put me in the twenty-year club, at least. Though I missed a few years along the way, my heart has always been right here in…this…place!"

He stomped his foot on the stage. The crowd roared its approval.

"I just returned from the source, from Cairo and Khartoum, the birthplace of this music we all love so much. I played with wonderful people there and every one of them, even if they couldn't speak a word of English, knew and respected our St. Louis style. A couple of those players are here with me today."

He turned and nodded to the musicians and two slender Arab guys, an oboist and the bass player, waved to the crowd.

"One day in Cairo, I took a walk. I wandered through the neighborhoods, the markets, past the monuments and the mosques. Eventually, I found my way down to the river—the Nile—and I stepped in. Got my feet wet. And you know what I found? That it was brown and warm and full of mud, just like our mother, the Mississippi."

The crowd cheered once again.

"As that river flowed over my bare feet, I realized that our music is born of two parents—the father, the Nile, and the mother, the Mississippi. When those rivers of music join together, a miracle arises, alive with power, beauty, and sweetness. It fills our hearts and tingles our bones. It's what we crave, what we need, and what saves us. Can you feel it with me tonight?"

The crowd exploded with the loudest screams and stomps of the night. Milo let out another long, looping wail. The band shifted into a different rhythm, the horns took off, and a new song was born.

Everyone who was not already standing leapt to their feet. Mary Jo and her friends pulled Billy into a mass of dancers in front of the stage. He looked around to see stout matrons, lanky teenagers, and angelic children all swaying in a kind of belly dance motion, with their arms above their heads and their eyes closed. He spotted the two young musicians he had first seen outside the Asian market. They were in a blissful trance, gazing up at Milo. Billy thought these South Siders certainly were a livelier, more fun-loving bunch than the ones he had grown up around.

He kept dancing, following Mary Jo's lead. Every now and then, Walt worked his way out of the scrum then returned with more beers.

"Milo never stops," Mary Jo shouted to Billy, who could barely hear her. "The whole show is one long, magnificent song!" Billy nodded as he danced and drank. He was getting drunk for the first time in years. He didn't mind it one bit.

Billy lost himself in music, sweat, and movement. He relished each rhythmic metamorphosis of the beat, each howl from the horns, and each sparkling arpeggio from Milo's blindingly quick fingers. He hadn't done anything like this in years. He was blissed out, like he had been at raves back in the 1980s.

After some period of time—he had no idea how long—he started to slow. Then, suddenly, he was overcome with nausea. Too much beer. He mouthed to Mary Jo, "Be right back," then elbowed his way through the dancers toward the sidewalk. He was going to throw up any second. Eventually, he found some open space in front of a building. He put one hand on the wall and began to heave. His ears began to ring. The music began to recede, as if fleeing down a long, echoing corridor. His stomach convulsed and all the beer, pasta, and sausage spewed onto the sidewalk. He took a deep breath. Then he panicked. The music was gone. He stood up and turned to face Grand Avenue, empty at midnight on a Saturday night. A lone car passed by, its broken muffler clattering on the pavement.

"Shit!" Even though his head was clouded by the beer, he knew what had happened. He had gotten dumped out. He looked up and down the block, trying to visualize where the stage was, where Mary Jo and the other dancers were still dancing, where Milo and the band were pumping out the rhythms of the Nile and the Mississippi.

But it was all gone. He started walking the several blocks to his car. There were a handful of people here and there. He watched his shadow race ahead of him as he passed under each streetlight. After a little while, his disappointment subsided and was replaced by elation. He had just had the most wonderful night of his life.

Own a Piece of the Future

1939

Colossus Magazine, December 1939
The Mighty Metropolis on the Mississippi
By Jonathan Ormrod

Move over, New York, St. Louis is right behind you and coming on strong!

The 1930s has been one of the most remarkable periods of growth in American history. But, because of pioneering developments in St. Louis, the very heart of the country, the 1940s will, in all likelihood, leave this decade in the dust.

From the Mississippi riverfront to the acres of gleaming factories under construction in its western reaches, the city is humming with raw energy and fresh ideas. St. Louis is changing the way business gets done, the way that cities are built, and may, in the near future, usher in a revolutionary concept in electricity.

The Citizen Shareholder Plan, or CSP, as everyone in St. Louis refers to it, is the brainchild of the brilliant financier, J. Whittemore Hines. Despite all the acclaim he has received, he remains remarkably modest. "I'm not important," he recently told an interviewer, "The CSP is a success because of the people of this city, not because of me." Hines avoids the spotlight and is shy when he is the subject of attention. He is a very private man who prefers not to answer questions about his childhood, education, or family. "My personal story makes no difference. We should all keep our eye on the ball. That's the CSP and its ability to harmonize capital and labor for the benefit of all."

Hines conceived of the CSP when St. Louis faced the gravest peril in its long history. Swaths of the city lay in ruins after the earthquake of May 28, 1931. Businesses were closing and thousands of survivors packed trains and boats to abandon the city for new lives elsewhere. Bridge collapses had cut off rail and road access to large parts of the country. Finance had dried up.

Yet money was desperately needed to rebuild. Hines proposed a funding plan so audacious that many St. Louis leaders were certain that it would fail ignominiously. But they had no other options. No banks wanted to take chances on St. Louis' recovery. Today, a mere eight years later, the CSP earns universal accolades, not to mention handsome returns for its growing number of shareholders.

On the fateful day of June 26, 1931, in a meeting that has already been memorialized with a bronze plaque outside the New Southern Hotel, Hines explained to astonished city leaders that a massive source of capital, both monetary and human, was waiting to be tapped. It was the people of the city themselves, even those packing up to leave town. "If we turn them from mere residents into owners, we will unleash more money and energy than this city needs to rebuild—ten times over."

Hines proposed that St. Louis convert itself from a traditional city government into a joint-stock enterprise, with the city residents—and no one else—as stockholders. Every adult resident would be issued shares and given the opportunity to buy more. Annual dividends would be paid. Only residents could keep their shares; when moving away, they would have to sell and forfeit future returns. To maintain the scheme's democratic nature, no individual or confederation of individuals would be allowed to own more than $1/1,000^{th}$ of shares extant.

With the city on the brink of collapse, leaders agreed to Hines' plan, though with trepidation. From that moment, he took the reins. Commandeering one of the first speech projection systems in the city, he traveled the streets tirelessly, explaining the new plan to all who would listen and signing them up for their CSP shares on the spot. Despite the initial bewilderment of most St. Louisans, share purchases began to rise after the first month. And, just as Hines had foretold, city coffers were full by September, when the first reconstruction contracts were let.

But the most remarkable effects of the CSP became apparent when the rebuilding projects began, as scenes like this played out around the city:

A contractor repaving a shattered street was laying down asphalt that was thinner than the contract specified. A passing tradesman stopped to observe. He boldly approached the supervisor.

"Don't mean no disrespect, sir, but that don't look like no four inches of asphalt."

"Move on with your business and stop harassing me."

"My money is paying for that asphalt, so this is my business."

"I'll call the police on you!"

"Please do, sir. I will ask them to alert Mr. Hines about this paving."

The supervisor fumed, then directed his workmen to increase the asphalt to four inches.

No detail was too small to escape the notice of St. Louis' new citizen shareholders. Crooked contractors quickly reformed or were booted out.

Not surprisingly, CSP shareholders elected Hines to be the managing director of the enterprise, responsible to invest the growing mountain of money for their and the city's benefit. After the basic reconstruction projects were funded, he branched out to invest CSP funds in every major business operating in the city. New buildings started going up right and left.

Most notably, CSP investments are allowing St. Louis' premier corporation, the Hydraulic Brick Company, to erect a spectacular new skyscraper, after its previous headquarters was leveled by the earthquake. Hydraulic's chairman and chief designer, F.L. Wright, promises a structure that will dazzle the world. He coyly hints that it will showcase a new form of electricity that will be the envy of the nation.

So, just eight years after its earthquake-caused nadir, St. Louis has assumed its place as the metropolis of the heartland. The city is bursting at the seams as trains and riverboats bring fortune seekers, eager to make it their home and claim their share of the CSP cornucopia. Smaller municipalities surrounding St. Louis are clamoring to be annexed by the burgeoning behemoth. Dignitaries from near and far visit to study the CSP and glean nuggets of wisdom from its enigmatic, visionary leader.

And a new tradition has emerged. Every June 26, the anniversary of the CSP, the day when annual dividends are distributed to all shareholders, the city now holds a massive celebration with parades and outdoor suppers. It goes by the name of "Dividend Day" or "D-Day." Some observers opine that this annual event will soon surpass the opulence, mirth and excess of New Orleans' Mardi Gras.

What do the coming years hold for St. Louis, other than continued progress and growth? A plaque in front of the New Southern Hotel immortalizes these words of J. Whittemore Hines, "When a man owns a piece of the future, every sunrise is a magnificent opportunity."

Interference

2010

Back at home, Billy realized, with some pleasure, that the other St. Louis had become his hobby. He thought about it constantly, he made time to pursue it, and he was developing expertise in an obscure field that wasn't about making money. Yes, at age forty-five, Billy Boustany finally had a hobby! Whatever happened, that was something to be proud of. He figured that he might know more about visiting this other St. Louis than anyone else in the world.

He had no way of testing that theory because he couldn't talk about it with anyone. On a Thursday evening, a few days after the amazing night at the Sons of Rest street supper, Billy was at his sister Anita's for yet another barbecue.

He was standing in the back yard next to the pool with other men. Some expounded about baseball, others about rock climbing. The brothers-in-law commanded rapt attention with tales of golf derring-do and craft beer revelations. Billy gave every appearance of listening dutifully, but, inside, the urge to tell stories of his trips to a parallel universe, if that's what it was, was melting his brain. He could give these jokers something to think about!

But he knew he had to keep his mouth shut. He couldn't imagine any scenario in which people would either believe him or react positively. In his head, the scene played out like this:

"I had a really interesting time in the parallel universe a few days ago."

"Parallel universe?"

"Oh, yes. You haven't heard about it? I just stumbled into it by accident, and I've found it to be very fascinating."

"What in God's name are you talking about, Billy?"

"I'm not sure if it's a complete parallel universe or just a parallel St. Louis, another city that overlays the regular city. Most of the time, you can't see it, hear it, or touch it, but it's there all the same."

"Billy, are you okay? Do you need to sit down?"

"I'm fine, thanks. Slipping back and forth between our city and the other was tricky at first, but I'm getting the hang of it. I've moved up from beginner to intermediate level."

The men stare down at their drinks and shoot sideways glances at each other. A few drift away, as nonchalantly as possible. "I think I need a refill." "Time to hit the head."

Billy continues on to his dwindling audience. "The crowds and the odd clothes are the first things you notice over there. The cars are pretty weird also. Last time I got to hear some live music. It was unbelievable. Totally different from anything we have. I wish I had some photos or video for you, but, of course, our phones and cameras don't work over there...."

Then he feels a tap on his shoulder. It's Carol, looking at him with her "concerned teacher" expression.

"Are you all right?"

"Yep. The best. I was just talking about last week in the other St. Louis and ..."

"Jeff said that you might be a little delirious." She gave him her deeply sympathetic, "I know what's best" smile as she led him toward the driveway. "Let's call it a night."

Every conversation that Billy came up with, no matter what its twists and turns, ended up more or less the same way. Some went further, to the awkward conversation in a psychiatrist's office, with Carol expressing her grave concerns about Billy's nervous exhaustion.

So he just stood there smiling at the stories about the latest craft brewery in town and its special Belgian or Czech concoctions. Then it hit him. He not only had a hobby, he had something far cooler—a secret. A huge secret, an earth-shattering secret.

Any small-time asshole could have a hobby, but did anyone else in this back yard have a secret that was worthy of the name? A couple of them were probably hiding affairs, but those were tawdry secrets. His had scope and depth and mystery.

Billy remembered a documentary he had watched on the History Channel one night after Carol and Meredith were asleep. Scientists from the Manhattan Project talked about their time in the New Mexico desert building the first atomic bomb.

For years, they came home at night unable to breathe a word of it to their wives and families, who thought they were working on obscure, boring military engineering projects, like waterproof radios or self-repairing tank treads. Then, the day after Hiroshima, they were able to spill the beans.

Though he couldn't see how it could ever come to pass, Billy relished the imaginary moment when he could tell a rapt audience about his little jaunts to the parallel universe. He would, of course, be very matter-of-fact and modest, almost reluctant, but his listeners would beg him for more and more details. The guys with the craft beer and golf stories would be reduced to silence.

Over the next few weeks, Billy went back to the other city whenever he had spare time. Or made spare time by blowing off responsibilities at the store. It wasn't like his efforts there were turning the business around. So, he had nothing to lose.

Every time, the bar on Gravois was his first stop. He enjoyed the camaraderie with Walt and other regular customers. He tried one of the "sidie" inhalants at their recommendation. But it just made him feel lightheaded and a little manic. An additional level of strangeness that he didn't need. Everyone got a big kick out of his confused reaction.

"It's a St. Louis thing," Walt said. "Outsiders take a while to get used to it."

Billy especially enjoyed becoming friends with Mary Jo, the bartender, who was quick to smile and had a subtle sense of irony and humor. She and Billy continued their bantering from his first visit.

"What do you think about the World's Fair?" asked Billy. He was thinking of the 1904 fair that was legendary in his city as the highwater mark of its history.

"Which one?" she asked.

"Uhhh... the big one."

"2004? It was pretty amazing. I had more fun in one summer than I had in my whole life before then"

"Did you think it was better than the 1904 fair?"

"Is an ocean liner better than a rowboat?"

After an hour or so, Billy would leave the bar and explore the surrounding neighborhoods on foot. In some ways, they reminded him of his childhood. Tree-lined streets were lined with well-kept houses with fancy brickwork. Though, the brickwork here was much more colorful and elaborate than anything he had ever seen. Houses looked like gingerbread confections, with patterns on top of patterns, fringed with three-dimensional designs, made of materials he couldn't identify. From his one college art history class, which a girlfriend had convinced him to take with her, he remembered the word "baroque." It seemed to fit.

Every block brought new revelations. Children played in fountains in tiny pocket parks on almost every corner. How did these places get here? Who thought that all this was a good idea? And he never got tired of watching the cars—some of which reminded him of the Oscar Meyer Wienermobile—the people in their odd clothing, and the buildings with moving walls and awnings.

After some thought, Billy decided to call this other city "HD St. Louis" or HD for High-Definition. At his store, the new sharper, more vivid high-definition TVs had rapidly driven the older standard-definition (SD) TVs—which had once been called just TVs—into obsolescence. He found this vivid HD St. Louis vastly more fascinating than the SD St. Louis he had lived in his whole life.

One day, on his way to the Southside National Bank building, Billy noticed an abandoned building at the corner of Grand and Shenandoah, just a few blocks from his old home on Flora Place. It was once the site of Pelican's Restaurant, a seafood place that his father loved.

Billy went there often as a kid, eating shrimp cocktails while his father held court, regaling the other diners as only the Duke of Discounts could. He remembered both its famous turtle soup and the faded undersea murals on the walls. Tuna and groupers glided between fronds of kelp as lobsters scurried below.

On Billy's tenth birthday, the family had his party at Pelican's. His father gave him a ten-dollar gold piece from the 1850s. It was smaller and thinner than a dime.

"This is worth a lot more than ten bucks. I worked damn hard to get it for you. Don't lose it."

Big Bill, in his awkward way, was trying to make up for the humiliation of the turkey baster incident. Billy still kept the coin in his desk.

Billy experienced an odd sensation as he drove by. He parked and got out to take a closer look. The building was boarded up. Its neon sign of a giant pelican was long gone and every bit of copper gutters, downspouts, and flashing had been stripped off for scrap. Billy walked around to the back of the building so he could see how it looked. He felt a twinge of a vertigo that had become familiar to him. Was this another place where he could cross over? He saw two long dumpsters in the vacant lot behind the Pelican building. He walked in between them. The vertigo got stronger in the confined space. He closed his eyes, waited, then took a step.

First, empty space. Then his foot crunched onto a hard surface. He opened his eyes. The dumpsters were gone.

He turned toward the Pelican building. Instead, he saw a much larger structure. He ran around to Grand Avenue to see it from the front. The façade was a cross between a totem pole and a cuckoo clock. Columns shaped like giant black-and-white painted eagles, with hooked beaks and glaring eyes, rose from the sidewalk to the roof.

Billy studied the intricately carved shapes between the columns—vines of various types, hanging globes of fruit and musical instruments—violins, French horns, and flutes. There were also images of tools and small appliances.

Carved doll heads, like putti, peeked out from behind apples and oboes.

On the top floor, between two tall windows, was the face of a large clock. As Billy watched, the minute hand of the clock reached twelve. Lights flickered and danced from behind the carvings and a chirping, wheezing symphony of sound rose up. Billy detected echoes of the music played by the buskers outside the Asian market. This time it sounded like a calliope, with accordion, drums and tuned bells. After about thirty seconds, the music ended with a flourish and the lights went dark.

A man wearing a suit with shorts came down the sidewalk.

"May I help you?" he asked.

"I was just admiring the building. "

"Would you like to see the inside?"

"Sure!" Billy responded.

The man opened the front door, which was made of glass etched with floral patterns and little birds. A brass sign next to the door said "The Refugees Club." Billy followed him inside.

They entered a large room, which appeared to be as wide and tall as the building. It contained fig trees in huge planters and a sky-lit ceiling. People sat in small groups at long tables that were scattered here and there. A shuffleboard game was going on. Others were playing chess at a giant chessboard with beautifully carved wooden pieces about three feet high. It was quiet, like a library.

"What brings you to us?" asked the man, who looked to be about Billy's age, but pudgy with soft pink cheeks.

"Curiosity, I guess."

"That's how many of us start."

"I was in the neighborhood and I never saw your building before. It's pretty wild."

"We want to be welcoming to the people who need us."

"Who needs you?"

"Many people. Maybe you." The man smiled as he looked at Billy. "May I ask you some questions?"

"Okay."

"Are you alone?"

"Yes."

"Are you far from home?"

Billy had to think about that one for a moment. "I'm not sure, but it's hard to get there from here."

"Have you failed?"

"Not yet, but it may be coming."

"Do you despair?"

"Wow! No one has ever asked me that."

"I'm sorry that no one has cared to ask."

"It's not that. It's private. People just don't ask those kinds of questions."

"We do here. Because despair is a terrible burden that weighs on far too many people. This club is a haven for those who need refuge from our sometimes cruel world—the lonely, the lost, and the fearful."

"Is it a church?"

"No. Just a club. For companionship and mutual support. Nothing more. May I show you around?"

The man, George, led Billy through the enormous room. He explained the history and philosophy of the club. It was organized years ago by civic-minded citizens who saw that the city's rapid growth left some people behind. Billy asked if it was for poor people.

No, George explained, many of the members were well-off. The club was for those who couldn't quite connect, who couldn't find their way, who had been overwhelmed by the vagaries of life. It could be a person who speaks softly, and is ignored. Or a person who does her best, but is never judged to be good enough. Billy felt an unpleasant pang of self-awareness. Did he know how to find his way? Was he good enough?

On one wall, Billy saw rows and rows of tiny portraits that extended far up toward the distant ceiling.

"What are those?"

"Portraits of members who have passed on. Without families, they risk being forgotten by the world. We remember them here."

George introduced Billy to some of the people in the room. They were as pleasant and friendly as he was. They spoke enthusiastically about the club's potluck dinners, sports teams, singing groups, and help for the troubled. Back at the front door, George handed Billy a paper application for membership. It had the same questions that George had asked him earlier.

Out on the sidewalk, with the eagles looming over him, Billy thought to himself: Was this a scam, a cult, or something wonderful? Above his head, the music started its mechanical clanging and chirping. Whatever it was, this was the damnedest place he'd ever seen. Which was saying a lot, given the past few weeks.

One day, after Billy had made a few visits to HD St. Louis, he was once again prowling city neighborhoods to look for spots that might have potential for another slip across. He didn't know what exactly would make a place promising, but his eyes were open. Suddenly, a vivid memory popped into his mind—John Little, his childhood mentor in the repair room at his father's store showing him the invisible world of shortwave radio.

John had lived his whole life in the same apartment. He was an only child who lived with his mother, Lily, until she died. Lily had been the Boustanys' maid. She had begun working for them in the early '60s, before Billy was born, when his father, his mother, Rose, and his sisters lived in a little bungalow off Gravois, near the store.

Even though his store's fortunes were still touch-and-go in those days—he had not yet invented the Duke of Discounts character—Big Bill managed to cobble together enough money to hire a maid to help Rose. It was one of the early milestones on Big Bill's life journey to success and respectability.

Years later, Lily made the transition with the family to the big house on Flora Place. She took the bus to the Boustany home every morning, then spent her day dusting, vacuuming and preparing dinner. Lily was present throughout Billy's childhood, though he barely noticed her. She went about her work silently. Sometimes Billy saw her sitting at the kitchen table during her breaks, drinking a cup of tea and reading her Bible. He occasionally overheard muffled conversations between Lily and his mother.

He remembered them because he could hear his mother laughing, something so rare that it startled him. Lily made grilled-cheese sandwiches for Billy and his sisters when they came home from school. She engaged the sisters with small talk about their outfits and their homework, but had little to say to Billy.

One afternoon, when Billy was about twelve, he raced through the house with a friend, laughing and hollering. Lily grabbed him by the elbow and scolded him for making such a racket when his poor mother was upstairs with a migraine. Her strong grip and the fierceness in her eyes scared him. He steered clear of Lily for a long time after that.

John didn't venture very far from home. The only times he was ever on an airplane were in 1963 and 1964, during his tour of duty in the army. Fortunately, he had been drafted during a safe period, after Korea was over and before Vietnam heated up. The army trained him as a radio technician and sent him to a base in Germany. He spent most of his tour there inside a windowless Quonset hut, hunched over his repair bench or at the base's ham radio club. There, he learned to talk with other enthusiasts all over the world and to bounce radio messages off the moon.

John saw little of Germany other than the small town outside the base, where he would sometimes go with other soldiers for a stein of beer. These rare occasions were his only social moments. He would loosen up with the beer, laughing loudly at jokes, and telling long, involved stories, about his mother, St. Louis, jazz and classical music, that left the others baffled.

He didn't fit in with either the white or black soldiers. After the first few months, they stopped inviting him on their outings. He barely noticed. He spent his evenings talking with ham operators in Australia, India, and occasionally, the Soviet Union, who appreciated his stories much more than the other GI's in the beer hall.

When John's tour was over, he returned to St. Louis and moved back in with his mother. Lily worked up the courage to ask Mrs. Boustany if there might be a job for him with the Duke of Discounts. Rose broached the subject with Big Bill, but he was dismissive.

"My customers don't want to buy a TV from a negro! I got a business to run here."

His store was in the heart of white South St. Louis, where the civil rights movement was bringing prickly attitudes and resentments to the surface. But Rose persisted until Bill reluctantly agreed to interview John.

At the interview, Bill sized up the tall, young black man with close-cropped hair and thick glasses. John spoke clearly, but slowly and awkwardly. He didn't get Bill's jokes. Black or white, this shy giant was not salesman material. When Bill asked him about his army experience, John perked up.

"I fixed radios and walkie talkies every day for almost two years. AM, FM, short wave, medium wave. You name it."

"What about TVs?"

"Didn't do a lot of those, but electronics are electronics."

Bill's last technician had recently quit to open up his own repair shop. This kid wasn't going to do that any time soon. He would be in the back room, where customers wouldn't have to deal with a negro. And Rose would be happy.

So, that day, John got a job at the Duke of Discounts. "We always give our BOYS in uniform a great big-hearted BREAK!" proclaimed Bill as he introduced John to the staff.

John settled into the back room of the store on Gravois and stayed for twenty-four years. He spent his days in the repair room surrounded by shelves of TVs, stereos and radios that weren't working. Each waiting patiently with its little tag taped in place. John never shot the shit with the salesmen. He only talked to Big Bill when an unhappy customer was asking why his TV wasn't fixed yet. Without a murmur, John made good on Big Bill's reckless promises.

He was still working there when Billy had to close the store in 1988. By then, Lily had died and John liked the idea of becoming "semi-retired." He turned down Billy's offer of a job at the Crestwood store. It took too long to get there by bus—and John had neither a driver's license nor a car.

As a kid, Billy liked hanging around with John in the repair room after school. John taught Billy how to solder and use a voltmeter. He showed him what resistors, transistors, and capacitors were, and how to find the right ones in the bins on the wall. Billy loved the burning smell of vacuum tubes covered in dust. John had a shortwave radio receiver on a shelf above his workbench.

Late one December afternoon, as the sun was going down, John said, "Want to go someplace really different?"

"Sure," Billy said, "Are we going to drive there?"

John laughed. "No. It's right here."

He turned on the shortwave receiver. As his thick fingers twirled the tuning dial, Billy heard swooshing squeals, followed by staccato bursts.

"That's Morse code," John said. "Probably from a ship."

He turned the dial a little more and a voice of a man came in. It sounded a little hollow, like talking through a pipe. The man spoke with an odd, stilted, extremely formal accent.

"The leaders of the freedom-loving nations met today to protest the imperialist plans to dominate Africa. Chairman Brezhnev welcomed them with warm greetings..."

"Radio Moscow," John said. It was the coolest thing that Billy had ever heard. John showed him the proper way to record the station in a logbook, with the time and frequency, so they could find it again.

Another day, Billy was hanging around John's repair room watching a "Speed Racer" cartoon on one of the many TVs.

John asked, "Billy, what do you like better, radio or TV?"

Billy didn't need to think about this one. "TV!"

"Why?" John said.

"Cartoons. 'Star Trek.' Cop shows."

"Those are just shows. There can be shows on radio, too."

"No there's not. Just music and ballgames."

"There used to be shows on radio. Kids like you listened to them every day."

"They don't have them anymore because TV is better," Billy said triumphantly.

John laughed. "Anyway, I'm talking about TV itself, not the shows. Do you know how TV and radio work?"

"Uhh, you turn the set on and the show is there. If there's static, you move the antenna around."

"Both travel through the air from a transmitter to a receiver. But TV can only go as far as you can see from the transmitter. Radio can go all over the world after the sun is down at night."

"Wow," said Billy, politely, though he didn't understand what John was talking about. The commercials were over and he wanted to get back to "Speed Racer."

John went on. "I think radio is the best because signals from stations all over the world are in this room, right now. Messages from ships, programs from Germany, Japan, Brazil, stuff in Spanish, the news. All of it right here all the time. Just waiting for us to turn on our receiver and tune them in. I think that's a lot cooler than 'Speed Racer'."

"Huh," said Billy, trying to digest John's words. Billy turned back to his cartoon. John went back to repairing a stereo. The usual silence reigned.

The next time Billy was in the repair room after school, he asked John, "What are your favorite TV shows?"

"I hardly ever watch TV."

Billy could not imagine such a thing. "What do you do at night?"

"I listen to the radio and talk to people. It's called ham."

"What do you talk about?"

"Mostly about radio."

Billy pondered that. What if there were a TV show that was all about other TV shows? Might be cool.

Billy hadn't been in contact with John since he retired more than twenty years ago. He recalled John's specific address, 4049 Enright Ave., from when he signed paychecks after he took over the store.

Somehow, Billy knew that he had to talk to John right now. He turned onto Enright, west of Grand Avenue. Enright was just north of Delmar, which, for decades, had been the dividing line between the black and white sides of St. Louis. Billy felt a tinge of nervousness as he crossed Delmar—a fear that he didn't belong there, along with a bit of guilt that this racial divide was somehow his fault.

Billy saw the house number on a classic St. Louis brick two-family. He parked and got out, looking around warily. He walked up the steps and rang a doorbell next to the name "J. Little."

After a few moments of silence, he rang again and heard an irritated voice, "Coming, coming!" Billy felt a reflexive tug of shame in his chest. His mother and father had scolded him throughout his childhood for being impatient.

The door opened. A haggard face, with white stubble and big black glasses, stared out at him through the screen door.

"John," Billy said. "It's Billy...Billy Boustany...from Duke of Discounts."

John blinked.

"I was in the neighborhood, so I thought I would stop by to see how you were doing."

"I'm doing all right...getting by," John said, trying to sort out who this was in front of him. No one had come to his door in four months. The last person was a little girl with her mother, selling Girl Scout cookies. He did not buy any.

"That's great. You look good." Actually, Billy felt a chill at the sight of John. He had shriveled and appeared to be no taller than Billy. He looked frail and confused.

"John, I'd love to catch up. Would you like to go get a beer or something?"

"I don't drink beer."

"We could go over to Steak 'n Shake."

"Come inside. We can talk here." John opened the screen door. A cat darted out.

The small living room was dark and stuffy. A sofa was covered by a gray blanket. A coffee table overflowed with dirty plates and silverware. Billy saw the next room through an archway. A dining room table was piled with electronic equipment. Shelves and a sideboard held old records and more equipment.

"Sit here," John said as he picked up a bunch of newspapers from an easy chair across from the sofa.

Billy pointed to the other room. "Looks like you're still fixing electronics."

"A little bit."

"Do you still listen to shortwave radio?"

"Sometimes. But there isn't as much traffic as there used to be. I talk with other hams now and then."

"That's great. I just want to say, John, that you taught me a hell of a lot. I tell my kid about the time you played Radio Moscow for me."

John nodded, still a blank look on his face. "Would you like a glass of water?"

"Sure."

John went to get the water from the kitchen. Billy looked around. Everything in the apartment was old and faded. A table with lace doilies. Sepia family pictures in tiny oval frames. Besides the equipment covering the dining room table, John had probably not changed one thing since his mother died.

Billy was suddenly embarrassed to have intruded on John. This pathetic old man was no longer the guy who had inspired him about the vast world of radio and its invisible, space-shattering force fields.

John returned with two glasses of water. He had perked up a notch. "So, how's the business going, Billy?" It was the first time he seemed to recognize Billy.

Billy smiled and began to tell the story. The slowly fading sales. The ways customers used his stores to window shop and try stuff out, but then walked out without buying. The killer low prices from Amazon. How he had closed the service department. You didn't really fix anything these days. You just sent them back to the manufacturer who would send a replacement. Who knows what they did with them?

"Good thing I got out when I did," John said. "You wouldn't need a guy like me anymore."

"If it doesn't get better, I may not need a guy like *me* anymore," Billy joked.

"That'd be too bad," John said. "Your dad worked his butt off to build that place. He cut a lot of corners and could be a bastard, but he made it work."

Billy nodded. They sipped their water in silence.

"There is something else I wanted to ask you about," Billy said. "You know that tall bank building up at Grand and Gravois."

"Yeah. I used to change buses at that corner on the way to your dad's store."

"Is there some kind of market that's been built right next to it?"

"I don't know. Haven't been there in a long time."

"I was there a few weeks ago and there was this extra building. Full of people selling food, trinkets, and weird stuff."

"Uh-huh," John muttered.

"Then, when I drove away, it was gone. Just a vacant lot next to the bank. Then, another time, I went to an outdoor party with like a thousand people. Then I felt sick and, a minute later, the street was empty."

John stared straight at Billy. The thick glasses magnified his cloudy brown eyes.

"Have you ever heard of anything like that?" Billy asked.

"Not exactly."

"It's been driving me nuts. Between this and the business, I'm having a hard time."

They were both silent for a few moments.

John said, "It's probably best to let it go. Strange things happen." John took off his glasses and wiped them on his shirt. "Interference."

"What?"

"An interference pattern. Say two stations are broadcasting on the same frequency. Their signals interfere with each other. Sometimes you pick up one, sometimes the other, sometimes a garbled mix of both of them. You hear station A at one place and station B a few steps away.

In some places—nodes—the signals cancel each other out. You get silence. Interference patterns constantly move around. They can be affected by weather, sunspots, even a garage door opener. You can't predict them or pin them down. It's all analog...very temporary. It doesn't last."

Billy nodded as he tried to make sense of John's sudden monologue. John leaned in a little closer and looked Billy directly in the eye, with a stern expression on his face, "I strongly advise you to forget about this. Things can turn out bad."

The conversation with John unsettled Billy. It reinforced his obsessive speculation about HD St. Louis. Whether at work, driving his car, or standing in the shower, thoughts of HD St. Louis were always with him. He relived the sights and sounds of each visit in his head. He imagined all the places he could explore on his next visit.

Every time he turned a corner in HD St. Louis, he came across something unforgettable. It could be a tiny detail, like the lavender sweet buns, or an amazing sight, like the swirling curlicues of lights that snaked through the trees of Tower Grove Park. What further wonders and delights would he see in this place that was both the same as the city he knew and completely different?

Thinking about HD St. Louis was more confounding than just remembering a great vacation or planning the next one. A dark, ominous anvil of questions hovered over every sweet and pleasant HD St. Louis daydream: What the hell was this place? Was it real or just some sort of midlife-onset schizophrenia? Should he see a doctor? Should he share his secret with Carol? How did he get there? And get back?

Billy struggled with these questions every day. They frequently spiraled him down into a pit of despair that was almost as bad as thinking about his business problems. Now, when lying awake in bed at three in the morning, he had his choice of two different unsolvable dilemmas.

He decided to logically address the questions:

Was HD St. Louis real? It sure seemed so. The times he was there felt exactly like real life—there were no hints of hallucination or feeling high. And he had the souvenirs— the bun wrapper, the Kahok beer coaster, the application from the Refugees Club. He could pull them out of the desk drawer in his home office in the basement. He could turn them over and over, hold them up to the light, look at them with his magnifying glass. They were as real as real could be.

Could he be experiencing some kind of mental illness? It was hard to rule this out completely. Billy had seen the movie "A Beautiful Mind" and he remembered how Russell Crowe had been totally convinced that he was being pursued by spies who turned out to be figments of his imagination. It was quite possible that something like this was happening to him.

He remembered his late-night college bullshit sessions when someone said, "What if the entire world was created five seconds ago, with all the fossils and geological layers? And we were created at the same time, sitting right here in this room, with all of our memories? How could you prove that it wasn't true?"

No matter how many bong hits they applied, none of them were able to answer that question. However, it didn't make a damn bit of difference the next morning when Billy went back to class. The world was still there, just as always.

Billy admitted he was stressed about the business, but who wouldn't be? Was stress making him crack? But, honestly, he didn't notice anything weird or hallucinatory going on most of the time. HD St. Louis only existed when he made a specific decision to go there.

Should he see a doctor? Or tell Carol? He had a very strong instinct about this. No fucking way—at least for now. If he opened his mouth, one thing was sure: somehow, he would be prevented from going back. The thought terrified him. HD St. Louis was just too cool to turn his back on.

How did he get into HD? This was the question that fascinated him the most. It was much more interesting than being afraid of mental illness.

Billy began to develop a theory of slipping over. He realized there were several things going on at the same time:

1. He had to be at a certain place. Grand and Gravois obviously worked. And he had made one successful crossing behind the vacant Pelican Restaurant building at Grand and Shenandoah. But that was it. He had tried several other places with no luck.

2. It's like seeing something out of the corner of your eye. If you look directly, it disappears. Billy practiced noticing things with his peripheral vision. When you have the hint of something new at the edge of your vision field, you have to be able to see it without turning your head or eyes.

3. A surprise or a startle helps—something that interrupts your train of thought. Once, he slipped over because of a sneeze. Before the sneeze, he was in one place. Then, after the sneeze and its involuntary blink, he was in the other place. Billy had read once that it was physically impossible to sneeze without blinking.

Slipping back was even easier. Actually, too easy. On some of his first visits, Billy found that the slightest stumble, blink or distraction popped him out of the other St. Louis. He learned to be more mindful and focused while he was in the other St. Louis and, with practice, he could usually stay as long as he wanted.

The whole process of slipping over and slipping back was like learning to juggle or play an instrument. You fail over and over again. Then, at some point, you do better for no apparent reason. What had been awkward suddenly becomes natural.

The more skill that Billy developed at slipping over, the more he came to appreciate it as a subtle art that required finesse and surrender and faith. He thought it must be like what sky divers feel right as they take the step out of the plane's door. For a brief instant, he experienced a twinge of fear and disorientation, followed by the sweetest feeling he had ever known. Just like that, he stepped into a different world.

Billy also figured out a few practical things he could put in the guidebook that he imagined writing someday:

1. Don't say that you're from St. Louis. People start asking questions that you can't answer and the conversation quickly descends into confusion and puzzled faces. Better to say that you're visiting from out of town. (Billy had chosen California because he was a big fan of Hotel California by the Eagles). Say that this is your first time in St. Louis. People may be taken aback at that idea and seem to pity you for having led such a narrow life, but at least they accept the statement.

2. Don't ask about specific people or places that you know—like the Duke of Discounts or Stan Musial—people give you funny looks like you're delusional.

3. Get people talking by asking very simple, general questions, like those an ignorant stranger would ask.

A Universe Less Traveled

4. Bring cash. They don't seem to use credit cards, and yours would probably not be accepted anyway. Apparently, there is some other kind of payment that we haven't figured out yet. Fortunately, cash works, but you won't see many other people using cash. And, even though their bills look a little different from the ones you bring, no one seems to notice or care.

5. Leave phones, cameras, watches and other battery powered devices behind. Batteries are always dead when you enter HD. When you return, plan to recharge them or replace them. This is a big hassle that smart travelers avoid.

Billy also pondered the nature of the existence of HD St. Louis. What is the relationship of this place to our regular world? How is it possible that he could move back and forth, but nobody else could—at least as far as he knew?

HD St. Louis appeared to be a perfect overlay of SD St. Louis, street by street. The corner of Grand and Gravois was the corner of Grand and Gravois in both places. The other crossing place he had found, by the Pelican building at Shenandoah, also matched in both places—though the buildings were different. The time scale was also a complete overlay. It was always the same time, same day, and same year in both places.

As he strolled the sidewalks of regular St. Louis or picked out lettuce in the supermarket, Billy now imagined that people in HD were also there, passing right through him, even though he couldn't see or feel them at all. It brought back his college physics class, which he hadn't thought of one bit since graduation.

The professor gave a lecture on neutrinos, tiny particles with no mass and no charge that flooded the universe, but didn't interact with anything else. Zillions of neutrinos were zipping through your body every second, but you don't notice a thing. If it works for neutrinos, why not for HD St. Louis?

Billy decided there must be a thin veil or membrane that separated the two cities. It floated everywhere, like a gauzy curtain of neutrinos billowing in the breeze. Somehow, he had stumbled across weak spots where he could slip through from one city to the other. Obviously, not everyone could do this, or the cities would be filled with people from both places. Maybe he had a rare psychic ability—not the bullshit kind that you see on TV—that enabled him to sense porous places in the membrane.

He had discovered Grand and Gravois by accident, but the other crossing points he had found—and would find later—were the result of his semi-purposeful wanderings through the city. His strategy was to walk quietly, then, if he felt any slight hint of a difference, to stop, close his eyes, and listen.

He didn't know what to listen for but, over time, found that various phenomena could signal a crossing point. It could be a temperature change, a breeze from nowhere, a humming or throbbing in his ears, a tinkle of distant sounds, lights rising behind his closed eyelids, or a moment of dizziness.

There were a lot of dead ends and false positives. He blew an entire Saturday walking around the Soulard area. As one of the oldest neighborhoods in St. Louis, he figured it was a good bet for crossing points. But nothing happened. He spent almost an hour on one corner, right outside one of the many Soulard bars, that felt like it would be perfect. He closed his eyes, shifting a few steps here and there, over and over again, to no avail. All he got was a sunburn and weird glances from people entering and leaving the bar.

One day, while riding the exercise bike at the gym, another theory came to him—the carousel theory:

Imagine that our world is a carousel spinning around. When we are on it, it seems to be perfectly still and stable. We can happily sit on a painted reindeer as it pumps up and down. Now, imagine that there is a second carousel, spinning in the opposite direction. It almost touches ours. Most of the time, we have no idea that the second carousel is there, but it is just as real as the one we are on. When our painted reindeer comes around to the place closest to the other carousel, we may, if we pay attention, catch a whisper of breeze from it.

Then, imagine that we climb off our reindeer and stand on the floor of our carousel, toes right at the edge. The next time we come around to the point close by the other carousel, the floors of the two carousels almost touch. They are moving at the same speed, so, for a moment, they are stationary relative to each other.

If we are standing on the edge at that moment, and we have the nerve, all we have to do is take one small step across to the other carousel. It's a tiny distance, but it feels like a leap into the void. Our foot lands on the other carousel and we join that world as it spins away. Our world disappears.

Billy thought that the carousel theory was pretty slick. It perfectly captured the feeling he had at the moments when he crossed over into HD. He imagined he had somehow developed the knack for knowing when he was at the right place on the spinning carousel where the other, invisible, carousel was right there waiting for him. But this theory didn't account for the way that HD St. Louis seemed to overlay the regular city. Would there have to be millions of carousels all over the place?

So, for a while, Billy was torn between the membrane theory and the carousel theory. One or the other of them must be wrong. Then he remembered back to the college physics class. The professor had talked about Einstein's general theory of relativity, which perfectly explained gravity, motion, and other large-scale phenomena.

He described quantum mechanics, developed by Max Planck, Niels Bohr and other buddies of Einstein, which explained light—either a particle or a wave, depending on who's measuring—and the behavior of subatomic particles.

The problem was that the two theories, which both worked well at their own scale, created nonsensical predictions when applied to the other scale. This discrepancy bedeviled Einstein, who didn't like the randomness and uncertainty that were central principles of quantum mechanics. He spent much of his life trying to reconcile the theories, without success.

So, Billy decided that he didn't have to choose between his two theories. He could accept both of them as true. If Einstein couldn't figure these things out, then Billy Boustany wasn't going to worry about them.

PRECESSION

1982

BLEEPS, BURBLES, AND TRILLS echoed through John Little's headphones as his blunt fingers tenderly turned the tuning dial on his shortwave set. He heard a passing snippet of voice and backed up the dial as gently as possible to part the tangle of sounds and bring it to the foreground. It was a woman speaking soft spongy Portuguese—all zh's and oo's. He listened for a moment to determine if it was ham or broadcast. A tinny jingle began. Broadcast. John noted the frequency and time in his logbook. Later, he could look it up in his international station guide to confirm the location. Somewhere in Brazil, no doubt.

Then he moved on.

John was sitting in his bedroom at a desk he had used since childhood. It was way too small for him now, but large enough to hold his logbook and radio, a Heathkit SB-100 he had bought with his first paycheck from the Duke of Discounts back in the 1960s. A wire ran out the window and up the side of the building to the antenna he had set up on the roof. Almost every night, after his mother went to bed, John got a Coke out of the refrigerator and spent a few hours roaming the world.

He traversed the dark spectrum ocean seeking voices and signals bobbing in the vastness of static and throbbing thumps. Anything could turn up. An Australian fishing report. Germans declaiming incomprehensibly in ordered rows of complete certainty. Mexican game shows. British seaman's broadcasts, which provided news and encouragement to lonely, far-flung sailors, reading letters from wives and mothers without embarrassment, for all the world to hear.

During his nightly voyages, John also sought out other ham operators for conversation. There was a group of regulars, Arturo from Buenos Aires, Wendell from Bozeman, Montana, Steve from Tucson, and others. Most were from the Western hemisphere, where the common hours of darkness enabled their signals to ricochet off the ionosphere and travel the farthest. They mostly talked about equipment—antennas, transmitter sets, and microphones—and DXing, the sport of making contact with the most distant signals. Politics and religion were considered topics unworthy of discussion. These fellow navigators of darkness were John's best friends.

After checking in with Arturo and Steve, the only members of the group who were transmitting that night, John set out on a solo voyage, steering by thumb and forefinger. He tuned to a portion of the band he rarely visited, then inched his way methodically across the dial in tiny nudges, pausing if he heard a flicker that might be another ham. If that operator, say AB2GD, was CQing, calling to find other hams, John responded with his own amateur radio call sign, NØJL.

"AB2GD. AB2GD. This is NØJL. November-Zero-Juliet-Lima."

Most operators only wanted to exchange call signs, then end the conversation. Their goal was to rack up as many contacts as they could. But now and then, John found operators who wanted to talk longer. That's how he had acquired his group of radio friends.

When he found a frequency that was silent, John might send his own CQ to see if anyone else around the world was tuned to that frequency at that moment.

"CQ. CQ. Calling CQ. This is NØJL. November-Zero-Juliet-Lima."

He would repeat this a few times. If someone responded, he had a new contact for his logbook. If not, he sailed on.

John came to a set of frequencies that were primarily used to transmit rapid-fire Morse code, cacophonous chirps meant to be decoded by machines. These weren't very promising for conversations, and he usually skimmed through them quickly. But tonight he heard a faint voice signal jammed in a narrow band between pounding waves of automated traffic.

"Ahoy. Ahoy. Does anyone go there? Does anyone go there?"

John nudged his finetuning dial to try to lock in on the signal. He adjusted his squelch dial to reduce the adjacent interference. The voice was a little better, but still faint and oddly distorted.

"Ahoy. Ahoy. Does anyone go there? Does anyone go there?"

John responded.

"Please identify yourself. This is NØJL. November-Zero-Juliet-Lima."

"I am Leo 1764. Leo 1-7-6-4."

"Do you mean Lima-Echo-Oscar 1-7-6-4?"

A pause, then "I do not understand."

This operator was not following amateur radio protocol. Perhaps he was someone who didn't know how to use shortwave.

"Are you in distress? Do you need assistance?"

"No distress. I am seeking radio contact."

The voice continued to distort. It seemed to speed up, then slow down. John had never heard interference like that.

"What is your location?"

"St. Louis, Missouri."

John was baffled. A signal from a nearby station should be loud and crystal clear. "I am also in St. Louis, Missouri. Your signal is very weak. What are you transmitting with?"

"Federov AB12 unit. This is my first time using this channel."

"I'm not familiar with that manufacturer."

The voice laughed. "You don't know Federov? It's the most popular apparatus that…"

Noise welled up and the signal faded away. John noted the time, frequency and call sign in his logbook, with the comment "unusual call." He took the last sip of Coke, switched off, and got ready for bed. How could an operator from St. Louis sound so bad? Must be a piece of junk transmitter. What kind of call sign was Leo 1764? It didn't comply with the FCC regulations.

The next day, John was at his post repairing cassette recorders, turntables, and televisions in the back room of the Duke of Discounts. John listened to music on headphones as he worked, and he liked Bach when he was troubleshooting. The logical, intricate castles of sound that arose, transformed, and melted away helped him visualize the flow of current through a device and spot problems. Ellington was best for the more mundane tasks of disassembly and reassembly. The infectious rhythms kept his focus and energy levels up as he meticulously replaced tiny, hard-to-reach components.

The strange call from the night before kept percolating in John's mind. The voice sounded thin and reedy, though it was hard to tell with such a weak, distorted signal. Maybe some kid who didn't know what he was doing and had no business being on the air. Just messing around with his father's radio, then, when John answered, spouting off goofball nonsense.

That night, John had dinner in front of the TV with his mother. They watched *The Jeffersons,* Lily's favorite show. Lily took great delight at the predicaments George Jefferson got himself into.

"Black men and big ideas—a surefire recipe for trouble!" she shouted out with a loud guffaw. John had heard this saying his whole life. It was how she always shut down John's questions about his father. John had only a few clear memories of him. John Sr. liked to play records and dance around the living room. He would get so excited that he would pick up the needle in the middle of a song and plunk down a new record, something totally different. His mind had raced ahead of the record. He talked a mile a minute. Lily would playfully tug him away from the record player.

"Let me hear the whole damn song for once!"

Then they would dance around together, lifting young John in their arms.

Those memories ended abruptly. John Sr. disappeared when John was six. Dancing and laughing were replaced by lectures on responsibility that always included "Black men and big ideas—a surefire recipe for trouble."

John was eleven the last time he asked about his father. Lily grabbed him by the shoulders, shook him, and told him to never, never mention John Sr. again. Then she ran into the bedroom and didn't come out until dinner time. John could hear her sobs through the thin wooden door. From that day, he knew that she was in profound pain, but he never found out whether her tears were about something bad his father did or something bad that was done to his father.

Lily went to bed when *The Jeffersons* was over and John settled into his cramped desk chair and switched on his radio. He checked his logbook entry from the night before, then dialed in the frequency of the strange call. It was earlier than the time of yesterday's contact, but he gave it a try anyway.

"CQ. CQ. Calling CQ. This is NØJL. November-Zero-Juliet-Lima."

No response. He repeated the CQ a few more times. He was reaching for the tuning dial to go find his buddies, when a garbled voice came through.

"Ahoy, November-Zero-Juliet-Lima. This is Leo 1764. Can you hear me?"

The signal was stronger than the last time, though the pitch of the voice still gyrated up and down.

"Yes, Leo 1764. I can hear you. A little better than yesterday."

"I moved my apparatus to a different location. Now, I'm on the twenty-fifth floor of my building."

"Where is your building?"

"The corner of Russell and Jefferson."

John couldn't think of a tall building near there, but he didn't know that area that well.

"Where are you?" asked Leo 1764.

"Enright, west of Vandeventer."

"Yes, I know it. Near where the subway lines cross." John was baffled. St. Louis had no subways. For a few seconds, all John heard was the rise and fall of wheezing background noise. Then, Leo 1764 asked, "What's your real name?"

"John. What's yours?

"Leo."

Another pause. Then Leo continued. "I think I know why it's hard to hear each other. A barrier separates your side of St. Louis from my side of St. Louis. Somehow, this radio channel is seeping through."

What did Leo mean by "your side of St. Louis?" Some kind of racial thing? Black north side vs. white south side? John was pretty sure he didn't "sound black" on the radio—it had never come up with any of his ham friends—but he had told Leo where he lived. The Enright address, north of the "Delmar divide," was a clear message understood by all St. Louisans. The whiff of race intruding on his pristine radio world annoyed John, but he wasn't going to bring that up.

"What kind of barrier?"

"Possibly a standing etheric wave that blocks energy and matter from passing. It may be weaker on this channel, which allows us to talk."

Now John was really confused. Was this kid punking him?

"Would you do an experiment with me?" said Leo. "If we both moved about the city while transmitting, we might be able to locate a place where the etheric barrier is weakest."

"Walk around with our radios on?"

"Yes."

"Why don't we just meet in person?"

"Not possible."

"Why not?"

"I can't explain. If the experiment works, you'll know."

John was dubious about this bizarre request, but a technical challenge always piqued his interest. His radio was heavy and required AC power. He would have to rig up something to make it portable. In a few days, he could pull it together.

"Okay. But not until next week."

Despite the distortions of the signal, John could hear the excitement in Leo's voice.

"Yes! Yes! Next week would be fine."

"Monday, 9 p.m.?"

"Yes! Monday, 9 p.m. This channel. Thank you, John! This is Leo 1764 switching off."

Leo was gone. John took a sip of his Coke, then wrote the time and channel of the contact in his logbook. He couldn't think of a comment to put down.

What the heck had he gotten himself into?

John stood in the back yard of his building, checking his radio rig. He had spent the weekend assembling it. He bought a beat-up rucksack at a thrift shop. He got a motorcycle battery and AC inverter that fit in the rucksack's lower pouch. He could squeeze his radio into the upper part. He realized that he wouldn't be able to control the radio as he walked, so he took a dead car stereo from the junk box at the Duke of Discounts and wired the tuning and volume controls into his radio.

He attached the little car stereo to a strap he could hang around his neck and have the controls in front of him. The rig was completed by headphones and a lavalier microphone clipped to his shirt. To get good signal coverage, he needed to get his antenna up in the air. He found a long fly fishing rod at a pawn shop and attached the antenna to its tip.

John turned the radio on, hoisted the rucksack onto his back and tried tuning to some of his usual stations. If he held the fishing rod high, they came in loud and clear. He was ready. It was almost time for his rendezvous with Leo.

But what would happen when he walked out into the street? This rig would surely attract attention. Kids hanging out on a summer night could give him a lot of crap. And how would he explain himself to a cop, suspicious of a big black guy walking around at night with a rucksack and a fishing rod? It was too late—he was committed. He would walk in alleys as much as he could and try to be inconspicuous.

At 9, he went on the air.

"CQ. CQ. Calling CQ. This is NØJL. November-Zero-Juliet-Lima."

The response came right away, still with the odd speed and pitch changes. "Good to hear you, John. Leo here. How do I sound?"

"You're distorted, but I can copy you."

"Where are you?"

"Outside my house. 4049 Enright."

Leo asked him to walk west on Enright for a few minutes. John switched off. He broke down the fishing rod into its three sections so it was less conspicuous, then walked up the alley. Fortunately, no one was around. Two blocks west, he turned the radio back on and called again. The wheezy interference was louder. Leo's voice swirled in and out. John could barely hear it. This location obviously didn't work. Leo said to turn around, walk east to Grand, and then call again.

He walked briskly. He wondered if he might be the victim of a practical joke to get him wandering up and down the street looking like a fool. But who could pull that off? Certainly no one in his neighborhood, and his ham buddies wouldn't do anything like that.

At Vandeventer, a couple of little kids shouted, "Hey, whatchu got there, man?" But John ignored them and pressed on. The VA hospital was at the corner of Enright and Grand. Near one entrance to the hospital, he ducked into a clump of bushes bordering the parking lot. He raised the antenna, switched on, and called CQ.

Leo's reedy voice answered, "I can hear you fine." Leo's voice was much clearer this time.

"Where are you?"

"Nearby."

"I don't see you."

"We'll work on that. Walk around and keep talking. Let's see if we can get any clearer."

John cautiously moved out of the bushes and walked through the parking lot. He prayed that there were no security cameras. "I'm walking in the parking lot on the south side of the hospital."

"Hospital?"

"Yes, what did you expect?"

"It's a little different for me." Suddenly, Leo's voice was clear as a bell.

"You're coming in great, Leo. Best ever."

John stopped to wipe his glasses, which were fogging up. Suddenly, the air felt thick and soupy. Maybe steam was venting out of the hospital.

"Stay there," said Leo, who sounded even closer in John's headphones. "Close your eyes. Now walk."

John didn't know what to make of this. But he'd come this far. He closed his eyes and breathed in the humid August air. He started to take a step, but his feet felt like they weighed a hundred pounds each.

"Walk…walk," Leo said.

Though he was afraid he was about to faint, John lifted his foot with great effort.

"Fantastic! Yes. Almost…" he heard Leo say. Then silence. John almost stumbled, then sank to his knees with the awkward weight of the rucksack. He opened his eyes. It was dark. He was kneeling on grass. He saw a person running toward him, jumping up and down.

It was a woman. Short, with close-cropped hair and a big smile. At first, he thought she was white, then he saw her eyes better—Asian. She held a box in her hands. She put the box down and reached out to John. She was talking but he couldn't hear her. She lifted his headphones off his head.

"We did it! We did it! We did it!"

"Leo?" John asked.

"Yes. I'm Leo. Leonora Matsui. Pleased to actually meet you, John."

John shook her hand. He was so far beyond confused. He looked around. Grass, trees, a gravel path.

"Where are we?"

"Corner of Enright and Grand."

John ran his hand through the grass he was kneeling on.

"You're on my side now."

"Your side?"

"The two cities. You live in one and I live in the other. I'd heard about this, but I didn't know if it was real. But it is. You're really here!"

John started to feel scared. What had happened to him? Who was this person? He put the headphones back on and tried to tune in something on his radio. Silence. He took off the rucksack and the pulled the radio out. He toggled the on/off switch. Nothing lit up. The battery must have died. It should have been good for several hours. He looked around some more, at Leonora, at the trees.

"What happened to the hospital? The VA?"

"There's no hospital here. This is a park. Grand Avenue is right over there. I'll show you."

She led him down the path to a corner. He saw the street signs "Grand" and "Enright." Some cars whooshed down Grand. They looked like smooth cylinders with barely visible wheels. John looked at Leonora in a near panic. He was hyperventilating.

"I want to go back. I don't like this."

"You'll be fine. I'll get you back home soon. I promise." She patted his arm to reassure him. Leonora wasn't sure if she could get him home, but she'd figure something out. "Let's talk first. I know a place we can get coffee. We'll hide your radio under the bushes."

John didn't want to part with his radio, but he was too disoriented to resist. Leonora gathered up the rucksack and fishing rod and slid them under a big boxwood bush.

Then she took John's hand and led him to Grand Avenue, where they headed south. "We'll go to the Met. It's open all night."

John looked at her more closely. She was wearing a bright yellow, loose, jumpsuit kind of outfit. A polished wood object was slung over her shoulder.

"What's that?" John asked.

"My radio."

As they walked, Leonora led the bewildered John by the hand like he was a child. She chattered away, but nothing she said registered with him. He was transfixed by the strange surroundings. More of the sleek, rounded cars zoomed past them. In vain, John searched around for the familiar landmarks on this part of Grand, Powell Hall and the Fox Theatre. Instead, he saw a string of high-rise buildings. Their brick walls glowed faintly, some pink and some pale green. He dragged his fingers across a wall as he walked past. They left dark streaks in the iridescent bricks.

After a few blocks, they came to a building with an ornate stonework façade. Elegant tendrils of script etched into glass above a revolving door spelled out "Metropole."

"Are you hungry?" Leonora asked.

John followed her into a vast, noisy room. A forest of marble columns supported a high ceiling of interlocking domes that were covered with painted designs. Crystal chandeliers hung from cables that were so slender they were almost invisible. People sat at tables scattered throughout the room. Some read newspapers while others were immersed in lively conversations. Waiters carrying huge trays weaved precariously around the tables. The walls were covered with mirrors that reached to the ceiling and multiplied the tables and diners and waiters almost to infinity.

Leonora led John to an empty table in a far corner. "They have great coffee here and every pastry you can imagine."

People stared up at him as he passed their tables and sat down. It was like the white people's "What are you doin' here, boy?" gaze that had terrified him as a child.

"They're looking at me."

Leonora turned to see what he meant. The people staring quickly averted their eyes.

"It's your clothes. Very strange, if I say so myself."

John was wearing his usual summer outfit, a short sleeve shirt over a white T-shirt, loose jeans, and hi-top sneakers, all from Sears. John paid no attention to clothes and had never been accused of looking like anything, certainly not "strange." He glanced around the room. Including the mirror reflections, there appeared to be hundreds of customers, all wearing shiny outfits of intense reds, oranges, yellows, and blues, many with matching hats.

John began to relax a little. Leonora smiled her big smile. She could barely contain herself. Because of an accidental radio connection, she was sitting across from someone from the other side, a near-mythical creature she had only heard about indirectly in her uncle's cryptic hints. With his black glasses and dazed expression, he was a bit of an odd duck. He had no idea what had happened to him. But, only a few weeks ago, she would have been equally confused.

A waiter appeared. He silently presented a tray filled with pastries. John, whose dessert experience included only ice cream and his mother's pies, didn't recognize any of them. He saw a miniature mountain range of whipped cream, chocolate shavings, and tightly layered strata of cake and fillings.

"They're famous for their strudels and tortes, but my favorites are the éclairs," Leonora said.

John nodded vacantly, still bewildered by the whole experience.

"Two éclairs and two coffees," Leonora said. The waiter disappeared without a word.

"John, we're pioneers! Like Columbus or Magellan or Tesla. It's amazing!"

John looked at her. The panic inside him was rising up again. Leonora saw his frightened look and patted his hand. She continued talking nonstop. That's what she always did when she was stressed or didn't know what else to do.

"My uncle told me it's some odd, mysterious thing. But it's not. We did it with our radios! We found a gap in the etheric barrier. There are probably more of these gaps. No one knew how to look for them. Until now. You could be famous, John. You will be! The barrier has kept our two cities apart, so we couldn't see or touch each other. But it can all be different."

John was trying to listen to her, but he was getting more and more confused. "What two cities?"

She held up her hands and wiggled her intertwined fingers. "They're both right here. Each going its own way with no hint of the other."

"Like different radio frequencies?"

"Yes! That's perfect, John. Brilliant! And we just discovered how the frequencies can interact."

"Interfere with each other?"

"Yes, you interfered your way over here tonight."

"Interference isn't good. It garbles the signal."

"These are physical frequencies, not radio. Etheric waves are like walls. We found a door."

The waiter returned, set the éclairs and coffee on the table, and left, all without a word. The coffee cups were piled high with whipped cream. John had never seen anything like it. He took a bite of the éclair. The fluffy filling tasted as smooth as the opening clarinet in *Rhapsody in Blue.*

"Do these people know about the waves?" John gestured to the others in the restaurant.

"No. It's a secret. I'm not even supposed to know. I heard about this—about your city—from my uncle Martin. He's in the Knights."

"Who?"

"The Knights of the Carnelian. They're an extremely secretive bunch. Uncle Martin is one of them, I think. He never comes out and says so. He likes me and we talk a lot. Sometimes, after he has a few glasses of wine, stuff slips out. That's how I heard about the two cities. He probably wasn't supposed to tell me, but he did. So I know. And now you do, too."

"Were you looking for these gaps when you found me on the radio?"

"No, I was just messing around with my new apparatus. I got lucky."

John picked up his coffee cup with its soft white mounds. He wasn't sure how to approach it and when he took a sip, he mostly got whipped cream. Darn good whipped cream. He thought for a moment.

"The gaps must move. If they stayed in one place, someone would have found them a long time ago."

A bell rang in the crowded room, echoing off the vaulted ceilings. The lights dimmed. All the customers stopped talking. In a far corner of the room, a woman stood up and began to sing. A long gyrating melody. It reminded John of the hymns heard every Sunday in church services with his mother.

Leonora leaned over and whispered to John.

"It's singing time. We'll pick up our conversation when it's over."

"What's singing time?"

"It's a spontaneous thing. Anyone can start and anyone can join in. I think the tradition started in the time of the earthquake. People love to do this wherever there are good acoustics, and the Met is one of the best. They come here for the singing as much as for the coffee and food. Singing time lasts for ten minutes out of every hour."

The song grew richer and deeper as voices from all parts of the room picked up the chorus. Some people stood up; others remained seated. A waiter set down his tray of pastries and launched into a baritone harmony.

Though John didn't recognize the melody or the lyrics, it felt both completely fresh and bone-deep familiar. The first song ended with a long, sustained note, then a new song began on top of it. This one had a quicker rhythm. Rapid arpeggios from different directions built on top of each other. Leonora swayed back and forth in her chair as she joined in. John recognized it as a Bach piece, but transformed.

He closed his eyes and let the music wash over him. He could feel the vibrations from his toes to his head. Shimmering curtains of color slowly rotated through the darkness behind his eyes. The music brought him back to the hospital parking lot and again he felt the gap opening in front of him in the dizzying, but now delicious, moment when he slid into this new place. He saw it through the music and now it all made sense.

The final chorus slowly faded to silence. The bell rang and the lights came back up. People around the room nodded and smiled to acknowledge each other, then went back to their coffee and conversations. John opened his eyes. Leonora was looking at him. He said one word.

"Precession."

"What?"

"If the—what do you call them—etheric waves cancel each other out in certain places, then it's an analog interference phenomenon. Large scale wave patterns are never static. Not in the real world. They change and move. It's precession. Like a top that spins on its axis and also slowly moves around on the table."

Leonora wanted to reach across the table and hug him.

"That's brilliant, John. You're a genius!"

John smiled. The last person who told him he was brilliant was his father.

As they finished their coffee and éclairs, John and Leonora hatched a plan to map the gaps in the barrier. They would establish radio contact again over the next few days, beginning in the parking lot where John crossed over, to see how the gap moved.

John suggested trying it during the day, when he thought he might be less of a target for curious troublemakers— or the police. He was pretty sure their signals could still get through at that time. John savored the last bite of the éclair. He would remember its exquisite flavor for the rest of his life.

They made their way to the front door of the Met. John avoided the suspicious gazes from customers who glanced up at him as he passed their tables. As they walked up Grand Avenue, John was again struck by the faintly iridescent buildings.

"Why are these walls glowing?"

"Ampies. Amperic bricks that generate power. That's what I work on in my regular job."

"How do they work?"

"When different metals and minerals are mixed in with the clay, the bricks generate electricity as temperatures change. Hydraulic invented them back in the 1940s. People like the glow—it's become kind of a trademark. But, actually, it represents wasted energy. I lead a team that works on improving brick efficiency. We're trying to eliminate the glow in the new formulation."

John was impressed. He touched the bricks with his fingers and watched the dark marks they left fade away.

Back at Grand and Enright, they retrieved John's radio from under the boxwood. Leonora wasn't sure how to get John back to his side, but she pretended she knew what she was doing.

She positioned John in the same place in the park where she had seen him first appear. She told him to walk slowly in a circle with his eyes closed. She prayed that it would work. Nothing happened. After his first circle, she told him to make the circle wider. He moved tentatively, afraid of bumping into a tree. His foot caught a protruding root and, as he lurched forward, he disappeared.

Leonora felt a slight rush of air filling the vacant space where his body had been.

John didn't sleep that night.

The next morning, as he rode three buses to work, he minutely analyzed the evening's startling experiences. On the Delmar bus, he retraced each step through the parking lot, Leonora's ever clearer voice in his headphones, then the dizzying moment when he found himself on his knees in the grass with a dead radio. Then, on the long ride south down Grand Avenue, the sights and sounds of the Metropole washed over him. The mirrors, the unwelcome stares, the transcendent singing, the silky delight of the éclair.

As the bus passed the Fox Theatre, he tried to imagine exactly where the Metropole had been—somewhere around here. On the final leg of his journey, as the Gravois bus carried him to the front door of the Duke of Discounts, one image overwhelmed all the others—Leonora's smile.

Over the next few weeks, John and Leonora, each working on their own side, mapped the movement of the etheric gap. To avoid harassment, John abandoned the rucksack rig for his radio. He found a junked shopping cart in an alley and placed his radio and battery inside, wrapped in an old blanket. Wearing his most beat-up clothes and a cap to conceal his headphones, he looked like just another harmless, homeless man wandering the streets, occasionally muttering to himself.

As they crisscrossed the city on their respective sides, Leonora kept up a constant stream of chatter about her work on bricks, theories about the dynamics of the gaps, and the weather, which was different on each side, even at the same place and time.

Like ham enthusiasts everywhere, they compared notes about their radios. Leonora was fascinated by John's description of printed integrated circuits as a replacement for elaborate configurations of tubes. She told him about her portable pneumatic power supply, a baseball-sized metal sphere that emitted a tiny stream of compressed air to turn a turbine and generate electricity to run the radio.

"The best thing is that it recharges in just a couple of minutes."

John couldn't wait to see it for himself.

They found that the gap moved southeast about fifty yards a day. Near downtown they discovered a second gap, which was moving north at a similar rate. Leonora meticulously tracked the data points on a pocket-sized map of the city.

She was elated about their project and kept babbling away as they wandered their two cities in tandem. She speculated about the causes of the gaps, daydreamed plans for what they would do when they were both famous, and made jokes. John had never met anyone whose mind moved as quickly and unpredictably as hers. He was enthralled.

For the first time since he was hired in 1962, he called in sick to the Duke of Discounts so he could devote more time to the explorations with Leonora.

Of course, Leonora was eager to cross over and see John's side for herself. John found a relatively well-hidden spot where the gap would be the next day—behind a building near the corner of Compton and Olive. He left his radio at home and waited for her at the appointed time. To his amazement, it worked perfectly. Leonora stumbled out from a poof of squiggly air. She hugged him.

"I want to see everything."

John's idea was to take her to the Highway 40 overpass where there was an open view of downtown. As they walked, she took in every detail, from billboards to passing trucks to trash cans.

"Where is everybody?" she asked. She had expected an intense, bustling corner with pedestrians and tall buildings, like in her own city. Instead, there was open space with grass along Market Street—the result of depopulation and failed urban renewal. John shrugged his shoulders.

"That's what it is."

At the highway overpass, cars and trucks zoomed underneath them. Leonora was fascinated.

"They had to tear down a lot to build this."

"Yeah, but people want to be able to move around fast."

"Why not build subways?"

"I don't know. Too expensive?"

Leonora pointed toward downtown. "What's that curved thing?"

"That's the Arch. On the riverfront. Don't you have the Arch?"

"Nope. Can we go see it?"

"How about lunch first?"

A few minutes later, John was opening a sack of hamburgers for Leonora at the White Castle on Olive Street.

"They're tiny, so you have to eat several to fill up, but they're great."

Leonora took a few bites and nodded her agreement.

John had a lifelong history of making awkward jokes that fell flat—with his army buddies, with the salesmen at the Duke of Discounts, and even with his fellow radio voyagers. He saw the world in his own way and he could never figure out what would be funny to other people. So he had given up on telling jokes. But, today, inspired by Leonora's ebullience and ceaseless energy, John worked up his courage to try one.

"These hamburgers taste fantastic, but they're not going to inspire anyone to start singing."

Leonora laughed hard and had to struggle to avoid spewing hamburger bits all over the table. The joke worked!

The next day, a Sunday, John crossed over to Leonora's side, using the same spot. She wanted to show him more of her city, including the riverfront. When he appeared, she handed him a loose purple shirt and a floppy, broad-brimmed hat. "Wear these so you fit in better."

Broad sidewalks were crowded with throngs of people. Streamlined streetcars and the lozenge-shaped cars whooshed silently past. Tall, brick-clad buildings lined the street in both directions as far as John could see. As he and Leonora threaded their way through the busy sidewalk toward the riverfront, he heard people speaking many unfamiliar languages. John was dazzled. These sights and sounds would haunt him for years.

When they reached downtown, Leonora pointed out a shiny, multicolored skyscraper that towered over the rest of the skyline. "That's where I work—the Hydraulic Building."

They approached the riverfront. Instead of the grassy park surrounding the Arch, they entered a tangle of narrow streets with a mix of old and new buildings. Large signs advertised restaurants, bars and boutiques. Balconied apartments above were festooned with trees and trailing vines. A small square was filled with café tables and musicians.

"They call this place Leveetown. It's pretty quiet on a Sunday morning, but you should see it at night," Leonora said.

On the side of the square closest to the Mississippi, there was a building with three outdoor elevators running up its side. People were lined up waiting for an elevator.

"I thought we could take the gondola to the amusement park across the river. It's a great view. And this is the last year for the amusement park. They're tearing it down to build apartments. A lot of people are unhappy about that. Including me."

They got in line for their turn to ascend an elevator to the gondola station. Leonora suddenly called his name. John turned to her in surprise and she snapped a picture of him with a small silver camera.

"Hey, what was that all about?"

"I couldn't resist. The look on your face was priceless," she laughed.

John, who was shy about having his picture taken, went along with the fun. Anything that Leonora did was fine with him.

As they waited for the elevator, Leonora glanced around idly. She spotted a man with binoculars on a balcony. He was scanning the square below. A chill shot up her spine. She looked around some more and saw a few men standing alone at different places in the square. They seemed to be watching the groups of café patrons and musicians. She briefly made eye contact with one of the men.

"John, we need to get out of here. I have a bad feeling. Someone may be looking for us. Let's go back to your side."

She hustled John out of the square. When they got to a quiet corner, Leonora took out her pocket map to figure out where the gap near downtown would be. It was about ten blocks away. They headed in that direction. John could see that Leonora was agitated. She was silent for once and kept looking around nervously as they walked.

"Who would look for us?" John asked.

"It could be the Knights or their people. You don't want to get mixed up with them. We'll be safe once we cross over."

A little while later, they were standing in a deserted lot on the edge of downtown in John's city. Leonora breathed a sigh of relief. John suggested that he could show her the electronic equipment where he worked.

"Sure!" Leonora brightened up. She was always ready for technology and gadgets.

"The store is closed today, so we'll have to stop by my house to get my key."

They rode a Delmar bus out to the corner near John's apartment. Leonora didn't like the noisy diesel bus and the smoky exhaust it spewed out. When they entered the apartment, Lily was there in her Sunday best outfit.

"Where have you been? Everyone at church was asking about you."

"Mom, this is my friend Leonora."

Lily looked her up and down with a skeptical eye. John hadn't brought anyone to the house in years, much less an Asian woman.

"Pleased to meet you, Mrs. Little. John has told me a lot about you," said Leonora, reaching out to shake Lily's hand.

Lily responded with the limpest handshake imaginable.

"Leonora's one of my ham radio friends. She's visiting from out of town and I'm taking her to see the store."

"Be home for supper."

Three noisy and smelly buses later, John and Leonora were at the Duke of Discounts. He unlocked the front door to the darkened store. Inside, he flipped the switch that turned on the wall of TVs on display. Leonora ran up to get a closer look.

"What do you call these?"

"Televisions, TVs."

"We call ours moviolas. Yours are different. So many sizes."

They went around the showroom looking at all the various products—videocassette recorders (VHS and Betamax), audio systems (eight-tracks, cassette recorders, record players, radios, boomboxes, Walkmen), and combination living room consoles with wooden cabinets.

Leonora was overwhelmed by the range of products. She peppered him with questions about how each one worked and why there were so many different formats and types of devices.

"Do people actually buy all of this?"

"Most of them. Some don't sell and they disappear."

He took her over to a CD player and held up a CD.

"This is the latest. One disc can hold more than an hour of music. It uses a laser to read the information. They're expensive, so I don't know if they'll catch on." John had to explain to her what a laser was.

They went to the repair room in the back of the store. Leonora was doubly fascinated to see the innards of TVs and audio equipment. John described how repairs and troubleshooting were changing.

"Equipment used to have discrete components wired together—transistors, diodes, tubes in the oldest models. I used diagnostics to isolate the piece that was malfunctioning and replace it. It was an art, and a lot of fun. Now, everything uses integrated circuits with thousands of components printed on a little board. All I do is replace the whole board."

"Sounds like a waste. Throwing the whole board out."

"That's progress for you. Someday, nobody is going to fix anything and I'll be out of a job."

They heard a voice from the showroom. "Hello? Johnny boy, is that you?"

"Yes sir," John answered.

Big Bill Boustany, wearing a beige polyester leisure suit and tinted glasses, sauntered into the repair room.

"I got a call from a neighbor that someone was in the store. So I rushed over. You can't be too careful with the crime these days." Bill turned to look at Leonora. "What have we here?"

"This is my friend Leonora Matsui, Mr. Boustany. She's visiting from out of town and wanted to see the store."

"Leonora Matsui. A beautiful name for a beautiful lady. A pleasure to meet you. No visit to St. Louis is complete without going to the Duke of Discounts. The best deals on the planet!"

"It's wonderful to see your store, sir. It's very impressive," Leonora said.

"We'll always do right by any friend of Johnny boy here. Just tell him what you want and you'll get the best price in town. Right, Johnny?"

"Yes sir."

"I'm just an old softie. That's our slogan, in case you haven't heard it."

"Very nice," Leonora said.

As Big Bill turned to leave the room, he gave John a wink and a nudge and whispered, "You're a sly dog, Johnny boy."

John and Leonora grinned at each other after Big Bill left.

"I have something for you for the bus." He reached in a drawer and pulled out his Sony Walkman. He put the headphones over her ears. "Have you ever heard Duke Ellington?"

He clipped the Walkman to Leonora's belt and pushed play. The sounds of Ellington at Newport from 1956 filled Leonora's head. She didn't say a word on the long bus rides back to John's place.

On the Grand Avenue bus, she and John made eye contact. He saw the dreamy look in her eyes. She put his hand in hers. She held it the rest of the way back. He was both bewildered and delighted.

As they came around the corner onto John's block, Leonora stopped suddenly and gasped. She pulled the Walkman headphones off her head.

"Damn!" She pointed toward John's house. Two huge men in purple suits were standing on the sidewalk. One of them turned toward John and Leonora. She recognized him as the guy with the binoculars.

"Who are they?" John asked.

"The same ones I saw down at the square on the river this morning. They see us now, so there's no getting away."

John and Leonora continued up the block to his house. He could hear the tinkle of Ellington from the headphones dangling around Leonora's neck. He reached over and turned off the Walkman, still clipped to her belt. One of the purple-suited men went into John's apartment.

"Let me do the talking," Leonora said.

John and Leonora walked up the front steps onto the porch. The second man stared at them, but said nothing. Leonora led John past him into the apartment.

In the small living room, John's mother was sitting on the sofa with a slender, elegantly dressed Asian man with a reddish-brown carnation in his lapel. Teacups and small plates were on the coffee table. The big purple-suited guy was standing in the corner, arms crossed.

"Hello, Leonora."

"Hello, Uncle Martin."

"This gentleman has been waiting for you, John," said Lily. "He's your friend's relative. We've had the most delightful conversation."

"And the most delicious pecan pie. Your mother is quite a cook, John."

Martin smiled at Lily, who enjoyed the flattery.

"I'm afraid that I must speak with Leonora outside," Martin said. "Please excuse us."

He got up and ushered Leonora out the front door. The big guy followed silently.

John and Lily sat there in awkward silence. She offered him a piece of pie, which he declined.

"He's one of the nicest people I've ever met," said Lily. "We talked for at least an hour."

John said nothing. The longer he sat there, the more anxious he got. Martin and Leonora came back after about ten minutes. She didn't make eye contact with John.

"John, can we talk outside?" Martin said.

John tried to figure out what was going on with Leonora, but her face was expressionless.

On the porch, Martin looked into John's eyes.

"Very impressive, your discovery. Finding weaknesses in the barrier with radio. Very impressive."

"It was her idea."

"Perhaps, but you identified the mechanism for the movement of the weaknesses. What do you call it?"

"Precession."

"A brilliant contribution! It advances our knowledge of the barrier and should be celebrated." Martin leaned closer. "But, of course, it must never be spoken of. Travel between our worlds is unwise, extremely unwise. Leonora should have known that. I apologize for her recklessness."

"I didn't know what was happening."

"How could you have? She was taking advantage of your curiosity and good nature. But there's another aspect of the travel process that Leonora doesn't understand."

"What's that?"

"Individual ability. Only a small percentage of people have the capacity to cross the barrier, under even the best of circumstances. You and Leonora seem to both have it. But most do not. I don't know if this ability is a blessing or a curse, but you have it."

Martin reached into his pocket and pulled out a cigarette case. "May I smoke?"

John nodded. Martin lit his cigarette, inhaled and looked around, taking in the unfamiliar sight of John's block with red brick two-family houses interspersed with ragged vacant lots. He continued, now with a harder edge in his voice.

"John, I've enjoyed this conversation about science, but we have a more critical task to attend to. You have a choice to make—now. You must stay permanently in one world or another. If you decide to come with us—and you would, of course, be welcome—there can be no coming back. Crossing would be forbidden."

John didn't like the sound of "forbidden."

"To everyone here, such as your mother, you would have disappeared without a trace."

Those words gave John a chill. They reminded him of his long absent father.

"And if I want to stay here?"

"Then you stay permanently. Don't attempt to visit us—also forbidden."

"What about Leonora?"

"She has already decided to return with me. She's sorry to have involved you in this foolish escapade."

John's head was swimming. He had never faced a big decision about anything. His life had plodded along with little strife, except for the hole left by his father. Now, he had to choose either Leonora or his mother—forever. His chest began to heave. He squeezed his eyes shut. He just wanted all of this to go away. Martin was getting impatient.

"Time's almost up, John. Leonora and I are leaving in five minutes. We mustn't let uncertainty linger."

"I can't leave my mother." He struggled to hold back tears.

Martin patted him on the shoulder. "Of course. Family is the most important thing, I always say. A wise decision."

Martin looked intently at John to get his full attention.

"Never speak of this episode to anyone. There are others, less forgiving than I, who would frown on any disclosure. Do you understand?"

John squirmed.

"These people frown upon things most decisively. You don't want to find out how decisively."

John nodded weakly. Martin shook his hand.

"It's settled then. Your mother has been a lovely hostess for a stranger who appeared out of nowhere at her doorstep."

A few minutes later, Martin and Leonora, flanked by the two purple-suited giants, walked down the front porch steps. She glanced at John sheepishly. He was still in shock from the decision he was forced to make.

As they headed down the street, never to return again, John saw that she had the Walkman in her pocket. Before turning the corner, she broke away from the group and ran back to John standing on the porch steps.

"You've been wonderful. I will never forget our time together. And thanks for this." She discreetly patted the Walkman in her pocket.

She gave John a long kiss. It was the first kiss of his life. He didn't expect to ever get another one.

"I love you," she said. John was dumbfounded. He watched her disappear around the corner with one giant leading the way and the other following behind. He felt like he had been kicked in the stomach.

Lily joined John on the front porch. She waved to Martin, who cheerfully waved back.

"Lord have mercy!" she said. "I'm way behind on fixing supper and we got *The Jeffersons* tonight!"

A Partner in Crime

2010

ONE SATURDAY MORNING, Meredith Boustany took her clothes out of the dryer and dumped them onto a table in the basement laundry room. She followed the advice that her mother had drummed into her since she was a child, "Prompt folding prevents wrinkles and saves you time in the long run." As she worked, Meredith mulled over the dilemma that had tormented her for months: how to tell her parents that she wanted to major in art, with a focus on multimedia. They were pushing her to major in business or finance. "There is always a demand for people who can run a business," her father had said to her about a million times. Her mother, the queen of practicality, was on the same wavelength.

Meredith hated the business classes she had taken and the boring, predictable business majors who were in them. Still, she was afraid she might not have the talent to make it in art or media. The only way to find out was to give it a shot. Her friend Amy, a screenwriting major from New York, encouraged her to take the chance. "Girl, you need an adventure."

Meredith had to declare a major in a month, before the fall semester began, so she couldn't put off the moment of reckoning much longer. But she had no desire to rock the boat with her parents by forcing the issue. Somehow, her father hadn't brought up the subject in the last several weeks. "Thank God for small favors," Meredith thought.

She put her folded clothes into the laundry basket and carried it towards the stairs, passing Billy's home office. The door was slightly ajar and the lights were on. "Hey, Dad," she said as she nudged the door open with her shoulder.

Billy wasn't there. Just his desk, cluttered as usual, and the shelves filled with his weird old college books, *Zen and the Art of Motorcycle Maintenance* and stuff like that. She noticed something new on the back of the door. She put down her basket and closed the door to see it better. It was a map of St. Louis, covered with scribbled sticky notes that made no sense: "Asian market," "bar," "street supper" "fountains," "lights in trees."

The door opened. Meredith jumped back to avoid getting smacked in the face.

Billy's head poked out from the other side of the door. "Meredith? What are you doing?"

"Getting my laundry. I thought you were in here."

Billy stepped into the room and closed the door behind him.

Meredith gestured to the back of the door. "What's this?"

"I've been doing a little research...for the store."

She looked puzzled.

Billy continued. "They say the city could really take off again. We may want to open a new store down there. I'm trying to get out in front of a trend."

She pointed to the sticky notes. "Lights in trees? Fountains? What do these have to do with a computer store?"

Billy just looked at her with a pained expression on his face. His discomfort unsettled her.

"Dad, you may think that I don't notice, but you've been gone a lot recently. It's not like you."

Billy didn't know what to say. The burden of his secret was wearing him down. He took a long breath.

"There's something I want to tell you, but you've got to promise not to tell a soul."

Meredith felt a wave of foreboding. "You're not having an affair, are you?"

"What? No. Nothing like that."

Billy sat down behind his desk. Meredith sat in the lumpy armchair.

"I've run into some really strange stuff down in the city. It doesn't make any sense." He took a deep breath. "I found this other place. We can't see it, but it's right in front of us. The regular place is there and the other place is there too. At the same time, on top of it, kind of mixed up. The other place looks almost like the regular city, but buildings and people are different. I went into this amazing indoor market, right here."

He pointed to the map and the sticky note "Asian market." "But when I went back a second time, it was a vacant lot."

Meredith listened in disbelief. The shocked look on her face unnerved Billy. He knew he should've kept his mouth shut. Too late now. Somehow, their roles had reversed. He was the teenager with the wild story that he desperately wanted her to believe and she was the skeptical adult.

"Are you okay, Dad? This is pretty far out in left field."

"I'm fine."

"Were you taking drugs? Hallucinating?"

"No! It was completely real."

"I know you used to be a pothead. I heard you and mom talk about it."

"That has nothing to do with this."

"Sounds like good drugs to me."

"I'm not making this up!" Billy opened his desk drawer. "Here's a wrapper from a pastry I bought there." He handed it to her. "See the phone number? I called it when I got back. They hung up. Wrong number. I also Googled the market. Nothing."

Meredith looked at the wrapper. She turned it over and held it up to the light. "Did you take pictures?"

"When I go there, my phone dies."

"So, all you have is this wrapper and your story?"

"And these." He pointed to the Kahok beer coaster, the Sons of Rest program, and the Refugees Club application tacked to the door. Billy watched her play with the wrapper. Her expression softened.

"So, is it cool when you're there?"

Billy grinned. "Insanely cool."

Then everything tumbled out in an avalanche of words. The street supper, Milo Riley, the dancing, the magical lights in Tower Grove Park, Chuck Cherry. Billy was elated to finally tell someone.

Meredith listened in amazement. What was going on with her dad? This didn't sound like something he would, or could, make up.

"How do you get there?"

"It's hard to explain. I get a weird feeling in certain places. My ears pound. Sometimes, a noise startles me. I take a step into nowhere. Then, boom, I'm there."

"Wow. Can you take me? Today?"

"Here? This is where you go into the parallel universe?"

Meredith studied the corner of Grand and Gravois. It looked like a dump. A bunch of sketchy, low-rent stores, a White Castle, and this creepy old bank building.

"This is the first place I used and it still seems to work best."

"So what do we do?"

Billy showed her the entrance alcove of the Southside National Bank building. "We go in there, turn our backs to the street, and wait for the feeling to come."

"This is so goddamned weird."

"Do you want to do it or not? We can go back home."

"Yes, I want to do it."

"First, take a good look at everything on this corner, so you remember."

Meredith rolled her eyes and looked out at the corner dutifully. Billy pointed out the vacant lot next to the bank building. Then he led her into the alcove, where they stood side by side, facing the wall. He told her to be still, let her mind empty, and do what he said. After a few moments, Billy began to feel the faint throbbing in his ears. He waited for it to ripen.

Meredith started to giggle.

"Dammit, Meredith, be quiet!" he hissed, without opening his eyes.

"I'm sorry." She kept giggling.

Billy opened his eyes and turned to face Meredith. "Did you feel anything?"

"Not really." She was trying to hold back a smirk.

Billy didn't know what to do. He had never done this with another person. Meredith pleaded that she really, really wanted to try—and wouldn't laugh any more.

Billy decided to change his approach. He took her hand and they both faced the wall again. He told her to take a step forward when he said "Go," but not a moment before. He squeezed her hand as the throbbing began again. He waited, longer than he had ever before, as it got stronger and stronger.

Finally, he called out "Go" and they both stepped into thin air. After a tiny instant, their feet landed on the tiles of the alcove. Meredith looked at him, "Was that it?" Billy nodded and turned her around to see the street.

In front of her was the billboard with the smiling lady, the green glass building, and spidery cars gliding by. The sidewalk was filled with people. Meredith was speechless.

"I told you," said Billy, beaming. Meredith kept looking back and forth with panicked eyes, like a cat that had just been let out of its carrier in a strange house. He put his hand on her shoulder. "It's the best."

She slowly nodded, but was unable to speak.

Billy led her out onto the sidewalk and turned toward the Asian market. He heard hurdy-gurdy and flute music, then saw the two street musicians in their usual spot. He magnanimously dropped a few coins into their instrument case, nodding to them like an old friend.

He and Meredith entered the market. She stopped and looked right and left, up and down, to take in every detail. She still didn't say a word, but now she was smiling. Billy savored every ounce of her pleasure. It amplified the excitement that he had felt at every new sight in HD St. Louis. And, it brought back a joy of fatherhood he had lost long ago—showing his child the shining wonders of the great wide world.

The market was packed on this Saturday. Billy and Meredith edged their way through the crowd and squeezed past a group of the young men in suits and shorts who were carrying their scooters. Billy didn't like the way they eyed Meredith up and down.

At the stall with the pastries, Billy picked out a purple bun and gave it to Meredith. She took a bite and said her first word since crossing over, "Incredible."

They left the market and headed east on Gravois. All of a sudden, Meredith was talking nonstop.

"What the heck is this place?"

"A different version of St. Louis. I call it HD."

"Like a TV?"

"Something like that."

"How come we never saw it before?"

"Good question. I have no idea. But here we are."

He guided her across the busy intersection of Grand and Gravois. He had to hold her hand because she kept turning her head whenever she noticed something new. And everything was new.

"We'll get lunch at a place up ahead. It's quiet, so we can chill a little."

A few minutes later, they stepped into the dark, cool hush of Whittemore's. Mary Jo lit up with a wide smile.

"Hey, Billy. How's ol' Chuck Cherry doing?"

"He asked about you," replied Billy as he shook her hand across the bar.

"This is my daughter, Meredith. Meredith, this is Mary Jo, who runs this place."

Mary Jo shook Meredith's hand. "It's a pleasure to finally meet you."

Walt wandered over from his perch at the end of the bar. Billy introduced him to Meredith. She was bewildered by the attention, but knew how to be polite to her parents' friends. Billy ordered sandwiches and Kahok beers. He and Meredith sat at a table in the back.

"How do you know these people?" she asked.

"I've been coming in here for about a month. We're friends. They took me to that amazing party I told you about."

Meredith was struggling to reconcile this story—and this whole day—with the father she had gotten used to in the last few years. The one who was always either at work, falling asleep in front of the TV, or giving her crap about her messy car.

Mary Jo brought the sandwiches and beer to the table.

"What are you up to today, Billy?"

"I was thinking we would go downtown. We haven't seen it yet."

"Can't go wrong with downtown on a Saturday. Everybody's got to see the Mezz."

"Exactly."

Mary Jo went back to the bar as Billy and Meredith began to eat.

"What's the Mezz?" Meredith asked.

"No clue. But it's a lot easier if you act like you know what they're talking about. Don't you love these sausage sandwiches?"

With her mouth full, Meredith could only nod. Billy kept talking.

"They don't know that we're not from here, not from HD. If anybody asks, say you're from California. They seem to buy that."

They finished their lunch. Billy put cash on the table and they got up to leave. Meredith got sidetracked by the sight of a customer taking a big hit from one of the steel tubes of the innie dispenser. There were heartfelt goodbyes from both Mary Jo and Walt. Hugs this time.

Out on the sidewalk, Meredith looked relaxed for the first time. "What an awesome place! I can't believe you found this."

The city streamed past Billy and Meredith in a majestic procession. They sat on the upper level of a double-decker streetcar that was gliding along Gravois toward downtown. Every direction they looked, fresh and intriguing sights greeted them. Men and women in broad hats and loose clothing strolled the tree-lined sidewalks. Shrieking children ran gleefully through fountains in a pocket park. A small crowd gathered in front of a bowling alley to watch men cajole reluctant llamas down a ramp from a truck. An elderly accordion player stood at the entrance to a restaurant. Long, ovoid cars and trucks, and flocks of scooters with slender silver frames zipped along in both directions.

Most buildings were five and six stories tall and dotted with balconies. On one side of the street, where the sun was shining, opaque windows and blank surfaces predominated. On the shady side, the windows and walls had opened up. Thin, gauzy curtains rippled in the breeze. Billy and Meredith could see right into the apartments, like they were doll houses.

They were enraptured by every scene that swept by. Meredith nodded dreamily. She was watching the world's greatest IMAX 3D movie.

"Let's get off here," Billy said.

The streetcar had stopped right next to City Hall—the same one that Billy knew—a Renaissance Revival structure of pink and yellow stone, built at the height of St.

Louis' wealth around 1900. Here in HD, City Hall looked cleaner and better cared for.

Like most St. Louisans, Billy spent little time downtown. He attended baseball and hockey games, of course, and he brought out-of-town visitors to see the Arch. That was about it. When he first took over the store, the bankers and lawyers were mostly downtown, but they had long since moved to the suburbs, just as his business had.

Billy had an imprinted sense of downtown geography from coming there with his father. The traumatic turkey baster incident had taken place at a TV station downtown. Billy had a happier memory of eating lunch with his father in an old-fashioned, somewhat shabby, cafeteria, where the denizens, mostly old men, were thrilled by the presence of the Duke of Discounts himself.

Many of the buildings in Billy's mental map were long gone, replaced by parking garages championed by a string of city governments to "revitalize" downtown by making it easier for suburban workers and visitors to get in and out quickly. But each time an office building was demolished for a parking garage, there was one less reason to go downtown.

Today, Billy and Meredith saw a completely different place. A forest of slender towers rose up as far as they could see. Some were brightly colored red, blue, and orange. Shrubs and small trees grew on balconies and platforms all the way up, thirty or forty stories. One building in the distance loomed much taller than the rest. Its glass spire gleamed in the afternoon sun.

As they crossed the street, they had to dodge a swarm of young men on scooters who swooped by uncomfortably close.

"Watch it!" Billy yelled. One of the riders leered back with a nasty grin.

They headed east on Olive Street, which was lined by buildings old and new. One had an ornate façade with terra cotta figures of mythical beasts framing huge circular windows on the second floor. The building next to it was clad in etched glass and narrow brick tendrils. It reminded Billy of the giant beanstalk in the fairy tale. They came to a narrow side street that was paved with black-and-white stones. Above, hundreds of colored discs hung from wires to form a fluttering canopy. A sign said *Needle Street Arcade*.

Meredith and Billy strolled into the arcade, which was filled with high-fashion boutiques. Women in glittery dresses window shopped arm-in-arm with men with broad hats and suits with short pants. Other people wore loose African or Arabic robes. Tall men with long black hair and elaborate face tattoos escorted tattooed women carrying shopping bags. Meredith pulled out her phone to take a picture.

"Crap, it's dead," she said.

"I warned you."

Billy saw a store window displaying odd-looking devices. Upon closer inspection, he realized they were televisions and audio components.

"I have to see this place!"

Meredith didn't share her father's nerdy tech obsessions. And she was becoming more comfortable in HD.

"I'll look around and come find you in a few minutes," she said.

Billy looked concerned.

"I'll be fine. I won't go far."

Billy reluctantly let her go. Then he entered the store. Shelves lined both walls and glass tables displayed a bewildering mix of items. A clerk approached.

"May I help you?"

"No thanks. I'm just looking."

"Very well. We carry radios, moviolas, sonographs, filing assistants, and pretty much everything you might want."

Billy worked his way down one aisle. Moviolas were apparently televisions. They had elliptical screens on top of wooden consoles with sliders and buttons. One TV was on. It was showing a travelogue about mountains. The image was incredibly sharp. Billy reached up to scratch an itch on his neck. The picture changed to a baseball game (the Browns). He raised his hand again. The picture changed to a woman in white talking about Jesus. He pointed his hand down a couple of times and the picture changed back to the travelogue. Gesture recognition! Totally cool.

The clerk finished helping another customer and approached Billy to ask if he had any questions.

"Do you sell PCs?"

The clerk looked puzzled.

"You know, computers for calculating things, finances, writing?"

The clerk took a moment to decipher what Billy was saying.

"Difference Engines. DEs. Yes. In the back room. We carry both continuous and discrete models."

Now Billy had to decipher. It came to him—analog and digital. Just as Billy was heading to the back room, Meredith appeared.

"Hey Dad, ready to go?"

Billy knew it was impossible to get Meredith interested in technology —even if it was mind blowing. He followed her out.

On the street, Meredith was bubbly.

"You won't believe what I found. First this." She handed Billy a small paper bag. "It's the most amazing snack. A fried pickle on a stick, dusted with cinnamon."

Billy pulled it out of the bag and looked at it skeptically.

"I know it sounds gross, but it's fantastic."

Billy took a bite. He had to admit that it was pretty tasty. Meredith was indifferent to technology, but she had a sixth sense for great food.

"And," she said triumphantly, "we don't need a camera!" She held up a handful of postcards. "Here's a cool one. It was the tall, tapering skyscraper with a glass spire at the top. The back side said "The Hydraulic Building, St. Louis."

"Here's the place that Mary Jo was talking about." The postcard showed a greenspace with walking paths on top of a building. The back side said "The Mezz. St. Louis' Oasis in the Sky."

They scanned Olive Street in both directions. A block away, a bridge spanned over the street about five stories up. A smartly-dressed man with a broad straw hat directed them to an elevator around the corner.

The sign by the elevator door said "Direct to Mezzanine St. Louis. Scooters strictly prohibited." A few minutes later, they emerged onto the Mezz. They were in a sun-dappled plaza dotted with trees and umbrella-shaded benches. People were reading, chatting, and walking their dogs. Puffy pillows of red and yellow flowers filled planters and formal beds.

It was remarkably quiet, compared to the street below. A breeze-producing tower, like the ones at the street supper, cooled the space. Across the plaza, they saw the entrance to a blue office tower, which rose up twenty stories or more.

Billy and Meredith soon figured out that the Mezz was atop the base of a building and the tower was the narrow center portion of that building. They could walk all the way around it. There were bridges to other buildings, all configured in more or less the same way. More bridges zigzagged into the eastern distance. The Mezz went on for blocks.

Meredith pointed. "Where's the Arch?"

The Gateway Arch, the stainless steel emblem of St. Louis to the world, wasn't there.

Each time they crossed a bridge to a new section of the Mezz, it was different from the others. They wandered through parks of various styles. Some had ponds and tall trees. Others were formal gardens. They watched people playing handball and listened to impromptu concerts and poetry readings. Several of the Mezz "districts," as they were called on the maps posted at each bridge, had restaurants and food stands.

Billy found fried pickles on a stick at a stand advertising itself as "The Original Stickpickle!" He and Meredith shared one and agreed that it was a little bland—not as good as the one she had bought down on Needle Street. Billy noticed the sun was getting low.

"Time to go. Your mother's probably been calling."

They found an elevator and soon were back on the streetcar heading toward Grand and Gravois.

"We've got to tell people about this, Dad! You may be the first person to ever come here," Meredith said as they got into the car.

"No one will believe us. They'll think we're nuts."

She pulled the postcards out of her pocket. "We can show them these."

"No! I don't want to screw this up. I still don't understand what's going on."

"But, Dad, it's a real place. We saw it, we talked to people, we ate pickles!"

Billy turned their car onto the Highway 40 ramp at Grand to head toward home. The new reality hit him hard—the secret was no longer his alone.

"Actually, I don't mind if people think I'm crazy. But it's way too soon to talk about this. Let's keep our mouths shut."

"Can we just tell Mom?"

"No! I'm not ready for that. This isn't your mother's kind of thing."

"Will you take me there again?"

Billy sighed. He was getting in deeper, but he couldn't turn back now. "Yes. Will you keep quiet about this?"

"Will you promise to take me back?"

"I promise. But no talking to friends. No Facebook. Keep the postcards to yourself."

"Okay. Deal!"

Billy glanced over at Meredith. They both smiled.

Rabbits and Zippers

1941

"Look this way, Mr. Hines…Smile…We got it… Thank you, sir."

J. Whittemore Hines dropped the shovel in the dirt and started to walk away to a round of applause. This was the third groundbreaking in a month—another building funded by the CSP was going up. He hated having his picture taken. The relentless attention was an unwelcome side effect of the transformation of St. Louis he had unleashed.

One of his assistants, an eager, industrious young woman, rushed up to him. "Dr. Cantwell at the Asylum says he needs to see you right away. An urgent matter." Vernon Cantwell was Jim's first new friend in this St. Louis and an upstanding member of the Knights.

Jim waved to the crowd one final time before he got into his highly polished, black limousine, "Cancel the rest of today's appointments," he said to the assistant as he drove away.

187

Cantwell greeted Jim, then shut the door to his office.

"A very disturbing incident occurred today and the staff is in an uproar. I thought you needed to know." Hines settled back into the office sofa, expecting to hear that another Visitor had surfaced.

"We have a patient, Irene Watkins, who suffers from grand mal epilepsy, as well as a host of psychiatric problems. This morning, there was a mix-up with her medication orders. A nurse came into her room to administer an anti-seizure medication. She didn't realize that another nurse had just given Miss Watkins a different anti-seizure medication. After swallowing the second pill, the patient went into convulsions. Apparently, instead of suppressing seizures, the combination of drugs induced one."

"Vern, what does this have to do with me?"

"The nurse did her best to stabilize Miss Watkins' convulsions, then ran into the corridor to call for help. When she returned, the room was empty. The patient wasn't there. Several nurses and a doctor frantically searched the entire floor, but could not find her. After about five minutes, they heard a scream from Miss Watkins' room. She was back in her bed, in the final throes of her seizure. It subsided, then she fell asleep."

Jim's interest perked up. "What do you think it means?"

"The medications may have triggered a seizure that sent her over to the other side and brought her back. When she woke up, she rambled incoherently about being in a green room full of strangers. There isn't a single room in this hospital that is painted green."

Jim started to game out the implications of this event. As usual, he was three steps ahead of everyone else on the chessboard. Could travel between the duplicate cities be more than an accidental phenomenon? What if someone could choose to move back and forth? That could be dangerous—a lot more people might cross over and create all kinds of havoc. Or, could there be an advantage—especially if Jim controlled the means of travel?

He told Vern to calm the staff. "Dream up a story to throw them off the scent. Then, find out if you can make the travel happen again."

Vern went to work on the problem. He knew not to quibble with Jim's directives—Jim was almost always right. Vern recruited a small team of researchers, all sworn to secrecy. Because of the great risks involved in causing seizures (and disappearances), they began with animals. They systematically injected rabbits with various combinations of anti-seizure drugs. Could they induce seizures in animals with no previous history of epilepsy? The two drugs that Miss Watkins had accidentally received had no effect on the rabbits. But when they added a third drug, convulsions occurred. After the convulsions subsided, the rabbits appeared to have no ill effects.

Vern and his team gradually increased dosage levels of the promising combination of drugs. One day, a convulsing rabbit on the experiment table disappeared. The astonished researchers hugged each other and danced around the room in joy. A few minutes later the rabbit reappeared, looking no worse for the wear.

They continued to vary the doses on the rabbits. One level of the medication caused the rabbits to disappear, then return. But, with a slightly lower level, the rabbits disappeared and didn't come back. A one-way trip? If there were a hospital in the same location in the other city, Vern wondered if people there were puzzled by a sudden plague of rabbits hopping around.

Hines and Cantwell met at the Racquet Club to review the good news. Jim was pleased, especially by the discovery of the one-way dose. "It's no use to travel over there for five minutes. You need to go for as long as you want. Of course, you carry a second dose to bring you back."

"Rabbits are all well and good," he continued, "but can you make it work with people?" Vern worried that experiments on humans would pose ethical issues and liabilities. Jim reassured him that he would cover any financial exposure. "I'll find volunteers if you need them."

Hines and Cantwell clinked their brandy glasses in the wood-paneled private room at the Racquet Club to toast this new venture.

While Vern was doing the rabbit experiments, Jim was consumed by CSP business and his new duties as the recently installed leader of the Knights of the Carnelian. The St. Louis boom continued and, if anything, was picking up steam. Newcomers poured in each month. Businesses were expanding to meet the demand. Entrepreneurs and scoundrels of all stripes wanted to get in on the action. Plans were needed for more housing, offices, and factories. Every day, Jim had to make a dozen decisions, and answer a hundred questions. He was on a thrilling, but exhausting, ride.

Whenever he had a free moment, he mused about what he might do with the ability to travel to the duplicate city. Over the years since 1929, he had often wondered what was going on in the world he had exited so abruptly. He would like to see the people and places he had left behind. Would he reveal himself? Or would he be more like Tom Sawyer surreptitiously watching his own funeral? These had always been idle speculations—until now.

What was the angle that could make this new travel ability worthwhile? To put it bluntly, was there money to be made? Sooner or later, the CSP boom would slow down. How could he keep it going, keep the new businesses making profits? Everyone else was intoxicated by the current prosperity; only Jim Hines was looking far enough ahead.

He thought back to the early days of the CSP when he traversed the city, speaking to any group who would listen to convince them to purchase shares. He remembered the primitive, crappy loudspeakers he had used (called "speech projection systems" in this weird new world). They were a pain in the ass. The ones in his old city were much clearer and more powerful. What if he could travel across and bring back products like that from the duplicate city? Or, better yet, bring back plans and designs?

He had been gone twelve years; they must have come up with all kinds of new inventions since then. Their patents wouldn't matter. They didn't even know his new city existed. He could patent the designs himself, then sell them to companies he wanted to help—and who would pay him top dollar.

He would make St. Louis a "city of inventors."

After a few more weeks, Cantwell was almost ready for a human test. Jim wanted to go, but Vern pleaded with him not to be the first guinea pig. The risk was too high and Jim was irreplaceable. He knew that Vern was right. Jim had always disdained cautious people, and now he was becoming one.

So Jim began to cultivate a volunteer, Peter Tomlinson, a young member of the Knights, who was smart as a whip and ambitious as hell. He reminded Jim of himself. Peter

Tomlinson was pumped up by the attention he received from the great man. Then, Jim explained the mission to him: Travel to the other side, find products and technologies that were different from anything we have here. Bring back samples, designs, or manufacturing specifications. Use bribery if you can; theft if you must.

Peter Tomlinson was shocked, and more than a little afraid of this crazy-sounding scheme. Jim used all his persuasion skills, even revealing to Peter that he himself had come from the other side. Peter agreed to everything. He desperately wanted to please his new mentor.

The first test was scheduled for midnight in the Asylum's library. Cantwell's thinking was that, if there were a similar hospital in the other city (as Irene Watkins' wild rantings had suggested), the library would be empty at this time. No one would see a human being popping out of thin air. Peter Tomlinson was ready, though visibly nervous. Jim was there to observe and also make sure he didn't get cold feet. Vern began with what he estimated would be a round-trip dose for an adult male, though he gave Peter a return dose to keep in his pocket just in case.

Peter stood in the middle of the room. Jim, Vern, and two researchers were watching. Jim gave Peter a thumbs up and he took the pill. A few seconds later, he began to convulse and crumpled to the floor. His body shook for a few seconds more, then he disappeared in a thwoop of rushing air. Jim smiled. After about six minutes, and a few nervous glances between Jim and Vern, the air shimmered and they heard a faint hum. Suddenly, Peter was back, lying on the floor in a daze.

He regained consciousness and looked extremely happy to see Vern, Jim, and the researchers.

"I was in a dark room. From moonlight coming in the windows, it looked a lot like this library." He opened his hand. "I took this off a desk."

It was a name plate, "Margaret Berra, Chief Librarian." Vern quickly checked a staff directory. "No one by that name works at this hospital."

After Peter recovered his strength and ate a sandwich, they moved on to the one-way dose. Jim handed him a briefcase. "Hold this. Let's see if it crosses over with you." Peter still had the return dose in his pocket. He took the one-way pill, convulsed, and disappeared, along with the briefcase. This time he was gone about fifteen minutes. He was still holding the briefcase when he reappeared.

A week later, Peter was ready for his mission. Jim spent hours briefing him on everything he remembered about the other city. He gave advice about where to look for interesting products and how to approach potential sources. On the day of departure, Jim gave him a bag of gold coins to finance his journey and the cost of obtaining product designs.

"I don't care if it takes two weeks or two months. Come back with something we can use."

It took two months.

Peter returned with three suitcases and a big grin. A limousine whisked him to Jim's private office, where Jim and Vern awaited.

Peter opened his suitcases on the conference table.

"A lot of their products are no better than ours, but I found three that could be very lucrative. The first is a fastening system for clothes which eliminates the need for buttons. I saw it everywhere, in ladies' dresses, children's outfits, and heavy coats for men. They call it a 'zipper.'"

"Could give our garment manufacturers a leg up," Vern said.

"Do you have the plans?" asked Jim.

"I couldn't find them anywhere. But we can easily copy the "zipper" design from the samples. It's not complicated."

"Next, I have this." Peter opened a small jar and poured brown powder into an ashtray. "Instant coffee. You stir a spoonful into a cup of hot water and you have coffee, instantly. A housewife can make one cup at a time, with no waste. A restaurant doesn't need to buy a big coffeemaker. And there's no risk of boiled, sour-tasting coffee. I drank this every day I was there. The process is called "freeze-drying." I have a complete set of specifications. They didn't come cheap.

"The last product is my favorite. It's very new, even over there, and I've never seen anything like it."

He pulled a thick, silvery disc out of his suitcase and unwound it a little bit. "It's a fabric-backed, highly-adhesive tape. They call it 'duck tape,' I think because it's water resistant."

Peter went on to describe the many uses of duck tape—pipe sealing, closing window leaks, small repairs, and more.

"The sky's the limit with this stuff." He added that he had complete formulations for both the adhesive and the backing material.

"Well done!" Jim said, clapping Peter on the back. "Let's have a drink to celebrate."

"One more thing," Peter said. "A few days ago, the country went to war. After that, I couldn't get anyone's attention."

"Who are they fighting?"

"Japan and Germany. Apparently, there's been a war in Europe for a few years. Last Sunday, Japan attacked Hawaii with flying machines. Now, everyone is in a frenzy."

Jim was the only one who knew about the other war with Germany just over twenty years ago. He didn't say a word.

BRICKS AND TAFFY

2010

A FEW DAYS AFTER THEIR PREVIOUS VISIT, Billy and Meredith were back to HD St. Louis. They decided to see the Hydraulic Building. To avoid the long streetcar ride, Billy looked for a place to cross that was closer to downtown. He had a good feeling near the YMCA, so they gave it a try in the alley behind a homeless shelter. Success! Minutes later they were crossing the wide boulevard near City Hall in HD.

"Look what I brought!" Meredith pulled a cheap, disposable camera out of her pocket. "No batteries, no electronics. We can take pictures!" She snapped one of Billy on the sidewalk with one of the Mezz bridges behind him.

The Hydraulic Building was hard to miss. It dominated the skyline from every direction and filled a full block between Chestnut and Market streets, just west of the nineteenth-century Old Courthouse, a landmark that looked the same in both SD and HD St. Louis. The Mezz was connected to three sides of the Hydraulic Building. Though most other HD skyscrapers had setbacks above the Mezz level, the Hydraulic tapered smoothly in a continuous line all the way to its distant glass spire.

Billy and Meredith were struck most by the building's surface. Shimmering curves and zigzags covered it like an ephemeral basket weave. From the sidewalk across the street, it was hard for Billy to tell where the windows began and the frames ended. A passing cloud briefly shaded the sun and the building appeared to flicker slightly and subtly change color.

The side of the building that faced the Old Courthouse had a two-story arched entrance, framed by inlaid ribbons of multicolored brickwork. Above it the words "Hydraulic Brick Corporation" were inscribed.

Billy and Meredith crossed the street to go inside, again dodging young men on scooters who swept past. In the lobby, polished marble floors were creamy with red and gold swirls. A large mosaic in the center of the floor depicted a brick with the word "Hydraulic" stamped into it. Walls were decorated with designs that echoed the building exterior—patterns of glazed bricks of many shades from light tan to purple

The lobby was half-filled, mostly with businessmen wearing the summertime uniform of downtown strivers—buttoned up suits, shorts, and colorful knee socks. Women wore similar outfits, but with flared shoulders and sharper creases in their shorts.

Off to one side of the lobby, they saw a sign, "The Saga of Bricks."

"Hey, Dad, let's check that out. Looks educational!" Meredith said.

"Ha ha," Billy said. She was paying him back for all of the boring "educational" destinations he had dragged her to when she was a kid.

They entered a darkened room of photos and exhibits. The floor was made of rough bricks, each one stamped with the word "Hydraulic." Clumps of people were milling about. The first exhibit was beneath a sign that read *"Bricks Are as Old as Civilization Itself."* A glass case, illuminated from within, contained a small, brown lump of burnt clay and an ancient tablet, inscribed with cuneiform scratches. Middle Eastern music played quietly. A plaque said that the lump was one of the oldest bricks ever discovered, from ancient Sumer. A second plaque translated the tablet, a prayer to the Sumerian god of bricks.

The exhibits moved swiftly through the succeeding centuries, breezing through ancient Rome (a brick from the Colosseum) and the Middle Ages (a trowel from Chartres). Apparently, little had happened in the world of bricks.

Billy and Meredith approached a brightly lit area which contained a machine about the size of a car, with pipes and springs and various unidentifiable protuberances. A shiny plaque announced:

> "In 1868, brick science took a great leap forward when the Hydraulic Press Brick Company was founded in St. Louis. E.C. Sterling revolutionized brick making with a process to mold highly durable brick in a hydraulic press."

A photo showed a man with a bowler hat and mustache standing stiffly next to a machine like the one in front of Billy and Meredith, which, another plaque announced, was a meticulously crafted replica.

People were lined up to take pictures of each other in front of the machine. Meredith positioned Billy there and snapped one of him.

The next part of the exhibit, *"The Path to the Sky,"* continued the Hydraulic story.

"Hydraulic's second president, Henry Ware Eliot, set the company on its course to greatness in 1906 when he hired a young Chicago architect, F.L. Wright, to become its lead designer, a position he would hold for fifty years, even after he also became Hydraulic's chairman. Wright transformed the company into a powerhouse of brick art and science. He hired chemists to create ever lighter formulations of brick in myriad colors, shapes, and textures, and mathematicians to devise advanced methods to lay these bricks in complex patterns that brought the designer's visions to life or, as Wright liked to put it, 'conjured dreams in brick.' Wright maintained strict quality control through teams of Hydraulic experts, who came to be known as 'brickitects,' who supervised the construction of every project. Structures clad in Hydraulic brick proliferated across the U.S. and around the world."

The next part of the exhibit, entitled *"Brick Power— the Amperic Brick®,"* showed cutaways of bricks bathed in ultraviolet light to reveal webs of different colored minerals and metals inside.

The plaque read:

"The Hydraulic Brick Company revolutionized the world of electricity with the introduction of the Amperic Brick® in 1943.

F.L. Wright and his team of genius metallurgists and ceramicists developed a method to generate power from the natural thermal expansion and contraction that bricks experience every day. By incorporating admixtures of phosphorus, magnetite and copper tendons into the clay material, each brick produces a tiny current as it heats and cools. Multiplied by the tens of thousands of bricks in a building, this process brings abundant power to our everyday lives. From Moscow to Melbourne, brick electricity flows to factories and powers vehicles. Modern life would be inconceivable without the billions of Americ Bricks® that Hydraulic manufactures each year.

"And still we don't rest! Research to create the bricks of tomorrow continues. Pixelated Americ Bricks® from Hydraulic will bring new dimensions of color and patterning to enrich everyday life for all.

"We don't just see the future, we mold it - Hydraulically!™"

A friendly guide wearing a shirt with the Hydraulic Brick Corporation logo stood by to answer visitors' questions. Billy and Meredith picked up snippets of his practiced spiel.

"Mr. Wright himself led the design of this building. Construction began in 1936, after the destruction of the original Hydraulic Building in the 1931 earthquake. Construction was frequently halted, sometimes for months, as Mr. Wright revised the design to keep up with new brick technologies emerging from the fertile minds of Hydraulic engineers. Insect wings inspired the iridescent surface effects we see today. Mr. Wright spared no expense to make this structure the pinnacle of the brickitect's art. Because of the many design changes, the building wasn't completed until years after his death."

Meredith and Billy looked around a bit more, then headed to the exit. They squinted as they emerged back into the bright lobby.

"That sure was educational," Meredith said.

Billy laughed.

They wandered out onto the street, gazing up at tall buildings, peeking into store windows, and marveling at exotic pedestrians. Meredith got great shots of Billy surrounded by the sidewalk crowd. Downtown HD seemed to attract people of all shapes, sizes, colors, styles and persuasions. They were buying, selling, conversing, arguing, flirting, and hurrying to their next appointments.

Meredith discovered a small shop tucked away in an alley around the corner from the Hydraulic Building. "Everything, since 1965," a sign in ornate script announced.

The shop sold curios, knick-knacks, embroidered decorations, and iced tea with fruit. One counter was covered with large glass jars filled with pieces of taffy in individual paper wrappers. A photo hanging above them showed a dapper man in a suit with the caption "The King of England has tasted our taffy. Why don't you?"

A handful of customers milled about examining the wares and sipping tea. The shopkeepers were two elderly ladies with perfectly coiffed white hair. They looked almost identical, but their habits were quite different.

One of them constantly scuffled about the shop straightening displays or dusting with a duster made of peacock feathers. She cheerily greeted every customer who entered. She had a sing-song voice and a faint accent that

Billy couldn't place. The other lady sat very still behind the counter with the cash register. She was reading a magazine and smoking a cigarette in a long holder. It looked like she hadn't moved all day. When a customer approached to pay for an item, she put down her magazine, then stated the amount of money that was due, speaking with the same unidentifiable accent. The customer handed over a bill and, with great ceremony, she opened the cash register, got the change, and precisely counted it out for the customer.

"Thank you so very much. We appreciate your kind patronage."

She used the exact same wording every time.

As each customer left with their purchase, the other lady would look up from her dusting and tidying to say: "So nice to see you. We eagerly anticipate your next visit. Shipments of many new items will arrive next week."

After a little while, Billy and Meredith were the only customers in the shop. Meredith asked if she could have a piece of taffy. The lady at the register said, "Take your pick," without removing her cigarette holder or lifting her eyes from the magazine. Meredith selected one, unwrapped it, and popped it into her mouth.

"Omigod!" She chewed a little longer. "Omigod!" She took another piece and gave it to Billy.

"Dad, taste!"

She watched, beaming, as Billy took a bite. He chewed, stopped, then chewed some more.

"Wow!

"What flavor is this?" Meredith asked.

The dusting lady scurried over to where they were standing by the taffy jars. She peered at the wrapper in Meredith's hand.

"Ambrosia, my dear" she said.

"It could be nectarine," said the other lady, still buried in her magazine. "They're quite similar."

"Excuse me," said Billy, "I hear your accent, but I can't place it. Where are you from?"

"South Africa," said one.

"Cape Town," said the other.

"That's a long way away. What brought you here?"

"It's both a long way and quite a journey," said the lady behind the counter.

"This may come as a surprise, but we are sisters," said the dusting lady.

Billy smiled. It was blindingly obvious. "Really?"

"Yes," said the dusting lady. "I'm Churcha Crockett"

"I'm Scienca Crockett," said the other.

"Nice to meet you both. I'm Billy Boustany. This is my daughter, Meredith. We're visiting from California."

Scienca put down her magazine and asked Meredith, "Are you enjoying your visit to St. Louis, my dear?"

"Oh, yes."

"And do you have a beau back in California?"

Meredith wasn't sure what a "beau" was.

"A young man," offered Churcha helpfully. "A special young man?"

Billy's ears perked up. He had been wondering about this same question for quite a while, but didn't know how to broach it without being accused of prying.

Meredith blushed slightly. "No. Not really."

"Then, be very careful while you're here," Churcha said. "St. Louis is full of sharpies and deceivers who would take advantage of someone as lovely as you."

"Oh yes, it's known for the sharpies," Scienca said.

"That's how we came to be here," Churcha said.

"Seduction and deceit," Scienca said.

"Most unscrupulous deceit," Churcha said, giving Billy a knowing glance.

"We were wholly unprepared."

"What happened?" Billy asked.

"It was many years ago," Scienca said. "No longer of interest to anyone."

"I'm interested!" Meredith said.

"It might be instructive for the young lady," Churcha said to Scienca. "So she can avoid a similar fate."

"I suppose you're right. Tell it we must," Scienca said.

Meredith fished more pieces of taffy from the jars and handed a few to Billy as they sat on stools in front of the display cases to listen. Despite their modest demurrals, Billy had the distinct impression that the sisters had told this story many times before, to anyone who displayed the slightest bit of interest.

Like seasoned performers, Churcha and Scienca smoothly handed the narrative back and forth, complete with dramatic pauses and knowing glances.

Churcha began.

"As young ladies in Cape Town, we were suffocating. Everyone there was so pinched up and afraid of what 'polite society' and 'the better people' thought about them. It was dreadfully dull. And the 'respectable' young men were complete bores.

"'Drips' we called them, commented Scienca, taking a long drag on her cigarette.

"We took consolation in each other and dreamed of a day when we could get away and begin to live with air and adventure. We joined a correspondence club and, before long, we were exchanging letters with people all over the world. As it happened, we both hit it off with young men from St. Louis. It was thrilling. The letters flew back and forth. New ones arrived almost every day. We fell in love with those letters and the handwriting.

"My young man," Churcha said, "had the most graceful, flowing script. Every word revealed his deep sensitivity. His name was Adalbert Kunz and he was from a family of prominent merchants. He was no drip. He wanted to live a remarkable life."

"Mine," Scienca said, "was completely different. His letters were in a strong, tight script that proclaimed integrity and noble purpose. His name was Lucas MacNeil. He was studying to be a dentist so he could give people beautiful smiles. So high minded!

"We suggested exchanging pictures but they told us that the rules of the correspondence club forbade that. Its mission was to encourage a focus on character, not surface appearances."

"We were in love."

Billy and Meredith listened raptly. Billy felt himself slipping into a hypnotic reverie as the story unfolded. He opened another piece of taffy.

"The letters were becoming our real lives and Cape Town just a minor annoyance. Then a moment of truth arose. A choice had to be made. Adalbert and Lucas declared their love for us. We had shown them our true characters through words alone.

"So they said."

"Adalbert invited me, and Lucas invited Scienca, to come to St. Louis. We agonized over the choice to leave our home."

"You agonized. I was ready to get out of there."

"And so we did. A few weeks later, we arrived in St. Louis.

"What did your family say?" Meredith said. "Didn't they hate seeing you just leave like that?"

"They wailed that we might as well be going to a different world, but Adalbert and Lucas had sent us tickets, so we didn't need anyone's permission."

"Adventure doesn't call every day, you know," Scienca said.

"A porter met us at the St. Louis train station who said that both Adalbert and Lucas had been detained. He took us to a hotel in Leveetown."

"Just a few blocks from where we are now.

"In those days, Leveetown wasn't like it is today. Instead of tourists, there were unsavory characters everywhere. Rude people and loud music at all hours. Danger was in the air. This wasn't the St. Louis we had expected."

"A note from Adalbert was waiting for me at the hotel. He asked me to meet him that evening in the restaurant across the street."

"A note from Lucas said he was detained until the next day. He suggested that I rest from the long journey."

"Did Adalbert and Lucas know each other?" Meredith asked.

"Not at first. They had only met after we gave them each other's address in our letters. They became friends and each considered the other to be a fine fellow."

"With great trepidation, I crossed the street to the restaurant that evening. A tall, strikingly handsome man approached. 'Churcha, I'm Adalbert.' Ever the gentleman, he kissed my hand. I wanted a mad embrace. We had a lovely dinner. We talked and talked, never taking our eyes off each other. We kissed goodnight. Briefly, of course.

"She was walking on air when she returned to the room. As I reeled her in, I hoped that Lucas would be even half as charming. The next day, I took a cab to meet him for lunch. He was modest and serious, but his eyes glowed with love. We had vichyssoise with floating cucumber slices in a courtyard of potted palm trees. I remember it like it was this morning.

"Now I was the one who had to reel Scienca in. We talked for hours about the grand lives that we were about to have in St. Louis. I dressed to meet Adalbert again that evening. I was running late, so I rushed out quickly. I didn't want to give him the impression that I was flighty and unreliable.

"I noticed that Churcha had left without one of her earrings. I grabbed it and raced down the stairs—this seedy hotel had no elevator—to catch up with her. She was ahead of me on the sidewalk on her way to the corner. Just as I was about to call to her, I saw Lucas across the street. I froze. He was walking toward Churcha. They met, and he was bowing to kiss her hand when I called out his name.

"Both Adalbert and I turned when we heard Scienca's voice. He was still holding my hand when she ran up to us, in tears. She said 'Stay away from my Lucas!' 'But this is my Adalbert,' I protested. He looked at me, then at her, then back at her. You can't imagine the look on his face. He dropped my hand, turned, and ran as fast as he could. He dashed out into the street and, WHAM, he was hit by a bus."

"Oh, no!" Billy and Meredith said in unison.

"Sadly, he survived. The ambulance people assured us that he would."

"But he never bothered us again."

"Who was he really?" Meredith asked, unwrapping another piece of taffy.

"A cad and a sharpie," Scienca said.

"We were well to be rid of him," Churcha added.

"What did he want?"

"His likely plan was to meet us both and then to take his pick."

"These sharpies have no consideration. They'll stoop to anything."

"Remember this lesson, my dear," said Scienca triumphantly.

"What did you do next?" Billy asked.

"We were alone and practically destitute. Then, some wonderful people came to our aid. The Refugees Club."

"I know them!" Billy said.

"You do?" Meredith said in amazement.

"They helped us survive, then get back on our feet."

"It would have been too shameful to go home. We needed a livelihood here. We thought of our grandmother's taffy recipe."

"It was famous in Cape Town. But it required a special ingredient, available only in Africa. The club lent us money to order a shipment of the spice. At first, we sold the taffy to the club members. Before long the demand grew and grew, so we opened our own shop."

"And here we are."

All were silent. Meredith and Billy were each chewing their fourth or fifth piece of taffy. They had kept reaching into the jars throughout the story.

"It's late," Billy said. "We have to be going."

"Can we buy some taffy to take with us?" Meredith asked.

"Of course," Churcha said. She picked out an assortment from the different jars.

"Will you come back and see us again?" Scienca asked.

"Yes. Very soon," Meredith promised.

Meredith asked the sisters if she could take their picture. They posed behind the taffy jars, with the photo of the King of England above them.

"What an odd little camera," Scienca remarked.

Billy and Meredith left the taffy shop to head back toward the crossing place. Meredith waved the bag of taffy with delight.

"Dad, we could make a fortune with this! It's the most amazing thing I've ever tasted. I couldn't stop."

"Me, neither." A thought flickered through Billy's head that, somehow, the taffy had contributed to the strangeness of Churcha's and Scienca's story.

"People at home would go nuts for this stuff. I bet I can get them to give me the recipe."

They continued west, weaving through throngs of pedestrians. People on scooters whizzed by on Market Street, like flocks of geese in formation. At a corner, they stood in a crowd waiting to cross. A group of tourists was babbling in Chinese. The light changed. More scooters shot by just as people began to move forward. Billy and Meredith had to jump back onto the curb to avoid getting hit. A few teenagers pushed up against them, almost spinning them around. "Hey, watch it!" Billy shouted.

"Sorry, sir," said one of the teenagers. His friends laughed as they ran across the street.

A couple of minutes later, Billy realized that his wallet was gone. At first, he was mad at himself, then he laughed it off. A rube in a strange city. Now he would have to cancel the credit cards and get a replacement driver's license.

At home that night, Billy, Carol and Meredith barbecued hamburgers on the patio. Carol, who was tired from a long day teaching summer school, noticed they both were in an uncharacteristically good mood.

Usually, Meredith was in a hurry to leave right after she ate and Billy moped silently, stewing about the troubles at the store he never wanted to talk about. Carol was thankful for any uptick in his attitude. Still, she had a suspicion that something might be up with them. But she said nothing. Billy and Meredith were terrible at keeping secrets from her. She knew she would figure it out before long.

As they finished the burgers, Meredith ran into the house and returned with the bag of taffy.

"Mom, Dad, try this for dessert."

"What is it?" Carol asked.

"Taffy. I was down in the city with friends last night to listen to music. We came across one of those popup kiosks."

"Honey, you've got to watch out for street food. You can't trust those places," Carol said.

"It's fine. We ate some last night. No one got sick."

Carol and Billy each took a piece.

"Wow!" said Carol. "That is good. Tastes like nectarine."

"Or it might be ambrosia," Billy said.

They watched the sun set over the trees and got into a long reminiscence about a car trip to Florida they had taken when Meredith was eight. They all laughed about how scared she had been of the crabs on the beach. Carol had three more pieces of taffy and became looser and more talkative after each one. Each time she opened a piece, Meredith flashed Billy a sly wink.

Billy was finishing breakfast the next morning. Carol had just left for school. Meredith walked in the back door and threw a photo envelope on the table.

"I dropped these off last night. They're all screwed up."

Billy took the photos out. They were blotchy and overexposed. White and green globs obscured most of the detail. He was able to pick out a few things, the outline of the Hydraulic Building, himself in front of the brick press, and Scienca's awkward smile. But if you didn't already know what you were looking at, they were a jumbled mess.

"I'm sorry, honey. I guess that whatever wipes out our phones when we cross over—magnetic fields, radiation, or something—ruins film as well."

Meredith was in a funk. Billy tried to cheer her up.

"We can enjoy it without pictures."

"I want to go back today to get the taffy recipe."

For a change, Billy actually had something he wanted to do at the store, but he couldn't resist her. This was their great adventure, after all.

Churcha gave Meredith a big hug when she and Billy entered the shop. Scienca glanced up from her magazine and nodded. Soon, Churcha, Scienca and Meredith were deep in conversation. Meredith was charming the hell out of them. And they were charming her. She loved how they talked, the way they fussed over her, and their endless trove of stories and quips. They saw their younger selves reflected in her innocence and enthusiasm.

Other customers who came in received minimum attention. Billy explored the shop, checking out the curios in much more detail than they deserved. Of course, he couldn't resist a piece or two of taffy.

He was examining whimsical figurines of chipmunks made out of tiny seashells when he heard all three of them giggling. A moment later, Meredith came over to tell him that they were going to make taffy now. Churcha followed behind her and shooed Billy toward the door.

"You'll just be in the way. Come back in two hours and you can taste Meredith's taffy."

As she shut the door behind him, she flipped the sign in the window to "Closed."

Out on the sidewalk, Billy thought about the best way to kill a couple of hours in downtown HD. He decided to go back up to the Mezz. He had explored only part of it the first time.

He took the elevator inside the Hydraulic Building to the Mezz stop and emerged into a manicured garden with trees and shrubs trimmed into pyramids, globes, cones and other geometric shapes. He strolled along a shaded path that provided relief from the hot summer sun. Teenagers were lounging on a bench deep in conversation, oblivious to everything around them. Several Argentinian tourists were listening to their tour guide expound on the wonders of the Mezz. Billy remembered just enough Spanish from high school to have a general idea of what the guide was saying.

He rounded a corner and started to cross another bridge. This one was covered by arched trellises with thick foliage. Thousands of fragrant purple flowers were blooming above his head. Bees were everywhere, darting from flower to flower. Billy stood still in the middle of the bridge to breathe in the sweet scent and listen to the faint buzzing of the bees all around him. Another perfect moment in HD.

The bridge led to a part of the Mezz he hadn't seen before. It was easy to get lost up here. He heard a guitar playing up ahead and saw a man on a bench under a large maple tree. The man, who looked a little younger than

Billy, sang, "She's gone, but I don't worry, I'm sittin' on top of the world." His fingers danced up and down the guitar neck, releasing bent, funky notes. The song sounded more familiar to Billy than anything he had heard over here.

A handful of people stood around listening as the song ended. They tossed money into the open guitar case on the ground, then drifted away. The man was tuning his guitar as Billy approached.

"Great song," Billy said. "I've heard it before."

"Maybe from me. I play up here every day. The Mezz is the best place in town—the top of the world."

"No, I think I heard it when I was in college."

"Where was that?"

"California."

The man played a few quick, bluesy licks. "I've never been to California." Then, he gave Billy a piercing look.

"You ain't from the other side, are you?"

"Huh?"

"You know, the other side of those lonesome invisible tracks." His fingers pulled some long, train whistle notes out of the guitar.

Billy got real quiet.

"Don't want to talk about it? I understand. Probably a wise policy."

"Yeah," muttered Billy weakly.

"Be careful my friend. Don't end up like me—stuck. It's no fun."

"I'm careful," whispered Billy, who was now both confused and uncomfortable.

"Could you do something for me?"

The man took a piece of paper out of his pocket, wrote on it, and handed it to Billy. There was a name, Sharon, and a phone number.

"If you get back across, please call her and say that Chris loves her and misses her."

Just then, people started to appear—the Argentinian tour group. The private conversation was over. Billy dropped a couple of dollar bills into the guitar case.

"Thank you, sir. And watch out for those spy boys."

"Spy boys?"

"They don't come up here much, but down there …" he pointed to the street below, "they're everywhere."

The man began another song as people gathered around him, "I got my mojo working, but it just don't work on you…"

Billy backed away. He wandered the Mezz for another hour, but he paid little attention to what he saw. He was consumed with questions. *What was that guy all about? Why did he dump an obligation onto me?* Something wasn't right.

Back at the shop, Billy saw a big bag of taffy next to the cash register.

"Try one," Scienca said. "They're still warm." Meredith was sitting on a stool. She was strangely silent.

"Time to go?" asked Billy. Meredith nodded. She picked up the bag of taffy and gave hugs to Churcha and Scienca. They urged her to come back real soon and she said she would. But Billy could tell her heart wasn't in it.

When they got outside, she unloaded her disappointment. "Damn!"

"Did you learn the recipe?"

"No! Well, almost. They showed me how to mix it. Sugar, butter, cornstarch, fruit flavors. And, how to cook it. Then Churcha said, 'Time for the secret ingredient.' Scienca made me turn away as they got it out and put it in the batch. She said, 'My dear, we love you, but we haven't shared this secret with anybody for forty-five years.'"

"So, I can't make it right." She held up the bag in disgust, "This is all we have."

They walked in silence. They reached City Hall, just a few blocks before their crossing place.

Billy noticed a park on the other side of City Hall they hadn't seen before. He was searching for a way to take her mind off the recipe debacle.

"Can we check out this place?"

"Sure," Meredith said, without a shred of interest or affect.

The square had a graceful band shell and a large statue of a man next to a piano. The paths through it were paved with black-and-white bricks in the pattern of piano keys. According to the sign, it was Joplin Square. The plaque at the base of the statue identified the man as Scott Joplin. Billy explained to Meredith, "He was a ragtime music guy from around 1900. His music was in a big movie when I was a kid. That's all I know about him." They read the plaque.

> Scott Joplin (1868-1944) was one of the greatest American composers and St. Louis' most famous citizen. From his early work, such as "Maple Leaf Rag" and "The Cascades," he became nationally known at the first St. Louis World's Fair in 1904. He went on to compose operas and ragtime symphonies, including the monumental 6th. His greatest musical legacy was the Mountains and Rivers Suite of 1924, an inspired collaboration with the Russian, Igor Stravinsky. It is widely considered to be one of the most important musical works of the 20th century. Joplin's funeral on June 6, 1944, was the largest public event in the history of St. Louis.

Next to the bandstand was a billboard plastered with posters for musical events. Meredith pointed to one of them. "Dad, is this the guy from the street supper?"

ONE NIGHT ONLY!
Milo Riley
Friday, August 13th
Uhrig's Cave
DON'T MISS IT!

"Yep. That's him."

At home that night, Billy stared at the scrap of paper the musician on the Mezz had given him. Should he call Sharon? What would he say? It could get really awkward really fast. He put the paper in his desk drawer so he wouldn't have to look at it.

People bumped and jostled Billy as he tried to worm his way through the crowd. He was at the Fourth of July celebration on the riverfront with a few hundred thousand other people. It was hot and the sun was beating down. He heard a loud roar above him and looked up. Three biplanes, trailing red, white and blue plumes of smoke, swooped low over the vast throng of people, then curved out over the river. He saw them framed by the Arch as they flew away.

He was headed toward the stage overlooking the river, though he wasn't sure why. Loud music echoed everywhere. As he got closer, people in outlandish clothes were dancing wildly. He came to a roped-off clearing. Someone lifted the rope so he could enter.

"It's about goddamn time," his father said, "I can't do this without you." Billy mumbled an apology for being late. The old man was wearing a white sequined jumpsuit. Carol and Meredith were brushing his hair and making the final adjustments to his suit. Carol threw a disapproving glance at Billy as she worked.

The old man waved for everyone to back away and he began a ceremonial walk toward a tall scaffold above the steps that led down to the river. The crowd parted to let him through. A phalanx of cameramen walked alongside him, recording his every move. Big Bill climbed a ladder to the top of the scaffold. Billy noticed that a wire stretched across the river to another scaffold on the distant Illinois bank. Giant TV screens around the Arch grounds showed close-ups of Big Bill at the top of the scaffold. He waved to the cheering crowd.

The music settled into a powerful, throbbing beat. It was Milo Riley! Milo spoke:

"Ladies and gentlemen, the one, the only, the original Duke of Discounts will now attempt the impossible. He will cross over our ancient mother Mississippi to the promised land, then return to us again. And why does he do this death defying feat? Because he's just an old softie."

Everyone cheered. Big Bill waved, then picked up a long balance pole to steady himself on the wire. A washing machine dangled from one end of the pole and a dryer hung from the other. Meredith was right next to Billy. She hugged his arm. "Daddy, this is his greatest ad, ever!"

The old man stepped out onto the wire. The washer and dryer flopped around, but he kept his balance. He tossed a handful of gold coins to the crowd below. Billy saw that he was wearing dainty ballet slippers so his toes could grip the wire. He stepped gingerly out over the river. A couple of times he stumbled and nearly lost his balance. The crowded cheered louder with each recovery. When he got to the middle of the river, he turned around, and bowed back to the crowd. Boats of all sizes and shapes, which dotted the river below, tooted their horns in response. Billy was amazed by his father's poise and showmanship.

He got to the far bank, did a little pirouette, then came back toward the Missouri side. When he reached the scaffold, the crowd went wild. Billy watched the close-up on the TV screen. Big Bill waved and smiled his crooked, goofy smile. Then he turned to look directly at Billy. He scowled and mouthed the words "Now, you little runt!" Billy was confused. Then he realized that he was holding a small metal box with a big red button on it. He pushed the button. The whoopee cushion "heart" began beating under the old man's jumpsuit. The crowd erupted with adulation.

Big Bill climbed down from the scaffold and embraced Billy.

"Your turn," he said.

A circle of people stood around, chanting "Bil-ly, Bil-ly!" He saw Carol, Meredith, his sisters, Mary Jo and Walt from the bar, Churcha and Scienca. Panic overwhelmed him.

"Do you want to sell TVs or not?" the old man said, as he nudged Billy toward the ladder. Churcha came up and shoved a piece of taffy into Billy's mouth. "This will get you across."

Milo's band was gone from the stage, replaced by Chris, the blues singer. As Billy climbed the ladder, he could hear Chris:

"Here, ladies and gentlemen, is Billy Boustany, the best friend that anyone could ever want. He'll never let you down." Then he launched into "Sittin' on Top of the World."

Billy reached the top of the scaffold. The people below looked like ants. Didn't they know he was terrified of heights? How had he let everyone push him into this? But there was no turning back now. He saw his own face on the giant TV screens. He grabbed the balance pole, which now had televisions and PCs dangling from the ends, and prepared to step out onto the wire. He looked down and saw that he was wearing thick, clunky shoes with hard soles. Way down below, he could see his father, Carol, and Meredith looking up to him with such deep love.

He took a step forward, almost slipped, then took another. It was working. *Maybe I can do this*, he thought. Before long, he was out over the middle of the river. The cheers of the crowd were well behind him, and he began to feel elated. He paused to wave to the boats below. As he raised his arm, he realized he had made a huge mistake. He lost his balance and fell, the brown water of the river rushing up toward him ...

Billy woke with a start. Carol lay in a deep sleep next to him. He felt the caress of cool air from the ceiling fan. He blinked and tried to orient himself. Sights and sounds of the dream shimmered vividly. For a few moments, it was the most spectacular movie he had ever seen. Then, one by one, the images and faces began to crumble, like icebergs splitting off a glacier to crash into the ocean. By dawn, all that remained was the shame and humiliation of his fall.

The dream hung around Billy like a shroud for the next few days. The July sales numbers didn't help. People who could afford to buy electronics tended to leave town every year during the sweaty inferno of the St. Louis summer. Still, sales this July were noticeably worse than last year. He kept signing receipts for inventory that was accumulating for the back-to-school season, but he didn't have much faith that it would sell. He might as well be sinking into the muddy oblivion of the Mississippi.

Justin, the retail consultant, was in Duke's Digital day after day, observing and taking notes on a clipboard. Sometimes, he hung back in a corner, watching from a distance. At other times, he followed salespeople around, scribbling from inches away as they demonstrated products to customers. If they looked at him, he just smiled cryptically and gestured for them to continue. After a salesperson complained that Justin's creepy presence was making customers uncomfortable, Billy asked him to back off.

"This is my process, Billy. The process that's going to rejuvenate your brand."

"Just don't stand quite so close to the customers."

"Of course, I'll disappear into the shadows, like a ninja."

"What ideas have you had about us so far?"

"None. I'm merely collecting data points." Justin pointed to the scribbled symbols and arrows on his clipboard. "I make no judgments until the data begin to speak."

"An idea or two wouldn't be such a bad thing, given what we're paying you."

Justin put his hand on Billy's shoulder as if he were calming a nervous child.

"Right now, I know nothing. But when I see the whole field of data before me, there will be a moment when I'll go from knowing nothing to knowing everything. That's the moment you're paying for, Billy. Allow it to ripen organically."

Justin turned and went back to lurking in a corner by the wall of TVs.

That afternoon, Billy got an email from Dan the banker with the date, a few weeks out, for Justin's presentation of his strategy for Duke's Digital. It felt like a court summons.

SUPREME PROTECTOR

1942

AFTER PETER TOMLINSON RETURNED with the three products, patents were filed, deals were made, and money—quite a bit—changed hands. Jim's plan was off to a great start. Now he wanted to see the other city for himself and begin the next phase.

Vern protested once again. Jim mollified his fears by agreeing to go for only two days, and to be accompanied by Peter.

"We'll be careful. I'll come back." Jim mostly wanted to see his old home for himself. When Jim and Peter were ready to depart for the other city, Jim patted his lapel to assure Vern that he had the drug in his pocket.

"I have my return ticket."

After they crossed, Jim and Peter hailed a cab to go downtown. Jim peered out the window intently during the whole ride, spotting places he remembered. They got out of the cab at Seventh and Olive, in front of Jim's old office building, where he had taken his fateful fall on the day of the 1929 crash. It looked just the same. Jim took a deep breath. Even the scent of the air brought back memories of his earlier life.

In fact, all of downtown was remarkably unchanged. There was no sign of any earthquake and almost no new buildings had gone up in the intervening years. Since Jim was used to the construction frenzy in his St. Louis, this stagnation unnerved him. It was as if nothing had been built in more than twelve years.

After a few hours of looking around downtown, Jim proposed that they take a cab to the Chase Hotel to have dinner at one of his favorite old haunts, the Chase Club, the swankiest place in town. The lobby of the Chase was swarming with military men in transit on their way to war.

Jim saw two black soldiers, officers by the look of their uniforms, arguing with the Chase Club *maître d*, who was refusing them admission to the restaurant. They pointed to empty tables. The *maître d* shook his head. Reluctantly, they left.

Jim hadn't witnessed a scene like that in quite a while. It annoyed him. What a stupid way to run a business! The CSP, which granted equal share rights to black citizens of his new St. Louis, had begun to wear down racial separation and animosity there. Jim was glad.

Unlike the black officers, Jim and Peter were seated without delay. The *maître d* led them through the large, high-ceilinged dining room, fringed with palm trees in large planters. Tuxedo-clad waiters floated about, handing out menus, lighting cigarettes, and pulling back chairs so ladies could sit. A small combo performed tasteful swing music. At their table, Jim ordered champagne and shrimp cocktails. He was elated to be here again.

Jim was eager to discuss the smuggling project. He told Peter that there were much bigger opportunities than zippers, coffee, and duck tape. "I don't know what they are yet, but we'll find them."

Continued success depended on absolute secrecy. No one in either city must know about the existence of the other. If that knowledge got out, the value of the smuggled product designs would plummet. Jim planned to set up an elite inner group of Knights who would be the only ones to know the truth about the drug and the smuggling scheme. He wanted Peter to run the operation. Dr. Cantwell and a couple of patent lawyers would be the other members. Jim would enlist the full Knights organization to protect the secret of the two worlds, but would concoct a cover story that would not expose the smuggling scheme to them. The waiter brought a bottle of champagne in a silver bucket and filled their glasses. They toasted. Jim's words meant that Peter's future career was assured.

Jim looked out over the tables where elegant men and women drank, smoked, and laughed.

"We are shepherds, Peter, and these are our sheep. As long as we don't frighten them, they will supply us with wool forever."

Just then, Peter saw Dr. Cantwell entering the Chase Club.

"Look who's here!" Before Jim could tell him that it was the wrong Dr. Cantwell, Peter bounded over to greet him. Cantwell was startled by this young stranger shaking his hand. Peter led him over to Jim's table. Cantwell recognized Jim and scowled.

"Jim Hines, you miserable, lying scum. I'd like to wring your neck."

"Nice to see you, Vern."

"You've got a lot of nerve showing your face around here. Everyone thought you were dead."

"I nearly was."

"We drank a toast and said, 'Good riddance! May he rot in hell.'"

Jim signaled to Peter to step away so he could speak with Cantwell privately.

"Vern, I understand why you're angry. No one feels worse about those times than me. I think I can make it up to you, make you whole for your losses. But I need some help from you in return ..."

From across the room, Peter watched them talking intensely, leaning in closer and closer to each other. After several minutes, Cantwell stood up. He and Hines shook hands, then he left to join his companions at another table.

Peter came back and sat down. Jim refilled their glasses with champagne.

"Another sheep added to our flock."

From the Most Secret Archives of the Knights of the Carnelian. For Founders Circle Members Only.

May 12, 1942
Address of Supreme Protector J. Whittemore Hines to the Knights of the Carnelian Annual Meeting at the New Southern Hotel

My Fellow Knights,

Both our beloved city and this esteemed Order of Knights are at a crossroads. We have made great progress building the long-term future of St. Louis. The Citizen Shareholder Plan, endorsed and promoted by you, the forward-looking members of this august organization, has made this past eleven years the most prosperous in the city's history. We have much to be proud of and much to be thankful for. As our friends in the Sons of Rest say, "Life is sweet."

Note: At this point, Supreme Protector Hines instructed the waiters and other staff members to leave the hall. Only Knights remained.

Gentlemen, an ever-darkening shadow looms over St. Louis. Our citizens have not seen it yet. Many of you think it is trivial, a mere curiosity to be discussed over cocktails in this hall. But let me assure that it is, in fact, a grave threat to our stability and our future.

We are all aware of the stories that have emerged over the past thirty-four years about odd people appearing in our city who were bewildered and confused. Some of them had fantastic stories about people and events that we know nothing about. Dating back to 1908, the Knights have assumed an informal responsibility to investigate these incidents, and have kept the records in our archives, subject to our sacred oath of secrecy. A few of you have interviewed these poor souls, who often disappeared as suddenly as they arrived. We have spent many a pleasant evening debating and speculating about the cause and meaning of these incidents. Are they the result of excessive exposure to the sun or toxic fumes? Has some sort of delusion or mental condition struck these individuals? Some of the more scientific-minded among you have even proposed that these people have somehow ingested vision-inducing plants, like those the Indians of Mexico are said to use.

But you have long agreed that this subject is no more than an obscure puzzle, suitable for our amusement and intellectual pursuits, but not a matter of practical importance.

But, today, I'm here to tell you that all of these ideas are completely wrong. This phenomenon of the strange Visitors has the very real potential of upending our way of life and destroying our city's peace and prosperity.

So, what is going on? These Visitors are actually people from a near duplicate of our city, one that exists alongside of ours, or inside of ours, or is tangled up with ours in some

mysterious ball of twine. I don't
pretend to understand the details.
Perhaps none of us ever will. But
the time has come for we Knights to
confront this situation seriously.

Each of these visitors may have a
different story, but they all come from
the same place, this duplicate city.
If we do nothing, sooner or later the
general population will get wind of
them. When that happens, there will be
a panic like none we have ever seen.
It would make the earthquake seem like
child's play. The idea that there is
another world under our feet, or in the
air, or wherever it is, will confuse and
confound people. Such knowledge is too
much for the average citizen. They will
question the meaning of their world,
the value of their actions. Commerce
could grind to a halt. The government
might step in to take control, or
quarantine the city, or worse. What
would happen to your businesses? What
would become of our city's great,
shining future?

As sworn Knights of the Carnelian,
we cannot allow such a fate to ruin St.
Louis.

I'm sure you are skeptical of what
I'm saying, and some of you may be
inwardly laughing at me. But before
you doubt any further, let me tell you

why I am 100 percent certain that I am correct—I myself, the Supreme Protector of this Order, am one of these Visitors.

Note: An audible rumble of shock permeated the room at this remark.

I lived in the duplicate St. Louis and was completely unaware of you and this city. Just over twelve years ago, in the fall of 1929, events that I cannot explain suddenly landed me here. Let me assure you that it is not a matter of mental illness or toxic fumes or Mexican plants. The other city is real and some small number of people seem to be able to travel from it to here. Though I come from that city, I have no idea how to go back to it. At first, I was lost and confused here. But now this city is my home and you are my brothers. I have cast my lot with you and have no desire to return.

I propose that the Knights of The Carnelian remake this sacred organization to combat this threat. We can leave the debutante balls, parades, and social niceties to others. I assure you that your daughters will still find suitable husbands. We must provide a deeper level of protection to them and to all of St. Louis.

Our new mission must have three elements: vigilance, containment, and inquiry.

Vigilance: We must detect these illegal Visitors as soon as they arrive. The most dangerous situation that I can imagine is to have a Visitor in our city without responsible people—namely, we Knights—being aware of their presence.

Containment: Once we find a Visitor, we must act quickly to isolate them. Who knows what they might say to an average citizen? What information might they let slip? What uncomfortable questions might they ask? Every moment of unsupervised contact between a Visitor and a citizen risks starting a wildfire that could go out of control.

Inquiry: We must learn more about this phenomenon. What is this duplicate city? How do people travel from there to here? What other possibilities exist? This is a vital subject for scientific investigation, but we cannot open it up to the broad community of scientists. The impact on business must be our foremost concern. I propose that we Knights maintain tight control over all investigations. Only qualified members of our Order should have access to information about the phenomenon. If secrecy delays the development of a full picture of the phenomenon, so be it. As Knights, we are patient. We have a long-term perspective. We are committed to the future health of our community. Our commitment extends to the lifetimes of our children and grandchildren. No calling is higher than that.

So, I ask this body tonight to commit to protecting our city, now and forever, with vigilance, containment, and inquiry.

I know that I can count on you noble Knights of The Carnelian to make the right decision, the wise decision for St. Louis' future.

Thank you.

Note: A long and vigorous debate ensued. Supreme Protector Hines had previously instructed the staff to lock the doors to the hall as they left. All Knights would remain in the hall until a decision was ratified.

Knight Wright spoke eloquently against the Supreme Protector's proposal. He stated that the city had nothing to fear from these Visitors and was strong enough to withstand any knowledge, no matter how bizarre and disturbing. He further objected to the idea of limiting scientific inquiry, which he called an affront to light and truth.

Knight Cantwell drew upon his expertise as a physician to confirm the substantial risk of mass hysteria and nervous breakdowns if the public gained knowledge of the other city. While he sympathized with Knight Wright's concern about restricting scientific inquiry, he believed that the well-being of the patients, the citizens of our great city, must come first. Furthermore, he doubted that anything useful could be learned about the mysterious phenomenon of the Visitors without an investment so massive that it would deplete the Knights' resources. It might take decades to gain even a rudimentary understanding.

Debate continued until dawn on May 13. Ultimately, the Supreme Protector's view prevailed and his proposal was adopted. In the spirit of noble unity, Knight Wright moved that the decision be made unanimous and that it remain secret for all time. And so it was agreed.

Respectfully submitted,
Christopher Sherman, Jr., Esq.
Recording Secretary

THE PERMEABILITY PROBLEM

2010

THE BACK-TO-SCHOOL SEASON had begun for Duke's Digital and Billy was consumed with work. Meredith was racing to complete her summer school assignments. So HD St. Louis had been on the back burner for a couple of weeks. One morning, amidst the flood of bills, catalogs, and useless solicitations in the mail, Billy saw a plain envelope addressed by hand to "William H. Boustany, Jr." There was no return address. He opened it and saw his missing credit cards and driver's license. There was a note on plain paper. *"We need to talk. Lobby of the Hydraulic. Wednesday, August 11. 10:00 a.m."*

He froze. Oh, shit.

On Wednesday morning, Billy entered the Hydraulic Building. In one corner of the lobby, a kiosk of miniature glazed bricks rose up from the floor. A brass sign arching over it said *Answers*.

Billy looked around, unsure what to do. Another kiosk was festooned with newspapers, magazines, and candy bars. Its sign read *Diversions*. Billy started walking toward the *Answers* kiosk when he felt a tap on his shoulder.

"Mr. Boustany?"

Billy turned to see a young man in a dark suit with a white carnation in his lapel. "Yes."

"You're expected upstairs. Follow me."

They walked past the big bank of elevators, then turned a corner to reach a single door with no handle. The young man took a key out of his pocket, inserted it, and the door slid open to reveal a large elevator, inlaid with polished wood. The control panel had only two buttons, "L" and "KotC."

As the elevator ascended, the young man said, "There is a dress code here. We'll lend you a jacket and tie."

Riding in silence, the ascent seemed interminable to Billy. The young man did not make small talk or eye contact. When the elevator stopped, the door opened to a high-ceilinged room with a mosaic floor, dark paneling, and indirect lighting. There was no furniture other than a table in the center of the room with a massive vase of flowers. Billy looked up to see skylights. Some were clear, showing the blue morning sky, others had stained glass in abstract patterns.

"Wait here," said the young man. He opened a door in the paneled wall and took out a dark blue blazer and striped tie, which he handed to Billy. Billy put them on. The blazer didn't fit well. The young man stepped in front of Billy, adjusted the tie and brushed something off the shoulder of the blazer. He stepped back to appraise the effect.

"That will do, for now," he said and ushered Billy toward the far end of the room. The paneled wall looked completely blank, but the young man touched a spot on it and a door opened. He gestured for Billy to step through, though he did not follow. The door closed behind Billy.

This room was darker—no skylights. A voice said, "Mr. Boustany, thank you for coming."

As Billy's eyes adjusted to the dim light, a man approached with his hand extended. Billy shook it. "Yeah, sure. I'm happy to help."

"My name is Giles Monroe," the man said. He was a tall, thin black man with wire rimmed glasses and an impeccably tailored suit, of course with short pants, and a reddish-brown carnation in his lapel. For a moment, Billy felt like he was in a funeral home.

"This way, please," Giles said. "These are my two colleagues, Martin Matsui and Jennifer Logan." Billy shook hands with a small, older Asian man and a slender white woman with a gray pageboy. Like Giles and the young man in the lobby, they had carnations in their lapels.

"May we offer you some coffee?" Martin asked.

Giles gestured toward two facing leather sofas. Martin went to a silver service on a sideboard. From a large samovar, he drew a cup of coffee and handed it to Billy. They all sat down. Giles slid Billy's wallet across the coffee table. Billy took it.

"You were the victim of some of our many pickpockets who prey upon visitors. As your wallet worked its way through the chain of traffickers who deal in stolen goods, it came to the attention of one of our spotters."

"Spotters?"

"People who discreetly watch for unusual items. We don't get them very often, but we like to be informed when they appear," Giles said. "May we call you William?"

"Everyone calls me Billy, except when I'm in trouble."

Billy smiled. Giles, Martin, and Jennifer did not smile back.

"Of course, Billy. You probably have some questions, but let's begin with ours. How many times have you been to our city?" Jennifer asked.

"Nine or ten. I haven't been counting."

"Did anyone teach you how to get here?" Giles said.

"No, I sort of stumbled into it."

"But you have come back several times. How did you learn to do it?" Martin asked.

"I guess I'm self-taught. My first crossing was an accident. Then I tried different things to make it happen again. I closed my eyes, turned around, stuff like that."

Jennifer was taking notes intently. Billy took a sip of coffee.

"Eventually, I figured out if I feel a hint of dizziness or throbbing, and then wait until it's just right, crossing becomes the easiest thing in the world, like slipping through a thin curtain in the breeze."

Giles and Martin looked at each other. "That's consistent with what we've heard before," Martin said.

"Before?" said Billy. "Do other people know how to do this?"

Giles leaned forward. "Have you told anyone about your visits?"

"No. I didn't want people to think I was crazy."

"Good. No one, then."

Billy paused. "Actually, I did tell my daughter."

"A child?"

"She's twenty...and...I brought her with me a couple of times."

"This child has visited also?" Giles said, a look of horror on his face. "Has she told anyone?"

"No, no. Meredith wouldn't do that. I made her promise."

Giles turned to Martin and Jennifer. "Uncertainty," he said. They nodded. Billy didn't like the way they were looking at each other.

"What the hell is going on here?" Billy demanded.

"Please don't get upset," Giles said.

"In many respects, we are as baffled as you are, though we have been studying this phenomenon for quite a while," Jennifer said.

"Who are you, anyway?"

"We are members of the Knights of the Carnelian," Giles said.

"The people who put on fireworks on the Fourth of July?"

"In your city, yes, that's what the Knights do. Once we were the same organization. But like our cities, we have diverged," Giles explained.

"What if I took a few minutes to brief Billy on the big picture?" Martin said to Giles and Jennifer. "Then we will be able to have a more productive conversation." They nodded, then Giles and Jennifer got up and left the room.

"Follow me," Martin said. He led Billy to another door, also hidden in the paneling. He opened it to reveal a narrow spiral staircase. "Please go first. At my age, I may take a little longer."

Billy climbed the staircase about twenty feet and emerged into a sunlit room whose entire roof and walls were made of glass. He was at the pinnacle of the Hydraulic Building. He could hear Martin breathing heavily as he climbed. "Be there in a minute."

Billy walked over to one wall. The city was spread out below. Buildings, streets, and people on the sidewalks.

The zigzag bridges of the Mezz. He saw the Mississippi a few blocks away. Boats, large and small, dotted the river. On the far bank, tall, gleaming white towers lined the riverfront. Three of them were joined at the top by a long platform, shaped like a giant surfboard, which formed an aerial park, with trees and terraces. He noticed that many of the buildings on the St. Louis side also had shade trees, elegant canopies, and restaurants on their flat roofs.

Martin, wheezing, arrived at the top of the stairs. "Amazing view, isn't it? Sadly, I don't get up here much anymore. Tell me what you see. What stands out to you?"

"I see the Eads Bridge, but the other bridges don't look familiar to me. And there's no Arch."

Martin chuckled. "Ahh, your famous Gateway Arch. No, we don't have that. I only know a little about your city, but I think we have very different views about the role of the river and the riverfront. It did not occur to us to clear out some of the most valuable real estate in the country—and one of the city's biggest attractions—to install a giant piece of sculpture, as striking as it might be. We do have the marriage of the rivers in Forest Park. A similar form, but made of water." Martin led Billy to the other side of the room to look west. "It's out there about six miles, but it's only visible once an hour."

"Where's the ballpark?"

"Baseball? Up that way, on the north side, in its traditional home." Martin pointed to a stadium in the distance.

"I don't see any highways."

"Your rivers of automobiles? One of the most prominent features of your city. We have avoided those. Probably just as well. They haven't helped your city all that much, have they?"

Martin pointed to a pair of wicker chairs. "May we sit? My knees are acting up." Martin sighed in relief as he sat down. He poured two glasses of water from a pitcher on a table, gave one to Billy, then took a sip. "It's best to start with a metaphor."

Martin closed his eyes slightly. "Consider a snowflake. It falls on a mountaintop in Colorado. Tossed about by the wind, the snowflake could come to rest either on one side of the mountaintop or the other, just inches apart. When the sun shines, the snowflake melts into a drop of water, which might flow down one side of the mountain or the other. It could end up flowing east to the Platte, then into the Mississippi and the Gulf, or west into the Colorado and, eventually, the Pacific."

Billy wasn't sure where this was going.

"Excuse me," Martin said, a little flustered, "Did I mention that this mountain lay right on the Continental Divide?"

"No, but I get it."

"A tiny, insignificant difference leads to completely different outcomes. Next, imagine that the snowflake splits in two, with each snowflake in its own independent world. They have nothing to do with each other. In one world, the snowflake falls east and, in the other, it falls west. And events go on their merry way in each world, with no awareness of the other.

"How could that happen?"

"We don't know." Martin gestures to the windows and the city below. "But, apparently, it did. We have observed—and now you have, as well—that our two worlds are not completely separate. Ninety-nine point nine-nine-nine percent separate perhaps, but not one hundred percent. Otherwise, you and I would not be having this conversation."

"What do scientists say about this? It's got to be one of the biggest discoveries ever. I mean, Jesus ..."

"Very few scientists are aware of this phenomenon of occasional permeability. Our organization has worked very hard to keep it under wraps."

"Why?"

"Imagine the panic. If masses of people found out that there was another version of their world where their actions and choices didn't matter, or where they did not exist, all because of chance, they would be paralyzed by despair."

"I've survived it. My daughter survived it."

"Have you not thought that you might be insane?"

"Yes, at first. But now I'm okay."

"We can deal with it as individuals, but not on a society-wide scale. The level of uncertainty would be devastating to everyone—definitely to business, which would not be able to function in such an environment."

Billy leaned forward, put his elbows on his knees, and cradled his head in his hands. He stared at the floor. He was trying to take it all in, to compare what Martin was saying to all the amazing things he had experienced over the past two months. Martin sat patiently. He had seen this reaction before.

After a minute or two, Billy said, "Are there only two separate worlds? Why not millions?"

"We're only aware of two. There could be millions of worlds that are one hundred percent separate. We wouldn't have any way of knowing. Perhaps the anomaly is the slight permeability between our two worlds."

"Is this permeability just in St. Louis?"

"Again, we don't know. It happens here from time to time, but we have not heard of it anywhere else."

"When did the separation start?"

"Excellent question. Our predecessors in the Knights first became aware of it in January 1908. As the leading citizens of the day, the police approached them for advice about a strange situation."

Martin told Billy the story of the two Edward Runklemanns, both claiming to be married to the same woman, and who had identical stories of the wedding. How they fought over a "missing" baby and were arrested by the police and then interviewed by the Knights. How they had identical scars. How one had a newspaper with articles about events that didn't happen.

Martin opened a drawer in the table and pulled out a large, leather-bound photo album to show Billy a picture of two men, each about thirty years old with dark hair, parted in the middle. Both stared straight into the camera. They looked exactly the same. One seemed mightily peeved about something. Martin pointed to the peeved one.

"He was the visitor from your city. In your world, he and his wife had a baby, over here they did not. So we think the separation of the worlds occurred after the wedding in 1904, when the two men were still one person, and before the conception of the child. That would put it in in late 1904 or early 1905. But we have no idea what caused it."

"Do I have a double over here?"

"No. Right after the split, the people in the two cities were identical. Then the snowflakes began to accumulate. In each world, accidents occurred, different choices were made, different marriages, different children. So, a century later, the populations are completely separate."

Martin turned the pages of the photo album. "Over the succeeding years, more of these occasional incidents came to our attention." Billy saw pictures of men and women dressed in the styles of the teens, twenties, and thirties.

"Each visitor had similar stories and questions. One, in particular, told the Knights in great detail about a man named Albert Einstein, the speed of light, and something called 'relativity.' He couldn't explain it very well, though he insisted it was behind everything."

"Everyone learns about it in school. But I couldn't explain it either."

"One of the Knights took it upon himself to research the story. He went to Switzerland, where the man said Einstein had lived. All he found was a newspaper obituary of an obscure patent clerk who had died in a hiking accident in 1905. Snowflakes in the wind, I suppose."

"So, where does that leave me?"

"The conditions for permeability are unpredictable. The boundaries between the worlds seem to thin out at various times in various locations, with no clear pattern. And, only very few people—like you—seem to be able to move across."

Martin continued to turn the pages of the photo album. Billy saw more people wearing clothes from various decades. Martin turned one more page and Billy froze. There was a picture of a man with a round face and black-rimmed glasses, standing in a crowd.

"I know him," said Billy. It was John, his father's radio repairman, though younger with dark hair. "John worked for my father. I talked to him just a few weeks ago."

"What a small world! I visited John's home and met his mother, back in the 1980s. He was brilliant and she was charming. I still remember her delicious pecan pie. I had the responsibility to put a stop to his crossings. An unpleasant assignment.

"You need to know something else, Billy. Each person's ability to cross over disappears after a while—a few months or maybe up to a year. It's impossible to know when it will happen, and you don't want to be in the wrong place when it does."

"Why does it disappear?"

"Excellent question. The current theory is that the stress of crossing over the barrier causes a resistance in the body at a molecular level. The resistance increases with each journey. At a certain point, it prevents the person from making further crossings."

As Martin closed the album, Billy noticed a copy of his driver's license on the last page. Martin looked at his watch. "Time for the fountains. Let me show you."

They stood up and walked to the western window. Martin pointed toward Forest Park in the distance. "There they are." Billy saw two columns of water forming an arch hundreds of feet tall. "They are especially beautiful at night when they are illuminated. I often wonder if your Mr. Saarinen slipped across and saw them. But we have no record of a visit by him. Let's rejoin the others."

Martin slowly descended the spiral staircase. Billy took one final look at the city spread out below. Until he heard the sad story from 1908, he hadn't considered the possibility of having a double in HD. Now he was disappointed that there wasn't a second Billy out there that he could meet. It would be so cool, like finding a long-lost brother.

Giles and Jennifer were ready for them in the paneled library.

"I trust that Martin brought you up to date on our situation," Giles said, sipping his coffee.

"Yes. It's a real mind-blower. The last few months make a lot more sense to me now."

Jennifer offered Billy a pastry. "I'm sure you can appreciate our concern about this problem."

Billy was too excited to listen to her. "I want to see more. Your city is amazing. You must be very proud of it. When I lose this power, or whatever it is, I'll be gone. Game over."

"That would be a very dangerous plan, Mr. Boustany," Giles said. Billy noticed that he wasn't calling him "Billy" anymore.

"Isn't that my business? My chance to take?"

Giles peered intently over his glasses. "Mr. Boustany, I admire your sense of adventure. But risky behavior, however satisfying in the moment, is foolish. As a businessman, I'm sure you appreciate that."

"No risk, no reward," said Billy. "As a businessman, I'm sure you understand *that*, Giles. Whoever you are."

Billy smiled and leaned back in the leather sofa. He was pleased with his snappy comeback.

"Let me put it more directly," Giles said. "We want you to go back to your side—today—and stay there. Don't come back and don't bring your daughter back."

"This is the biggest thing ever and you want me to just walk away from it? I don't think so."

"We have seen your city," Jennifer said, "and we don't care for it. People are leaving. The place has been taken over by cars. It's a disaster."

"And there is the absurd fear and conflict between your black and white citizens," said Giles. "Who would want to do business in such a place?"

"Hey! We're not all racists," protested Billy, though, deep down, he knew they had a point.

"We don't want your people and your ways over here," Jennifer said.

"Billy," Martin said, "remember, we discussed the potential for panic if people became aware of the two cities."

"Do I look panicked?"

"Maybe you should be. You could lose your crossing power and get stranded here," Jennifer said.

"And we could assist you with that," said Giles softly.

His words hung in the air. After a long pause, Billy stood up.

"We're done. Thanks for the coffee."

Giles gave him a stern warning. "Be reasonable, Mr. Boustany. Go home. Enjoy your life. Don't come back."

Billy ignored him and started toward the door. Martin followed him. In the entrance hall, Billy took off the jacket and tie and threw them at the young man, who was waiting there. Billy and Martin got into the elevator.

"They're serious," Martin said. "And they're right. Crossing over, as fascinating as it is, is very dangerous."

"I don't think they care about my well-being."

"We have kept the cities separate for a hundred years. It has worked well. Wouldn't you agree?"

"Hell, I don't know. Until a few months ago, I had no clue."

"Yes. And you were secure in your world."

"Not as secure as you think, but it's none of your business."

"Fair enough. But our world is none of your business, either."

"Who are you to tell me what to do?"

"I'm an architect. I solve problems and do my best to create beauty out of ugliness. But Giles and Jennifer, like most of the Knights, are businesspeople. They see their only duty as protecting the shareholders."

"What goddamn shareholders?"

"Everyone in this city is a shareholder. The Knights are management."

The elevator door opened. They walked out into the lobby.

"I beg you to consider two facts, Mr. Boustany. One, the Knights will do whatever it takes to protect the shareholders. Two, as the letter you received demonstrates, they can enter your city also."

Billy recoiled slightly. Martin shook his hand. "I wish you the best of luck."

Billy walked through the revolving door to the sidewalk. The crowd of pedestrians flowed by. He turned and looked up at the Hydraulic Building, then back down to the busy street. A new reality was sinking in. He had been threatened for the first time in his life.

That night, Billy looked for an opportunity to talk with Meredith alone. He, Carol, and Meredith ate dinner on the patio—grilled chicken and one of Carol's signature salads. Carol was in an especially good mood, talking about the camping trip she was taking with her students the next weekend.

"We're joining up with a group from a charter school in the city. I wonder how these kids from two totally different worlds will interact with each other. They'll all be in a new environment."

"That sounds awesome, Mom. Kind of 'Lord of the Flies' meets 'Glee.'"

Carol laughed. "I hope it doesn't go that far." She invited both Meredith and Billy to come along. They both begged off. Meredith cited unnamed "plans" and Billy said he had to work on Saturday. As they cleared the plates, Billy said he was going to make a run to Costco. He hoped that Meredith would pick up on his hint. Carol disliked Costco.

"I'll come with you, Dad."

In the car, Meredith had a big smile. "Do you really have to work this weekend? It would be a great time for more exploring."

"Things have changed. I had a very weird meeting this morning."

"What?"

"Remember when my wallet got stolen? A couple of days ago I got a letter. It came here. It had my credit cards in it and this." He handed Meredith the note.

"Wow."

"I went over and met with these big shots in the other St. Louis. The Knights of the Carnelian."

"The people who put on fireworks and debutante balls?"

"Kind of. But they're very different over there."

Billy gave her the highlights of his meeting at the top of the Hydraulic Building, including the revelations that other people had gone there in the past and that his ability to cross over would disappear. Also, that they had threatened him if he or she came back.

"That sucks. What's their problem?"

"They think that people from our world are inferior or undesirable. Illegal immigrants sneaking in."

"Like Mexicans swimming across the Rio Grande?"

"Something like that. The bottom line is we're done. It's too risky."

"But there's so much more to see. I'll miss Churcha and Scienca."

They pulled into the Costco parking lot and got out of the car.

"Screw the Knights!" Meredith said.

"They know how to find us. Let's not mess with them."

"Are they afraid we're going to tell the other Mexicans how to swim across the Rio Grande?"

"Worse. They're afraid that we're going to tell the other Mexicans that there *is* a Rio Grande."

Meredith didn't say another word the whole time at Costco or on the ride home. When they pulled into the driveway, she stormed into the house. A minute later, she came out again, got in her car, and drove off.

As Billy brought the Costco stuff into the kitchen, Carol asked, "What's with her? She blew right passed me."

"She got a text while we were at the store and wouldn't talk about it. Probably something from one of her friends. A post-adolescent emergency. It'll blow over."

The next day, Billy skipped out of the store at lunch and drove down to the city as fast as he could. But this time he wasn't going back into HD. He headed straight to Enright Avenue. He had to tell John that he now understood everything—interference patterns, snowflakes—and about meeting Martin. He parked, ran up onto the porch, rang the doorbell, then pounded on the front door. He didn't care about seeming impatient.

There was no answer. He peered through the lace curtain behind the glass door. He could see the worn-out living room furniture and the pile of electronics on the dining room table. He kept knocking. After a few minutes, the door to the next apartment opened. A haggard-looking woman smoking a cigarette looked out.

"What do you want?" she asked.

"Do you where John is? I have to talk with him. It's urgent."

"They took him to the hospital last night."

Billy felt like he had been punched in the gut.

"Which hospital?"

"The VA. Up the street."

Because he wasn't a relative, Billy had to use all of his wits and charm to get past skeptical gatekeepers and be allowed into John's room.

"He had a heart attack," the nurse said, "They're going to do an angioplasty and put in stents to open his coronary arteries. He's very weak. You can have five minutes."

John looked haggard and limp. His eyes were half-closed. An oxygen tube ran under his nose.

"John, it's Billy. You're going to make it. Doctors know how to treat this."

John nodded weakly.

"I know you were there. In the other world. I saw your picture."

John opened his eyes a little wider.

"I met a man who said he knew you. Martin Matsui."

John turned his head away. He didn't like hearing that name.

Billy held John's hand. "I'll come see you when you're better." John squeezed Billy's hand back. Billy asked, "How did you do it? How did you get over there?"

"Radio."

Meredith participated in the dinner conversation that night—to a point. Billy was relieved that she was home and acting more or less normal. A little distant, but not in a way that Carol would notice.

After dinner, Carol got a call from a parent about the upcoming camping trip and went into the living room to take it. Billy was loading the dishwasher. Meredith brought some plates into the kitchen and set them on the counter.

"How are you doing, kiddo?" Billy said.

She didn't answer and went back to the dining room to get more dinner dishes. When she returned, she said, "I don't know why you let those jerks scare you."

"You weren't there, honey."

"Dad, you found the most awesome, wild thing that anyone could ever find and now you want to turn your back on it. That's crazy."

"Trust me, I've looked at the pros and cons. I know what I'm doing."

"Man up, Dad."

She stormed out of the kitchen. A few minutes later, she yelled from the front door, "I'm going out with some friends. Be back late." The door shut.

The next day, Billy was at the Crestwood store until it closed at 9 p.m. When he got home, Meredith's car was in the driveway. Carol was packing for the camping trip and told him that Meredith's friends had picked her up earlier. Billy was exhausted and fell asleep watching the news.

He got up early on Saturday morning to give Carol a kiss as she left for the camping trip. He checked his phone over coffee. There was a text from Meredith:

> **Dad, I've learned from watching you. I'm going to give it a try. I understand the risks. But, nothing ventured, nothing gained. CARPE DIEM! Love, Meredith.**

The message was time-stamped at 10:15 the night before. Billy called her. No answer. He raced up the stairs to her room. She wasn't there. He looked outside. Her car was still in the driveway. He called again. Nothing.

"Fuck. Fuck. Fuck." He buried his head in his hands.

THREE CITIES

1958

CLAIRE MOORE HAD NEVER BEEN FIRED BEFORE. She had always been a high achiever, a star, the girl that others envied. She got scholarships, showed up early, stayed late, and produced brilliant work. She did it all with good cheer and relentless optimism. She was a friend to everyone, so even people who were envious when they compared themselves to her couldn't help but like her.

She had married Bennett Adamson, the golden boy to her golden girl, on a sunny afternoon under the towering columns of water that formed the Fountain Arch in Forest Park. Claire wore a wreath of flowers in her hair. Friends and family surrounded them, though many eyebrows were raised by their surprising union. Claire was a blond beauty from the Illinois farm country. Bennett was a dark-eyed Ojibway from the Northern Minnesota forests. They had met as students in a doctoral program in archaeology. Though they were living on a shoestring as they entered adult life, no one doubted that they were destined for great things.

But now, five years later, she sat next to Bennett in the office of the chairman of the Washington University Art and Archaeology department as he fired them both. It was a genteel, oblique, academic-style firing, with a smokescreen of words like "research priorities," "funding challenges," and "thinly supported hypotheses,"—but it was a firing all the same.

Claire drifted into a fog of shock and shame as the department chairman puffed his pipe and droned on. For once in her life, she couldn't think of anything to say. Then she heard Bennett speak up, cutting off the chairman in mid-sentence.

"Nine hundred years ago, Cahokia is one of the great cities of the ancient world. We're on the brink of a new paradigm in the understanding of the history of American Indians. After this year's excavations, we will have the evidence needed to publish. Washington University's name will be forever associated with this achievement. And you want to cut us off?"

"Faith in your so-called 'achievement' is much weaker than you think it is, young man. I've consulted eminent archaeologists, both at this university and elsewhere, who say your theory is preposterous. The idea that primitive Indians of the Midwest built a great city is hogwash!"

Bennett fought back. "Who said that? Let them criticize me to my face! Claire and I will gladly explain our hypotheses, methods and evidence."

His defiance roused Claire out of her shame. "We have maps, field notes, photographs. Everything is meticulously documented, which is rarely the case for hogwash."

Bennett was fired up. "At the benefactor's reception last month, Mr. Wright of Hydraulic was very impressed. He said our theory was revolutionary and should be expounded everywhere."

"Wright is a doddering, senile fool who would think a cheese sandwich was revolutionary. We invite him to these events only out of respect for his past accomplishments and the Hydraulic Endowment. After that reception, several major donors called me. They were outraged by your behavior. They said you cornered them and pestered them relentlessly about Cahokia.

"When donors come to an Art and Archaeology Department reception, they want to hear about Greece, Rome, and exotic places. Not about Indians piling up mud in a swamp across the river." The chairman paused for effect. "You will recall, Dr. Adamson, that we've had this conversation before. Last winter you commandeered the discussion at the annual medieval conference to insist that Cahokia must be recognized as a major city of that period, on a par with London or Paris."

"Actually, it surpassed them in some respects, such as hygiene," Bennett interjected.

"Be that as it may, several European scholars vowed never to attend another Washington University event."

Claire was incensed. She knew that Bennett could be abrasive when he was excited, but the chairman was going too far.

"Don't blame my husband for being passionate! We've spent years in the hot sun excavating Cahokia inch by inch, building the evidence that supports our theory. Our students are inspired to be part of this work."

The chairman put down his pipe. "I've heard all of this many times. Inspiring students is all well and good, but upsetting donors is quite another matter. My mind is made up, Mrs. Adamson."

"My name is Dr. Claire Moore."

"You'll have to use that name somewhere else. That is, if you still have a profession. Your termination is effective immediately. Good day to both of you."

Claire and Bennett staggered out of the chairman's office and silently walked back to their apartment in one of the new highrises on Lindell. They had rented the twelfth-floor apartment overlooking the park to celebrate their two Washington University jobs—a step on the long ladder to their expected success. The place was expensive. It was a large semicircular space with louvered floor-to-ceiling windows overlooking Forest Park utilizing the latest convection ventilation system, which pulled cool evening air into the apartments and up a central shaft to the roof. They had a Friday ritual of cocktails and carryout East African food with friends to enjoy the magnificent view. Now those happy evenings seemed like a million years ago.

Claire flopped on the sofa and began to cry, for the first time in years. Bennett stood at a window and stared at the traffic below.

"Those goddamned ignorant bastards," he muttered after a while. He turned to Claire. "What in hell are we going to do?"

She stopped crying, wiped her eyes, and looked at him with a determination he had only seen once before—the time she got a B on her Archaic Greek pottery paper when she felt she deserved an A ("When you're blonde and cute, they assume you're stupid."). "We'll find other jobs. Plenty of universities will want to support our research."

"That will take a while. How will we afford the rent on this place?"

"The CSP check will get us through the summer. I hear the dividend is going to be big this year. By fall, we'll be working again. Everything will be fine, like always."

Within a few days, Claire and Bennett had developed a list of targets, universities that might hire them and foundations that might fund their research. They scoured through directories at the library and assembled the names of people they had met at the annual Archaeology League conventions. Bennett began drafting letters of inquiry that Claire—as always—edited and improved. They spoke by telephone to several of their best contacts, who were encouraging about their prospects.

Meanwhile, Claire had to break the news of their firing and the cancellation of the summer dig at Cahokia to their students. They were upset and vowed to protest to the department chairman. But final exams were looming and the students had to scramble to make alternate summer plans. The protest fizzled out before it had even started.

Claire and Bennett's friends, faculty members themselves, insisted that the Friday evening cocktail party go on as usual. There was a lot of commiserating and grumbling about the dictatorial ways of the university administration. More bottles of wine than usual were consumed.

Claire's best friend, Molly, an English professor who studied mythology, took her aside.

"Job hunting is rough. You find out who the fair-weather friends are."

"We'll be fine. We have a lot of promising leads and Bennett is putting together some brilliant proposals."

"Claire, you've never had to do this before. People come up with all kinds of creative reasons for not hiring you. It took me three years to get this job—the longest three years of my life. You and Bennett don't have to go through this alone. If it ever gets to be too much for you, call me. Promise?"

"I will. But, really, I know it will all work out."

For the next several weeks, Claire and Bennett continued writing letters and making phone calls, systematically working through their list of targets and contacts. To prepare for interviews, Claire assembled a binder that summarized their research—hypotheses, photos, and preliminary findings—along with plans and budgets for future excavations. Everything was indexed, tabbed, and color-coded.

Claire checked the mailbox every day. At first, it was empty. Then letters from universities and foundations began to appear. She opened each one with excitement. But they all had more or less the same message:

Funding constraints prevent us from taking on new faculty at this time …

Our research focus does not align with your proposal.

We will keep your information on file and we wish you the best in your future endeavors.

The telephone calls were no better. People took a long time to return their calls, if they did at all. A few made vague offers of assistance with reaching higher-up decisionmakers "when the time is right." Follow-up calls were awkward, as even their best contacts tried to avoid them or dodge questions about the referrals they had (sort of) agreed to make on Claire and Bennett's behalf.

One day in early August, the truth became clear. They were on the phone with a professor from the University of

Nebraska who had admired their research and conference presentations about Cahokia.

"I probably shouldn't be telling you this, but Washington University has put out the word that you're troublemakers. They say that you reject any critical discussion of your work and that you argue with donors. No one is going to touch you with that story going around."

Claire and Bennett were shocked. They sat on the sofa and stared out the windows at the park below. "They can't stand it when an Indian is right about something," muttered Bennett. From an early age, he had turned away from the 'superstitions' of his tribe and fiercely embraced science and logic. He believed that rigorous research and meticulous data would overcome the furtive sneers at his Native background. Now, painful experienced had crushed that dream. Claire couldn't think of one hopeful thing to say. The afternoon slowly faded into evening. As the light drained away and tiny lights winked on in the distance, Claire and Bennett felt their futures dissolving into a black void. Eventually, they dozed off on the sofa.

The next day, Claire suggested they drive to Cahokia. "I need to see it."

They walked from Monk's Mound—the Great Pyramid—across the Grand Plaza. Half of the land had been developed as a suburban subdivision with no regard for the remains of ancient structures. A new train station to take commuters into St. Louis was under construction.

"How will we finish our research?" lamented Bennett. "We have no funding, no institutional backing."

"We've always found a way before," Claire said.

"That was before we became 'troublemakers.'"

They had identified four sites around the Grand Plaza as priorities for the now-canceled summer excavation and negotiated permission to dig from the landowners. They were low mounds, one conical and three oblong, all covered with grass and weeds. Claire and Bennett walked around the perimeter of one of the oblong mounds. Neighborhood children were playing on top. Bennett sank to his knees and pushed his hands into the soft grass.

"Secrets of the ages are just a few feet away. And we can't reach them."

Though he was usually the optimist and hard charger, Bennett started to cry. Claire knelt down next to him and hugged him.

"Don't worry, we'll get there. Somehow, we'll find the proof of our theory. We'll show them."

Back at the apartment, they clung to each other all night.

"You were right, Molly. This is the hardest thing I've ever done."

Claire and Molly were having pastries and coffee at the Metropole on a bright August morning. "We've done everything we could think of. We sent out a hundred letters and made a hundred phone calls. But the university is sabotaging us."

"Have you gotten any promising leads?"

"Not a one."

"What's the worst part?"

"I have no idea what's next. Do we have to give up on archaeology? Become high school teachers or insurance salesmen? I've always known where I was going and how to get there. Now there's nothing."

The waiter refilled Molly's coffee. She sipped and thought.

"I may have an idea that could help. Someone I ran across in my research for my next mythology book. There's a woman here in town who has amazing gifts."

"What do you mean 'gifts'?"

"She can look right into people and see things about them—like where they're going."

"A fortune teller? That's absurd. I'm a scientist!"

"I didn't believe it at first either. But now I do. She's an Indian. That might mean something to you. Call it anthropological field work."

"This is so ridiculous, I don't know where to start. Bennett would laugh me out of the room. He doesn't want anything to do with spiritual mumbo-jumbo."

"Don't tell him. What have you got to lose?"

Claire was stumped. She didn't have anything to lose.

"I don't get much chance to talk to live Indians. It's all been bones and pottery."

"Exactly. Field work."

The next day, Claire and Molly rode the streetcar toward downtown. It was one of the new ones, completely silent except for a mild whoosh when it stopped or started.

"What's the fortune teller's name?" asked Claire.

"Deirdre. She doesn't like being called a fortune teller."

"What then?"

"A 'speaker.' She communicates with spirits."

"What have you told her about me?"

"Nothing. I just said I had a friend who wanted to meet her."

"What should I say?"

"Don't tell her about archaeology or Cahokia or being out of a job. See what she comes up with on her own."

When they reached downtown, they transferred to a southbound Broadway streetcar. They passed the construction site where the Riverfront subway was being built. Molly sensed that Claire was nervous and tried to engage in small talk.

"Sorry about the long ride. It would be a lot faster if the subway were finished."

"I feel like a fool," Claire said. Molly patted her on the knee.

The streetcar continued south for about five miles, passing breweries, office buildings, and hundreds of homes and apartment buildings under rapid construction—all part of the city's scramble to keep up with the horde of newcomers who arrived every year. From the streetcar window, Claire watched huge yellow cranes lifting pre-built apartments to be stacked and attached to central columns that contained elevators, utilities, and ventilation ducts.

Molly and Claire got off at the corner of Osceola and Broadway and started walking toward the river. They passed rows of nearly identical bungalows built of deep red St. Louis brick, then turned onto Ohio Avenue where Claire saw a small, plain house perched next to a large oak tree on top of the only hill in this otherwise flat neighborhood.

Claire did a bit of a double take. The shape of the hill eerily reminded her of some of the mounds at Cahokia. Could it be? But she decided not to say anything. She and Molly ascended stairs to the front door and Molly knocked.

A young woman opened the door. She had long black hair and wore an unremarkable, but fashionable, dress. She was about the same age as Claire, not the wizened old hag that Claire had expected.

"Hello, Deirdre," Molly said. "This is the friend I told you about, Claire."

Deirdre welcomed them into the house and offered them tea in the front room. Molly and Deirdre exchanged a few pleasantries. Claire began to relax. Maybe this wouldn't be so weird after all.

Deirdre turned to Claire. "Come with me into the back, so we can talk more comfortably."

"I'll wait here," said Molly, nodding to Claire that she should go.

The curtains were drawn in the back room. A few candles were burning. Deirdre gestured for Claire to sit down, then she sat in a facing chair. She clasped Claire's hands in hers and looked into Claire's eyes. Her gentle, welcoming smile put Claire at ease.

"Why did you come to see me?"

"Because I don't know what to do next. I can't see my future. Can you help me?"

"I can look into parts of your dream that you may not see yet. The Pale One teaches that what occurs around us reflects our own mind and shows us the dream we are weaving."

"Who is the Pale One?"

"A teacher who came to the people of North America thousands of years ago, long before the current age of darkness. He brought great wisdom."

"Are we in an age of darkness?"

"Look around. Decide for yourself. But this age is coming to an end."

Deirdre picked up a small bundle of dried plants. She held it over a candle until it began to smoke. Claire smelled sage. Deirdre waved the smoking bundle toward each corner of the room.

"Let's begin. Breathe calmly and clear your mind."

Deirdre raised her arms above her head in an invocation.

"Wise protectors they are giving. Serenity it resounds. Mother Earth and Father Sky are giving. I am thankful. It is well."

She closed her eyes and began to chant in an Indian language. Claire tried to clear her mind, as Deirdre had said. It was harder than she expected. She kept trying. She smelled the fragrant smoke and watched it swirl up and around Deirdre. As Deirdre chanted, Claire noted that her face and her dark hair seemed to glow softly. The chanting continued. Afterward, Claire couldn't say if it had gone on for two minutes or for twenty minutes.

Deirdre was silent. She opened her eyes and, once again, took Claire's hands in hers. She spoke, but her voice had a different timbre than before.

"You will unearth three cities from the same ground. The first by your hands. The second by your voice. The third by your silence."

Claire struggled to make sense of what she had heard.

"How can I unearth a city by silence?"

"The third city is hidden from view."

"Is it real?"

"Very real, but it can't be seen from here. Silence means that you must never speak of the third city."

Claire nodded, though she still didn't know what to make of this prediction. Deirdre continued. "And, when you become an elder, many children will gather around you and call you 'mother.' That is a great blessing from the Pale One."

"Is this my fortune? Will it come true?"

"I'm telling you the prophecy. Prophecy is always true. But how it manifests depends on you."

Molly stood up when Claire and Deirdre returned to the living room. Claire was beaming.

"Thank you so much. I feel like a cloud has lifted."

"I'm thankful to have met you. May your path continue to be blessed."

"What tribe are you from?"

"Your people call us the Osage. We call ourselves *Wazhazhe*."

As soon as they left the house, Molly turned to Claire. "Well?"

Claire didn't respond. She sat on a low stone wall, deep in thought. After a few minutes, she said, "Now I know what to do. Forget about universities. We can raise Cahokia into the light. I have to tell Bennett."

CORN MOTHER AND MORNING STAR

2010

BILLY DID HIS BEST to blend into the Saturday morning crowd of shoppers and tourists. He felt a bit silly wearing sunglasses and a hat pulled low over his eyes, but it didn't seem smart to walk past the Hydraulic Building without some attempt at disguise. And the sisters' taffy shop was right around the corner.

"Mr. Boustany!" shouted Churcha with delight as he came through the front door. "We just made a fresh batch of your favorites." She held up a platter of green taffy with pink stripes, each piece wrapped in wax paper.

"Have you seen Meredith?"

"She came a half hour ago with a nice Cahokian fellow," said Scienca, with a sly wink. "Very handsome."

"She wanted him to taste our taffy."

"He liked it very much."

"And was extremely polite."

"As those Cahokians are, you know."

"Do you know where they went?"

"They didn't say," Churcha said.

"Dear, you weren't paying attention. He said 'let's take a look at the river.' So I imagine they are out on the Eads."

"The perfect place for young people on a Saturday morning. Very romantic."

Billy's mind reeled. She had pulled it off. What if the Knights or one of their "spotters" saw her?

He ran north to Washington Avenue, weaving through the crowd and dodging a gaggle of banjo players who took up most of the sidewalk. He turned east on Washington and kept running toward the Mississippi. Another question hit him between the eyes—who was this "nice Cahokian fellow"?

He stopped where Washington Avenue sloped up to become the top deck of the Eads Bridge. Billy had seen this bridge countless times as the backdrop to the Fourth of July celebrations under the Arch—the ones put on by his version of the Knights of the Carnelian.

Built in 1871, it was the first bridge over the Mississippi and a St. Louis landmark. But, like most people in his St. Louis, Billy had never set foot on it. Light rail trains used the lower deck and the top deck was a third-rate automobile route to East St. Louis, which Billy thought of as a dilapidated, dangerous place where no one wanted to go.

Here, Billy was just one of hundreds of people strolling on a different Eads Bridge. Trains still crossed on the lower deck, but the top deck was a linear park with trees in raised beds, wrought iron benches, and mini cafes serving crepes, coffee, soup, and popcorn.

Billy looked south and had his first clear view of the riverfront where the Arch should have been. It was densely packed with buildings. Many were older brick ones of three and four stories. Taller glass and steel structures popped up here and there. Almost all of them had rooftop spaces with tables and canopies. These were the settings for the Leveetown nightlife he had heard about. "Too touristy," some of his informants on South Grand had said, as they disparaged the riverfront hoopla as unworthy of their patronage.

A tree-lined promenade ran along the riverbank and a floating pier curved out into the river. Boats were parked along it at an angle, so more could fit in. Some were in the style of nineteenth-century steamboats, others had large open decks with the tables and umbrellas he saw everywhere in this town.

He looked over to the Illinois side. Instead of the empty plain and grain elevators he was used to seeing, there was a line of white and pale blue high-rise buildings, gleaming in the early afternoon sun. He saw the three buildings topped with the giant park platform, thirty stories up. More boats were parked on that bank and Billy saw still more entering and leaving the river through a cut in the riverbank framed by an arched bridge.

Billy was briefly hypnotized by the beauty of the scene, but this wasn't the time. He had to find Meredith. He walked out toward the center span of the bridge, looking right and left. Families with children were lined up at an ice cream stand. A group of Russian tourists was staring at the city while their guide, holding a white, blue, and red flag, prattled on in a practiced spiel. A similar group of Italian tourists gathered around their own guide, who was giving the same spiel in Italian. Young couples strolled dreamily, holding hands. No Meredith.

As he got to the center of the bridge, he saw a roped-off section marked with a fluttering banner, "A.B. Lambert

Aero Club—Kite Flying Today." Inside the ropes, parents and children launched kites into the cloudless sky above the bridge—boxes, diamonds, dragons, and compound forms. An instructor dashed back and forth, showing proper technique and untangling strings.

Billy saw Meredith's light brown ponytail on the other side of the bridge. She was leaning on the rail, looking out over the river next to a tall, slender man who was pointing out something to her.

"Meredith!" Billy shouted.

She turned to him with blank amazement.

"Dad?"

The man with her turned around. He was wearing a conservative outfit, a solid color shirt and pants. His black hair fell below his shoulders and his face was covered with geometric tattoos.

"How did you find me?" she asked.

"The taffy ladies."

"Dad, this is Diyami."

"It's a pleasure to meet you, sir," said the young man as he shook hands with Billy. "Meredith speaks very highly of you."

"Thanks." Billy turned to Meredith, "I thought we had an understanding that we weren't doing this again."

"Excuse us a minute, Diyami. I need to calm my dad down."

She took Billy's arm and led him to a slightly more private spot along the railing. "You're embarrassing me."

"Embarrassing you? Oh, God, Meredith, it's not safe. What have you told Di— what's his name?"

"Diyami. Everything is okay. I told him the California story."

"How did you get over here?"

"Last night, I had my friends drop me off at Grand and Gravois and then I just tried doing what you do, and it worked!"

She looked at him with a big smile on her face.

"Remember, we saw the poster about the Milo concert? After hearing you talk about him, I had to go. He was as amazing as you said."

"Is that where you met him?" Billy nodded toward Diyami, who was looking out over the river. "He doesn't look like the right kind of guy for you." Billy gestured to his face, suggesting the tattoos.

"Daddy! We're in a fucking parallel universe. Let it go!"

Billy shut up.

They walked back to where Diyami was gazing at the river. Meredith was cheerful again.

"Diyami was telling me about Cahokia. He said we could go there this afternoon."

Billy remembered Cahokia as a sleepy state park a few miles east of the Mississippi. With grass-covered mounds built by native Americans hundreds of years ago, it was primarily a destination for school field trips.

"We can see the mounds, of course, and the whole city, Sir," Diyami said. "Come with us."

"Diyami grew up there."

Something behind Diyami's shoulder caught Billy's eyes. The kite-flying instructor was staring straight at him.

"Yeah. What are we waiting for?"

They started walking toward the east end of the bridge. A horde of children rushed toward them, laughing and screaming. Billy, Meredith, and Diyami, hugged the railing to let them pass. The adults accompanying them smiled and nodded silent apologies for their exuberant charges.

Billy whispered to Meredith. "There's a guy looking at us. I don't like it."

She bit her lip, like she did when she was scared as a kid. Billy asked Diyami if they were going to drive to Cahokia.

"No. Speedboat."

At the eastern end of the bridge, they took an elevator down to a large floating dock. Twenty or thirty people were standing around, mostly Native Americans. Many of the younger ones had tattoos and long hair like Diyami's. The men's tattoos were angular designs, dark blue and black. The women's tattoos were more delicate patterns in yellow and red.

Diyami went to a ticket booth and returned with the tickets.

"The boat will be here in three minutes."

Billy scanned the crowd, but didn't see the kite-flying instructor. He made conversation to keep calm.

"How long have they had speedboats to Cahokia?"

"They started running right after the canal was finished," Diyami said, "in 2004. Part of the World's Fair."

"And you live in Cahokia?"

"I grew up in Cahokia, but now I live right over there to be closer to my job."

He pointed to a high rise on the Illinois bank, one of the three towers with the platform on top.

"He's on the twenty-third floor, Daddy," Meredith said. "The view is unbelievable!"

"Look." Diyami pointed upriver. A white boat was headed toward them. A large plume of water behind it sparkled in the sun. It was a hydrofoil, speeding along with the hull completely out of the water. It shot under the bridge, then made a wide U-turn. The hull sank down into the water as it slowed. The boat was about eighty feet long and narrow. It had a large raised prow with a carved eagle head that reminded Billy of a Viking ship. Curved windows along the side revealed rows of bench seats. A raised deck at the stern had a small pilot's house.

As the boat pulled up to the dock, Billy noticed the name painted on the side, *Corn Mother.* Below the name was a logo of a pyramid and the letters *ABSOM.*

After the passengers disembarked, Billy, Meredith, and Diyami were first in line to board. They went to the front row. "Best view for first-timers," Diyami said, with a wide smile.

The boat quickly filled with passengers, then pulled out into the river. Billy looked up at the bridge. He thought he glimpsed the kite-flying instructor looking down at them.

The boat turned upstream and accelerated with the engine roaring. It lifted out of the water and the ride became smooth as the boat glided north. The windows shielded them from the wind. Billy looked over at downtown St. Louis. He was struck by how unfamiliar it was. He spotted the Hydraulic Building, the tallest of the skyscrapers, and even saw the tiny glass cupola at the top where Martin had explained everything to him. Then he noticed the old power plant on the river, with its arched windows and smokestacks. It was the only building he recognized. He had been there on his bicycle just a few weeks earlier on a ride up the Riverfront Trail. That seemed like a thousand years ago. The boat began a graceful turn to the east to enter a canal and leave the Mississippi behind.

From talking with thousands of customers over the years, Billy had cultivated a knack for quickly and gently finding out the pertinent facts about someone. On the way to Cahokia, Billy used his skill to learn about Diyami. He had grown up in Cahokia. His parents were professors at the university. "Washington University? SIU?"

"No. Five Hundred N-U," Diyami said. Billy didn't understand. "Five Hundred Nations University," Diyami clarified. Billy nodded, pretending to know what that was. Diyami went on to explain that he had graduated from that university with a degree in civil engineering and had moved to the apartment overlooking the Mississippi to be closer to his new job in downtown St. Louis.

"What kind of work do you do?"

"Dams, canals, irrigation. Many projects like that are in the long-term plan for Cahokia, and I want experience so I can be part of them."

Meredith pointed to another hydrofoil coming toward them. As it sped by, Billy saw that it was identical to theirs, but with a different name on the bow, *Morning Star*. A few of the passengers waved.

They slowed down and entered a lock on the canal. The gates closed behind them and water poured into the lock from pipes on either side.

"I love stuff like this!" Diyami said, shouting over the din of the rushing water. The water level rose about twenty feet in just a few minutes. The upper gates opened, and the boat accelerated out of the lock.

As the hydrofoil rose up, Billy could see cornfields and pastures on both sides of the canal. Large numbers of deer grazed in the pastures, which were studded with trees. Herons flew up from their perches in trees along the canal as the hydrofoil approached, circled once, then landed back on the same branches after it passed—just as they did several times a day.

After a few minutes, houses began to appear. They were modern, with so much glass that Billy could see right through them. Many had painted crests along their rooflines that reminded him of the tattoos on the people in the boat—stylized birds, corn stalks, and abstract designs. Larger structures were up ahead in the distance.

The hydrofoil slowed, settled down into the water, and pulled up to a dock. A swooping, curved roof on tall, slender columns provided shade. A sign read: "Welcome to Cahokia, the Capital of Native America."

As the passengers lined up to disembark, other boats with freight were being unloaded. Workers, young men with tattooed faces, operated cranes to lift pallets of boxes onto carts. Other young men drove the carts away with silent, electric-powered trucks.

"We can walk from here," Diyami said as Billy and Meredith stepped onto the dock. He led them across a paved plaza, bordered on three sides by white buildings. Covered arcades along the front of each building revealed small shops inside. Signs advertised "White Buffalo Fashions," "Caddo Spice Emporium," and "Oneonta Fine Photography."

"Can we look at some of these shops?" Meredith asked.

"These are for tourists," Diyami said, dismissively. "I can show you much better ones later. Are you hungry? There's a great lunch place nearby."

Billy and Meredith agreed that lunch was a fine idea. They walked out of the plaza, then along a tree-lined street. The buildings were all one-story with blank, windowless walls. Occasional doors were framed with stylized animal designs. The street was completely flat, with no separation between street and sidewalk. There were no cars. People were walking or using the same little scooters that were everywhere in St. Louis. A tram, like an oversized golf cart with several rows of seats, pulled up in front of one door to drop off a passenger.

Billy, Meredith, and Diyami rounded a corner and entered a small tree-lined square. They took a table at an outdoor café.

"The grilled venison sandwiches are amazing. Also, the spiced lemon tea," Diyami said. Billy saw a taller building across the square. The roofline was a series of wooden arches. The walls were glass.

"What's that?" Billy asked.

"My elementary school," Diyami said.

"Do only Indians live here?" Meredith said.

"Everyone is welcome, but it's mostly native people."

"Looks like a nice little town," Billy said.

"You haven't really seen it yet. Just wait."

A waitress brought their lunches. She was tall and slender, like Diyami. The tattoos on her face were of lacy flowers, almost imperceptible.

"Hi, Diyami," she said.

"Hi, Willow. These are my friends, Meredith and Billy. Their first time in Cahokia."

"Nice to meet you. Maybe I'll see you later, Diyami?"

"Yeah, maybe."

Meredith didn't like the way Willow and Diyami looked at each other.

The lunch was excellent.

"Close your eyes," Diyami said as they came to the end of a block. Billy and Meredith complied. He took their hands and led them around the corner of a building.

"Now, open…the Grand Plaza of Cahokia."

They saw a vast space. Billy later estimated it to be about the size of twenty-five football fields. Small clumps of people stood here and there. Some were tourist groups whose guides waved flags to keep them together. Out in the center of the plaza, children were running back and forth, playing some kind of game.

To their left, at the north end of the plaza, stood a stepped pyramid, ten stories tall. It was the same mound of grass-covered earth he had seen many times before, driving by on the interstate highway to Chicago. But here, it was groomed and restored. The edges were sharply defined and a structure with a steep roof stood on the top level.

"That's the ancient Cahokian pyramid," Diyami said. "We call it the Temple of the Ancestors."

To the right of the pyramid, across the open space from where they stood, was a row of white multistory buildings. They had balconies and terraces at every level.

"That's the university. My parents live in the second building from the left."

The largest structure stood at the south end of the plaza. Its shape mimicked the ancient pyramid, but it was about four times the size. And it was made of glass. Smaller structures were visible inside it.

"That's the new pyramid, the Temple of the Children. It has the museum, visitors' center, city government, things like that."

"Why do you call it the Temple of the Children?" Meredith asked.

"Because the new Cahokia is for us, the children, and for the generations of children still to come."

Billy and Meredith took it all in. Billy had a huge grin. Even after the many surprises of HD St. Louis, he was stunned.

"There's an observation deck at the top of the Temple of the Children. It's a great place to see everything."

The elevator rose swiftly. Billy, Meredith, and Diyami stood on the open platform with several other people. The elevator cables and mechanism were in a column at the back of the platform. Diyami pointed out the engineering details with great enthusiasm.

"This is the largest cantilevered elevator in the Midwest. It can hold up to forty people." He pointed to the glass skin of the pyramid. "Those louvers open and close automatically based on temperature and wind direction. The idea is to create an updraft in the summer to vent heat out the top and to trap solar heat in the winter."

"Awesome!" Meredith said.

Billy noted the sparks between her and Diyami.

The roof opened up as the elevator approached the top. It stopped and the railings lowered into the floor. Diyami guided Billy and Meredith toward the edge of the roof overlooking the plaza. All of Cahokia lay spread out below. It was surrounded by a series of lakes connected by concentric canals. The Grand Plaza was at the center. Wide, straight avenues led out from the Plaza north, south, east, and west, with bridges crossing the canals. Billy could see both the dock where they had gotten off the hydrofoil and downtown St. Louis six miles to the west. A white wake trailed a hydrofoil speeding toward St. Louis.

Diyami pointed to where an additional ring of canals was under construction. "Those will provide water access to the new neighborhoods that will be going up."

The tallest buildings were closest to the Plaza and shorter structures were further out. As Diyami explained, most residential neighborhoods were on the west and north sides, the university was on the east, and the business and industrial districts were to the south. Looking south, Billy saw a large Kahok Beer sign on the roof of what he assumed was a brewery.

Pocket parks in spaces between buildings near the plaza preserved many of the smaller mounds that remained from ancient times. The Plaza itself was surfaced in packed dirt, like a baseball infield. From this observation deck, various designs etched in the dirt could be seen. There was a huge spiral in front of the old pyramid, a sun on the west, a warrior in the center, and a frog closest to the new pyramid. Diyami explained that these designs were only visible from above. Groundskeepers touched them up with rakes each morning and drew new ones every few months.

Teenagers were playing a game in one corner of the Grand Plaza. They were using sticks about six feet long to push a rolling rubber disk. It looked like some bizarre version of hockey.

Billy pointed, "What's that?"

"Chunkey. It's an ancient game that was popular at the time of the old Cahokia. People have revived it and now almost every tribe has teams. I played in high school and still mess around with a group of guys on Sundays. We're not that good, but we have fun."

They rode the elevator back down to ground level. Diyami pointed out the large museum.

"It's got a lot of great exhibits, from ancient times to the architecture of the new city and the plans for the future." A long line of people were standing in line to enter. "We'd have to wait an hour to get in. Maybe next time."

A group of dancers in feathered costumes were performing in front of the museum. Drums and song echoed throughout the pyramid, making it hard to talk. Billy noticed a raised platform near the entrance. A beat-up, old green station wagon sat on top behind a railing. People were gathered around taking pictures of themselves in front of it. He wanted to ask Diyami what it was, but the drumming was too loud.

Diyami excused himself to make a phone call. Over the din of the drumming, he mouthed, "I'll be back in a minute."

Billy leaned close to Meredith so she could hear him: "Do you remember when we came to Cahokia? You were in seventh grade. It was the spring equinox. Your class came to watch the sun rise over the mound. We were over there."

He pointed through the glass toward an area to the left of the old pyramid. There was a colonnade of logs stuck vertically in the ground. "We had to be here at 5:30 in the morning. It was cold as hell."

"I remember a little bit."

Diyami returned. "You're invited to have dinner with my parents and me at their apartment. Can you stay this evening?" He looked at Meredith, hoping for a positive response.

"We would love to," Billy said.

"Don't you have plans later?" Meredith asked.

"Canceled."

Diyami opened the apartment door.

"Dad, Mom, we're here."

He, Meredith, and Billy stepped into a living room with white walls and a gray carpet. An image of a falcon was outlined in the center of the carpet. One wall was lined with bookshelves, the other held a collection of artworks, mostly tapestries and ceramics. The opposite side of the room was floor-to-ceiling glass, with a patio beyond. A fireplace with a stone chimney was in the center of the glass wall.

A man and woman emerged from the kitchen.

"Welcome!" said the man. He looked a little older than Billy, with glasses and long black hair, with accents of gray, pulled into a ponytail. He had a small tattoo under his left eye.

"This is my father, Sahale Red Hawk," Diyami said. "And my mother, Menara Red Hawk." She was about the same age as Sahale, also with long hair going from black to gray. Diyami introduced Billy and Meredith as visitors from California.

"My Indian name is Sahale, but, actually, I've been Herbert most of my life. The young people want nothing to do with English names, but I'm from a different generation. So please call me Herbert."

"And I'm Juliet," Diyami's mom said.

Diyami rolled his eyes with a universal "my parents are so embarrassing" look that Billy was all too familiar with.

"Dinner won't be ready for a while, so please relax. Diyami, could you and Meredith help me in the kitchen? I need some tasters and stirrers," Juliet said.

"Sure," Diyami said, pleased to have Meredith included.

"Billy, I'll show you the patio," Herbert said. "Would you like a beer? I have Kahok Lager and Pale Ale."

"I've had the Lager, so I'll try the Pale Ale."

Billy and Herbert stepped through a sliding glass door onto the patio. The Grand Plaza lay before them, with the new pyramid to the left and the old pyramid to the right. Billy looked over the patio railing to see the apartments below. Each floor was stepped back from the one below. The view was spectacular.

"We're very fortunate." He turned to Billy with a sly smile. "University housing."

"What do you do at the university?"

"I'm chairman of the Linguistics Department. Juliet is a professor of microbiology. What about you, Billy?"

"I'm in the electronics business, in California. Computers."

Herbert looked confused.

"Difference engines," Billy said.

"Of course. I may be a linguist, but I'm easily baffled by technical language. Do you like the Pale Ale?"

"I do."

"Kahok Beer is one of our economic success stories. It's in ten states now and still growing. The fellow who started it is a friend of mine. A Potawatomi from Wisconsin. He thinks it's hilarious for an Indian to be selling alcohol to the whites."

Billy chuckled.

Their small talk continued. Herbert pointed out various landmarks and Billy used his fact-finding skills to learn about Cahokia. Most Cahokians worked in St. Louis, but they were developing more local businesses, banking and insurance, in addition to the brewery. The university planned to add a medical school, which Herbert hoped would happen soon enough so Juliet could be part of the faculty before she retired.

The best time to visit was in October for the Three Worlds Festival, when the Grand Plaza was filled with thousands of costumed musicians and drummers representing the five hundred nations of native America and the pyramids were bathed in elaborate light shows each evening.

Billy sipped his beer, leaned on the railing and thought, *I like this guy.*

After a little while, Juliet, Meredith, and Diyami joined them on the patio, with additional beers and a tray of snacks. It was Meredith's turn to be amazed by the view, and Diyami pointed out of landmarks.

"I told Billy about the Three Worlds Festival," Herbert said. "They should come back here for it."

"You definitely should," Juliet said. "We have an excellent view from this terrace."

They sat in a half-circle of chairs facing the outdoor side of the fireplace. Though it was summer, Herbert started a small fire.

"We must have a warm hearth to welcome our guests."

Billy raised his bottle in a toast, "To Diyami, Herbert, and Juliet, our favorite Cahokians."

"Coming here on the boat, I noticed that the two hydrofoils were called *Corn Mother* and *Morning Star*," Billy said. "And they both had *ABSOM* written above the names. What does that mean?"

Herbert chuckled, then replied with mock seriousness, "Mr. Boustany, you have just asked a very big question. One that requires a long story. Do you really want to hear it?"

"We do, for sure!" Meredith said. She stole a glance at Diyami, who smiled back at her.

Herbert opened another beer. "Let's start with ABSOM, which stands for "As Before, So Once More." It has become the motto of Cahokia. Nine hundred years ago, Cahokia was a great city, the largest in North America north of Mexico, and also larger than London and Paris. The center of a culture that influenced what is now the entire Midwest and South. So that history is the "As Before." "So Once More" is the city you see today, which is again the greatest Native American city in the

United States. Forty years ago, when native peoples started to move back to this area, their goal was to build both a modern city and a center of native culture. Those early pioneers came up with ABSOM, and it stuck."

"And that's when Corn Mother and Morning Star came in," Juliet said.

Diyami leaned over to Meredith, "You'll love this."

Herbert and Juliet took turns telling the story, one that everyone in Cahokia knew.

It was an Indian man and a white woman who first taught about the wonders of Cahokia. We revere them because they lit a tiny match, which native peoples later grew into a life-giving fire. Their names were Bennett Adamson and Claire Moore, though, today, every Indian within a thousand miles calls them Morning Star and Corn Mother, because we believe they were messengers of the two gods with those names. Morning Star and Corn Mother were important figures in the mythology of the ancient Cahokians. In the early 1950s, Adamson—Morning Star—and Moore—Corn Mother—were archaeologists in the Art and Archaeology Department at Washington University in St. Louis.

From their research and excavations here at Cahokia, they discovered that they were standing on the bones of a great civilization. But no one else could see it. They tried to explain the story to academics and to leaders in St. Louis. Morning Star said, 'You have a treasure that must not be ignored. It's Babylon, Carthage, Pergamon right here at your doorstep. But, forgotten in the mud beneath the cornfields and houses.' (Yes, a subdivision of little houses had been built right out there on the Grand Plaza.) They had pictures, maps, everything. But they were seen as kooks and cranks. People in St. Louis laughed at them behind their backs and said: "There can be no Indian city here. The French, starting with Marquette, had met only scattered bands living in tiny villages, traveling by canoe, trapping beavers. They were simple people who knew little. Not members of a great civilization."

Washington University grew tired of Adamson and Moore and their obsession, so they were fired. They could not find another university to support their research. But the spirits were not finished with them. They moved to a little house in Collinsville, just a mile from here, inside the territory of ancient Cahokia. It is said that the Earth spirit of Cahokia talked to them at night. They continued to dig, map and photograph. They searched the libraries, looking for more pieces of this story that was hidden in plain sight among the farms, the small towns, the five-and-dime stores. The whites of Collinsville were completely ignorant of the soil they plowed and lived on. They were sleepwalkers, aliens. It was not their story. The spirits did not speak to such people.

The seasons of sun, rain, and snow, of row crops and blacktop, of aluminum siding and roof shingles, of short-haired boys and curly-headed girls laughing on concrete playgrounds, all continued. Cahokia sank further into the silence of the earth.

But Corn Mother and Morning Star were two seeds that the barren earth could not destroy. In those days, no native people lived here. Not a one.

Only the whites and the black white people, who were equally ignorant of the soil under their feet.

Corn Mother and Morning Star were in despair. No one to talk to. No one to sponsor their digging and studies. Morning Star had one job after another in Collinsville, but he had no interest in business affairs and lost them all. Eventually, he was reduced to working at a gas station. Corn Mother was a secretary at a farm implements dealer.

One day, a car pulled into the gas station. Morning Star went out to pump their gas, as was the custom in those times. He saw that they were a family of Indians. The children ran inside to get candy and sodas, the mother went to buy sandwiches from the diner next door for their lunch. Morning Star talked to the father as gas flowed into the tank.

"Where are you from?" Morning Star asked.

"Oklahoma. We were up in Ohio for a tribal event. One of my cousins got married."

"What tribe?"

"Osage."

"Like us!" interjected Diyami with a grin like he was eight years old again.

"I understand that the Osage used to live around here in Missouri and Illinois."

"Yes. But they were scattered and driven away a long time ago."

"Do you know that there was once a huge Indian city right near here?"

"What are you talking about? An Indian city?" The man shook his head.

"No, really. We don't know when, exactly, but it was about a thousand years ago."

"Yeah, right." said the man, "C'mon, kids. Get in the car. We've got to make time if we want to get home tonight."

"I'm not kidding. They built a big pyramid. Just about a mile from here. I can show it to you."

"An Indian city? With a pyramid? Here? You've smoked one peace pipe too many, my friend."

Morning Star moved a little closer and looked the man in the eye. "I know what I'm talking about. Let me show you. Twenty minutes, then you can be on your way."

The man, whose name was Robert Weatherford, looked closely at Morning Star and said nothing. He had a sense. A whisper from the spirits, or so he said, years later. "Kids, we're going to see an Indian pyramid."

The children and wife were puzzled as they got into the car. Morning Star said, "Follow me." He got into his car, a green 1950s station wagon with wooden sides.

"You saw it in the museum!" Diyami said, bubbling with enthusiasm.

They drove about a mile. Morning Star pulled over to the side of the road and got out of his car. Weatherford pulled up behind him.

"Where's the pyramid?" he asked.

"Right there," said Morning Star, and he pointed to a grassy hill to the right of a subdivision of new houses.

"That's just a hill, man," Weatherford said.

"No, it's an earthen pyramid with four straight sides and two levels and a flat top. Some people call it a mound, but it is *not* a hill."

"Don't pyramids have pointy tops?" one of the kids asked.

"The ones in Egypt do. The Indians built them differently, flat on top for a temple or for the king's house. This one is similar in shape to many in Mexico."

Weatherford, his wife and kids looked at the pyramid, then back at Morning Star.

"You know about that, right?" Morning Star said. "Mexico. The Aztecs. The Mayans. The people here were inspired by the cultures in Mexico to build a great city. You're standing in that city."

"Why are those houses there if this is an ancient city?"

"No one around here gives a damn."

"That's the story of the Indians," Weatherford said. He, his wife, and Morning Star looked at the pyramid in silence for a minute or two. The kids played in the grass, chasing butterflies. Weatherford closed his eyes. He turned to face the north, then to the three other directions.

"Our people don't know anything about this," he said. "What do you call this place?"

"Cahokia."

"Would you like to come to Oklahoma and give a talk about this? We have a tribal meeting four times a year. They might like to hear it."

"Sure," Morning Star said. They exchanged phone numbers and shook hands. The family drove off toward Oklahoma. And that's how it began.

A few months later, Morning Star and Corn Mother drove their green station wagon to Oklahoma. They had put together a slide show about Cahokia and written a small booklet to hand out, just mimeographed sheets stapled together. They spoke at Weatherford's Osage tribal meeting. Eight people showed up. Morning Star and Corn Mother each did their part of the presentation, one running the slide projector while the other spoke, as they had practiced in the tiny living room of their Collinsville bungalow. Everyone listened politely, but only a couple asked questions. Corn Mother and Morning Star were disappointed at the lack of response.

They spent the night at Weatherford's home. The next morning, as they were packing their suitcases, he asked them: "Could you stay another day? Some people who didn't come last night would like to hear you."

The second night, there were twenty people. Weatherford asked them to stay over once more. The third night, there were almost fifty and many asked questions. The booklets ran out. At the end of the third evening, one man asked, "How many Indians live at Cahokia now?"

"Only me," Morning Star answered.

A murmur of disbelief rippled through the group.

"Maybe you should be the first," Corn Mother said.

Word got around. Over the next few months, Corn Mother and Morning Star made several trips to Oklahoma. They spoke to the Cherokee, the Pawnee, the Miami, the Creek, and more. Corn Mother ended each talk the same way, "There's room for you at Cahokia —you can make it a great Indian city once more."

Then, one day, back in Collinsville, just as they were sitting down to dinner, Morning Star and Corn Mother heard a knock at their door. They opened it and there stood Robert Weatherford with his wife and kids.

"We're ready," Robert said. "Do you know of any homes for rent near here?"

Others followed over the next few years. Mostly young people, just out of high school who didn't see any future on a reservation and who wanted to be part of something. Others were families, like the Weatherfords. Morning Star and Corn Mother kept traveling and talking —to the Ho-Chunk and Chippewa in Wisconsin, the Ojibway in Minnesota, even to the Sioux in South Dakota. They put thousands of miles on their worn-out green station wagon.

And the new city of Cahokia began to emerge. By 1975, Native Americans became the majority population in the town of Collinsville and the surrounding countryside. They petitioned the state of Illinois to annex the entire ancient site of Cahokia. After that, the first large construction projects began.

Sadly, Morning Star did not live to see those projects come to fruition. He passed away in 1978. Corn Mother lived until 1994. She spoke at the first university graduation ceremony just three weeks before she died.

"I met her when I was little." Diyami said proudly. "She had the softest hands and the brightest eyes."

"How did you decide to come here?" Billy asked Herbert.

"Robert Weatherford was my father's first cousin. 500NU had just been founded when I got my Ph.D. from Michigan and Juliet was finishing hers at Yale. Robert worked hard to convince us that Cahokia needed the best and brightest of our people. He was very persuasive."

Juliet and Diyami brought out plates of food and set them on the table next to the fireplace.

"Before we eat the main meal, we must make an offering to the Great Mystery," Juliet said. She took a bundle of dried plants, held it in the fire to light it, and placed it in a bowl. She picked up small pieces of food from each platter and threw them into the fire.

"Juliet is a speaker as well as a microbiologist," Herbert told Billy. "She has the power of communicating with the spirits of this place."

"Let us gather," Juliet said.

Herbert and Diyami gestured for Billy and Meredith to stand with them in a circle around Juliet. She picked up the bowl of smoldering plants and moved it back and forth in front of each person as she sang, alternating between an Indian language and English.

"We offer this day and its miraculous light so that you may continue to bless our family, our home, and our new friends, who have traveled a great distance to see this holy city. Please guide us, your people, as we continue the work of Corn Mother and Morning Star. And guide our friends on a safe journey to their home by the ocean," she said.

Juliet set the bowl down on the table and stood between Billy and Meredith, facing the center of the circle. All five of them held hands.

"Let us close our eyes and release all our desires and cares so we can hear the wisdom of the Great Mystery."

She began to sing softly and sway gently back and forth. Billy opened his eyes slightly to see that Herbert and Diyami were swaying also. Billy smelled the smoke from the fire and listened to Juliet's beautiful, hypnotic voice. After a few moments, her hand clenched. Once, twice, three times. Billy opened his eyes and saw that Herbert and Diyami were staring wide-eyed at Juliet. Billy closed his eyes quickly so they wouldn't see him looking.

Juliet's song became deeper and more staccato. It didn't sound like singing any more, but like a string of yelps and moans. She was shaking. Billy began to feel uncomfortable. Was she having a seizure? Juliet let out a shriek, then was silent. She let go of Billy's and Meredith's hands.

Everyone opened their eyes. Herbert rushed over to Juliet and helped her into a chair. She looked weak and was breathing heavily. Diyami motioned to Billy and Meredith to sit down.

"When the spirits enter a speaker, things can get unpredictable. It will all be okay," Herbert said.

Diyami got his mother a glass of water. No one spoke. After a few minutes, she said: "The spirits of Cahokia were very agitated. I couldn't tell if they were telling me to be glad or fearful."

She sat up straight and looked at Billy and Meredith. "Where did you come from? Where? Not from California." Billy didn't know what to say. She continued, "The spirits say you are from here, but not from here." She slumped back in the chair. "What does that mean?"

Diyami turned to Meredith, "Do you know what she's talking about?" Meredith had a panicked expression. She looked at Billy. He closed his eyes, took a deep breath, and opened them again.

"Now I have a long story to tell."

It took the rest of the evening for Billy to explain the events of the last few months to Herbert, Juliet, and Diyami—as best as he could. The sun set and night fell. They ate dinner by the fire. Herbert, Juliet, and Diyami listened carefully without skepticism. They had many questions:

"What does it feel like when you slip across?"

"It's like stepping off a diving board with your eyes closed."

"Is it scary?"

"Not really. It happens quickly."

"What is your city like?"

"There are fewer people and more cars. A huge thing called the Arch is on the riverfront."

"Do you like it here?"

"Yes, it's incredible. That's why we keep coming back."

"What is your Cahokia like?

"Nothing like this, just a park."

"Do people in your world know about us?

"In general, no. I have one friend who may know, but he's old and sick."

Herbert and Juliet, as academics, asked more scientific questions about how the two worlds interacted and the potential for multiple dimensions. Billy had to say that he had no idea, beyond John's vague talk of interference patterns and Martin's analogy of the snowflakes.

When he mentioned the Knights of the Carnelian, Herbert said: "I've heard of them. People say they pull the strings on everything in St. Louis. It's all rumors. No one even knows who they are."

"From what they told me, their mission is to keep this whole thing a secret. They tried to scare me into not coming back."

"They did a pretty good job of that," Meredith said.

"Well, Meredith, they made some threats that weren't very subtle. And, I think that one of their people saw us on the bridge today." Billy told them about the kite-flying instructor and how he was watching them when they boarded the hydrofoil.

"What will you do now?" Juliet said.

"I think we have to avoid the Knights and get home."

"Not tonight," Herbert said. "It's far too late. The speedboats have stopped. Stay with us and we'll figure this out in the morning."

Billy realized there was no other option and agreed. Herbert went to prepare places for them to sleep. Diyami and Meredith took the dishes inside.

Juliet and Billy walked to the railing at the edge of the patio. He could see the lights from buildings across the Grand Plaza and, in the distance, the flashing beacon atop the Hydraulic Building.

"Now that you know our story, what do you think the spirits were telling you?"

Juliet looked up to the sky. "Do you have the same stars in your world?"

Billy looked up. He pointed. "Uhh, yes. The Big Dipper. Cassiopeia. The Milky Way."

"In our tradition, we call the Milky Way the Path of Souls. It's the road we follow at death from this earth to the Below World." She turned to Billy. "The spirits sensed that you have a great gift. They were vibrating, or dancing, in your presence. Their dance is what overwhelmed me."

"I'm sorry."

"Don't be sorry. Be glad. Very few people have such a gift. What counts is how you use it."

Billy awoke on the living room couch the next morning. He could smell breakfast being made in the kitchen. Through the glass wall, he could see Meredith and Diyami talking on the terrace. He had slept deeply and felt refreshed. After a moment, he realized that he also felt peaceful, remarkably peaceful.

Juliet walked in from the kitchen. "Good morning." She opened the glass door and asked Diyami and Meredith to come inside. Billy pulled off the blanket and stood up, straightening his clothes. Juliet asked Diyami to retrieve Herbert from his study. Breakfast was ready.

Everyone got their breakfast—cornmeal pancakes with maple syrup, bacon, and coffee—and carried it outside, where they sat at the table bathed by the sweet morning breeze.

"We could hardly sleep last night," Herbert said. "We kept going 'round and round with the possibilities and implications. Each question leads to more and more questions."

"I know the feeling," Billy said.

"It hurts your brain to think about it," Meredith said.

"Thank you for not thinking we're out of our minds."

"Perhaps we should, but the ancestors believe you," Juliet said.

"What now?" Herbert asked.

"We have to get back today, or we'll be missed. After that, I don't know. As I said, I'm pretty sure that my ability to cross is going to disappear at some point."

"I know you're worried that the Knights are looking for you. I called my friend at the Kahok Brewery this morning. One of his trucks can drive you to wherever in St. Louis you need to go. That will be a much lower profile than using the speedboats."

"Good idea. Thanks," Billy said.

"I want to go with you," Diyami said. "I want to see your world."

"Diyami, that could be dangerous," Billy said.

"You have come here many times. Why can't I go there?"

"You belong here, not there," Herbert said.

"Meredith told me about their city, their Cahokia. I need to see it."

"Dad, please," Meredith said. "You can bring him back in a couple of days."

"I would be back here by Tuesday," Diyami said.

They sat silently. Meredith knew not to press the issue any further.

Juliet stood up. "I must consult the spirits." She walked inside.

Billy climbed into the cab of the truck and shook hands with the driver, Anak. He had full-face tattoos like Diyami. Meredith got in next, followed by Diyami. Herbert and Juliet stood outside the truck. They waved cheerfully, but looked anxious.

The truck pulled out of the parking lot behind the university buildings and headed north. As it turned left onto a main road, Billy could see the back side of the old pyramid and the new pyramid at the other end of the Grand Plaza. Billy looked at everything closely. He was pretty sure that he would never see it again. He was sad, because the previous day had been one of the best days of his life.

They passed several boys playing the stickball game with the rolling rubber disk. Billy remembered that Diyami had said it was called chunkey.

In a few minutes, Cahokia was behind them. Billy wondered if the ancestors would ever speak to him.

They crossed the Mississippi into St. Louis, skirted downtown and headed west on Olive, which, like in Billy's St. Louis, turned into Lindell Boulevard. Yesterday, Billy had used a new place to cross over in the Central West End, far from his usual haunts in south St. Louis. He had figured that the Knights' spotters wouldn't be watching for him there.

Billy and Meredith had not seen this street in HD St. Louis, so they soaked up every sight—the people on the sidewalks, the stores and restaurants, the shapes and colors of buildings—in the hope that they would be able to remember these images someday while they lay awake in bed at four in the morning.

Lindell, like most major thoroughfares, had a streetcar line down the center. The wide sidewalks had painted lines separating the bike and scooter paths from the pedestrian areas. As they crossed Grand Avenue, Billy looked to the right for the Fox Theater, a gaudy 1920s movie palace turned concert hall that was a fixture in his St. Louis. Instead, he saw a nondescript row of glass office towers.

A few blocks further west, they approached the Catholic cathedral, which was the same as the one he was familiar with—a limestone Byzantine structure topped by a green dome. Opposite the cathedral, on the other side of Lindell, there was a deep square with colonnaded buildings on either side. At the far end of the square stood a second large building whose brick-covered façade was a mountain range of slender arches upon arches. Thickets of tables covered with colorful umbrellas dotted the square.

"What's that?" Billy asked.

"Cathedral Place. Lots of fancy restaurants. Not really my style," Diyami said.

Anak chimed in: "That's the Opera House at the back. I went there once with my school."

A few blocks later, they stopped at a red light at Euclid. Billy knew this street for its restaurants, antique stores, old homes, and his favorite bookstore, from long ago when he had had time to read books.

"This is where I like to come," Diyami said. "Live music everywhere. Goes on all night—gypsy beat, jump bands, throat singers, you name it. Big time players on tour."

"Wow!" Meredith said. "I want to see that."

"We can," Diyami said with a smile.

"We'll see," Billy said.

Billy told Anak to turn right at the next corner, Kingshighway. He had crossed over near the churches a few blocks north. But right before they got there, Billy noticed the clock on the dashboard—11:51.

"Let's take a little detour. Keep going straight."

They continued west. Forest Park was on their left. People were jogging and riding bikes and scooters. On the right, Billy noticed some of the same mansions that he was familiar with. In his St. Louis, a string of them lined Lindell for two miles, all the way to the end of the park, sitting on large lots with leafy trees.

In this city, an old mansion appeared here and there between the ten- and fifteen-story apartment buildings that dominated the streetscape. Most were wrapped with wide balconies on every floor. Spiral cylinders of wind turbines spun slowly on their roofs. After about a mile, Billy told Anak to pull the truck over and stop. It was 11:57.

"I want to see this up close," Billy said. "One of the Knights showed it to me from downtown."

He pointed toward the Art Museum, which sat upon a hill about half a mile away. A couple minutes later, two jets of water shot up from the basin below. When the feathery columns of water were hundreds of feet tall, they slowly tilted toward each other to form a soaring vault that framed the museum and sparkled in the sunlight.

Meredith jumped up and down with excitement and hugged her father's arm.

"That's their Arch!"

"Yeah. Pretty cool."

Diyami and Anak shook their heads and looked at each other like "What's the big deal?"

A few minutes later, they arrived at the corner of Kingshighway and McPherson. Four large churches were visible in front of them. Because the services had just ended, the sidewalks were packed with people. Everyone was in white. Men wore starched white suits, with shorts, of course. Women wore flowing white dresses that shimmered in the sunlight and white hats in various styles. Children ran around in miniature versions of the same.

"Why do they all have white clothes?" Meredith asked.

"It's Sunday. That's what people wear at church," Diyami said.

"We'll stick out here, so we need to move quickly," Billy said. "Diyami, stay close and do exactly what I say."

"Dad, I've already told him how it works."

Diyami picked up the backpack he had brought. He reached across the cab and clasped hands with Anak. They said something to each other in Cahokian.

Diyami, Meredith, and Billy got out of the truck and Anak drove off. They walked toward the first church. As they weaved through the throngs of churchgoers, some people looked at them with annoyance, like they were interlopers. Billy didn't like that. Right next to the church, he spotted what he was looking for—a narrow space between the church and another building. He led Meredith and Diyami into it.

"Give me a moment," he said. He stood still and lowered his head. He swayed back and forth slightly. Meredith and Diyami watched him closely. After a minute, Billy reached out his hands, beckoning each of them to hold onto one.

"Close your eyes, breathe slow, and relax. When I say 'go', take one step forward –and keep your eyes closed."

The three of them stood there. Diyami listened to the bustle of people behind them, just twenty feet away on the sidewalk. Billy waited patiently for the first feathery brush of the membrane between the two worlds to touch his cheek. Meredith opened herself up as well, hoping to feel it at the same time as her father. A few more seconds passed. Billy could sense the membrane thinning out in front of him. The sounds of the sidewalk receded. A car honked. Billy said, "Go!" They stepped forward.

Diyami felt a swirl of vertigo. He grabbed Billy's hand tight. Then his foot landed on solid ground.

"We did it," Billy said.

Diyami opened his eyes to see the same narrow space between the church and the building. Meredith grabbed his hand, turned him around, and dragged him to the sidewalk.

The same churches were there, but the sidewalk was practically empty. None of the people were wearing white. The streetcars and tracks were gone. Strange, boxy cars drove by.

"See, it's real!" Meredith said. "Welcome to *my* world!" She gave him a huge hug.

They walked about a half-block to Billy's car. Diyami's eyes kept darting back and forth, trying to figure out what was different and what was the same. Some of the houses and buildings looked familiar, but he was unsettled by the line of bizarre parked cars they passed.

Billy unlocked his car. As they got in, he pulled a ticket off the windshield.

"Damn. I hadn't planned to leave it here this long."

They drove south on Kingshighway. As they crossed Lindell, Diyami looked around excitedly. Now, he could see that all the buildings were new to him. When they turned west on to I-64, he marveled at the vast number of cars speeding through the city on this ribbon of concrete.

As they drove toward Chesterfield, Billy rehearsed Diyami on his cover story. He was a new student at Webster University. He was staying with them for a couple of days until his dorm room was ready. He was from Norman, Oklahoma, and his parents were professors at the University of Oklahoma.

"No one here has tattoos like yours," Billy said. "So some people may stare at you. If they ask you about them, just say that they are what your tribe does."

As they continued toward home, Meredith showed Diyami the cool stuff she could do with her iPhone.

"Hi, Mom. How was the field trip?" Meredith said as Carol trudged into the kitchen from the garage.

"The kids had a wonderful time, but I'm exhausted," Carol said, collapsing into a chair.

"Mom, we have a guest," Meredith said, as she led Diyami into the kitchen. "This is Diyami Red Hawk. He's a new student at Webster, but there's a problem with his dorm room. So I said he could stay here until it's ready."

"It's a pleasure to meet you, Mrs. Boustany," Diyami said, reaching out to shake Carol's hand.

Billy and Meredith could see the skeptical look on Carol's face as she absorbed Diyami's tattoos and shoulder-length black hair.

"The school really screwed up and he can't get into his room until Tuesday," Meredith said. "I set him up in the guest room."

"Of course. It's very nice to have you here, Diyami."

"Who the hell is *he*?" Carol asked Billy after Meredith and Diyami had gone outside to the pool.

"Just a student who needs a place to stay for a few days, like she said."

"He looks like he's in a gang."

"He's an Indian, obviously. His parents are college professors. He's seems perfectly fine."

"He's not her boyfriend, is he?"

"Of course not. She just met him this weekend. She's trying to help him out of a jam. She didn't want him to pay to sit in a motel."

"Every time I turn my back this summer, something weird happens," Carol said. "I need a shower."

On Monday morning, Billy, Meredith, and Diyami drove toward downtown. The night before, Meredith had taken Diyami out for pizza with her friends. They didn't get home until after midnight. Billy could only wonder about what that evening had been like. Neither of them had said a word about it this morning.

They went to a Starbuck's drive-through, which fascinated Diyami. Meredith asked him, "What do you want?"

"Coffee. Don't we have to go inside?"

"No. They give it to us through the window. What kind of coffee?"

"Black."

Billy ordered into the speaker.

"A skinny macchiato." He turned to Meredith, "The usual Frappuccino?"

"Yeah."

He turned back to the speaker. "Cinnamon dolce Frappuccino, and a vente dark roast coffee."

When they got the coffee, Diyami took a taste from both Meredith's and Billy's. He wasn't sure which was stranger, the drive-through or the bizarre drinks and their cryptic names.

They parked the car on the sloping cobblestone levee near the foot of the Eads Bridge. The August sun beat down on a smattering of pedestrians on the riverfront boulevard below the Arch.

Diyami looked across the river to the East St. Louis bank, which was an almost featureless expanse. Scrub trees, weeds, and a large gray building with the vertical flutes of a grain elevator. A little farther in the distance stood a casino surrounded by a huge parking lot.

"That's where I live!" Diyami said, pointing to a spot just to the right of the Eads Bridge. "What happened?"

Billy remembered the three soaring apartment buildings topped by a slab of park space in the sky.

"There's not much built in East St. Louis over here. Pretty desolate," Billy said.

They walked along the street toward the staircase that would take them up to the Arch. The massive concrete embankment was on one side and the river on the other.

Diyami turned frequently to look at the bridge, the levee, and the opposite bank, again and again. His brain was overloading with the contrast between what he was seeing and the place he knew so well. Billy remembered feeling the same way on his first visits to HD.

As Billy imagined how Diyami must be seeing this place, he began to feel embarrassed for its emptiness and loneliness. From this vantage point, the city didn't look like much. He worried that Diyami would tell his parents about the dull, barren landscape that he had seen. He didn't want Herbert and Juliet to think less of him because of it.

They ascended the staircase to the base of the Arch and stood below its center point. Diyami looked up at the apex, impossibly slender in the distant reaches of the sky. Billy pointed out the little windows of the observation platform up there.

"It's spectacular," Diyami said.

Meredith held his hand and put her other hand on his shoulder as she looked up with him. Billy breathed a silent sigh of relief. He need not feel embarrassed. Diyami had the same reaction to the Arch as most visitors. No picture can capture the object itself.

The Arch is the one thing that people around the world know about St. Louis—that is, if they don't draw a total blank at the mention of the city's name.

In popular photos and countless logos of plumbers, electricians, and accountants, the Arch is a simple symmetrical form that neatly frames a little stand of buildings that represents downtown St. Louis. Up, over, down, done.

But from up close, the Arch is completely different—a leviathan that commands attention. It bears no resemblance to a product of the human construction process. It's not a building, yet it encloses a space that feels larger than any building. It doesn't look organic or natural like a tree or a mountain. Rather, it seems to have thrust out of the ground fully formed for no purpose other than to shout its own strength, magnificence, and mathematical perfection.

Though the Arch has become the symbol of St. Louis, it has nothing to do with the city. It stands alone in its green park, where the original heart of the city once thrived. The city gazes at the Arch. It does not gaze back.

Billy led them to the north leg to show Diyami his favorite view. The cross-section of each leg of the Arch is an equilateral triangle, fifty-four feet on a side at the base, which tapers to seventeen feet on a side at the top. The point of the triangle at ground level is like the prow of a ship slicing the ocean in two.

Meredith and Diyami touched the vertex of the triangle. Following Billy's lead, they stood with their backs up against one face of the triangle and tilted their heads back to gaze straight up. From that vantage point, the Arch looks like a shiny image in a funhouse mirror or a tidal wave about to break on top of you. Nothing is straight or safe.

After a minute, they stepped away from the Arch itself and strolled the paths between green lawns, trees, and ponds. Diyami tried to correlate different spots with places he knew.

"Around here is a place with a great view of the river from the roof. It's famous for crepes. Very hard to get in on Sundays."

"The club where we went dancing is right here, Meredith."

"You should have seen it, Dad. The walls were made of colored blobs that moved in time to the music."

"Over by the other leg of the Arch is a little square with fountains. Kids love to play in there. I buy clothes in the store next to it."

After a while, Diyami looked around the area one last time with a slow 360-degree turn. Then he said, "Can we go to Cahokia now?"

They walked up the steps on Monk's mound at Cahokia. A mother was walking down, holding the hand of her five-year-old son. He pointed at Diyami as they passed.

"Mommy, that man has scribbles on his face!"

"It's not polite to point."

"Will he get in trouble for those scribbles?"

At the top of the mound, Diyami scanned the Grand Plaza. He was overwhelmed with sadness. "It's dead, destroyed."

"Not destroyed," Billy said. "The new Cahokia was never built."

To the east, where the University is in Diyami's Cahokia, including the building where his parents live, there was an empty field, with a rundown mobile home park at the far end.

Diyami, increasingly agitated, walked off by himself on the top of the mound. He began to sing like his mother had on the terrace of her apartment. Billy and Meredith stood back, not sure what to do.

Diyami doubled over and vomited into the grass.

After he recovered, they climbed down the mound and drove over to the Visitor's Center and Museum, which stood in the middle of what Diyami knew as the Grand Plaza. It was a low brick building with a large atrium, a gift shop, snack bar, a theater with a multimedia show, "City of the Sun," and a large space with exhibits of ancient life at Cahokia.

They watched the multimedia show, with gorgeous photography and a narrator who told the story of Cahokia in a deep, booming voice, emphasizing the mystery of its abandonment in the 1300s.

Besides Billy, Meredith, and Diyami, the audience consisted of a group of Cub Scouts, and a motley assembly of old and young people in T-shirts and shorts. At the end, the screen retracted into the ceiling to reveal a life-size diorama with scenes of life in ancient Cahokia. It had a variety of sculpted figures and thatched houses.

Billy, Meredith, and Diyami walked through the diorama and museum. They wandered from exhibit to exhibit, on agriculture, mythology, and building materials. Diyami took great interest. He was pleased that the exhibits were historically consistent with what he learned in school.

While Billy and Diyami were looking at a glass case with pottery and tools, Meredith went to see part of the diorama up close. She yelled across the room, "Diyami, Dad! Come here quick! Right now!"

They rushed over to her.

"Look." She pointed to two life-sized diorama figures on the other side of the glass. An old man was standing in front of a house made of sticks talking to a young man sitting on the ground. The plaque said they were exchanging goods.

"That's you, Diyami, that's you!"

Billy and Diyami bent closer. They were just a foot and a half from the figure of the young man. He had an angular face with high cheekbones, deep brown eyes, a straight mouth, and black hair falling over his shoulders. Two horizontal stripes running from ear to ear across his nose and vertical stripes covering his chin. He was a dead ringer for Diyami.

"Oh my God!" Billy said.

Diyami leaned in. His body started to shudder. Billy and Meredith put their arms on his shoulders to steady him. Billy was worried that Diyami was about to pass out. He took his arm and led him away from the diorama.

"Let's get something to drink."

They sat in the snack bar, drinking sodas. Billy noticed that some of the other people there were glancing at Diyami frequently. The adults didn't want to stare, but he was the only Indian in the place. The children looked at him without shame.

Diyami didn't notice them. He still hadn't said anything since they saw the figure in the diorama. He sipped his Diet Coke.

His silence and withdrawal were making Meredith uncomfortable.

"That was unbelievably weird," she said, hoping to get some kind of conversation started.

"Yeah," Billy said noncommittally. He sensed that Diyami needed time.

After a few more minutes, Diyami said, "A whisper."

"Huh?" Meredith said.

"A whisper from the spirits."

"What did they say?" Meredith asked.

"They were muffled. Like they were buried far below. I think they're calling for help."

Meredith and Diyami went out again that night and didn't return until long after Billy and Carol had gone to bed. The next morning, Carol eyed Diyami with suspicion throughout the breakfast small talk.

"What time can you get into the dorm room?" she asked him.

"Eleven o'clock."

"I'm taking him there," Meredith said.

"First day of teacher meetings for me," Carol said. "I could do them in my sleep."

"Thank you so much for your hospitality, Mrs. Boustany. I hope to see you again."

"I'm sure you will. Good luck with school," Carol said.

After Carol left, Billy said, "It's time. Let's get Diyami home."

"I'm coming!" Meredith said.

"Okay, but you're not crossing over. We're not taking any more chances with the Knights. I'm going to get Diyami over, then come right back. The whole thing will take two minutes."

Meredith gave Billy her sullen look.

The drive into the city was like a ride to a cemetery. In the rearview mirror, Billy could see the tears in Meredith's eyes as she sat holding hands with Diyami in the back seat. Even Billy was sad. He liked Diyami, and hated the idea that he would never see him, or HD, again.

Billy decided to go to Grand and Gravois, his most reliable place for slipping across. Even though the Knights might have people on the lookout there, he figured that he would be in and out so quickly it wouldn't make a difference.

He parked the car around the corner from the Southside National Bank Building. They got out.

"Meredith, wait here."

"Daddy, no!" she wailed.

"We have a deal. Diyami goes back. You wait in the car." Billy couldn't bear the idea of Meredith watching Diyami disappear.

"I'll be fine," Diyami said.

He hugged Meredith close. Billy turned away to give them privacy. They embraced and whispered to each other for several minutes. Fortunately, the sidewalk was deserted.

As Diyami and Billy walked to the entrance alcove of the Southside National Bank, he looked over his shoulder and waved to Meredith one last time. She waved back forlornly.

A couple of minutes later, Billy got back in the car. Meredith stared straight ahead, stone silent.

"Honey, we've had an incredible adventure. We've seen things that no one else has ever seen, and we've met great people like Diyami and his family. But it's over now. We can't take any more chances with this."

"Shut up!" Meredith screamed.

They drove home in silence.

The next few weeks were rough for Billy. For starters, Meredith completely ignored him. She found a reason to skip dinner every night, busy with friends or stuff at school. Dinner together as a family a few nights a week had been an unspoken tradition for the Boustanys since Meredith had started college. She was blowing it off.

Carol was consumed by the beginning of her school year—so she said. Dinner was just small talk between them and, claiming exhaustion, she went to bed before their nightly glass of wine. This bothered Billy, especially as the late summer evenings were turning so pleasantly cool that dusk on the patio was perfection. It seemed to him that Carol had been put off by Diyami's visit. She didn't say anything directly, but Billy knew her radar was up, that she sensed something fishy.

Then, there was the business. The back-to-school season had been moderately successful. A definite uptick in traffic, and a small, but decent, bump in sales. Still, Billy observed customer after customer doing the usual dance. Parents and teenagers intently looking over the laptops, iPads, and printers, asking involved questions of the salespeople.

The kid would get excited about one model or another, the parent would discreetly signal caution to them, then turn to the salesperson with a polite "Thank you for all your help, but we're still looking." Then out the door to go home and order whatever the hell they wanted from Amazon.

Whenever he could, Billy intervened to help customers himself—though, after the incident in June, he made sure to keep his feelings in check. He was good at charming them. He could flow smoothly from talking value to the parents to showing off cool features to the kids. He liberally repeated Duke's promise of free in-store support for 90 days.

"If anything doesn't make sense or doesn't seem to be working right, we'll get you through it. You won't have to hunt around through confusing tech support websites, or sit on hold for hours to talk to someone in India."

He was better at closing sales than most of his people, but, even for him, it was arduous and exhausting. And he lost more times than he liked.

Most depressing of all was knowing he was never going back to HD. It was like a hot air balloon had lifted him to glimpse a spectacular new landscape, and then collapsed. He was left standing in a field, covered in shrouds of now useless balloon fabric, tangled up in lines and pulleys.

He felt like someone had died. Images and memories came back to him in every quiet moment. The conversations with Mary Jo and Walt at Whittemore's, Milo's music, how the taffy ladies fussed over Meredith, the view from the top of the Temple of the Children at Cahokia, the amazing conversation with Martin in the cupola of the Hydraulic Building. It was all gone, all over. He wanted to talk with Meredith, but she was too pissed off.

Pickup and Delivery

1966

Jim Hines pressed a hidden button on his desk. A paneled wall in his office slid open to reveal a rack of dark suits.

"These are appropriate clothes for over there. I'm sure we can find one that will fit you."

Martin Matsui was nervous, and elated. He was alone with a living legend and was about to accompany him on a trip to the other side. He wasn't sure he deserved this honor, but he wasn't going to question Jim's decision. No one ever did. Even though Jim had retired as Supreme Protector of the Knights of the Carnelian and as Managing Director of the CSP, he was still the most influential man in the city.

Jim had tapped Martin for this project because he had an intuition that this young architect had the intelligence and vision to handle the delicate business of harvesting products from the other side to fuel the industry of St. Louis and fill the coffers of the Knights. Most of the other young Knights were far too enthralled by the money and power that came with membership, and couldn't see beyond their noses. Martin wasn't from an old family. He had ascended into the Knights based on his talent, not on connections. Jim liked that.

Over the years, Jim had auditioned a string of young acolytes. He couldn't rest easy until he found the right person, one who could do well everything that Jim did well. Someone who could succeed him. They had all been disappointing, each in his own way. Back in 1941, Peter Tomlinson had been the first. He courageously brought back the first products that proved the viability of the scheme, "the trade" as Jim liked to call it.

Peter turned out to be a top-notch administrator, but Jim thought he lacked the imagination to keep "the trade" laying its golden eggs. Now, Peter had taken over Jim's positions with the Knights and the CSP, and Jim was in the early stages of an uneasy retirement. Jim tried to stay out of Peter's way, but people continued to come to him for decisions. Over and over, he had to say "Ask Peter" or "Take that up with Peter." He was beginning to feel like a talking parrot.

The trips to the other side were the last responsibility Jim held onto. Martin was Jim's latest candidate for the role of protégé. He was not likely to become the overall leader—Peter could manage the Knights competently—but perhaps he could be a wise navigator who could keep the enterprise from drifting too far from its mission.

Jim was drawn to Martin because he had a soft spot for architects. He thought they were more strategic than mere businessmen. Maybe he had been influenced by his experiences with F.L. Wright, who had come up with the big invention, Hydraulic's Amperic bricks, which had brought billions into St. Louis.

And Wright had seen the potential of that nut job Fuller's vehicle designs and fuel cells when no one else did. Paired with the generating capacity of the bricks, they created a closed-loop transportation system, with each element controlled by St. Louis companies. Wright had been a huge pain in the ass, who always thought he knew everything, but he had made everyone rich.

"That one is perfect," Jim said after Martin tried on one of the suits. Jim had put on his own suit from the rack. "Let's go."

They took the private elevator down to the basement level of the Hydraulic Building, where Jim's gleaming black limousine was parked.

"Riverfront. The usual place," Jim instructed the driver.

On the way, Jim explained to Martin that he always crossed at the same spot. It was out of the way and deserted in both worlds. Martin took note of the details. He would be making this trip on his own before long. The limousine parked and they got out. The sky was gray and overcast. Jim brought his briefcase with him. They walked behind a stack of barrels on the levee. Jim pulled a small silver case from his pocket, opened it, handed a white pill to Martin and took one for himself.

"Don't be afraid. I've done this for years. It will be over before you know it." They swallowed the pills.

Martin found himself on his knees as the vertigo receded. Jim was standing, but he was breathing heavily.

"Are you all right, sir?" Martin asked.

"Yes. Give me a minute. It's just a little shortness of breath."

Martin looked around. The sun was shining brightly. The levee bricks looked the same, but, instead of the barrels, there was a large, rusty metal container.

Jim said, "I'm ready. Let me show you the sights."

They walked around the container. The river was flowing brown and angry from an early spring flood. Martin looked up. Above him was the most beautiful thing he had ever seen. Slender and almost weightless, like a bird's bone, it seemed to touch the blue sky. Blinding sunlight reflected off its smooth, featureless skin. Its two sturdy legs tapered with mathematical precision to a brushstroke that bisected the heavens into east and west.

Jim was amused by Martin's reaction. What do you expect from an architect?

"They just finished it a few months ago. I'll never understand these people. They bulldoze the riverfront into a wasteland, call it 'renewal,' then put up a piece of magnificent fluff. They'll never make a dime off it. At least it's not our problem."

They climbed the staircase overlooking the river so Martin could inspect the Arch from close up. Then they crossed a highway and entered downtown. Jim pointed out the building where he had worked as a young man, before 1929. It was a tall cube, faced with white terra cotta. A bustling department store filled its lower floors.

Martin wondered how the terra cotta generated power. Jim explained that Hydraulic's technology didn't exist here. Martin was entranced by the long, tail-finned cars that jammed the streets, like sculpted shingles. Nothing like the smooth, aluminum ovoids he was used to.

"Do these run on fuel cells?"

"No. Strictly gasoline. It's funny, because we got our automobile concepts from one of their inventors, an odd little man who never stopped talking. His name was just as odd as he was—Buckminster Fuller, if I remember correctly. Apparently, no one over here listened to him."

Jim said he needed to sit and rest for a little while. They found a restaurant and ordered coffee. Jim bought a newspaper. He liked to catch up on the news from this side. Martin scanned the room, inspecting the styles worn by men and women, the design of chairs, light fixtures, and salt shakers. Everything was similar to what he knew, but always just a bit different. Fascinating.

Jim put down his paper. It was a good time to begin Martin's education.

"Up close, they look quite harmless, no different from our people. But a deep insanity runs through them. I find it hard to believe that I grew up in this world. I was lucky to get out when I did."

"What kind of insanity?"

"They're addicted to war and mass murder. As soon as one war ends, they find an excuse to start fighting again." He pointed to a headline in his paper. "Here's a new one. In a place called Vietnam, wherever that is. When I was a young man, in 1918, I was a soldier in a horrible war in France.

"You know what the earthquake in '31 did to us. The destruction in that war was ten thousand times worse. Millions were killed. You couldn't escape the stench of rotting corpses. They called it 'the war to end all wars.' What a joke! Twenty years later, they did it all over again. That time, they went from killing soldiers on the battlefields to burning entire cities and everyone inside them. Now they have bombs that can wipe out cities anywhere in the world in minutes."

"They must be constantly terrified."

"When you talk to them, they're as calm as can be. They've accepted death and destruction as something normal, even patriotic. A good way to make a buck. They go about their business like these bombs don't exist."

Martin was shocked by this information and by Jim's scorn for this other world, the world he came from. Jim intended to shock him. He wanted the handful of Knights who knew the real situation to protect everyone else by keeping their world from being infected by the madness over here.

"Don't get me wrong. They do some good work. Cherry picking their ideas has been an excellent business for us." Jim leaned forward and looked directly into Martin's eyes. "As a Knight, it's up to you to guard our people, our city. Whatever happens, you must never allow this insanity to get a foothold."

Martin wrestled with these words for the rest of his life. He had to reconcile Jim's stark warning with his own tendency to seek compromise and consensus. He would make a lot of big decisions over the years, and never knew if he got them right.

"Time for our pickup and delivery," Jim said. They went out onto the sidewalk to hail a cab. Jim was walking more slowly than usual. Martin offered to carry the suitcase. The cab took them to South Grand Avenue. Martin stared out the window the whole way. The cab pulled up in front of a restaurant with a large neon sign of a pelican.

As they got out of the cab, Jim said: "This place is famous for its turtle soup. You must try it."

They settled into a booth in a far corner of the restaurant and ordered two bowls of turtle soup. "Our contact is often late," Jim said. "We're involved in a shady business, so we have to put up with some marginal characters."

Jim explained that, in the early days of "the trade," he and Peter Tomlinson had dealt directly with the businessmen and engineers who could provide the product plans, formulas, and diagrams they needed.

But in the late 1940s (between two of the endless wars), people here became very frightened of Russian spies. Jim himself was almost arrested as a spy twice. The first time, he was able to talk himself out of it. The second time, in the early 1950s, he took delivery of a satchel of plans. When he opened the satchel to review the contents, a packet of red dye exploded and covered his face, hands, and suit. It was a way of marking him as the spy if he tried to escape.

"I ran into a bathroom and locked the door. The police were banging on the door. I had to quickly take a pill to get away." He chuckled at the thought of the police smashing down the bathroom door to find no one inside. "I had to cancel my public engagements for a week, until I could get the dye off."

Because of that incident, Jim took a different approach. He searched for middlemen, people who would be less likely to have second thoughts and alert the authorities. Let them deal with the proper businessmen for him.

"I found that, with these people, like with everyone, cash unlocks many doors." He opened his briefcase and took out a small cloth bag. It was filled with gold and silver coins. "Nineteenth century. Exactly the same in both worlds, so everyone over here accepts them gladly."

After a few false starts, Jim found his middleman in 1956.

"He's delivered reliably ever since. I tell him what I'm looking for. A few months later, he has it."

"Does he know about the two worlds?"

"Of course not! To him, I'm just a man who wants things and pays handsomely for them."

"How does he get the plans and formulas?"

"I don't ask questions, and he doesn't either. That's our arrangement. Maybe he thinks I'm a Russian spy. He's not going to say anything. He likes the money too much."

Just then, a tall, gangly young man with thinning dark hair and a prominent Adam's apple came to the booth.

"Sorry I'm late, Mr. Hines."

"Don't think twice about it. We were having a most pleasant conversation. I'd like you to meet my associate, Martin Matsui. Martin, this is Bill Boustany."

Bill ordered his own bowl of turtle soup. He slipped a large envelope across the table to Jim, who opened it and studied the contents. "Excellent work, Bill. These are just what I was looking for." Jim put the envelope in his briefcase and discreetly slid the cloth bag over to Bill. With the business taken care of, they all enjoyed a delicious lunch—soft shell crab for Jim, broiled snapper for Martin, and fried catfish for Bill. Jim told Bill that, in the future, Martin would be his contact.

"This is a young man's game and it's time for me to step back."

"As you begin your golden years, Mr. Hines, remember I can always get you an AMAZING deal on a TV, a Hi-Fi or whatever you want."

"That won't be necessary, Bill, but thank you."

Bill reached into his jacket pocket and pulled out two cigars.

"Here, have a cigar. I'm celebrating. My son was born last week. William Junior!"

"Congratulations, Bill," Martin said. "Family is the most important thing."

Back at the riverfront, Jim and Martin took the pills to get home. After they crossed over, Jim was on his knees, sweating, gasping for breath, and pale as a ghost. Martin helped him into the waiting limousine and told the driver to rush to the hospital. Jim would never leave it.

Family is the Most Important Thing

2010

The day Billy dreaded had come—the long-awaited presentation by Justin, the hotshot retail consultant, on his vision of how Duke's Digital could reinvent itself.

To emphasize the actual power relationship, Dan the banker had scheduled the meeting in the bank's boardroom, not at Billy's office.

"It'll be more comfortable, and I'll order in lunch," he said.

Billy invited a couple of his store managers to the meeting so he would have some backup. Justin began his presentation with a slide of logos—Amazon and a bunch of other online retailers.

"This is the biggest threat you face, internet competition. Not the store down the street or within fifty miles of here. They don't matter. And if you don't fundamentally change, you won't matter, either."

Billy sighed inwardly. He had figured this much out five years ago.

Justin's next slide blasted in bold type: "Go Big or Go Home."

"You have two choices: either go online and fight it out with them there or play a completely different game. Either way, you've got to take risks and be way bolder than you ever have been before."

Billy glanced over to Dan, who he didn't think would be particularly enamored of the idea of "risks" and "bold."

"Now, I'm going to be brutally blunt," Justin continued. "I'm not doing my job if I'm bullshitting you with happy talk. Your brand isn't strong enough to make it online. No matter how much you invested in data centers and logistics and SEO, you'll never get to scale with your current brand, which is limited, old, and tired."

"What's SEO?" one of the store managers asked.

"Great question!" Justin said. Billy knew Justin had learned to say this in consultant school, even to stupid questions.

"Search Engine Optimization is the science of building your website so that your search results come up in the top ten hits when customers are Googling the products you sell. It's massaging your site with the right keywords, making smart AdWords buys, and stuff like that. It can be fiendishly complex and expensive to do it well."

"Thanks," said the store manager, who didn't have a clue what Justin was talking about. He figured he had made his contribution to the meeting and could shut up and hold on until lunch came.

Billy didn't like the criticism of his brand, which he had worked damn hard to create over twenty years.

"What about our brand is tired?"

"You spend a lot of money to advertise in a dying newspaper, read by old people. Nobody outside of St.

Louis has ever heard of you. The people who know you take you for granted. You're the courtesy stop if they're in the neighborhood. The brand has gone nowhere in the last ten years. It's dead in the water."

Justin was right about one thing. He was brutal.

"If online's not the way to go with our pathetic, tired brand, what's Plan B?"

Justin smiled and clicked to the next slide, which proclaimed "Liberate your brand! A destination experience with a twist!"

"We're going to transform Duke's into an essential resource for tech customers—in St. Louis today, but bigger in a few years."

Justin went on to describe his vision of interactive arcades for kids, giant screens on every wall, photography and video classes, and free color laser printing services with every equipment purchase—all ways to keep the curious coming.

"It's all about the buzz!" Justin said triumphantly.

"You said there was a twist," Billy said. "What's the twist?"

"Great question! It's 'retro high-tech'! I looked at the old ads your father made. They're hilarious. They've got this cheesy, ironic thing going that will blow today's young consumers away. This '70s and 80s nostalgia is big now. Have you seen this new movie 'Hot Tub Time Machine'? It's a megahit! We'll create a character, the Duke, leaving out the Discounts part. He'll be a digital animation, both for local TV ads enticing people to the stores, and in longer, even funnier pieces on YouTube, which can be an inexpensive way to expand the brand geographically. In the stores, he can be featured in jumbo graphics and inflatables on the parking lot."

Justin showed a slide with several mockups of the animated Duke character. They were tall and skinny, with exaggerated eyes and bulging hearts. Billy winced.

The banker looked at him. "Keep an open mind, Billy. No bad ideas in a brainstorm."

"We're brainstorming here?" Billy said. "Then I've got some ideas too. I like some of what Justin is saying, but what about something innovative and educational? Not cartoons and blow-up dolls, but floating holograms. Heads of the giants of technology—Charles Babbage, Guglielmo Marconi, Philo T. Farnsworth, Alan Turing, Hedy Lamarr! You can ask them questions, and there's voice recognition, and they can tell you about their inventions that led to the wonderland of products here at Duke's. It would be very Disney."

Justin looked baffled. He didn't know who Billy was talking about. "Kind of a nerd appeal thing?"

"Exactly. Nerds. Early adopters. Risk-takers. That's where I want to go."

The room fell silent. After a few awkward moments, Dan the banker said: "We're making great progress. Let's break for lunch."

Everyone filed out into the corridor where a table was filled with sandwiches and drinks. Dan pulled Billy aside. "He's a pretty sharp guy, right?"

"Yeah, revive my dad, like Frankenstein's monster."

"C'mon, Billy. Keep an open mind."

Billy pulled out his phone to check his messages as the others filled their plates. There were two voicemails and three texts, all from Carol. The texts read: "Where's Meredith?" "I'm worried" and "Call me right now!"

Billy went out into the parking lot and called.

Her first words were, "Where the hell have you been?"

"In the big meeting with Justin, the retail guru. I had my phone off. What's up with Meredith?"

"I haven't seen her or heard from her for two days. I kept calling and texting, then I saw her phone was in her room."

Oh, shit. Billy knew what that meant.

"Have you heard from her?" Carol asked.

"Not in the past few days."

"I'm calling the police."

"Hold on. I'll come home right away and we'll figure it out. Don't call the police. Wait for me."

Billy mumbled something to Dan about a family emergency and was in his car in less than a minute. Why hadn't Billy told Carol about HD, despite his countless chances? He stewed over this as he drove home.

At first, he didn't say anything because he was confused and unsure. He didn't know himself what was going on and, being a reasonable person, he questioned his own sanity. The "A Beautiful Mind" conundrum. The idea of opening up to Carol about this mess terrified him. It had never been the right time to bring her into this craziness that even he didn't understand.

Later, he didn't tell her because he was afraid she would somehow make him stop going into HD. It was so cool he couldn't bear the idea of cutting it off. Carol would certainly come up with a plan to "fix" the HD problem. Like the home decluttering that she ruthlessly applied from time to time.

The notion that she might want to share his adventure didn't cross his mind—even though the sharing strategy turned out fine with Meredith—at least until recently. Only much later, after everything had come crashing down, did Billy realize that ignoring the possibility of teaming up with Carol in HD St. Louis was a serious indictment of his attitude toward her and their marriage.

How did she change from his partner to his adversary? From a person for hand holding, wine sharing, laughter, and love to a force to be managed? Though this trajectory is common in many marriages, Billy was dejected to realize he had fallen into it. Like the day he woke up, glanced at the mirror, and saw that he looked like his father. No one enjoys that day.

In the last month, his rationale for not telling Carol had evolved into a third form: he couldn't tell her now because he had already not told her for such a long time. At this point, her first questions would be "Why did you hide this from me?" which was a much tougher question to deal with than "Are you out of your mind?"

The longer he had delayed telling her, the greater the weight of the not-telling. It was the Watergate Principle: the cover-up is worse than the crime.

After Martin told him that his ability to slip between the two cities would vanish before long, the only silver lining Billy saw was that this might relieve his guilt about not telling Carol. If HD St. Louis became a closed chapter in his past, then keeping it to himself didn't seem so awful. You can't share every little thing, even in a good marriage, Billy told himself.

But then he got Carol's panicked call. HD St. Louis would not go gently into that good night.

Now he had to tell her at the worst possible time. She was freaked out with fear for Meredith and would see everything as his fault. Which it was, though not completely. He had, after all, forbidden Meredith from going back and she had gone anyway. So much for his authority as a patriarch. But Billy knew that arguing the fine points of the reasons for

Meredith's disappearance into HD—to get back to Diyami, no doubt—was a losing strategy. He owned everything associated with HD—the full catastrophe—like it or not.

Billy pulled up next to Carol's car in the driveway. She was waiting for him.

"Billy, I'm scared. She doesn't do stuff like this."

"Have you checked with her friends?"

"Yes. They haven't heard from her either. Could it be something with that Indian boy who was here a few weeks ago? He was different from her other friends. He looked like…a drug dealer."

"Carol. He's not a drug dealer."

"How do _you_ know?"

"I spent more time with him than you did. He's a serious kid."

"None of her friends had heard of any student like that at Webster. It's not that big a school. He would be hard to miss. Something about him isn't right."

Billy had not seen Carol this upset in a long time. Still, he could delay no longer.

"It's possible that she's with him."

"Where?"

"Probably downtown or on the East side."

"What would she be doing there?"

"That's where he lives. And that's where I took her earlier this summer."

"Billy Boustany! You took our daughter to East St. Louis and you didn't tell me? Are you insane? I'm calling the police right now."

"You're wasting your time. I guarantee you that there is no way the police will be able to find her. But you and I can. We can make this be okay."

Billy sat Carol down on the couch.

"First, I need you to listen to me."

He began with the bad day he had been having back in June. Which led him to drive down to his old neighborhood to look around and clear his head. Which led him to the corner of Grand and Gravois and his first puzzling experience.

"Billy, this is no time to be kidding around. What does this bullshit story have to do with Meredith?"

He continued, briefly describing his multiple explorations of HD St. Louis, how Meredith had confronted him, and how he had taken her with him for a few, just a few, visits. And that she had met Diyami there. He left out the parts about the Knights—too disturbing—and about Meredith's previous unauthorized visit.

"I thought she could only slip over there with me, but she must have learned how to do it herself. I'm sure that's where she is."

Carol stared at him for an uncomfortably long time. He looked away. Through the window, he saw squirrels madly racing through the tree branches in their endless game of tag.

"You have been acting strange all summer. You were obviously hiding something from me. I know the problems at the store are a lot worse than you've let on. I'm not an idiot."

That cut deep. Billy assumed that he had been successfully concealing his panic about the business.

"Are you having an affair?"

"No! Of course not."

"Who's Sharon?"

"I don't know any Sharon."

"Then what's her phone number doing in your desk?"

Billy remembered the note that the musician had given him up on the Mezz. Crap! "Someone in HD gave that to me and asked me to call her. Which I haven't!"

"This is probably the lamest cover story for an affair I've ever heard of."

"Carol! I would never have an affair! I swear to you. This is not a cover story"

"Then what is it, Billy?"

"It's the truth, goddammit!"

"Why did you hide it from me?"

The Watergate question. "Because I knew you wouldn't believe me."

"Well, you're right about that. At this point, an affair doesn't seem so bad, compared to a having a husband who is delusional and psychotic."

More silence.

"I'll take you there. We'll find Meredith and we'll bring her back."

"Just hop on our magic unicorn and go for a little ride?"

"Mockery won't help, Carol. We both want to find Meredith. Come with me. When it's over, if you still think I'm delusional, I will happily go to the mental hospital."

"Don't you have anything looser and gauzier?" Billy asked. Carol gave him an exasperated look. She was holding up different outfits from a pile on the bed.

"Billy, why are we wasting time on clothes?"

"Because they dress differently there. We need to fit in, stay under the radar."

She pulled one more outfit, a pale yellow summer dress, from the closet.

"That one! It's perfect."

After she got dressed, Billy put on a wide brimmed hat that she had never seen before.

"Where did you get that?" she asked with a note of disapproval.

"Over there. You'll see a lot like this one."

They drove into the city. He got off the highway at Kingshighway and turned toward the Central West End.

"I thought Grand and Gravois was your special spot."

"There's a place near here that also works. It's more discreet."

Carol shook her head in disbelief. "Whatever." She was thinking about which type of psychiatric care would be best for Billy.

He parked on McPherson, near the cluster of churches. They walked past the first church and Billy found the narrow space between the buildings that he had used with Meredith and Diyami a few weeks earlier. He stopped, closed his eyes, and took a long, slow breath. Yep, it was still a favorable place to slip across.

Carol watched skeptically.

"Take a good look around," Billy told Carol. "It will all be different in a minute." He took her by the hand and they walked into the narrow, quiet space. "Close your eyes. When I say 'go,' take one step forward."

Billy waited for the waft of the membrane to flicker across his face. "Go!" They stepped forward. Carol almost stumbled from the vertigo. He held her up. "Open your eyes."

They turned around and walked back to the street. Carol looked around intently. The churches were all the same. What's the big deal? Then, a three-wheeled car with a mirror-like skin sped by. She saw a streetcar coming in the other direction. She frantically glanced back and forth. Billy put his arm around her.

"Take a minute to get your bearings."

A family, a mother and three children, all wearing loose fitting pastel clothes, approached them on the sidewalk. Carol studied them closely. They nodded nonchalantly to Billy and Carol as they passed by.

"Still think I'm delusional?"

They headed south on Kingshighway.

"Where are we going?"

"We're going to take the subway to East St. Louis. To Diyami's place."

"There's no subway."

"There is here."

As they walked toward the subway stop at Lindell, Carol continued to look around with saucer eyes, trying to make sense of every little scrap of information. The discrepancies kept piling up.

The ornate entrances to the private streets of Portland and Westmoreland were the same, but an animated sign read "Gilded Age Historic District. Carriage and scooter tours available." The sidewalk was a mosaic of black-and-white squares. Up ahead, instead of the Park Plaza building, a famous Art Deco St. Louis landmark, was a slender high-rise covered in intricate, multi-colored designs—the handiwork of craftsmen using Hydraulic Brick products.

"What is that?" Carol said, pointing to the bizarre structure.

"That's the style they like here. You'll see a lot more downtown."

They came to the subway stop.

"If we're going to East St. Louis, why didn't we just drive there?" Carol asked.

"I've never tried to slip across there, so I wasn't sure that we could. It only works in certain places. Besides, I didn't want to leave the car in East St. Louis—our East St. Louis."

They rode the escalator down to the subway platform.

They got off at the stop on the Illinois side of the Eads Bridge. Carol froze as she saw the majestic line of tall, glittering apartment towers along the riverbank.

"Oh, my God!" She looked across the river. "Where's the Arch?" she exclaimed with horror.

"They don't have it here," said Billy matter-of-factly. Billy took a bit of devilish pleasure in Carol's disorientation. It was nice to be right about something for a change. They would find Meredith quickly enough, then all would be well.

"Diyami lives in that second building. Let's see if he's home."

He had to hold her hand as they walked. She kept twisting back and forth to take in each new sight. They reached Diyami's building, one of the three that were connected by the platform at the top. In the lobby, Billy scanned the directory and found "D. Red Hawk." He pushed the button next to it. After a little bit, Diyami's face appeared on the screen.

"Hello?"

"Diyami, this is Billy Boustany."

"Mr. Boustany, what are you doing here?"

"We're looking for Meredith," interrupted Carol, "Is she with you?"

"Oh, hello, Mrs. Boustany. I haven't seen her since I was at your home."

"We're worried sick that something has happened to her."

"Can we come up?" Billy said.

Diyami opened the door. It was obvious that he had been hastily straightening up the apartment as they rode up the elevator. He needn't have bothered.

"Diyami, Meredith's been missing for more than two days," Billy said.

"None of her friends have heard from her," Carol said.

"And she left her phone at home. That's why I think she slipped across."

"What does the phone have to do with it?" Carol asked Billy.

"Phones are useless over here. The batteries die the minute you cross over."

Carol couldn't help but be distracted by the view. Despite her fears about Meredith, she was hypnotically drawn to Diyami's panoramic windows. The river and downtown St. Louis were spread out below. Most of it was strange to her, from the spiraling mosaic skyscraper that towered over everything to the jumble of buildings along the riverfront where the Arch should have been.

Countless rooftop and balcony gardens dotted downtown with green. Hydrofoils zipped up and down the river in between massive barges. She spotted a few familiar sights scattered here and there, like the Eads Bridge and the dome of the Old Courthouse, but the overall vista gave her a headache. Carol was not used to having her mind blown.

She turned away from the windows and rejoined Billy and Diyami's conversation. They looked worried.

"The Knights?" Diyami said.

"That's what I'm thinking," Billy said.

"Who are the Knights?" Carol asked.

"The Knights of the Carnelian. They don't like us."

"The people who put on the parade and Fourth of July festival?"

"Yes. But they're different over here."

"Why don't they like us?"

"Because we're here. They think that, somehow, we're going to mess up their city."

"Do they know where Meredith is? Should we contact them?"

"No. They may have kidnapped her. They threatened me with the same thing."

"Oh God, Billy! How could you drag Meredith into this?"

"Mrs. Boustany," said Diyami, "Meredith really likes it over here. If she came across, she did it on her own. No one forced her."

"Can we go look for her?"

"Not a good idea," Billy said. "The Knights are probably watching for me. Maybe for Diyami, too."

"Let's call the police."

"The police are going to do what the Knights want, not what we want," Diyami said.

They continued batting around ideas and decided to make phone calls to places that Meredith might have gone, like the taffy shop and Whittemore's bar.

"I can also check with my parents," Diyami said. "It's possible she went to their place looking for me."

"Don't your parents live in Oklahoma?" asked Carol asked.

"We made that up," Billy said. "They live in Cahokia. Meredith and I were at their home a few weeks ago."

"Goddamn you, Billy Boustany!" Carol exploded. "How many lies have you told me?"

The first phone call didn't turn up anything. Diyami's parents hadn't seen Meredith. Diyami dialed the taffy shop and handed the phone to Billy.

"Churcha, this is Billy Boustany." He exchanged pleasantries, then gingerly asked if Meredith had been in the shop recently. He didn't want to alarm her and Scienca. They had not seen Meredith—was she all right?

He reassured her. "I'm sure she'll turn up. You know how these young people have minds of their own."

Billy hung up the phone and paced nervously. Carol couldn't keep her eyes off the window. He walked over to her and put his hand on her shoulder.

"I'm sorry I didn't tell you about all this. I was pretty sure you wouldn't believe me."

She pointed to the city below. "I don't know what to believe."

"That's how I've felt all summer."

"Mr. and Mrs. Boustany!" Diyami said. "It's Whittemore's. They've heard from her."

He handed the phone to Billy.

"Mary Jo? It's Billy."

"Where have you been? Are you mad at us?"

"No. A lot has been going on. Did Meredith come in?"

"She called yesterday and asked if I'd seen you. She said to tell you she would come by tomorrow around three o'clock."

"Did she sound okay?"

"I think so... It was a short call."

Billy hung up the phone. "Tomorrow. Three o'clock at the bar."

Carol let out a long sigh of relief, "Thank God!"

"You can't go there, Mr. Boustany," Diyami said. "It's a trap. The Knights will be waiting for you."

"What do they want with him? We'll just get her and go home," Carol said.

"Honey, they don't want people in our city to know about this place. They told me if I kept coming over here, they would make me stay permanently so I couldn't tell anyone back home."

They sat quietly for a minute, each wondering what to do. Carol walked back to the window. She watched the city and the river.

"I'll go. They don't know who I am. Those Knights aren't as smart as they think they are."

Carol opened the door to Whittemore's and went from the bright afternoon sunlight into cool, dim shadows. Her eyes adjusted as she approached the bar, where Mary Jo was wiping the counter. Carol introduced herself. Mary Jo broke out in a large smile, came around from behind the bar, and gave her a long, enthusiastic hug. They talked for a little while, then Mary Jo took to her the last table at the back of the room. Carol sat facing away from the front door. Mary Jo brought her a drink and a magazine to read. Carol handed her something.

Fifteen minutes later, Meredith came in, accompanied by two tough-looking guys. Mary Jo greeted her warmly.

"Meredith, nice to see you! Who are your friends?"

"James and Josh. They're showing me around town."

The two goons with over-developed shoulders and arms nodded to Mary Jo without expression. She smiled broadly at them. "Welcome to Whittemore's."

"Is my dad coming in?" Meredith asked.

"I gave him your message. Can I get you something to drink?"

"Three iced teas," James said. They went and sat at an empty table. Carol, at the back, listened to the conversation, but did not turn around. Meredith didn't notice her.

Mary Jo brought the drinks. As she set them down on the table, she spilled a glass into Meredith's lap, drenching the front of her dress.

"I'm so sorry," Mary Jo said. "Go to the ladies' room and blot that out before the stain sets."

Meredith started to get up, but Josh, who was across from her, shook his head.

"Hey! I don't want to ruin this dress!" said Meredith said. James, who was sitting next to Meredith, stood up to let her out. He silently mouthed the words, "It's okay" to Josh.

In the ladies' room, Meredith pulled paper towels from the dispenser. A folded piece of notepaper fell out. She picked it up.

> Honey, we'll get you out of here. Stay quiet
> and act normal.
> Love, Mom

Meredith, shocked, stared at the note for a moment or two. Then she put it in the trash can. She soaked the paper towels and blotted the tea out of her dress as best she could. As she came out of the bathroom, she walked past Carol at the back table. Carol glanced up and made momentary eye contact with her.

Several minutes later, Carol looked over at the clock on the back wall of the bar. She took a final sip of her drink, then stood up. She picked up a baseball bat that had been hidden beneath her table and walked to the table where Meredith sat with the two goons.

"Meredith, it's time to leave. Thank you, gentlemen, for bringing her to me."

Josh grabbed Meredith's arm to prevent her from standing up. James looked at Carol and laughed. A second baseball bat, wielded by Mary Jo, tapped him on the side of the head.

"What's so funny?" she asked.

"Please let go of her now," said a voice behind Josh. It was Walt, who tapped him gently on the shoulder with yet another baseball bat. After a few tense seconds, Josh complied.

Meredith stood up and hugged Carol. "Mom!"

"Not now, honey." She gestured for Meredith to head for the front door.

"I don't know what you're doing or why you're doing it," Carol said to the two goons, "but don't ever mess with—us— again!" With those last two words, she whacked first James, then Josh, on the knees with her bat. They screamed in pain.

Meredith watched her mother with amazement. Carol took Meredith's hand. "Let's go." She turned around and waved cheerfully to Mary Jo and Walt, "Thanks for all your help!"

"Jesus, Mom!" sputtered Meredith, as they stepped onto the sidewalk. "That was awesome!"

"Hurry. We're supposed to meet your father any minute. We're going to get you home."

She started to walk briskly up the sidewalk toward Grand Avenue and the Southside National Bank building. Holding her baseball bat in one hand, she pulled Meredith along with the other. Meredith tugged her hand away and stopped.

"I'm not going home. I want to stay here."

"Don't be ridiculous. Look what those awful people were doing to you."

"That was my fault. I was careless. When I'm with Diyami, I'll be fine."

"No. You're coming home. Diyami helped us find you. He and your father are waiting for us."

Carol successfully got Meredith walking again. They saw Billy and Diyami standing at the next corner. A Kahok Beer truck was parked across the street. Carol sped up and Meredith stayed with her. Meredith ran up to Billy and hugged him tightly. After a moment, she let go and gave Diyami an even longer and bigger hug. Billy and Carol looked at them, then at each other.

"How did it go?" Billy asked Carol.

"Piece of cake."

"Mom beat the crap out of the Knights' guys! She was unbelievable!"

Billy had not seen this side of Carol before. She gave him a demure little smile.

"We have to cross back over quickly," Billy said.

"I don't want to go. I'm staying here, with Diyami."

"Are you out of your mind?"

"Dad, you know how amazing this place is. I've got to stay."

"Absolutely not!" Billy and Carol said in unison.

"Diyami will keep me safe. The Knights don't mess with the Cahokians."

"That's true, sir," Diyami said.

"I don't care. You're coming with us!" Billy said.

"I know how to get home when I need to."

The three Boustanys bickered back and forth. Diyami tried to get a word in here and there, but to no avail. He realized he had to let this family dispute play itself out. People passing by on the sidewalk gave this loud group a wide berth and disapproving glances.

Two young men on scooters came out of nowhere and buzzed by on the sidewalk. Carol had to jump out of their way. "These damn scooters are all over the place around here," explained Billy "They're a pain in the ass."

"Oh, shit!" Meredith said.

"What?"

"Dad, don't you know? The scooter boys work for the Knights."

Three more scooters came from the opposite direction and stopped about ten feet away from the Boustanys. Billy turned around and saw more scooters approaching on the street and the sidewalk. In a heartbeat, they were surrounded.

A man edged his way through the cordon of scooters. It was Giles. He was wearing a tailored, cream-colored suit. Just like when Billy met him at the top of the Hydraulic Building, he sported a reddish-brown carnation in his lapel. It was the first time that Carol had seen a man in a suit with shorts. She was not impressed by his knobby knees.

"Mr. Boustany. I wish I could say that it was good to see you again, but it's not. You people keep showing up where you're not wanted."

"Screw you, Giles."

"We tried to reason with you, but, apparently, you didn't want to listen. So now you can all take advantage of our 'guest' services."

"Don't threaten my family!"

Giles nodded toward Diyami. "Is this one part of your family now?"

"None of your damn business."

"Everything in this city is my business."

"Giles, I understand. You win. We'll go back to our city. You won't see us again."

"Daddy!" yelled Meredith in a panic. Billy motioned to her to be quiet.

"Back to 'your side of the tracks,'" Giles said with a chuckle. "Too late for that."

Giles turned to one of the scooter boys. "Keep them here. A car is coming to take them downtown."

There was a loud thwump of a metal sliding door. The back of the beer truck opened up. Eight tall, tattooed Cahokians, including Diyami's friend Anak, jumped out, carrying long wooden chunkey sticks. They let out high-pitched shrieks and charged the scooter boys, who scattered quickly.

Now Giles was surrounded. Diyami said, "Be careful when you talk about who belongs where."

Sirens wailed in the distance. Giles smiled. "It will take more than a few Indians with sticks to change the outcome."

"How about this?" said Carol as she popped Giles in the knees with her baseball bat. He crumpled to the sidewalk, howling.

The sirens grew to a deafening volume. Police cars pulled up, blocking Gravois in one direction.

"Let's go!" shouted Diyami. He grabbed Meredith's hand and started toward the beer truck. He waved for Billy and Carol to follow. Anak and the other Cahokians brandished their sticks to hold off the cops and the scooter boys.

Another police car roared up and got between Billy, Carol and the truck. Billy grabbed her hand tight and pulled her to make an end run around the car. Billy felt a cop's hand grabbing his shirt. He was cut off from Diyami. He pulled himself free and made a quick turn in the other direction, dragging Carol along.

Meredith screamed from the cab of the truck, "Mommy! Daddy!"

Billy jerked his head toward her voice. The sudden move brought on a wave of vertigo. "Shit, no!"

He looked to the truck. He saw Meredith's mouth open in horror, but he heard nothing. He held Carol's hand tight. He watched Meredith and the truck dissolve into a pale gray haze. The vertigo doubled him over.

A car horn blared. Billy jumped back as a Camaro with a bad paint job swerved around him. The driver gave him the finger as she sped by. Billy and Carol were in the middle of Gravois, in front of a nail salon. Back in SD St. Louis.

"Fuck, fuck, fuck!" Billy yelled.

He pulled Carol to the safety of the sidewalk. She looked around. "Where did they go? What happened?"

"We slipped back to our side."

"Why did you do that?"

"I didn't. It happened by itself. It's done that before."

"What about Meredith? Let's go back there. Now!"

"Give me a moment! I need some quiet."

Billy took a few breaths and looked around. He led Carol to the side of the nail salon. No one was around. He held her hand, closed his eyes, and waited. Nothing. He walked about twenty feet farther back and tried again. Nothing.

"It's not working."

Carol became hysterical. "Billy, what's the matter with you? We've got to get her away from those police!"

He dragged her a block and a half to the front of the Southside National Bank building, his most reliable crossing point. He tried every one of his tricks to slip back across. Nothing happened. He felt completely flat. The whole idea of crossing from one world to another started to seem absurd. How could it ever have worked? How could he have ever believed it to be true?

He felt like he had woken suddenly from a vivid dream and was trying to get back into it. With every attempt, a little more of the dream faded away. After twenty minutes, Billy gave up. He was exhausted. His special power had left him, just like he had been warned.

Carol sobbed and pleaded with him to keep trying.

"It's gone," he said. "I can't." Those were the hardest words he had ever spoken.

Billy called a cab to take him and Carol to their car. They drove home and walked in the front door to deafening silence. Their footsteps on the tile floor echoed hopelessly to every far corner of the house.

"She'll come back," Billy said. "Soon."

Carol started to cry. She lunged at Billy and began pummeling him with both fists.

"You bastard! You had your stupid adventure and now our little girl is gone."

Billy accepted the torrent of blows that he knew he deserved. Eventually, Carol's fury burned itself out. They both stood in the front hall, sobbing. He reached out to hug her, but she turned away and ran up the stairs.

He called out: "She'll come back. Just be patient." He heard the bedroom door slam.

At least she didn't have a baseball bat handy, Billy thought.

Billy and Carol hardly spoke the next few days. There was nothing to do but wait. For Meredith to show up, or for a sign from her, or something. Billy had never felt so useless. He and Carol went through the motions of work to get them through.

She had to be at school on the first day back from HD. She plunged right in. During the intense early days of the schoolyear, Carol barely had a moment to think about anything. That's just what she needed right now. Both the eager kids and the troubled kids demanded her attention. Their needs and problems were right in her face. That's what she had always liked about teaching—there was no room for vague, abstract musings. Her day was filled by clear-headed decisions and compassionate actions, which left her in a satisfied state of exhaustion.

It was tougher for Billy.

Driving to work that first morning, he resolved to turn his attention back to the store while he waited. He tried to act normal as he walked into the Crestwood showroom. But the news of his abrupt departure from the consultant's meeting had spread. The employees smiled, nodded briefly, and went about their work. Only Dennis, the store manager, had the nerve to approach him.

"How are you doing, boss?"

"I'm fine ... fine. Carol and I had to take care of a little family issue that couldn't wait."

"Was there an accident? Did somebody get sick?"

"Nothing like that. We worked it out. It's all good. All good. Everyone's healthy ... really."

Dennis looked at him with concern. Billy realized that he was babbling. He excused himself and went into his office, closed the door and turned off the overhead lights. Sitting in that little refuge, he made a few attempts to open mail and look at messages on the computer, but he was swamped by second-guessing.

His mind dragged him through hundreds of ways he could have avoided this nightmare. Through every missed decision, large and small, that could have led to Meredith being with them, not stuck somewhere in HD. All the way back to his first stupid, stupid choice—to tell her about HD—which had seemed like a good idea at the time. He got hopelessly lost in a circular labyrinth of regret until he flopped his head on the desk and sank into a silent sleep.

Billy and Carol avoided talking about Meredith as they made dinner that night. They were both afraid that speculating about where she was, what she was doing, and when she might come home would jinx things. Also, Carol was pissed at Billy. He had deceived her all summer.

The next day, Billy tried to pay attention to business. He drove over to the Belleville store to check on a reorganized showroom layout and actually had a productive conversation with the store manager. He felt semi-normal until he crossed the Mississippi on the way back. Seeing downtown and the Arch through the windshield about did him in.

Back in his office, he recovered enough to read sales reports. They were as depressing as he had feared. The problem was always the same: decent enough traffic, but not enough sales, and the sure knowledge that, sooner or later, he would drown in the rising online tide.

HD had given Billy a summer of distraction, but now he had screwed that up, too. All he had left were the same old bad choices about the store. Oh yeah, and one new bad choice. Did he really want to create a cartoon version of his father that would hover over him every day, leering at the awful, misguided mess the store had become?

The phone rang.

"Hello. Boustany here."

"What the fuck, Billy!" Dan the banker said. "You walk out of the meeting. You don't answer your phone for three days. Then I hear you're back at work, but you still don't call me."

"I told you it was an emergency."

"Yeah...and?"

"We took care of it."

"That's wonderful. But now you've got to focus. You need to make a decision on Justin's strategy."

"I didn't like what I heard from him."

"This is a big deal, Billy. There have to be some changes—soon. If you don't like his ideas, what else are you going to do?"

Billy was quiet. Then, in an instant, he went from knowing nothing to knowing everything.

"I want out, Dan. I can't do this anymore. I'm done."

"The stores have a lot of debt, Billy."

"Well, I did my best, but I guess it wasn't good enough."

"You want the bank to absorb the loss?"

"Why don't you see if Justin wants to take over? I'm sure his ideas will protect your investment."

Just like that, Billy Boustany was done with the electronics business. He left it in the same way he had entered it twenty-three years earlier—with a spontaneous decision that came out of nowhere.

That evening, Billy told Carol what he had decided. She gave him a long hug. "It's about time. I was wondering how long you would keep beating your head against that particular wall."

"What am I supposed to do now?"

"No rush. You'll think of something."

He wondered what that could be. He had been running Duke's since his early twenties. Besides Carol and Meredith, it had been his whole life.

That evening was the first step of a softening between them. Carol realized that she couldn't blame him for everything. He had tried hard to get Meredith back, after all. It wasn't *entirely* his fault that their daughter (their!) had chosen to stay.

Also, Carol's brief glimpses of HD St. Louis began to swirl around in her mind—the spectacular views from Diyami's window, Gravois as an elegant boulevard, the weird patterned buildings. She struggled to make sense of it all. Just as Billy had done after his first visits, she relived each moment to savor every image, every detail. Her curiosity began to supplant her anger.

A week went by, but Meredith did not come back.

Over dinners, Carol began to ask Billy about his experiences in HD. What had he seen? Where had he gone? Who did he meet? Billy was all too happy to answer her questions. He still felt guilty about having excluded her for so long. Also, it was a relief to be able to tell the stories. He described the street supper and the Refugees Club, the Mezz and the Hydraulic Building, and his visit to Cahokia. He told her about Churcha, Scienca, and the taffy shop, and about how much they adored Meredith.

"I remember that candy," Carol said. "It was the best thing I ever put in my mouth."

Carol sometimes picked up on a detail that Billy hadn't thought much about. She connected the vegetation-festooned buildings, the automated awnings, and the wind towers on many corners as elements in a strategy to cool the city without our kind of air conditioning. As they talked about these things, it made more and more sense. HD St. Louis was all about keeping people mingling outdoors, not hidden inside sealed cocoons.

They resumed their late evening glasses of wine on the patio. The conversations continued.

Carol asked Billy to take her around the city so they could be in all the places he had visited in HD. As they walked, he recounted what he had seen and done. Naturally, Grand and Gravois was the first stop. He described the stores, the Asian market, the animated billboard, and streetcars. They went to South Grand, where he tried to explain the Sons of Rest street supper, Milo's music, and the crowd dancing on tables. They stood in front of the boarded-up Pelican building as Billy described the fantastic sculptures and mechanisms that enveloped its HD counterpart, the Refugees Club. Downtown was trickier. So many of the buildings were different in HD that it was hard for him to get his bearings. The Hydraulic Building was across the street from the Old Courthouse, but Billy had trouble figuring out exactly where the taffy shop, Needle Street, and Joplin Square would have been.

Every place they visited, they stood quietly with eyes closed, trying to imagine what might be going on at that moment in HD St. Louis. Maybe Meredith was there, a neutrino ghost sliding right through them. Billy secretly hoped that his ability might be revived in these moments, but it didn't happen. Every time he opened his eyes, they were still standing on the sidewalk in plain old St. Louis.

After Billy and Carol had disappeared from HD in the chaotic confrontation with the Knights, Meredith, Diyami and the rest of the Cahokians took off in the beer truck, driving as fast as they could. The police cars were on their tail when they crossed a bridge into Illinois, but then they were in the clear. The power of the Knights didn't extend across the state line.

Meredith was frantic when they got to Diyami's parents' home. She felt terrible about her choice to stay in HD. She had wanted Billy and Carol to give her permission or, at least, to acquiesce to her decision. She knew that they had to be going nuts over the way it had worked out. Diyami, Herbert, and Juliet all tried to calm her down. Eventually, she collapsed and slept for fourteen hours.

She was in a daze when she awoke the next day. Diyami and his parents advised her to take it easy and get her strength back. Juliet said the effects of intense stress could last for a while. Meredith would be ready to cross back over in a couple of days. In the meantime, they thought she would be safest in Cahokia, well beyond the reach of the Knights. All three of them had to go to work, so Meredith was left on her own in the apartment.

She got a cup of tea and sat out on the patio where she could see the Grand Plaza and the great city of Cahokia. A chill of fall was in the air. Groups of schoolkids were playing chunkey on the Plaza. The morning sunlight refracted through the Pyramid of the Children. Damn, it was beautiful. What should she do? She felt an amazing connection to Diyami and this place. On the other hand, her parents didn't know what had happened to her and were fearing the worst.

By afternoon, she had decided that she needed to go back. That evening, she broke the news to Diyami.

"I'm going home. I love you and I love it here, but I don't belong."

"What if I came with you?"

"That's crazy."

"Hear me out."

Diyami said his two days in SD St. Louis had profoundly affected him—especially the visit to Cahokia.

It was so empty, so barren, with not an Indian for miles around. The images were with him every day, and they still made him cry. He could sense the muffled voices of the ancestors down in the earth.

"Over here, we know what Cahokia can be. We've already built it. It's real and alive. But, over there, nobody knows. Your world needs a Cahokia like ours—a city that can rise up from the earth, built by native peoples who can become strong after centuries of defeat and scattering. Someone needs to plant the seed, to show that it's possible. What if it was us? You and me?"

Meredith was floored. "But you would have to leave everything behind. You might not be able to come back—ever."

"I know."

They talked for hours. Diyami explained that it just felt right to him. They could be like Corn Mother and Morning Star. And travel to the tribes to tell the story of Cahokia, old and new. Maybe he was being called by the spirits—though he didn't completely believe all that stuff. Maybe, like Meredith, he just wanted an adventure, to see someplace new. But, certainly, he would be more needed in SD. His Cahokia could get along just fine without him.

None of the counter arguments that Meredith raised bothered him. She sensed his deep calm about this plan.

He broached it to his parents the next day. At first, Herbert was skeptical, almost dismissive. Juliet started to cry. How could her only son do this to her? Then she said, "We must consult the spirits."

Juliet suggested that she, Diyami, and Meredith pay a visit to her teacher, who, long ago, had taught her how to communicate with spirits. This question was too profound for Juliet alone.

They took an electric water taxi through a series of canals to an outlying neighborhood of Cahokia. They knocked on the door of a small, white stucco house.

"She's quite old and she rarely leaves her house. But her wisdom is much deeper than anyone's," said Juliet. "Her name is Deirdre."

A stooped, white-haired lady answered. She was pleased to see Juliet again and to meet Diyami and Meredith. Inside, she served them cups of fragrant tea.

"I was present to give your name blessing when you born," she said to Diyami.

Juliet explained that Diyami was seeking his path, but faced a difficult choice. "Can you ask the ancestors for guidance?"

Deirdre assembled ritual objects on the table—sage, blue stones, and carved antlers—lit the sage, and began the ceremony. She raised her arms shakily as an invocation.

"Wise protectors they are giving. Serenity it resounds. Mother Earth and Father Sky are giving. I am thankful. It is well." She began a long song in Cahokian.

Juliet and Diyami closed their eyes. Meredith watched Deirdre, who looked back at her with a radiant smile. Meredith expected her to start moaning and shrieking, as Juliet had done in August. This was altogether different, more delicate and modulated. Deirdre's voice paused and trilled occasionally, and she twitched a bit. Meredith closed her eyes and imagined herself drifting down a lazy river underneath the dappled shade of willow branches.

Deirdre stopped singing and began to breathe loudly and slowly. She chirped, twitched, and nodded, as if reacting to a voice only she could hear. After several minutes, she quieted and opened her eyes.

"I saw two houses twisted together, one dark and one light. Much birthing to be done. And a fistful of arrows held together, unbreakable. Your quest pleases the spirits, Diyami. Be steadfast. Gather the arrows."

"What arrows?"

"Allies. You cannot succeed alone."

She turned to Meredith. "You need stronger magic, my dear. You will find it. The Great Mystery showed me a good man from an evil tribe. He will help you."

"Who is this man?" Diyami asked.

"I could not see his face."

"Will this come true?" Meredith asked.

Deirdre laughed. "You white women all ask me the same question. Prophecy is always true. How it manifests depends on us."

They stood up to leave. Deirdre took Meredith's hands in hers.

"When I was young, I was blessed to meet Corn Mother as she began her journey. Now, I am doubly blessed to meet her again." She turned to Diyami. "And to meet you, Morning Star."

They said their goodbyes and went from the dim light of the house to the bright sun of the street.

One day, Billy and Carol went to Cahokia. Billy's dinner table descriptions of the gleaming Indian city baffled Carol. It wasn't just a different version of a familiar place, but something completely new, the product of a historical trend that had no parallel in her world. Carol taught middle school history, so she had a pretty good idea of what had happened to Native Americans.

They stood at the base of Monk's Mound, the Temple of the Ancestors. Billy pointed out where the various things he had seen would have been. The canals and residential districts were out to the west, instead of corn fields and occasional warehouses. The enormous glass pyramid, the Temple of the Children, rose up about where the visitor's center was. The terraced buildings of the university, including the apartment of Diyami's parents, stood on the site of the cheap trailer park.

Carol couldn't correlate what she was seeing to what Billy was saying. It was too much, too unbelievable. She shook her head and got back in the car. Her feelings were complicated even further by the thought that, of all the places they had visited, this one was where Meredith was probably closest to them.

That night, they lay in bed and hugged each other. They both cried.

Carol said, "Even if we never see her, I just want to know that she's safe."

Billy had an idea. "Maybe we can send a message."

Carol had never met John. He had retired by the time she first set foot in Duke's Digital. The squalor of his tiny apartment took her aback. Decrepit, sagging furniture. The cat smell. Boxes of papers and ancient electronic equipment gathering dust. John himself was gaunt and he shuffled around slowly, but his eyes were bright—a good sign. Billy had told her about his recent heart procedure.

Billy told John about the events of the past few weeks. His decision to stop going to HD. "You told me to do that, but I waited too long." Meredith's disappearance and their abortive rescue attempt. How his crossing ability vanished at the worst possible time.

"That's pretty rough," John said. Billy pressed him to tell them about his own HD experience. "I met someone from over there. We were trying to figure out how the two worlds interacted. It was great. Then the Knights, that guy Martin, shut it all down pretty hard."

"At the hospital, you said you got there by radio."

"I made the first contact over shortwave. It was an accident."

Carol jumped in. "Could you try again? We would do anything to talk to Meredith or just to get a message from her."

"Even if I got through, I wouldn't know how to find my friend over there again. It was a long time ago. Who knows if she's even alive?"

"Please, John, please," Carol said.

John shook his head. He had long accepted his solitary life. He was scared of stirring up the sadness from 1982 and he never wanted to tangle with the Knights again. But he also didn't want to disappoint Billy and Carol.

"Let me think about it."

Billy thanked him profusely and gave him both of their phone numbers. As they got up to leave, John grabbed Billy's hand.

"Be careful. You can't trust those people."

A time bomb lay in the desk drawer in Billy's basement office—the scribbled note from Chris, the blues singer he had met up on the Mezz. He had done his best to forget about it. The bomb had already gone off once, when Carol discovered it, and it wasn't finished with him yet. The singer's sad request to contact his girlfriend haunted Billy.

Now that he felt the black burning pit in his gut from missing Meredith, he understood the singer's loneliness— more than he wanted to. Ignoring it would be a pretty crappy move.

Billy had spent his whole life avoiding messy emotional conversations. He was really good at screwing them up. If he called the singer's girlfriend, what would he say? What if she started yelling at him or crying? What if he just made her more miserable? And, whatever he did, Chris would never know the difference.

The evening after the visit to John's apartment, while Carol was at a parent-teacher meeting, he decided to rip the Band-aid off. He dialed the number.

"Hello, Sharon?"

"Yes."

"My name is Billy Boustany. You don't know me, but I have a message for you. It's from Chris."

"What?"

"He gave me your number and asked me to call."

Sharon's voice became agitated. "That asshole? He went out one night to play a gig and never came back."

Billy heard a baby crying in the background.

"He told me to tell you that he loved you."

"I haven't heard squat out of him in over a year!"

"He would tell you himself, but he can't"

"Where the hell is he? In jail?"

"No. But he's far away."

"Don't they have telephones?"

"Please trust me. He's doing okay, but he can't call and he can't come home. I know that he loves you. He would do anything to be with you."

"Oh God. I was just getting over him."

At least she didn't hang up. Billy admitted to her that, even though he had only met Chris once, he was convinced of his sincerity. He realized that, as he defended Chris' good heart and good intentions, he was also vouching for himself. Yes, he made mistakes and stupid decisions, but he wasn't trying to hurt or take advantage of anybody.

Sharon kept asking where Chris was. Billy kept dancing around the question. He didn't know what to say that wouldn't add to her confusion or make her think he was a nut case.

"It's really hard to talk about this over the phone. I'd be happy to meet with you someday and I could explain it better."

The phone was silent. Just as Billy thought she wasn't there anymore, he heard her crying softly. She said, "I guess so."

Billy said that he would get back to her soon. She thanked him for calling. They hung up. Billy felt his tension drain away. He had done it. Sitting in his basement office, Billy began to cry. For Sharon, for Chris, and for Carol, Meredith, and himself. He wished again he could undo all this HD crap. Actually, no, he didn't. He just wished it didn't hurt so much. Did HD leave everyone feeling awful? How could it be so damn good—like dancing to Milo, like the sweep of Cahokia's grand plaza, like listening to the taffy ladies' stories—and so fucking hard?

He remembered a word from a long-ago English class, "bittersweet." His teacher, a bearded, would-be poet who ended up teaching obtuse, snickering boys at a Catholic high school, had used it to explain complex emotions. You could feel more than one thing at the same time. You could be both happy and sad, and that was something good and human and beautiful. You didn't need to run away from those feelings.

At the time, it sounded like a bunch of bullshit to Billy

and his friends. But now it made sense. Every feeling in the world was racing through him all at once. He couldn't stop them. But why bother? It wouldn't work anyway. And the feelings couldn't hurt him. He didn't have to do anything but allow the parade to go on. From nowhere to somewhere, then back to nowhere again.

Carol was feeling good as they got ready for bed that night. Maybe John could get through to Meredith. Billy tried to temper her optimism.

"He wants to help, but it's a long shot. He's still very sick."

After their return from HD, Carol had begun to take sleeping pills to deal with stress. She was snoring soon after they turned out the lights.

Billy lay there watching the shadows of the trees in the moonlight on the ceiling. He fell into a reverie about the gorgeous view from the top of the Hydraulic Building and his conversation up there with Martin. One of the pivotal moments of his adventure. The shadows shifted. Must be the wind coming up.

Just as Billy was drifting into sleep with the image of the two fountains converging in the distance, the lower window sash raised slowly.

Two dark figures burst into the room and grabbed Billy and Carol. In seconds, their hands were bound and their mouths taped shut. They were hustled down the stairs and into the back of a van in the driveway. Carol and Billy looked at each other in wide-eyed terror as the van sped away. It bounced around for several minutes, then stopped. The back door opened. Billy and Carol were dragged out onto a deserted parking lot. They thought this was when they were going to be murdered.

The two hooded figures ripped the tape off Billy and Carol's mouths. They shoved something down each of their throats and held their mouths closed with their hands. The convulsions began.

"I apologize for calling you so late," Giles Monroe told the chief psychiatrist at the State Asylum. "Two new residents are on the way to you. Put them in the Cantwell wing."

"Should they be sedated, according to the protocol?"

"No. That won't be necessary. Just isolate them."

John agonized all night over Billy's request. He wanted to help, but the thought of trying to contact the other world brought back the agony he had felt that Sunday afternoon in 1982, when the man from over there had forced him to decide his whole future right on the spot. He hated the choice he made, though he knew he would have hated the other choice just as much. John successfully buried his anguish for years, until Billy showed up at his front door. Now, Billy and Carol were the ones pushing him to make a big decision.

The stress caused the pain in his chest to throb. He considered taking the nitroglycerin pill they gave him at the hospital for an emergency. He held off and, by morning, he felt a little better.

He decided to call Billy to tell him that he couldn't do it. All he wanted was to get back to what, for him, was normal—living out his life in peace in the apartment.

He dialed Billy's number. There was no answer. John left a message for Billy to call him right away. An hour later, he called again. Still, no answer. He left another message. He tried Carol's number with the same result.

Something wasn't right. Given yesterday's impassioned pleas, they would call back right away if they could. He feared the worst had happened. He sat by the phone for a long time, praying that it would ring. It didn't. Now, he was all alone with the decision. There was no one to let him off the hook.

He started rifling through the boxes on his dining room table. It took him a while to find his logbook from 1982. He moved the oscilloscope, turntable, and records that were piled on his old Heathkit radio in the corner. He put it on the table, got a washcloth, and wiped off the thick layer of dust. He went into the kitchen and got a Coke out of the refrigerator. He plugged the radio into the outlet and put on his headset. He closed his eyes for a moment, then flipped the switch on the front panel. Would it work after all these years? The power light glowed green.

Billy and Carol awoke in a gray room. Gray walls, gray floor, gray ceiling. It had twin beds, a dresser, a table, and two chairs. All gray. A small window high on one wall revealed only gray sky. Though the door was locked, it didn't look like a jail, but it was definitely not a hotel or any place remotely welcoming. After the gray light in the window had brightened, a man in a white coat brought them trays with breakfast without saying a word. Billy and Carol were thankful that they hadn't been killed.

"I think we're in HD," Billy whispered. He signaled to Carol to speak carefully. They were probably being monitored.

The door opened and a man on crutches entered, Giles Monroe. Two assistants followed with a chair for him.

"Mr. and Mrs. Boustany, I hope you find the accommodations to your liking."

"What do you want, Giles?" Billy asked.

"Nothing." Giles smiled broadly, "I already have everything I want." He was in full gloating mode. "We warned you, as nicely as we could, but neither you nor your foolish daughter listened. So now we will do things by the book."

"Where's Meredith?" Billy asked.

"I thought she was with you."

"Don't bullshit us," Carol said. "If you touch one hair on her head, you'll need more than crutches."

Giles laughed. "Your days with a baseball bat are over, Mrs. Boustany."

"I only wish I had aimed higher than your knees."

Giles grilled Billy and Carol. Who knew about their visits?

"No one." Billy wasn't going to say a word that might get John in trouble.

Who was that Cahokian boy? "I don't know. Some kid Meredith met."

What did the people in the bar know? "Nothing. Just that they don't like you."

"You expressed a desire to see more of our world. Now you will have a lifetime to do so." Giles left and the two assistants described the procedure. They had given this little speech before. Stay here in the Asylum for six months to a year. Then, depending on your good behavior, you will be set up with an apartment and jobs. "Good behavior" meant not saying a word about where you came from. "Bad behavior" would bring you back here.

The assistants left them a stack of books and newspapers, so they could orient themselves. They also gave Billy and Carol a brochure about the CSP and two application forms to be filled out. "This will get you set up in the system."

Billy didn't think Meredith had gotten home, but he wasn't sure what had happened to her. She could be in Cahokia or locked up in a room like this one. He and Carol wondered if Giles really didn't know where Meredith was. Maybe he wasn't lying about that.

Carol devoured the reading material over the next few days. The books covered twentieth-century history. Despite her fear and despair, she was fascinated by the fantastical tale of a very different century—the long peace marred only by the vicious British-Indian war of independence, the rise of the Argentinian confederation, the spread of brick technology from St. Louis to the rest of the world.

Billy scanned the newspapers for anything that might shed light on Meredith's fate. There was nothing. He saw that a big Cahokian event was starting soon. Indians from all over were arriving to prepare for the "Three Worlds Festival." Herbert Red Hawk had mentioned this to him last summer. Billy also checked out the comic strips. He didn't think they were all that funny.

Herbert said that permission from the Cahokia elders was required for Diyami's mission. He spoke to the people he knew best on the Cahokia Council. Fortunately, he was a highly respected academic or no one would have listened to his bizarre request. A special meeting of the Council was scheduled.

The night of the Council meeting came. It was one of the strangest experiences of Meredith's life. The elders, a dozen white-haired men and women, listened to Diyami and Herbert tell the story of the two worlds, each with its own Cahokia, that interacted ever so slightly.

The elders asked Meredith, a supposed native of this other world, to explain herself. She awkwardly tried to repeat the theories about SD and HD that Billy had shared with her. A few of the elders scoffed that this whole thing was a waste of their time. Others were more sympathetic. They didn't trust the Knights of the Carnelian for one minute. If the Knights opposed something, that was a mark in its favor.

Then Juliet, as one of Cahokia's leading spirit speakers, weighed in. She said she had consulted Deirdre. The Great Mystery didn't like the idea that another Cahokia was shrouded in darkness. One elder, a speaker himself, backed her up. His own spiritual investigations had brought a similar answer.

The Council members began a heated debate. They kept switching back and forth between English and Cahokian, so Meredith couldn't follow what they were saying. But, in the end, they gave their approval. Diyami and Meredith could become Morning Star and Corn Mother for SD.

Now, they had to actually do it.

Diyami packed a bag with books and documents about the New Cahokia. He wanted to make sure that he had the complete story. The elders gave him a suitcase with ancient Cahokian artifacts, beautiful pottery and carvings. He could sell these for seed money to begin his work.

Meredith's job was to get them across. But she had never crossed from HD to SD on her own; she had always been with her father. And they had to watch out for the Knights. Diyami organized an escort of Cahokians for protection.

Late one night, he said his goodbyes to his parents and he and Meredith boarded a Kahok beer truck and headed to Grand and Gravois. As the escorts stood guard, Meredith tried to slip them across. Nothing happened. They went to a few other places that she knew—the Refugees Club and the church on Kingshighway.

Despite her best efforts, again and again, they got nowhere. Exhausted, they drove back to Cahokia as the sun was coming up. Juliet and Herbert met them. Diyami, who was normally very even-tempered, was dejected.

"What do we do now?"

"We wait," Juliet said. "The spirits are with us."

Leonora Matsui stood anxiously under a tree next to the Grand Basin in Forest Park. She had extrapolated from a tiny shred of data, then applied her flimsy results to precession equations that were almost three decades old. Was she correct? Not very likely, but without taking simultaneous measurements from each side, calibration was impossible.

It was the appointed time, exactly noon. Two columns of water erupted from the basin, sparkling in the October sun. As they bent toward each other to form the arch, Leonora felt a shot of air on the back of her neck and turned around as the shimmering subsided. She rushed to the figure slumped on the grass.

"John? John? Are you okay?" He lay still. Then, his back heaved violently as he gulped for air. He turned his face toward her. When their eyes met, the biggest grin she had ever seen lit up his face. She lay down and put her arms around him.

"Sorry," he muttered, still breathing heavily. "I had a heart attack a few weeks back." She hugged him close.

After a few minutes, he was able to stand. She helped him into her car parked nearby and drove toward home. Now she was grinning. "Our math was damn good!" John nodded.

They passed an entertainment district, with an amusement park, gaudy theaters, and the opulent, baroque

Opera House. John watched out the window to take it all in. Then he looked over at Leonora as she drove.

"We should have done this a long time ago."

"Yes."

"However," he said, "there's a problem I need your help with."

Billy and Carol had been in the locked room for a week. The food wasn't bad, but the reading material was running low, even with a fresh newspaper each day. Carol asked the silent orderly for a deck of cards, a pencil, and a pad of paper. With the next meal, he brought the cards, a crayon, and one sheet of paper. Carol figured that they weren't supposed to have enough paper to write a journal or make paper airplanes with letters begging for rescue. But they could play gin rummy and keep score.

She and Billy got more lax about talking. Even if they were being monitored, what could they say that the Knights would be interested in? They knew nothing and had no control over what was going to happen to them. It began to sink in that they might never be going home, might never see anyone they knew again. Fighting off despair became their main focus.

The days were spent reading (and re-reading), holding each other, and crying. Billy came up with the idea that they should sing to annoy the orderly when he brought their meals. "Ninety-Nine Bottles of Beer on the Wall."

Each time they heard his footsteps, they would start up at a different number. Billy hoped that he would think they were singing this song all the time when he wasn't there. If they were going to be in a mental hospital anyway, they had nothing to lose by acting crazy. You had to find a bit of fun wherever you could.

When they were finishing breakfast one morning, the door opened. They started to sing, at thirty-two, then stopped abruptly. Two people walked in, Martin Matsui and a woman, also Asian, a few years younger than him.

"Good morning, Billy. It's nice to see you again. I often think of our lovely conversation last summer. And you must be Mrs. Boustany." He shook their hands warmly. "This is my niece, Leonora. She's assisting me with your case."

"We have a 'case'?"

"I was distressed when I learned that you were being held here."

"Thanks. Your 'distress' (Billy made air quotes) is very comforting."

Leonora spoke up. "We're getting you out of here. You're going home."

"That's not what Giles said."

"He has reconsidered, at my urging," Martin said. "Occasionally, he listens to me." Martin enjoyed the shocked expressions on Billy and Carol's faces. "I suggest we move expeditiously. Giles has been known to change his mind."

Leonora handed Billy and Carol each a cloth bag. "Clothing that is more suitable." They took turns changing in the bathroom. When she came out, Carol stuffed as many books and newspapers as she could in the bag. It would be amazing if she could get them home.

"Don't make eye contact and let me do the talking," Martin said as he opened the door. They breezed down the corridor past orderlies and nurses. One began to protest, but Martin waved her off. Knights could not be challenged.

Outside, they hurried to Martin's long black limousine.

"We have a surprise for you," Leonora said. She opened the door. John sat in the back seat. Billy and Carol leapt in and hugged him. He was a little embarrassed. He wasn't used to such affection.

"Where are we going?" Carol asked Martin.

"To Cahokia. To see your daughter. There may be a delay at the river. The Cahokia festival is in full swing and it was decided that today, of all days, was a good time for bridge maintenance." Martin shrugged his shoulders in the universal sign to acknowledge dumb bureaucracies.

There was a lot of catching up to do on the way to Cahokia. John described how he made radio contact with Leonora.

"It was a fluke, really. It had been twenty-eight years since the last time." And how he had been able to cross. "Another fluke. We made a lucky calculation."

"Not luck. Skill!" Leonora joked. She gave John an affectionate jab.

Martin explained what would happen next. His deal with Giles was that they would all go home as soon as possible and—this was most important—they would solemnly promise never to talk about this other world with anyone. Billy and Carol quickly agreed. After a week locked in the asylum, they were not going to negotiate.

Martin had made arrangements with the Cahokian elders for a crossing tonight at midnight. Billy said he no longer had the ability to cross.

"I'll take care of that," Martin said. As predicted, they got stuck in a traffic jam on the bridge. Carol didn't mind. It gave her the chance to look at downtown St. Louis in HD one last time.

The limousine stopped at the back of the Temple of the Children. Because the road was clogged with people and vehicles, the driver suggested they would be better off walking the rest of the way. Billy checked with Martin and John, the two oldest in the group.

"My doctors want me to be walking more," John said. Martin waved his cane and was game to walk. They all got out of the limousine and set off to cross the Grand Plaza toward Diyami's parents' apartment.

When they rounded the corner of the temple, they saw the Grand Plaza filled with a vast throng of people. Phalanxes of ceremonial dancers wore feathered and beaded costumes of every style and color imaginable. Bells on thousands of ankles jingled to accompany drum, flutes and singing.

Onlookers in street clothes wandered among the dancers and along a midway of tents and booths. Most were Native Americans, but many other visitors mingled in the crowd. Small airplanes looped in the bright blue sky, drawing designs in red and white smoke. A raised platform, shaded by a canopy decorated with stylized images of mythical creatures, stood directly in front of the temple.

People crowded around the platform to take pictures of an old, green station wagon on top of it. It had been moved outside from its normal location inside the temple so more people could see it. Forty-foot tall banners on each side of the platform rippled in the breeze. Two of them were large blow-ups of old photos of an Indian man and a white woman.

Next to the woman was another banner showing a drawing of a seated woman with corn stalks growing out of her upraised palms. Next to the man was a drawing of a dancing man with a hawk-billed mask and feathers hanging from his outstretched arms. Billy pointed them out to Carol: "Corn Mother and Morning Star." With all the music, she couldn't hear him. "I'll tell you later," he said.

They passed a row of tents selling food, everything from buffalo steaks and fresh venison jerky to wild rice bowls to cranberry-maple pies. A huge tent, topped by an ornate sign, was selling Kahok Beer. After a week of asylum food, Billy was sorely tempted by the aromas all around him. Carol tugged on his elbow to keep him moving. Now was not the time.

As they made their way up the east side of the Plaza, they saw a rectangle of temporary bleachers. Tall video screens displayed the chunkey game under way on the other side of the bleachers. A cheer went up as a player scored. On the screen, the player raised his stick high in celebration. Diyami would later tell them that today's games were the semifinals of the national championship, with the final game, which would draw an even more enthusiastic crowd, taking place tomorrow.

Dodging exuberant chunkey fans, ceremonies, dance group rehearsals, and assorted revelers, they reached the University apartment building. They took the elevator to the fifth floor and entered Herbert and Juliet's apartment. Meredith leapt into her parents' arms. The three of them spun around until they almost fell over laughing.

Diyami soon joined the group hug and Herbert and Juliet patted them on the back. As everyone calmed down, Billy introduced Martin, Leonora, and John. Martin had spoken with Herbert by phone, but they had not met in person.

Billy, with his arm around John, said to Meredith, "Remember I told you about the guy at my dad's store who showed me Radio Moscow when I was a kid? This is him!"

A table was set with a spread of food that made Billy forget about the delicious smells from the midway. As they ate, Martin reminded everyone that the crossing was set for midnight. Juliet said that it would happen at the top of the Temple of the Elders, where the Cahokian elders were preparing a ceremony. Billy and Carol noticed that she was fighting back tears as she spoke.

Meredith took her parents aside. Carol asked her if she was ready to go back with them this time.

"Yes," Meredith said, "but not just me."

She explained Diyami's plan to build a new Cahokia in SD.

"But he would be leaving everyone over here behind," Carol said.

Meredith nodded. Diyami and his parents understood that and they still supported him. Carol broke away and went across the room to give Juliet a hug. She knew what it felt like to have a child disappear into another world.

After the meal, everyone was talking to everyone else except for John and Leonora who drifted into a corner and kept to themselves. The crush of the crowd on the Grand Plaza and the excited conversation in the apartment were too much for John. He was thrilled to be at Leonora's side once more, but he had been suddenly yanked out of his solitary life. Leonora sensed his discomfort and whispered sweetly to him.

The others were having quite a party. Herbert encouraged them to go out to the patio to watch the parade that marked the end of the chunkey game. Lines of feather-clad dancers with buffalo headdresses swirled around the players from the victorious team, which was from the Sioux of South Dakota.

The voice of an announcer introducing each player by name to the crowd echoed off the pyramids. Billy looked back inside and saw that Martin was alone on the sofa, sipping tea. Billy went in and sat down beside him.

"In all my years," Martin said, "I have never come to this festival before. It's remarkable."

"Yes."

"And this sassafras bark tea that Mrs. Red Hawk made is refreshing after a long day."

"Why are you helping us? You warned me to stay away, just like Giles and Jennifer did."

"That's the standard policy, but that doesn't make it always the right thing to do. Sometimes Giles lets his emotions get the better of him. He starts to think that he's the next Mr. Hines. I knew Mr. Hines, Mr. Hines was a friend of mine. Giles Monroe is no Mr. Hines."

Billy had no idea who Mr. Hines was.

"I still don't understand why you're taking a chance to help us. You don't owe us anything."

"Because of family. My niece Leonora came to me day before yesterday. A long time ago, I had to put an end to the work that she and Mr. Little were doing. He is so brilliant and we feared the consequences. I was harsher than I should have been and have always regretted that."

Billy listened. Hearing John described as "brilliant" flabbergasted him. What had he missed all these years?

"Then there was your father. He gave the Knights many years of valuable service. And we are an honorable organization. We remember our debts. I had to remind Giles of this. It all happened before his time."

Billy was doubly flabbergasted. "My father?"

"Of course, he never knew exactly who he was working for. Some things are better left unsaid."

"What could my father have possibly done for the Knights?"

Martin took a sip of tea as he searched for the right words. "Product development."

Billy had no idea what to say. He would spend the rest of his life trying to make sense of this information.

"So you can thank your father for today's events. I always say that family is the most important thing."

Billy wandered out to a far corner of the patio and leaned on the railing. He was in no way capable of talking to anyone. The festivities on the Plaza continued below.

What an ending to his five-month adventure! It had all worked out. His family was back together. Martin, Herbert, Juliet, and even John had come out of nowhere to get him here. Not to mention the others he had met along the way, like Mary Jo and Walt at the bar and the taffy ladies. Even his long-dead father had played a part! He couldn't begin to get his head around that.

He watched the masses of costumed dancers and the cheering crowds. The late afternoon sun glinted off the banners of Corn Mother and Morning Star in front of the Temple of the Children.

The spectacle reminded him of the last scene of "Return of the Jedi," when millions of people across the galaxy celebrated the destruction of the Death Star and the defeat of the Empire. Luke, Leia, and Han Solo hugged each other and C-3PO danced with the Ewoks. The ghosts of Obi-Wan Kenobi and Anakin Skywalker looked on beatifically. Everyone was completely happy.

But Billy wasn't so happy. What had he done to deserve a moment like this? He hadn't defeated anybody. An adventure was supposed to make you a better person, but he didn't feel like a better person. To be honest, he had to admit that he had stumbled through his whole adventure, and had messed it up more than once. He was damn lucky that no one had gotten seriously hurt in the process. Even that asshole Giles would recover from his shattered knees.

Billy wished that he had done something noble and courageous along the way, but he hadn't. And in a few hours, it would all be over. The sun was getting low in the west and clouds were rolling in. As it grew a little darker, he saw the beacon atop the distant Hydraulic Building flashing. He had an idea.

Billy raced inside and found Herbert. "Can your friend lend me a beer truck and a driver? I have to go somewhere."

"You're crossing tonight."

"I'll be back in time. This will only take a couple of hours. Please."

Herbert made the call. Billy found Carol, who was deeply engaged in comforting Herbert and Juliet about Diyami's impending departure.

"I'm going back to St. Louis for a little bit. Cover for me."

"What will Martin say?"

"I'm not telling him. It's easier to beg for forgiveness afterward than to ask for permission before."

Ten minutes later, he slipped out of the apartment and met the truck behind the building. Anak was the driver once more. He was glad to see Billy, but not pleased about having to leave the festival just as the hardcore partying was beginning. On the way, Billy told Anak to drop him at the Hydraulic Building, then to circle the block. He should be back in a half-hour or so.

Billy looked around warily as he got out of the truck in front of the Hydraulic Building. He figured that no one would be looking for him. If he moved fast, he wouldn't be noticed in the rush hour crowd. He crossed the lobby and took the elevator up to the Mezz. He crossed a few bridges from one roof to another.

Billy couldn't find what he was looking for, so he doubled back to the Hydraulic Building, then took other bridges in a different direction. Nothing looked familiar. He was lost. He was getting frantic and ran off over yet another bridge. He was breathing heavily when he saw some people standing in a park under a maple tree whose leaves had turned bright red. He heard a snatch of music. He ran toward it.

Chris, the musician he had met on the Mezz a few months ago, was singing for a handful of onlookers:

"Everybody wants to know why I sing the blues. Well, I've been around a long time, I really have paid my dues."

The song ended. People tossed money into Chris' open guitar case. Billy approached him.

"Remember me?"

He looked at Billy for a moment, then broke into a smile.

"Hey, California!"

"I gave Sharon your message."

"Bless you. What did she say?"

"She still misses you."

Chris could hardly believe what he was hearing. He embraced Billy. "My brother!"

"Want to see her yourself?"

"Yes, yes!"

"How about tonight?"

Chris hugged him harder.

Billy noticed a suspicious-looking character walking briskly toward them across a bridge. He pointed him out to Chris. The man broke into a run.

Billy suggested they get going, fast. Chris knew the Mezz by heart. He quickly found an elevator that took them to a busy sidewalk. He led Billy through some back streets toward the Hydraulic Building. They ran right past the taffy ladies' shop. Billy hesitated and watched them through the window. He longed to dash inside and be with them one last time, if only for a moment, but police sirens were echoing off the downtown buildings. He had to keep moving.

The truck rounded the back corner of the Hydraulic Building and Billy flagged it down. The sirens got louder as he and Chris hopped in. Anak took off, weaving through the traffic. After a few minutes, they raced over the bridge to Illinois and safety.

Everyone at the apartment had been alarmed by Billy's mysterious disappearance, and were relieved when he returned, even when accompanied by a stranger with a guitar case. Billy whispered to Carol that this was the guy who had given him the phone number.

Martin was annoyed. "I won't stand for any more surprises, Mr. Boustany." Billy took him aside to beg forgiveness and patch things up. It worked. Actually, Martin admired Billy's courage, though he didn't admit it.

Darkness had fallen with heavy cloud cover and a forecast of rain. Everyone went out to the patio to watch the fireworks display that marked the end of the day's festival events. After the last starburst, Juliet gathered everyone into a circle for a ceremony to prepare for the crossing.

She burned incense and led a chant, but did not enter a shamanic trance. She and Herbert both looked pretty glum as they held Diyami's hands. Martin made eye contact with them from across the circle. He nodded to let them know that he understood their grief.

Juliet reviewed the plans for the crossing at midnight. "The elders chose the time because the full moon is propitious, though we may not see it because of the weather."

John spoke up. "I'm not going." He was holding Leonora's hand. "I'm staying here."

"If you insist," Martin said, "then there will be five of you crossing, just as originally planned." Chris had been quiet since he got to the apartment because he didn't know these people or what to believe about the idea of going home. Now, he smiled. It was really going to happen.

Billy and Carol were shocked by John's announcement. It brought back memories of Meredith's resistance, which had begun the chain of falling dominoes that had led them all to be standing in Cahokia today.

They went over to him and Leonora. "Are you sure?"

"There's nothing for me over there. I'm worn out. You two are the only ones who will miss me." John took a key out of his pocket and pressed it into Billy's hands. "Go to my apartment. My radio and logbooks are on the table. They're yours."

"I wouldn't know what to do with them."

"Weren't you paying attention to what I taught you in the repair room?" John laughed. He had actually said something funny. Carol gave him a big hug.

"They might come in handy," Leonora said. "You never know."

Juliet and Herbert spoke with Martin. "The spirits prophesied that you would come to help Diyami on his mission. They said to expect 'a good man from an evil tribe.'" Martin got a kick out of that description.

Intermittent rain was falling as midnight approached. The elders of the Cahokia Council and a host of dancers, drummers and flute players gathered at the top of the Temple of the Ancestors surrounded by torches. Billy, Carol, Meredith, Diyami and Chris stood at the center of the circle.

The elders had prepared them for the journey by painting their faces, braiding feathers into their hair, and draping them with heavy necklaces. Billy felt like an astronaut at a rocket launch. Diyami's parents stood close by him, bravely holding back their tears.

A group of young men carried Martin, who was too frail to climb the steps, to the top of the pyramid. He spoke to each of the travelers.

To Chris: "Good luck, young man. Don't think too badly of us over here."

To Diyami: "If you can create something one-tenth as beautiful as our Cahokia, you will have earned your mythical status. I will keep an eye on your parents for you"

To Meredith: "Your adventure has a long way yet to go. I hope you continue it with the grace that you have shown us." He then gave her an envelope. "Don't open this until after you get across."

To Carol: "I wish we had more time to get better acquainted." He pointed to the cloth bag with books and newspapers she was holding. "We could have fascinating discussions about history."

To Billy: "Of all the visitors I've met over the years, you have been the most challenging and the most enjoyable. You caused me to break many rules. Fortunately, as an elder statesman, I can get away with it."

Billy asked him to take care of John.

"I will. He's family now."

The ceremony followed with music, dancing, and speeches in Cahokian. When it ended, Martin went over to the drummers and had a brief conversation. The lead drummer nodded. Martin turned back to the full group.

"I'm not used to doing this with an audience, so we're in uncharted territory." There were a few chuckles. "When you see me nod, be completely still and silent."

Martin lined the travelers up—Carol and Meredith in the center, with Diyami on the other side of Meredith and Billy, then Chris, on the other side of Carol. He walked along the line and handed each of them a pill. "Swallow these to ease your journey."

Martin took a place between Carol and Meredith and held their hands. A drizzle began to fall. The travelers closed their eyes and waited.

Martin whispered to them, "Good luck, children."

The drums began again. Chanting voices surrounded them. Billy turned around and saw John, who gave him a farewell wave. After a minute or so, Martin nodded. Everyone was quiet. A moment later, one of the Cahokians banged a drum as loud as he could. The single thwack startled everyone. Martin tugged at Carol's and Meredith's hands, signaling them to step forward. When they did, he let go.

The travelers found themselves standing alone atop the dark mound. Martin, the elders, the drummers, John, Leonora, Herbert, and Juliet were all gone. They looked at each other in silent amazement.

Chris, who had never crossed on purpose before, was shaken. Carol checked to make sure he was all right. The sky was clear and the light of the full moon was enough to guide them down the gravel staircase to the base of the mound.

They tried to flag down a couple of passing cars to no avail. They started walking toward Collinsville. Eventually, they found a run-down bar in a seedy cinder block building on the edge of town. Inside, there was a bartender and two half-drunk customers. The middle-aged bartender eyed them with suspicion. Five people in weird clothes, face paint, and feathers. One had long hair and face tattoos, another was carrying a guitar case. They looked like refugees from a bedraggled carnival.

Billy's plan was to get a cab to take them back to St. Louis, but in the excitement of the crossing, he had forgotten about money. After having been dragged out of his house in the middle of the night, he didn't have any. There was only the change in Chris' guitar case, which was not nearly enough and, also was in odd-looking HD bills and coins that a taxi driver might not accept.

Billy used all of his customer-facing charm to strike up a conversation with the bartender to convince him to lend them fifty bucks. He got nowhere. The bartender had heard hundreds of sad sack stories and sketchy schemes over the years. No one was going to con him out of his money. Then Billy tried a different approach.

"Did you ever watch ads by the Duke of Discounts when you were a kid? He was my father." The bartender's eyes lit up. "No shit? I loved those!"

All five of them crammed into the cab. As they crossed the Mississippi on I-64, the Arch never looked so good. They stopped in front of Sharon's four-family apartment building to drop Chris off. He embraced Billy.

"You don't even know me and you've done more for me than anyone ever has. I'll never be able to thank you enough."

Billy got back into the cab as Chris bounded up onto the front porch and rang the doorbell. After a few moments, a light on the second-floor turned on. Then, the front door opened. They watched a woman throw her arms around Chris and pull him inside.

As they drove off in the cab, Meredith patted Billy on the shoulder, "Way to go, Dad."

When they got home, Billy opened the door to find mail scattered all over the front hall floor. Carol got a bottle of wine from the refrigerator. They all toasted to celebrate, then collapsed into bed, exhausted.

Billy awoke late the next morning to the roar of the neighbor's leaf blower. Carol was already up. He threw on his bathrobe, then saw the HD pants from the day before draped over a chair. He searched through the pockets to find John's key. He put it carefully in the top drawer of his dresser. He had to get to the apartment soon, before anyone figured out that John wasn't coming back. He thought of Leonora's words: "You never know."

When he came down to the kitchen, Carol and Meredith were already up. Meredith was making scrambled eggs. Carol poured him a cup of coffee. She pointed him to look out the window. Diyami stood in the drifts of yellow and brown leaves that had accumulated on the patio. His arms were raised in front of him, palms up, and his eyes were closed.

"He's giving thanks to the Great Spirit for our safe passage," Carol said.

Billy watched and sipped his coffee. He could hardly believe that, after everything, the family had made it back here together. Somewhere, Ewoks were dancing.

Meredith handed him the envelope that Martin had given her before they crossed.

"It's so cool." He opened it and pulled out a note written in the shaky hand of an old lady.

> Dearest Meredith,
> We cherish every moment that we spent with you. We will never forget your sweet smile and the charming spirit that you brought into our little shop.
> Our old friend Martin (one of our first customers) said that we could help you with your long journey. The secret is: grains of paradise.
> Love always and forever,
> Churcha Crockett
> P.S. Martin promised that you wouldn't compete with us in the taffy business. We're holding you to that.
> Scienca Crockett

"What are grains of paradise?" Billy asked.

"The secret ingredient, Dad. It's real! I Googled it. Grains of paradise is an African spice. We can get it and make the taffy the right way."

Acknowledgements

Extra special thanks to:

My dearest Becky Brittain von Schrader, who supported, challenged, and sparkled me on every step of this journey.

Mac Mayfield, who understood the strange beauty of HD, dreamed up the CSP, and invented Amperic Bricks.

Special thanks to:

David Carkeet, who believed in a book that came to him out of the blue, and helped me make it better.

Bill Kwapy, who gave me detailed, insightful notes and suggested the cummings poem.

Marcia Meier, editor extraordinaire, who guided me through the mysteries of publishing.

Thanks to all who read various drafts and offered comments and encouragement, including:

Jerry Adler, Huntley Barad, Myra Blanc, Charlie Claggett, Katie Claggett, Tom Conway, BP Cooper, Brittain Cooper, Robert Fishbone, Laurie Justiss, Lee

Lawless, Barry Leibman, Erica Leisenring, George Mayfield, Bill McClellan, Tom Schlafly, Karen Techner, Sarah von Pollaro, Camille von Schrader, Will von Schrader, and Patty Wirth.

About the Author

Eric von Schrader has made documentary films, produced television shows, and worked as an instructional design consultant.

He was born and raised in St. Louis, Missouri, where he spent years exploring the city and imagining what might have been.

He lives in Carpinteria, California.

Visit his website at www.ericvonschrader.com

CPSIA information can be obtained
at www.ICGtesting.com
Printed in the USA
LVHW010724241220
674973LV00006B/1014